Gard

Cozy Mysteries ~~~~ Anthology III

Books 7-9

Hope Callaghan

FIRST EDITION

***

hopecallaghan.com

Copyright © 2017
All rights reserved

Visit hopecallaghan.com for special offers and soon-to-be-released books!

This book is a work of fiction. Although places mentioned may be real, the characters, names and incidents and all other details are products of the author's imagination and are used fictitiously. Any resemblance to actual events or actual persons, living or dead is purely coincidental.

i

Contents

Missing Milt – Book 7

Garden Girls
Cozy Mystery Series
Hope Callaghan

hopecallaghan.com
Copyright © 2015
All rights reserved.

A big **thank you** to Peggy Hyndman and Wanda Downs, for taking the time to preview *Missing Milt* - to make sure all my 'i's are dotted and my 't's are crossed – and always for their words of encouragement.

**Visit my website for new releases and special offers:
hopecallaghan.com**

Chapter 1

Gloria Rutherford rolled her car window down, letting the first hint of crisp fall air whoosh in. The fresh air was most definitely welcome. Summer had been long and hot. To Gloria, it seemed to have gone on forever.

She glanced out the window at the towering oak trees. The tips of the leaves had started to turn. The hint of colors lined the sides of the road as she headed into town. Soon, it would be time for the fall festivals, wagon rides, color tours and pumpkin patches.

The beautiful fall days reminded her that she had promised her grandsons, Tyler and Ryan, that they could sleep over and finish building the tree fort they had started the last time they had spent the weekend.

Brian Sellers, the owner of Nails and Knobs, the small town of Belhaven's only hardware store, had left a message on Gloria's answering machine, letting her know that the walls for the fort were ready for her to pick up.

She hadn't told the boys the fort was ready to go. She needed to talk to her daughter, Jill, first. School had recently started and Jill kept the boys on a tight schedule.

Gloria eased Annabelle into an empty parking spot in front of the post office. She squeezed out the driver's side door and scooted her way to the front.

The parking lot was full, although from what Gloria could see through the plate glass window, the residents of Belhaven weren't inside the post office.

She took a quick glance across the street. Many of them were in Dot's, a restaurant owned by Gloria's friend, Dot Jenkins, and her husband, Ray. The placed was packed.

Gloria stepped into the lobby of the post office and headed to the counter.

Head Postmaster, Ruth Carpenter, looked up when she heard the doorbell chime. She peered at Gloria over the rim of her reading glasses. "You're out bright and early this morning."

Gloria lifted a brow. She wasn't sure if this was a potshot at the fact that Gloria had been a bit of a recluse lately, since she had been staying close to home, trying to get everything organized.

On the heels of the fall festivals that were right around the corner were the holidays. This year, all of Gloria's children would be coming home for a visit and Gloria wanted to get a jump-start on whipping the place into ship shape for all of the company.

She set her purse on the counter and dropped a small stack of envelopes next to it. "Yeah, I'm just trying to get some stuff done around the farm."

Ruth tapped her pen on the counter. "You talked to Liz today?"

"Nope." Gloria shook her head.

"Liz" was Elizabeth Applegate, Gloria's sister. "What's she got cooking now?" Liz had a penchant for getting herself into some sticky situations. When she wasn't getting into trouble, she was vanishing for days at a time, putting everyone around her in an uproar. Namely, Gloria.

Eventually, Liz would return and wonder what all the fuss was about. Gloria tried to avoid the drama, but somehow Liz always managed to suck her into whatever was going on in her world.

Ruth picked up the stack of envelopes and dropped them in the large metal bin next to her. "Milt is still missing," she said.

Gloria frowned. Liz had called Gloria one day, out of the blue and in a state of panic. "Milt" was Milton Tilton. He was a resident at Dreamwood Retirement Community, along with Liz and Liz's best friend, Frances.

Gloria had promised Liz she would look into his disappearance. Gloria ended up sidetracked with other, more pressing issues, and had forgotten. She hadn't heard anything else so she assumed Milt had been found.

Ruth pointed at the back wall. "Check out the poster."

Gloria wandered over to the large corkboard. She pulled her glasses from her purse and slipped them on. Sure enough, a glossy 8-1/2x11 poster of Milt's mug hung on the wall. Below his picture was a plea:

"We desperately need your help. Milt Tilton, a resident of Dreamwood Retirement Community in Green Springs, Michigan is missing and we fear his life may be in danger.

Mr. Tilton was last seen near Dreamwood's main entrance on Friday evening, September 2nd, wearing plaid leisure pants and a gray polka dotted shirt.

If you have any information on the whereabouts of Milton Tilton, please contact Frances Crabtree at 626-1889. A reward of $500 is being offered for any information that leads to the safe return of Mr. Tilton."

Gloria scrunched her nose. "Huh. Frances is getting desperate. She's even offering a reward."

Ruth nodded. "Yeah. She and Liz were in here not 15 minutes ago. I think they were headed to your place to see if you could help track old Milt down."

Gloria had a bit of a reputation around, not only the small town of Belhaven, but also throughout the entire community. She had managed to end up right in the middle of several mysteries and murders. On top of that, she was good at solving them.

"I'll have to give her a call." Gloria stood upright. "I probably passed them on the road." She flung her purse on her shoulder and grabbed the door handle. "If they come back by, tell them I had to make a stop at the hardware store and then I'm heading home."

Ruth lifted her hand in a small salute. "Will do."

Gloria shuffled over to the car, opened the driver's side door and slid into the seat. She pulled out of the parking lot and veered left, in the direction of the hardware store. She got lucky and found a front row parking spot. Gloria climbed out of the car and made her way to the door.

Brian was standing on the front stoop talking to Carl Arnett, a longtime resident of Belhaven. Gloria stood off to the side and waited while the two of them finished their conversation.

Carl gave Gloria a brief nod then headed down the sidewalk toward Dot's.

Brian rubbed his hands together. "Let me guess. You're here to pick up the walls for the tree fort."

Gloria tucked a stray strand of hair behind her ear. "Yeah. I can't wait to tell the boys it's ready to go."

"Follow me." Brian waved her around the side of the building toward the back. "I have a surprise for you."

Gloria kept pace with his long strides as they made their way to the rear of the hardware store.

Brian lifted a metal latch, pushed the wooden gate open and stepped to the side while she followed him in.

The boards for the tree fort were propped up against the wall.

Gloria bent down and lifted one of the particleboards from the stack.

Brian had done an amazing job of cutting windows out on two of the boards, and a doorway for the front of the fort on a third board. On the other side of the wall panels were several long, wooden planks.

"Here's my surprise." Brian picked up a board. "I found these up in the attic. The boys can use these to build a railing to go around the fort."

Gloria studied the boards. "Brian, you went above and beyond what I asked you to do."

Brian's cheeks turned pink. "I always wanted a tree fort myself when I was a kid," he confessed. "Say, I can load these in the back of my SUV and bring them over on my lunch break."

Gloria was beginning to feel guilty. He could see from the look on her face that she was torn. "Tell you what - you make me lunch and I'll run by and drop these off," he bargained.

Gloria nodded. "That would be perfect. Do you think you can take a peek at the base of the fort while you're there? Make sure it's sturdy and all." The boys had done a great job of building the platform but it wouldn't hurt to have another set of eyes look at it to make sure it wasn't going anywhere.

"Anything for my girl." Brian grinned.

Gloria stepped out onto the sidewalk. Brian followed behind. He pulled the door shut and the two of them strolled to the front. "Your sister, Liz, was in here earlier looking for you."

He gave her a sideways glance. "Something about some guy that's missing." He shook his head. "She had another lady with her who was totally off the charts. She came inside the store and bought a long cable and combination lock."

Gloria chuckled. He must be talking about Frances. "I wonder why she didn't just call me on my cell phone."

She rummaged around inside her purse and pulled out her cell phone. Gloria flipped it over and stared at the screen. No wonder Liz hadn't called. The phone was off.

"Anyways, the two of them were trying to track you down," Brian added.

Gloria thanked Brian again and climbed into the car. She decided it would be best to wait until she got home to call Liz.

Gloria pulled Annabelle into the drive and made her way up the porch to the side door. She grabbed the handle on the screen door and something caught her eye. Tucked between the frame and the door was a slip of paper. Gloria plucked the folded sheet of paper, unlocked the door, and stepped inside her kitchen.

She dropped her purse on the table and reached for her glasses. She flipped open the note: "Help! Gloria, I am desperate. Please call me ASAP."

She rolled her eyes. This was typical Liz drama.

Mally, Gloria's Springer Spaniel, wandered into the kitchen. She held the note out so that Mally could see it. "Liz is in a tizzy." She peered down at her pooch. "I should probably get this over with and find out what in the world is going on."

Gloria grabbed the house phone and dialed Liz's cell number. Liz picked up on the first ring. "Thank God you called. I just left Frances. She's having a cow."

Gloria interrupted. "So Milt is still missing and Frances wants me to see if I can track him down."

Liz let out an aggravated sigh. "It may be too late. When I left her on the sidewalk out front of her apartment a few minutes ago, she had that look in her eye and mumbled something about staging a protest out in front of Dreamwood Eats."

Dreamwood Eats was the buffet-style restaurant inside Dreamwood Retirement community. It was the hub of Dreamwood – the main gathering place for the residents.

Liz went on. "She took a long cable and combination lock with her."

Gloria glanced up at the clock. It was already 11:00 a.m. Almost time for lunch. "You don't think she's going to…"

"Oh, I do think she's going to. She's been threatening for days now that she was gonna chain herself to the front doors of the restaurant. To bring attention to Milt's disappearance."

Liz begged her sister. "Can you please come by here and talk to her? I think you're the only person she'll listen to."

Gloria wasn't sure if chaining herself to a building on private property would get her arrested. Unless, of course,

9

Dreamwood decided to press charges. There was also the chance they might arrest her for disorderly conduct, disturbing the peace kind-of-thing.

"Brian is coming by for lunch with the materials for the boys' tree fort. After lunch, I'll head over," Gloria promised.

"Thank-you, thank-you, thank-you."

Gloria hung up and headed to the fridge. Luckily, she had just gone to the grocery store the day before and stocked up on all sorts of goodies.

She grabbed a package of deli turkey and sliced Colby cheese from the fridge. She set the food on the table and reached back in for the new jar of chipotle mayonnaise she'd been dying to try. She set that on the table along with the other ingredients and pulled the panini press from the top of the fridge. She blew a thin layer of dust from the top and then wiped her hand across the surface.

Mally let out a low whine when she smelled the grilling sandwiches. Gloria looked down. She knew there was no way she could refuse those doleful brown eyes. Right beside Mally was her cat, Puddles, with the same look on his face.

She pulled a slice of meat from the packet and tore it into small pieces. She put the small pieces in a bowl and moved it to the side for Puddles, out of Mally's reach.

Next, she took another piece of meat and dropped the entire piece in Mally's dish. The treat lasted but a second and she got the same pitiful look from both her pets.

Gloria shoved a hand on her hip. "Now you know that's a treat and I can't give you all of it."

Instead, she filled their dishes with pet food and added fresh water to their dishes.

After that, Gloria set the sandwiches on the plates and the plates on the table. She finished up just in time to see Brian's dark SUV pull in the drive.

She met him at the door. "Right on time. Sandwiches are hot off the press. Panini press, that is."

She gave Brian a light hug and held the door as Mally trotted over.

Brian bent down to pat her head. "Hey, girl. Haven't seen you in a while now." He scratched her chin. "Have you been naughty and Gloria is leaving you at home?"

Gloria frowned. It had been a few days since Mally and she had gone anywhere. "You're right." She turned to her beloved pet. "You can go to Liz's place with me," she promised.

Brian pulled a chair out and plopped down. "Did you find out what was going on with Liz and her friend?"

Gloria settled into the chair across from Brian. She lifted the lid on the new container of potato salad and scooped a large spoonful onto her plate before passing it to him. "Liz's friend, Frances, may have chained herself to a building in protest."

Brian had just taken a huge gulp of lemonade. He spewed the liquid from his mouth and it dribbled down his chin. He grabbed his napkin. "You're kidding."

Gloria shook her head. "I wish I was. Somehow, I can picture Frances doing that."

Brian took a big bite of his sandwich. "This is delicious."

Gloria tore a piece of her sandwich off and popped it into her mouth. He was right. It was good. The chipotle mayonnaise gave it the perfect level of heat.

Brian was curious. "What does this 'Milt' person look like?"

Gloria lifted a fork full of potato salad to her mouth. "Stop by the post office. Frances posted a picture on the community board."

Brian nodded, and then changed the subject. "What do you think of Andrea's new house mate, Alice?"

"Andrea" was Andrea Malone. One of Gloria's close friends. She was a young woman that Gloria had helped by solving her husband's murder quite some time ago. In fact, it was the very first murder that Gloria had solved.

The two of them had grown close and Andrea had purchased a big – some say haunted - house in the small town of Belhaven.

She had fixed it up and was now living in it, along with Andrea's childhood housekeeper, who had just retired and moved there from New York City.

Gloria was glad Alice was here. The house was too big for just Andrea. Now Gloria didn't worry about her young friend as much.

Andrea had had her share of odd things...and old bodies popping up on the property. The house was somewhat of a magnet for creepy, criminal activities.

"I think she's a great addition to the family." Gloria popped the last bite in her mouth. She swallowed the last bit of lemonade and set the glass on top of the empty plate. "Is she still after you?"

Alice had taken a real shine to Brian. Maybe that was too weak of a word. Alice was infatuated with Brian.

Brian chuckled. "Yeah. She hasn't given up yet. Of course, I think that's for show and she secretly hopes that Andrea and I will get married." He paused. "Let me clarify that. It's not 'secretly hopes.' Every time I go over there she bluntly asks when I'm going to propose."

Gloria's interest was piqued. "And?" She herself was curious. The two had dated for almost a year now and they seemed a perfect match.

Brian twisted his drink glass in a small circle.

Gloria could see the wheels turning in his mind. It looked like he was weighing the pros and cons of something.

Maybe he needed a little nudge...

"Are you going to ask Andrea to marry you?"

Brian didn't answer. Instead, he reached inside his jacket and pulled out a small jewelry box. He handed it to Gloria.

She grabbed her reading glasses from the center of the table and slipped them on. She lifted the lid on the box and gasped. Inside the box was one of the largest diamond rings Gloria had ever seen, if you didn't count gazing at them from the outside of a display case at a large jewelry store.

She looked at Brian over the rim of her glasses. "May I?"

Brian nodded.

Gloria plucked the ring from the velvet folds and pulled it close to her face. The diamond was a princess cut. Smaller, twinkling diamonds surrounded the large center diamond, then ran down both sides of the silver band. "This ring is beautiful," she gushed.

She held it up to the light. "Andrea and I must wear almost the same size ring," Gloria told him.

She slipped the ring back inside the box and closed the lid before handing it back to Brian.

He opened the lid and studied the ring. "I've been racking my brain, trying to plan something special. Something that's completely unexpected."

Gloria dropped her chin in her hand. "Hmm..." She gazed out the window. Andrea wasn't flashy. Although she had grown up in New York City, she was a down-to-earth, small-town girl

14

at heart. She did have a taste for the finer things, but they didn't define Andrea.

Her eyes wandered to the barn and beyond. Then it dawned on her. "Brian, I have the perfect idea."

Chapter 2

Gloria shared her idea with Brian, who promptly agreed it was the perfect setting for the upcoming proposal. He closed the lid and shoved the box back inside his jacket pocket.

Gloria carried the dirty dishes to the dishwasher and arranged them on the shelves. "It's time to take a look at that tree fort."

They headed outdoors. The base of the tree fort rested on several sturdy limbs of the large, leafy tree, which was smack dab in the center of Gloria's front yard.

Brian eyed the tree cautiously. "I haven't climbed a tree since I was a kid. Here goes nothing." He scampered up the tree so fast Gloria had to blink to make sure he had climbed and not catapulted.

He made his way to the center of the platform, spread his legs apart and swayed from side to side. The wooden frame shifted slightly under his weight. "It could probably use a couple long screws drilled into the tree to keep it from wobbling, but all-in-all, the boys did a great job of securing it," he hollered down to Gloria.

Brian waited in the tree while Gloria ran out to the garage to grab a cordless drill and a couple long screws. She handed them up and waited for him to secure the frame before he eased back down.

He pointed to the side of the tree. "Maybe you should put some slats in the side here to make it easier to climb up and down."

Gloria thought that was an excellent idea. There was still some scrap wood in the barn that would work perfectly.

Brian unloaded the materials for the tree house from his truck and propped them up against the wall, just inside the barn. He looked down at his handiwork. It had been fun, thinking of how much Gloria's grandsons, Tyler and Ryan, would enjoy this project. Someday he would have boys of his own and they would build a tree fort.

Brian wiped his hands on the front of his jeans. Gloria followed him to his truck and watched while he slid in the driver's seat. He stuck the keys in the ignition and started the engine. "You're not gonna..."

Gloria made a zipping motion across her lips. "My lips are sealed," she promised. "But, I'm so excited." It almost felt like one of her own children was about to propose.

Although Gloria was thrilled for Brian and Andrea, she couldn't help but wonder when her day might come. She and her boyfriend, Paul Kennedy, had been dating for quite a while now. She glanced down at her finger and the beautiful sapphire and diamond ring Paul had given her not long ago.

Gloria scolded herself. *Be happy with what you have, which is more than so many others.*

She shook her head to clear it, and then headed for the house. It was time to find out what was going on with Frances and Dreamwood Retirement.

Mally must've known she was going for a ride. She was waiting by the kitchen door, stuffed elephant clenched firmly in her jaw. "Ready to see what kind of bee Frances has swirling round her bonnet?" she asked her pooch.

She grabbed her purse, lifted her car keys from the hook near the door and headed back out. Gloria stood beside the car and waited while Mally took care of business, then sniffed around the dead and shriveled vegetables that littered the garden. "C'mon, girl. We gotta get going."

Gloria opened the door. Mally bolted across the seat and settled into the passenger side. Gloria followed her in, then reached over to buckle Mally's belt. She made sure the belt was secure around her before she fastened her own and started the engine.

Her mind wandered to Brian and Andrea. Andrea had the large, two-story mansion style house she had just renovated. Brian had a home of his own. His home was a big, beautiful, modern place that overlooked Lake Terrace. She wondered who would have to give up what house. They certainly couldn't live in both.

Their situation was similar to Paul and Gloria's situation. Both had acreage, farms and rambling farmhouses that had been in each of their families for decades.

Some time ago, they had discussed the fact that they both wanted to hang onto the homesteads and pass them down to the next generation.

Gloria wasn't sure which of her children would even want the farm. Her oldest son, Eddie, lived in Chicago with his wife, Karen. They had no children and showed no interest in moving back to Michigan, let alone Belhaven.

Next in line was her son, Ben, the middle child. He lived in Texas with his wife, Kelly, and their two children Ariel and Oliver. She doubted *they* would want the farm.

That left her youngest child. Her daughter, Jill, and Jill's husband, Greg, who lived in the nearby town of Green Springs. Their two sons, Tyler and Ryan, were closest to Gloria since they lived nearby and often came to spend the weekend. Now those two – they might fight over the farm.

Gloria adored her grandsons, not that she didn't love Ariel and Oliver just as much. She didn't get to see them very often, unlike Tyler and Ryan.

The thought of the boys reminded her that she needed to give Jill a call to see when they could spend the night and finish the fort.

Gloria slid Annabelle into Dreamwood's visitor parking spot, a straight shot across the parking lot from Liz's apartment unit. She opened the door, climbed out and waited for Mally to join her.

Mally tiptoed across the seat and hopped out onto the asphalt. She waited while Gloria closed the door and locked it.

As the two of them headed toward Liz's apartment, Gloria noticed a TV 8 news van parked at the end of the lot. Gloria wouldn't bet money on it, but she had a sneaking suspicion the van might have something to do with Frances.

She picked up the pace and darted across the parking lot. She and Mally headed to Liz's side door and rang the bell. From where she stood, she could see her sister frantically dart back and forth, from the kitchen to the hall.

Liz whirled around at the sound of the bell. Her eyes lit up when she spied Gloria. She hustled to the door and flung it open. "Am I glad to see you." She grabbed Gloria's hand, jerked her inside and Mally trotted in behind her.

Liz slammed the door shut behind them. "Frances chained herself to the front of the restaurant in protest. She's refusing to budge," she blurted out.

Gloria shook her head. This was not good. "But what can Dreamwood do to find Milt?"

Liz backed into the living room and plopped down on the sofa. "I have no idea. Frances is half out of her mind with this missing Milt thing. She figures if she can get the local news to pick up the story, maybe the police will open an investigation."

Gloria eased onto the other end of the sofa. Mally settled in at her feet. "I think she's got that covered. There's a Channel 8 news van in the parking lot."

Liz shot to her feet. "You're kidding me." She headed to the slider and peered out. Sure enough, the news van was still there. "We better get over there and try to talk some sense into Frances."

Liz grabbed her house keys from the counter and opened the side door. "Maybe you can offer to search for Milt or something."

Gloria frowned. Of course, she was willing to help in any way she could, but what if Milt wasn't really missing? What if he had vanished of his own free will?

The three of them headed down the sidewalk and in the direction of the restaurant. As they got closer, Gloria could see a large crowd had gathered out front.

The girls stopped near the outer circle and Gloria peeked over a woman's shoulder to catch a glimpse. Despite the gravity of the situation, she almost burst out laughing at the sight of Liz's best friend.

Frances had wedged her ample frame between the two metal handles attached to the front doors. Around her waist was a long, black cable. The cable looped around the door handles and Frances. In the middle of the cable, hanging right below Frances' belt, was a combination lock.

Plastered to the front of her shirt was a large piece of poster board. In the center of the poster was a picture of Milt. Above his mug shot, in large black letters was the word: *MISSING*.

Printed below his picture was the word: *REWARD*.

21

A reporter, holding a microphone, stood next to Frances. Gloria and Mally squeezed in and around the growing crowd until they stood next to the reporter. The young man was asking Frances a question. "How long do you plan to remain chained to this entrance?"

Good question. Gloria was wondering the exact same thing.

Frances crossed her arms and frowned. "Until the police assure me they will look into the disappearance of Milton Tilton." She lowered her voice. "Or until I have to go to the bathroom, whichever comes first."

The crowd snickered. Gloria rolled her eyes. The poor woman reminded her of a raving lunatic. Gloria needed to save her before she destroyed her reputation, what little she had left.

The reporter had turned to talk to the cameraman. This was Gloria's chance to have a word with Frances off camera.

She tugged on Mally's leash as they inched closer. Gloria leaned in. "If you free yourself from the restaurant, I'll help you search for Milt," she whispered in Frances' ear.

Frances' face lit up. "You promise? Today?"

Gloria nodded. "Yes. Free yourself from this fiasco and I promise I'll start today."

That was all the persuasion Frances needed. She promptly reached down, grabbed the combination lock and dialed some numbers. The lock clicked open and Frances pulled it from the cable loop.

Gloria helped her untangle it from the doors. A cheer went up in the crowd. Gloria wasn't certain, but she figured they were thrilled they could now go inside and enjoy their lunch.

The reporter stepped forward. He turned the microphone to Gloria. The camera was on her now. Gloria did not want to be on the evening news. She swallowed the lump in her throat.

The reporter thrust the microphone into her face. "What exactly did you say to Ms. Crabtree to convince her to abandon her protest?"

"That I would help her search for Mr. Tilton," she admitted.

Frances tapped the young man's shoulder. "This is the famous sleuth, Gloria Rutherford." Gloria, at that moment, wished the sidewalk would open up and swallow her whole. She did not want – did not need - this kind of attention.

The reporter lifted a brow. "Hey. I think I remember you from the night I interviewed you and a young woman after police caught two suspected killers in nearby Belhaven."

Gloria narrowed her eyes and studied his face. This young man was the one that had done the interview that evening outside of Andrea's place. The young reporter that begged for an interview, telling Gloria and Andrea that he was new.

She cocked her head. "I remember you. You were new."

He nodded eagerly. "Yeah, that was me. You gave me my first big break."

He covered the microphone with his hand. "I'm an anchor on the 6:00 evening news now."

"Congratulations," she said. "Now do me a huge favor and cut me out of your report."

Frances butted in. "No. You've gotta leave Gloria in the clip. She's nearly famous around these parts."

Gloria grabbed her arm and gave her a withering look.

Frances shrugged. "Well, it's true."

The crew wrapped up their interview. The reporter asked if he could get Gloria's number and follow up to see if she was able to crack the case. She shook her head no.

Liz was directly behind the reporter. Gloria hadn't noticed her move up. She blurted out Gloria's cell phone number, much to Gloria's dismay.

After the reporter and TV crew left, the girls wandered into the cafeteria for a bite to eat. Liz shuffled to the front of the restaurant while Gloria and Frances followed behind.

"I was about to give up the protest," Frances admitted. "I was starting to feel faint from hunger." She glanced around. "Plus, I gotta use the bathroom."

She darted off to the left, in the direction of the restrooms, while Liz and Gloria grabbed two trays and started down the line. Gloria wasn't the least bit hungry since she'd just eaten lunch with Brian.

She followed along behind Liz as she set two grilled cheese sandwiches on her tray, along with a couple bowls of piping hot tomato soup and several packets of saltine crackers.

Frances caught up with them at the cash register. "Here, let me pay," she graciously offered. The girls waited for Frances to pay and then the three of them and Mally wandered over to an empty table off to the side.

They no more than settled into their seats when a heavyset woman with shocking white hair and twinkling blue eyes approached the table and turned to Frances.

"I sure do admire your gumption," she gushed. "Why, I was just thinking as I watched you chained to the doors how we should get together and protest the food in this joint."

She leaned forward. "I'd like to see 'em put more meat and potatoes on the menu and less of those foo foo wraps and salads."

Frances' eyes lit up. "Get with me later, Agnes. Maybe we can round up a few more protesters and get some real changes around here." She thumped her fist on the table for emphasis.

Gloria sipped her soda and glanced at Frances from the corner of her eye. The woman had more spunk than Gloria had given her credit.

Frances gobbled up her sandwich and soup. Liz ate a bit slower and Gloria steered the conversation to lighter things – like grandchildren and the weather. No sense in getting Frances all stirred up – again.

They cleared the table and dumped the dirty dishes in the bin on top of the trashcan. Gloria trailed behind Liz and Frances. "Say, Frances, what happened to your walker?"

Gloria hadn't noticed with all the excitement, but Frances was getting around pretty darned good. She was no longer using a walker.

Liz held the door as Frances and Gloria stepped out onto the sidewalk. "I started taking these cayenne pepper pills a few weeks ago. Heard they were good for loosening limbs and joints. I also started walking around the neighborhood."

"In search of Milt," Liz pointed out.

Frances' head drooped. "True. In search of Milt." She lifted her shoulders and looked around. "I get this feeling that Milt is here, that he's with us. Close by."

Chapter 3

Frances' apartment faced Liz's apartment. If the two stood staring out their bedroom windows, they could look directly into one another's window.

Frances unlocked her side kitchen door and led them inside.

Gloria stepped across the threshold and caught a whiff of men's cologne.

Liz smelled it too. "Did you start wearing men's cologne?" She spun around and faced her friend. Her eyes narrowed. "What's up with that?"

Frances closed the door behind them. "I-I." She began to sniffle. "It's a bottle of Highland Nights, Milt's favorite cologne," she confessed. "I spray it in the house. It reminds me of him." She burst into tears, dropped her head in her hands and began to sob.

This was way worse than Gloria had imagined. This woman had an extreme obsession. She had no idea what the big draw over Milt was all about. The man's head was shinier than Mr. Clean's and he had beady, brooding eyes.

His voice an annoying pitch that was always three decibels too high and it grated on Gloria's nerves every time she heard him talk. On top of that, he was just plain slimy, for lack of a better word. Every time Milt shook Gloria's hand, she had the overwhelming urge to douse it in hand sanitizer.

Liz led Frances over to the dining room table and pulled out a chair.

Frances sunk into the seat. She dropped her arms on the table and laid her head on top of her arms. "I have to find Milt," she wailed. "I just have to."

Gloria pulled out the chair next to the heartbroken woman and settled in. "Now, Frances," she told her in a stern voice, "you have to pull yourself together if you want to help me find Milt."

"She's right, Frances," Liz agreed, "Gloria is a very busy woman and doesn't have a ton of free time to spend on this case."

Gloria's eyes shot up as she glared at her sister. Liz was making her sound downright heartless.

Liz gave a dismissive wave. "So we're gonna have to map out a strategy here to try to find him."

Gloria spied a small notepad and pen on the edge of the table. She grabbed the pen and the notepad, slipped her glasses on and lifted the cover. She needed to take a few notes if she was going to trace Milt's steps.

Her eyes widened when she spied the chicken scratch on the first sheet of paper. Frances had already started taking notes.

"Milt was last seen on the evening of September 2nd. He was talking to Clyde Ward out in front of the Rolling Green Clubhouse."

Rolling Green was the golf course located on Dreamwood's property, used exclusively by residents and their guests. Gloria had only caught glimpses of the golf course on her way in and out of Dreamwood, herself never having swung a golf club in her life.

Liz, on the other hand, was an avid golfer...or so she told Gloria. Whether she was or not hadn't been confirmed.

Gloria continued down the list. Next on the paper: *"Milt's habits."*

"7:30 a.m. Breakfast - Del's Diner with his buddies

9:00 a.m. Workout - Dreamwood gym

11:30 a.m. Lunch - Dreamwood Eats

1:30 p.m. Nap at home

3:00 p.m. Poker playing in the clubhouse

5:15 p.m. Dinner at someone's house. Rarely eats dinner at home. Frances had written a small side note. *Not certain that Milt knows how to cook.*

7:00 p.m. Walk with Frances."

There was a second list. This one listed Milt's preferences:

Milt drinks 2 cups of coffee every morning. Dunkin' Donuts original blend. (Purchased at Meijer, the local supermarket.)

Favorite food: Chocolate chip cookies. He eats at least a dozen cookies per week. The kind with the chunks. Milt likes to dip them in a glass of cold milk.

His favorite sports team is the Detroit Tigers and his second favorite is Dallas Cowboys, although I'm not sure why. (Frances had added additional commentary.)

Milt's favorite cologne: Highland Nights.

His dog, Fudge, died a couple years ago and he never got over it.

His favorite color is green. The color of money.

There were so many questions swirling around Gloria's brain. This was beginning to creep her out. How did Frances know that Milt napped at 1:30 every afternoon? Did she really want to know?

She closed the cover on the pad of paper and slid it across the table. "I guess the first thing on my list is talk to Clyde Ward to see if Milt said anything unusual."

Frances nodded. "I tried that already but every time I try to ask Clyde about Milt, he just clams up."

"That's because Clyde asked you to the afternoon movie matinee a few weeks ago and you shot him down, telling him he didn't hold a candle to Milt. You snubbed him," Liz pointed out.

Frances rubbed an imaginary spot off the table with the tip of her finger. "I know, I remember. Looking back, I shouldn't have said anything," she admitted. "He lives over at 726 Peachtree Lane."

Gloria slipped her glasses into her purse. "What about Milt's house phone and cell phone? Are they still in service?"

"Check," Frances answered. "I call them every single morning as soon as I wake up."

"Do you leave a message?" Gloria wondered.

Frances nodded. "I was leaving messages. Of course, now both the mailbox and answering machine are full and it won't let me."

"I also could've sworn I saw Milt talking to Trudy Gromalski the night he disappeared," she added.

Frances grabbed the notepad and pen and flicked the pad open. She scribbled a number down, ripped the sheet off and handed it to Gloria. "She moved to Dreamwood a couple months ago. She lives over on Wisteria Way."

"Did you try to talk to her?"

Frances jerked her head. "Of course," she snapped.

Gloria crossed her arms and narrowed her eyes.

Frances backed down. "No. I mean, of course I tried," she soothed. "Every time I go over there, no one is home."

Gloria rubbed her brow thoughtfully. She could kill two birds with one stone. Visit Clyde first then swing by Trudy's place. Hopefully, they would be willing to talk.

She grabbed her purse and rose from the chair. "If you think of anything else, let me know," she told Frances.

Gloria and Mally followed Liz out the door. Frances stood in the doorway. Her eyes filled with tears. "Will you let me know what you find out?"

Gloria assured her she would. Liz and Gloria slowly wandered across the meticulously manicured lawn toward Liz's place. "You want me to go over there with you?" Liz offered.

Gloria shook her head. "No. I'll go by myself. I might be able to get more out of them if I'm alone."

Liz had more enemies than friends at Dreamwood and Gloria wasn't sure what side Clyde and Trudy were on – friend or enemy.

The skies were clear and the temperatures perfect for a leisurely stroll. Gloria clipped Mally's leash to her collar and they headed down the sidewalk. Gloria admired the rich reds, buttery yellow and deep oranges of the fall flowers as they strolled along.

Gloria sometimes wished she had sidewalks near home. Of course, Mally and she took lots of walks. Through the fields behind the farm, to the creek that ran through the back of her property, but that was about it.

The road in front of the farm was the main road into Belhaven and there was a lot of traffic. No, it was not safe for them to walk on the side of their road.

Gloria was glad she had thought to hook Mally to her leash. A few times, she tried to dart off toward the old oak trees that lined the streets in hot pursuit of a pesky squirrel. The critter was bent on taunting poor Mally, who finally abandoned the chase and obediently trotted along next to Gloria.

Gloria turned at the corner of Peachtree Lane as she made her way to Clyde's place first. She was in luck. Sitting in a wooden rocker on the front porch was a dark-haired man, a pipe pursed between his lips. He eyed Gloria with curiosity as she made her way up the sidewalk to his front porch.

He took a puff off his pipe and studied her from his chair. The smell of maple and hickory floated in the air and drifted down the steps. The man pressed his foot on the porch floor and the rocking stopped. "Can I help you?"

Gloria shifted Mally's leash from one hand to the other. "Yes. My sister, Liz. Liz Applegate, lives in the complex. She was telling me that one of the residents, Milt Tilton, is missing and I'm making my rounds to see if perhaps some of the residents might know what happened to him."

Gloria left out the part about Frances saying he was the last person seen talking to him. She wanted to get Clyde Ward's take on things.

Clyde leaned back in his chair and studied her thoughtfully. "Yeah. It's the talk of the neighborhood, even more so now that that kook Frances chained herself to the front of the restaurant." He snorted.

"Do you know Mr. Tilton?" He seemed willing to talk. It was an encouraging sign. Gloria took a step up.

He nodded his head. "Yep. Old Milt and I like to play cards down in the clubhouse most afternoons. Poker. Not for much money though...just a few coins."

He changed the subject. "Pretty dog. Used to have a cocker spaniel myself. Good hunting dog."

Gloria glanced down at Mally. "Yeah, she loves to chase the birds, the squirrels. Just about anything, really."

Mally thumped her tail and let out a low whine. Gloria saw this as her opportunity to get closer to Clyde Ward and perhaps ask a few more questions.

They wandered up the steps and onto the covered porch. Mally trotted over to the rocker and Clyde patted her head.

"She's a beauty," he said admiringly.

"Do you think Milt took off or is there a chance something else happened to him?"

Clyde scratched under Mally's ears, which made her promptly drop to the floor and roll over onto her back for a belly scratch.

"You know, it's kind of odd. Can't see Milt as the disappearing kind. Course anything is possible."

He glanced up at Gloria. "Guess I was one of the last people to see him before he disappeared."

His eyes narrowed as he looked at Gloria suspiciously. "You seem awful curious about old Milt."

He leaned back in his chair. "Say...aren't you that nosy lady that's always coming across dead bodies?" He drummed his fingers on the arm of his chair. "Yeah. Yeah, you are that nosy lady."

Gloria stiffened her back. She wasn't nosy. She was a detective. Well, an unpaid sleuth. Her lips drew in a thin line. "I'm trying to help a friend that is very concerned for Mr. Tilton's well-being."

He snapped his fingers. The light bulb clicked on. "Frances is behind all this, isn't she?"

Gloria wasn't about to argue. "All I'm trying to do is make sure the man disappeared of his own free will." Gloria went in for the kill. "I would think any good friend would want the same," she pointed out.

Clyde Ward nodded. "True." He rose from his chair and shoved his hands in his front pockets. He stared down at Gloria. He was taller than he first appeared.

"Milt did make a bit of an odd comment the night he disappeared."

Gloria leaned in. This is what she'd been hoping for...

"He said something about someone lurking around his bushes the last few nights."

"Like a peeping Tom?" Gloria prompted.

Clyde nodded. "Yeah. Every time he went out to check, there was no one there."

Gloria nodded. "Huh. That's interesting." She stepped back down onto the sidewalk. "Is that all?"

"Yeah," Clyde rocked back on his heels. "Hope old Milt's okay. Good poker player, that one," he added.

Gloria fumbled inside her purse and grabbed a pen, along with small scrap of paper from her wallet. She scribbled her phone number on the slip of paper and stepped back up, pressing it into Clyde Ward's hand. "If you think of anything else, please call."

He glanced down at the paper. "Will do, ma'am."

He watched as Gloria and Mally stepped back onto the sidewalk and turned left. She could feel his eyes following them until they rounded the corner and disappeared from sight.

Chapter 4

Gloria and Mally walked to the next corner and stopped. She wasn't sure which way to go and where this Wisteria Way might be. They turned right and headed deeper into the neighborhood, farther away from the front where Liz and Frances' apartments were located.

They walked three more blocks. Gloria was about to give up and call Liz to see if she knew how far back this Wisteria Way was. At the corner, finally, she found the street.

The two of them made another right. It was a small cul-de-sac. Gloria let out a sigh of relief. She loved the walk and fresh air, but realized they would have to cover the same distance to get back to the car.

She looked down at her shoes – flats - and not necessarily the best pair of shoes for walking the neighborhoods.

The two of them made it to the end of the street when Gloria spied the address she had been looking for: 72709 Wisteria Way. She glanced at the name on the mailbox: *Trudy Gromalski.*

The driveway was empty and the garage door shut. The curtains were drawn. It appeared as if no one was home, but Gloria pressed on as Mally and she made their way up the drive to the side door that faced the drive.

She rang the bell and waited. No answer. She rang the bell a second time. Still no answer. After the third ring, she gave up and the two of them headed back down the drive.

She looked down at Mally. "We might as well finish the walk before we head back," she told her.

Mally's tongue hung out the side of her mouth. "Woof."

Gloria admired some of the houses on the street, and correctly guessed that this section of Dreamwood was a newer one. The houses were all Craftsman style with spacious covered porches and custom woodwork.

The homes were the complete opposite of Gloria's old farmhouse, which was in desperate need of a new paint job. Maybe she could hire Tyler and Ryan to paint it next spring.

She turned back to give Trudy Gromalski's house one last look and wondered if maybe her eyes were playing tricks on her. She could have sworn she saw the curtain move. She narrowed her eyes. Maybe someone was inside - avoiding her.

Back on the next street, she studied several other houses. The styles of these homes were a bit different, a little older and more of the traditional brick exteriors. She saw a few more curtains move and decided to make a game out of counting how many curtains moved and guessed at how many people were watching her – a stranger to their neighborhood – and Mally walk by.

Gloria didn't see Liz as she made her way through the parking lot and over to her car. She opened the door and waited for

Mally to climb in. She started the car and pulled out of the lot. At the stop sign, she debated. Should she make a run by Del's Diner to see if any of the employees or his buddies could recall anything odd Milt may have said or done or save it for another day?

It was already late afternoon. The first shift employees – the ones that probably waited on Milt and his pals – were long gone. She'd have to save that for another day. Maybe run by there for breakfast in the morning.

Gloria cruised into the small town of Belhaven and made a last minute decision to drop in to Dot's place. It didn't appear to be terribly busy since they were smack dab between the lunch and dinner crowd.

Dot was sitting at a back table with her husband, Ray, when Mally and Gloria stepped inside. The place was nearly empty. She wandered to the back table.

"Haven't seen you around in a few days," Dot commented.

Gloria slumped into a chair and Mally crawled under her chair. "Yeah, I'm trying to get ready for the kids' visit."

Dot frowned. "That's not until December," she pointed out.

Gloria nodded. "True, but Eddie and Karen will be here in a couple weeks for the fall color touring."

Dot crinkled her nose. "Oh, I forgot about that."

Ray got up from the table and grabbed a clean coffee cup. He set the cup in front of Gloria, reached for a fresh pot of coffee and poured. "You met Andrea's housekeeper, Alice?"

Gloria sipped the coffee. "Yeah, she's a real character."

Ray refilled Dot's cup, then his own before he sat back down. "She sure is. She came back in the kitchen to give me pointers on how to spice up the food."

Gloria grinned. She could picture Alice doing just that. Alice loved Mexican spicy food...the kind of food that roared through Gloria like fire.

Dot peeled the lid off the small creamer and dumped the liquid in her cup. "She got me to thinking...what about all-you-can-eat taco night?"

Gloria studied her over the rim of her cup. Dot served mostly comfort food: fried chicken, meatloaf, burgers and fries. "Yeah, I think that's a great idea. She can share some of her seasoning recipes."

Ray agreed. "That's what we were discussing. You know...a change from the same old, same old."

Dot got out of her chair. "You want a piece of pie? I'm trying a new pumpkin recipe."

Gloria's stomach grumbled. All that walking around had made her hungry. "Sure, I'd love to be your guinea pig."

Dot popped into the kitchen and returned with a generous slice of pie, topped with a dollop of real whipped cream. In her other hand, she had a small dish filled with diced chicken.

She slid the pie on the table and set the dish on the floor. Mally licked Dot's hand and chomped down on her treat.

Gloria lifted her fork and sliced off a piece before popping it into her mouth. The layered pie was delicious. There was something different about it. Gloria pointed her fork tines at the pie. "What's in this?"

Dot shook her head. "Nope. You gotta guess."

Gloria took another bite. She rolled the creamy pumpkin around on her tongue. "Hmmm...there's a creaminess to it. I mean, even creamier than pumpkin pie normally is."

Dot nodded. "It has a layer of cream cheese and white chocolate."

It was divine. It was heavenly. It was a hit – in Gloria's book.

She devoured the piece in record time.

Dot watched the pie disappear. "Did you ever catch up with Liz and her friend? They were in here looking for you this morning."

Gloria nodded and rolled her eyes. "Frances' love interest, Milt, has been missing for, I dunno, maybe a couple weeks now."

Dot nodded. "I saw the missing poster over on the wall in the post office."

Gloria picked up the last remaining chunk of crust and nibbled the edge. "Frances is going to be on TV 8's 6:00 o'clock news. She chained herself to the front entrance of Dreamwood's restaurant to draw attention."

Dot raised an eyebrow. "To draw attention to whom? Her or her missing boyfriend?"

Gloria picked up her coffee and took a sip. "Luckily, I was able to talk her into unchaining herself."

"In exchange for helping search for missing Milt." Dot finished the sentence.

"Bingo." Gloria wiped her mouth and dropped the napkin on top of the empty plate. "I need that recipe. I could make it for the kids when they come to visit."

"Or you could just order it from me." Dot winked.

"Yeah, maybe I should just have you make it. I'm probably going to have my hands full."

It had been years since all of her kids – and grandkids – had been home for the holidays at the same time. Gloria was excited. Not only would she get to see them, they would get to meet Paul. Of course, Jill had already met him.

Gloria grabbed her purse from the floor and stood. "I should get going. Lucy promised to come over for pizza and help me clean out my clothes closet."

Gloria had several close friends who lived in the small town of Belhaven: Ruth from the post office, Margaret who lived up on the lake and of course, Dot.

Gloria was closest to Lucy. Lucy was the most adventurous of her small group of friends and more times than not, she ended up in the middle of Gloria's adventures. Gloria had dragged all of the girls into her misadventures at one time or another, but Lucy was her main sleuthing sidekick.

"You want me to take a piece of the pumpkin pie for Lucy to try?" Lucy had the biggest sweet tooth in town. She was a bit of a confectionary connoisseur and Dot usually bounced her new dessert recipes off Lucy.

Dot shook her head. "She was in here earlier to pick up some cookies and such and she tried a piece."

Gloria wasn't surprised. It probably would've surprised her more if she hadn't shown up. Gloria waved good-bye to Dot and Ray and headed out the front door.

Chapter 5

Lucy's little white ranch was on Gloria's way home. She swung in the driveway and pulled in behind her friend's yellow jeep. She made her way up to the front door and tapped lightly on the glass pane as she peeked in the window. Lucy was nowhere in sight.

She waited for a few minutes before wandering around back to the storage shed. The single side door was closed and the padlock in place.

Mally and Gloria made their way over to the garage. The garage door was open but no Lucy there either.

Gloria started to grow concerned. It wasn't like Lucy to leave the garage door open and not be around. She headed to the car to grab her cell phone and give her a call. Hopefully everything was alright.

She was halfway back, phone in hand when what sounded like a dull roar echoed from the field directly behind Lucy's house.

Gloria stopped in her tracks. The sound grew louder. Mally backed behind Gloria, her ears flattened out and she growled. Gloria patted her head. "It's okay, girl."

A bright flash of red careened around the corner of the shed. On two wheels. It was a four wheeler. The ATV skidded to a stop. A cloud of dust swirled around the machine and drifted toward Gloria.

The driver shut off the engine, then reached up and unfastened the helmet, lifting it off a head of red hair. Lucy's red hair and it was standing straight up in the air.

Gloria stuck a hand on her hip. "What in the world?"

Lucy lifted her left leg and hopped off the quad. She set the helmet on the seat and peeled off a pair of black leather gloves.

Lucy patted the windshield. "Well, whatcha think?"

"What do I think? I think you have officially boarded the crazy train and lost your ever lovin' mind, that's what I think." Lucy had done some crazy things in the past.

Well, now that Gloria thought about it, Lucy had done a lot of crazy things in the past. Skydiving, building small explosives, hitchhiking to the Upper Peninsula by herself. Of course, that had been years ago when they were a lot younger.

Lucy held out the keys. "Here, give 'er a spin. It's fun."

Gloria took a step back. "No siree, Bob. I think I'll pass."

Lucy slapped the leather gloves across the front of her leg. "Oh, c'mon. Please?" she pleaded.

Gloria looked from her friend, to the menacing red machine, then back to Lucy.

Lucy could see she was starting to cave. "Then let me give you a ride. I'll go slow, I promise."

Gloria sucked in a deep breath. She led Mally over to the open garage and wrapped her leash around the leg of a work bench.

45

She bent down to Mally-level. "Now, if I don't come back in 15 minutes, call Paul and tell him to come look for me."

Mally let out a low whine before she yawned and slumped onto the cement floor. She closed her eyes. "Good watch dog you are," Gloria grumbled.

Lucy grabbed a helmet from the shelf and handed it to Gloria. "Strap that on."

Gloria pulled the helmet on her head and fastened the Velcro strap under her chin. Lucy had already pulled her helmet on. She reached forward and turned the key. The quad fired up. Lucy squeezed the handle and revved the motor.

"Climb on." Lucy reached behind her and patted the seat.

Gloria straddled the back of the seat and plopped down in the center. She gingerly placed her feet on the footrests before closing her eyes. "Dear God. Please protect me in my moment of insanity."

Lucy turned her head. "Hang on."

Without warning, Lucy pressed the throttle with her thumb and the quad lurched forward while Gloria jerked back. She grabbed the back of Lucy's shirt and pulled herself upright. *She wasn't kidding.*

Lucy made a sharp U-turn and the quad zipped by the shed to the open field out back. When the girls reached a semi-flat patch of ground, Lucy pressed down on the gas and the ATV raced across the field.

A couple of times, the quad hit a bump and Gloria flew off the seat. The girls made three trips up and down the long, open field before Lucy steered it back to the side of the shed. She killed the engine and Gloria slid off.

Lucy's eyes lit up as she pulled the helmet off. "That was fun, huh."

It was fun. Gloria enjoyed it much more than she thought she would. Her grandsons, Tyler and Ryan, would LOVE a ride.

Lucy took the helmet from Gloria and set that, plus her own helmet, on the garage shelf. She dropped the key in her pocket and waited while Gloria untied Mally.

The three of them walked to the house and stepped up onto the porch. "You think I could bring the boys by for a ride next time they're over?" Gloria asked.

Lucy grabbed the door handle and pushed the door open. "Sure. Yeah. Of course."

Lucy dropped down in a kitchen chair and slipped out of her work boots. She set them by the door before she shuffled over to the cupboard. "Tea?"

Gloria nodded.

Lucy pulled a pitcher from the fridge and filled two glasses. She reached to the back of the counter and grabbed a box of goodies. "I picked these up at Dot's earlier."

She opened the lid and slid the box toward Gloria.

Gloria eyed the contents. She had just eaten the piece of pumpkin pie. Of course, she'd also walked around Dreamwood so that had to count for something. She chose a small peanut butter cookie. "Thanks."

Lucy grabbed a peanut butter cookie, a lemon bar and a chocolate macadamia nut cookie before closing the lid and sliding it back on the counter. "We still on for dinner?"

Gloria nodded. "Yeah, I really need to get rid of some of those old clothes." She eyed Lucy critically. Although Lucy's main staple was sweets, she was thin...almost too thin.

Gloria wasn't big herself, but she had a lot more curves than Lucy and none of her old clothes would look right on her friend.

Lucy nodded. "I heard about the guy that's missing over at Dreamwood."

Gloria nibbled the edge of her cookie and sipped the tea. "Watch the 6:00 evening news on Channel 8. Frances chained herself to the entrance to Dreamwood Eats."

Lucy rolled her eyes. "Lord have mercy. That woman is crazy." She tasted her tea before reaching for the sugar bowl. "This needs a little sugar."

Gloria watched as Lucy dumped several large heaping spoons of sugar in her glass of tea and stirred. She lifted it to her lips and sipped. "Much better," she decided.

48

"How's Bill?" Bill was Lucy's boyfriend. Gloria had meant to ask about him the last time she'd seen Lucy. Gloria hadn't seen his truck in the drive for at least a couple weeks now.

Bill and Lucy had been dating for over a year now. Gloria liked him well enough, although she felt that it was a bit of a one-sided relationship. The one side being all in Bill's favor. Whatever Bill wanted to do, Lucy did it.

Lucy's lowered her eyes and shrugged. "Uh, I dunno."

Gloria paused, cookie mid-air. "Is everything okay?"

Lucy lifted her gaze. "We had a bit of a falling out. I haven't seen him for a couple weeks now," she confessed.

"Whatever happened, if you don't mind me asking?"

Lucy looked out the window. "I told him I didn't want to go bow hunting this year. That I wanted to hang out with you girls, maybe head to the outlet malls and do some shopping and such."

"And?" Gloria prompted. She could feel her face starting to grow warm at the thought that Bill was angry just because Lucy wanted to do something other than what he wanted.

"Well, he said if that was the case, that maybe he would give me a *lot* more free time to spend with my friends."

Gloria opened her mouth to speak and promptly closed it. What she really wanted to say was that Lucy was too good for Bill, but she knew if the two of them patched things up, there would always be that hanging in the back of Lucy's mind. The last thing she wanted was for her friend to think that she didn't support her 100% - no matter what choices she made.

"I'll pray about it," Gloria simply said.

Lucy nodded. "I appreciate that. In the meantime, I'm free to do – to hang out or whatever." Her voice trailed off.

Gloria finished the last bite of cookie and crumpled her napkin, envisioning Bill's head as the crumple. She squeezed it extra hard. "Great, you can help me with the missing Milt case," she said.

That suggestion seemed to brighten Lucy's mood. "You think so? Really? I mean, you know I'm all in."

And, indeed, Lucy was all in. Lucy was a good little sleuth and Gloria was glad they had something to work on together, to take her mind off Bill.

Romance and love was a tangled affair. Her mind drifted back to earlier that day when Brian showed Gloria the stunning engagement ring. Who wouldn't feel like a princess getting a ring like that?

She wondered if Paul would ever pop the question. She glanced at her friend and stiffened her back. *Who needed men anyways? They had survived just fine all this time without them.*

That resolve lasted until Gloria got in her car and glanced down at her phone. Paul had sent her a text. "I miss my girl."

There was a second text: "Dinner tomorrow night?" Although Gloria felt bad for Lucy, she texted back that dinner sounded lovely. Her heart skipped a beat at the thought of seeing her Paul.

Gloria parked the car in front of the garage. Mally followed her up the steps and into the kitchen. She set her purse on the chair and hung her keys on the hook. The afternoon had flown by. Lucy had promised to come down after she cleaned up, which gave Gloria just enough time to wash up herself and call her daughter, Jill.

Jill picked up on the first ring. "Hi Mom."

"Hello dear."

"Aunt Liz called earlier looking for you. She was in a bit of a tizzy."

Gloria grinned. "She found me."

"It was something about Frances' boyfriend."

Gloria sighed. "Yep. I guess I have a new investigation."

Jill snorted. "That's kinda what I thought."

Gloria could hear screams in the background. Her grandsons. "How are the boys?"

Jill groaned. "Driving me C-R-A-Z-Y," she said. "They have an in-service teacher day and the boys are off this Friday. I'm trying to figure out what to do with them."

Gloria nodded into the phone. "Good. That's why I'm calling. The tree fort is ready to put together. Brian dropped the pieces off earlier and I was wondering if they could come spend the night."

"Yes. A thousand times yes," Jill groaned. "You are a lifesaver, Mom. I don't even have to ask the boys. I know the answer already. In fact, I think I'll wait to tell them until Thursday night. Otherwise, they'll drive me even crazier than they already do."

Gloria talked to her daughter for a few more minutes then hung up the phone. She couldn't wait to see how the tree fort looked when it was done. They would need more nails and maybe even some cans of paint so the boys could customize it. Visions of painted walls and painted hair filled her mind.

Gloria wandered out to the front, screened-in porch, which she rarely used anymore. The porch was large and it ran the entire length of the front of the house. On one end was a deep freezer where Gloria kept all the frozen stuff that she harvested from the garden each summer: strawberries, corn, broccoli and green beans.

She headed to the opposite end – to the metal storage cabinet that had been a fixture on the porch for as long as Gloria could remember. She lowered the lever and opened the cabinet. Inside was everything the boys would possibly need for camping out. Sleeping bags, flashlights, bug spray...

She closed the door and watched through the front porch window as Lucy's yellow jeep pulled in the drive.   Gloria and Mally met her at the back door.

After placing an order for pizza, they headed to Gloria's small walk-in closet in the corner of her bedroom. The last time she'd cleaned the closet was after her husband, James' death.

Those had been some dark days and Lucy had come to her friend's rescue. The two women had painstakingly gone through all of his belongings.

Gloria donated most of it to charity. She kept a few items that had sentimental value to pass down to her kids and grandkids.

Gloria switched on the light and stepped to the side.

Lucy eased around her and stood in the center. "Good grief, Gloria." She plucked a shirt from the hanger and studied it. "This has to be from the 70's."

"I told you I needed help," Gloria pointed out.

Lucy shook her head. "Help? You need an intervention."

Lucy began pulling shirts from the hangers left and right, tossing them in the center of the floor. Soon, there was a small mountain.

Gloria grabbed Lucy's arm. "If you toss much more, I'll be walking around naked."

Lucy stopped her cleaning frenzy and glanced at the empty racks. "True." She looked at the pile on the floor. "I'll stop right here but we need to go shopping."

Gloria trotted to the kitchen and brought back a brand new box of heavy-duty lawn bags. The girls filled the bags – three in all – and carried them out to the kitchen. "I'm going to Green Springs tomorrow. I'll drop them off if you want," Lucy offered.

She changed the subject. "Where do we go from here on this missing Milt case?"

Gloria told her all that she knew so far. How Milt had commented he thought someone was lurking around outside his apartment and shortly after, he disappeared. How Frances was convinced he was somewhere in the vicinity.

"What do you think?" Lucy wondered.

Gloria wrinkled her nose. "Well, my next stop is Del's Diner in Green Springs. Milt and his cronies ate breakfast there every morning. I thought maybe I could head over there, do a little investigating and get his friends' take on his disappearance."

The pizza had arrived. Gloria paid for the pizza since Lucy had so generously offered to help de-clutter her closet.

Lucy cleared the table while Gloria grabbed paper plates and napkins. The girls munched on the pizza and talked about the upcoming holidays and the welcome relief from the summer heat.

Gloria was careful to avoid the painful topic of Bill. She lifted a mushroom from the top of her slice of pizza and popped it into her mouth. "Why don't we drop the clothes off together in the morning and then have breakfast at Del's?"

Lucy picked up her napkin and wiped her mouth. "Sure. Sounds good to me."

After they finished eating, Gloria took a leftover piece of pizza, sliced it into bite-size snacks and put them on two paper plates – one for Mally and one for Puddles. She shut the lid on the pizza box. "The leftovers are yours."

She walked Lucy to her jeep. The sun had set and it was dark out. The croak of bullfrogs filled the night air.

Gloria waited for Lucy to climb into her jeep before handing her the pizza box.

Lucy pulled the driver's side door shut and rolled the window down. "What time you want to leave in the morning?"

Gloria crossed her arms. If she remembered correctly, according to Frances' meticulous notes, Milt and his pals ate in the restaurant early. "Would 7:30 be too early?"

Lucy was a morning person. She nodded. "Okie Dokie. I'll be here at 7:30 with bells on."

Gloria watched Lucy's jeep until the tail lights disappeared in the dark. She stepped back into the kitchen and locked the door behind her. She looked down at Mally. "I guess I better head to bed if I'm getting up at the crack of dawn."

Chapter 6

Gloria had just finished her first cup of coffee when Lucy arrived bright and early the next morning.

She was happy to see that Lucy was a bit more chipper than the day before. Gloria didn't dare ask if perhaps she and Bill had talked.

Traffic was light and the drive to Green Springs flew by. On the way, the girls discussed the possibilities of what might have happened to Milt.

Del's Diner was packed and Lucy had to drive around the block a couple times to find an open spot. The inside was just as busy. The girls wandered around the maze of packed tables and squeezed into a corner booth.

Lucy studied the menu while Gloria studied the crowd. It was mostly men, which made it difficult for Gloria to try to figure out which group was Milt's buddies.

"Good morning, gals. Can I get you a cup of coffee?" A young woman wearing a black uniform and dark blue apron approached their booth.

Gloria nodded. Lucy shook her head. "I'll take a hot chocolate, please."

"Coffee for me," Gloria told the woman. When she walked away, she turned to Lucy. "You still on that hot chocolate kick?"

Lucy nodded. "Yeah. I think I'm addicted to it," she admitted, "chocolate, that is."

Gloria smiled. Had Lucy just figured that out?

Gloria perused the menu. She decided to go heavy on the breakfast and skip lunch since Paul was taking her to dinner. She glanced over the top of the menu at her friend. She didn't dare mention the dinner date.

The waitress returned. She set a cup of coffee in front of Gloria and an empty mug, packet of hot chocolate and pot of hot water in front of Lucy.

"I'll take the chocolate chip waffle and a side of bacon," Lucy told her. She turned to Gloria. "You should try chocolate and bacon together. It's to die for."

Gloria scrunched her eyebrows. Maybe she should follow Lucy's weight loss plan: eat all the sweets you can stomach and the pounds will melt away.

The thought of that much sugar made her stomach turn. "I'll take a western omelet, wheat toast and a side of sausage." She handed the menus back to the woman who turned to go.

"Wait."

The woman spun back around. She lifted a brow. "Yes?"

Gloria stuck her elbow on the table. "Say, you ever wait on a man by the name of Milton Tilton?"

The woman shoved her order pad in her pocket and clipped her pen to the front. "Yeah," she clucked. "Poor guy is missing. I saw some crazy lady on the 6:00 news last night. She had chained herself to some restaurant because of it."

She twirled her finger in a circular motion near the side of her head. "There sure are a bunch of lunatics in the world."

Gloria covered her mouth to hide her grin. If she only knew. "I heard he was a regular and that he came in with a group of men most mornings." She glanced around. "You wouldn't happen to know if they're in here this morning."

The woman tilted her head to a table not far from where the girls were sitting. "Yeah, that's them over there."

She leaned in. "Nothin' but a bunch of cheapskates. They come in here every morning, sit there at that same table for hours and drink coffee." She waved her hand. "Coffee and if I'm reaaal lucky...maybe a donut or two."

The waitress shook her head. "Lucky if I get a whole dollar tip from those tightwads."

She straightened. "Course Milt. He's a better tipper than most of 'em. He'd give me fifty cents no matter what he ordered."

The party in question was calling her name. "Hey Fran." She rolled her eyes. "I gotta go."

The girls watched as she headed over to their table with a fresh pot of coffee. "Looks like they're here for the long haul," Lucy observed.

That would give the girls plenty of time to finish their breakfasts and head over there for a chat.

Their waitress, Fran, came back a short time later with breakfast. Gloria's mouth watered as the woman set the piping hot food in front of her. The aroma of cooked sausage and onions wafted in the air.

Gloria eyed Lucy's chocolate chip waffle, which came with a side of melted milk chocolate and syrup.

Lucy promptly dumped the entire mini pitcher of melted milk chocolate on top of the waffle. Next, she poured the syrup over the chocolate. She picked up a slice of bacon and dipped it in the chocolatey-syrup concoction.

She took a big bite and closed her eyes. "Mmm. This is so good." She picked up a second piece, dipped that in chocolate and held it out. "Here, you have to try this."

Gloria scrunched her nose. She almost refused but it did look tasty - and fattening. She took the piece of bacon and bit the end off. It was good, but a bit too rich for Gloria's blood. "Delicious," she agreed and handed the rest of the piece back to her friend.

The girls ate their breakfast in silence. Gloria sipped her coffee – Lucy – her hot chocolate. Lucy lifted the steamy mug to her lips. "We should do this more often."

Gloria nodded. "I'd like that Lucy." She picked up her napkin and dabbed the corners of her mouth.

Lucy set her cup on the table. "I-I know that Bill took a lot of my time. You know, we were always doing what he wanted to do."

Lucy looked up and Gloria could see the unshed tears shining in her eyes. "Sometimes I miss him but you know, I'm just not sure he was the one for me," she confessed.

She drew a shaky breath. "The more he sucked me into his life, the less of me and my opinion seemed to matter," she said. "If that makes sense."

It did make sense. Standing on the outside looking in, Gloria felt that Lucy was losing her identity. Of course, Lucy had always been – and probably always would be – a bit of a risk taker and free spirit, doing things that Gloria herself would never even try. But somewhere along the way, Lucy began to change in small, subtle ways.

Gloria wrapped her hands around her coffee mug. "I love you, Lucy. You know that, and I never want to say anything to hurt your feelings but I have to agree that you lost a little bit of yourself when you started dating Bill."

She let go of the cup and grabbed her friend's hand. "If Bill isn't the one for you, the Lord will find the right one."

Lucy squeezed Gloria's hand and smiled. "You're right. I'm at peace with this." She reached for her check and lifted her purse. "You know what else? I'm okay if there isn't a 'Mr. Right' waiting in the wings."

Lucy lifted her chin in defiance. "Either way, after I got home last night, I made a list of all the things I want to do. You know, the bucket list." She pulled her wallet from inside the purse. "One of the first things on the list is that cruise we keep promising ourselves that we're going to take."

Gloria nodded. She picked up her handbag and set it in her lap. "Hey. That reminds me. Do you remember my cousin, Millie?"

Lucy tugged on her earring. "Oh yeah. She was married to that jerk, Roger. Wasn't he the guy that ran off with one of his clients?"

Gloria nodded as she pulled some bills from her wallet.

"Uh-uh," Lucy stopped her. "Breakfast is on me." She dropped a twenty on top of the check.

The waitress stopped by with a dash more coffee, picked up the money and the bill. "Be back in a jiff," she said.

"Thanks, Lucy." Gloria watched the waitress head to the back. "Anyways, Millie took a job on a cruise ship. Her daughter, Beth, called the other day to tell me her mom was having a blast." She went on. "What do you think about going ahead and booking our cruise on Millie's ship?"

Lucy placed her palm on the table. She leaned in. "Really? Can we? I mean, that would definitely give me something to look forward to."

Gloria nodded. "Let's all of us girls meet for coffee at Dot's and pick a date."

Lucy didn't have time to answer. Her gaze shifted to the table of men. One of them looked like he was getting ready to leave. She scrambled out of the chair. "I'll try to hold them off from leaving."

Lucy pushed in her chair. "Tell Fran to keep the change."

Gloria watched as Lucy headed to the table. The man sat back down as Lucy waved her hands in the air.

Gloria grinned. She had no idea what tactic Lucy was using to stall them.

Fran was back with a receipt and change.

Gloria waved her off. "You can keep it."

Fran looked at the five-dollar bill and coins in her hand. "Really? That's the best tip I've had all day."

Gloria got to her feet.

Fran held out a hand. "Say. I just thought of something. Milt was in here a couple days before he went missing. He came in with a woman."

She looked around then lowered her voice. "It was for lunch and the only reason I remember is that Milt was in here with his friends for breakfast and then came back a couple hours later with this woman."

"And?" Gloria prompted.

"Well, I could tell they were having a kind of serious conversation, you know. From the looks on their faces," she paused. "I'm a pretty good judge of that, what with having to deal with people every day."

Gloria's pulse raced. "Did you hear what was being said?"

Fran frowned. "Nope. Every time I came close, they would stop talking, which is another reason I think there was something to it. You know, more than just a regular conversation."

Gloria pointed to Fran's pad of paper and pen. "Can I borrow that for a minute?"

Fran handed it to Gloria, who grabbed her reading glasses and slipped them on. "Do you recall what the woman looked like?"

Fran tapped the side of her cheek and stared at the ceiling. "She was – uh." Fran snapped her fingers. "Yeah. She had gray hair with black streaks. It was kinda short and curly...like she permed it or something."

Gloria frowned. That could be just about anyone. "Anything about her stand out like a mole or a tattoo?"

Fran shook her head. "No. Not that I can recall."

Gloria scribbled her cell number on the pad of paper and handed that and the pen to the woman. "If you think of anything, anything at all, call me. Please."

Fran slipped the pad in her apron pocket. "Will do."

Luckily, Lucy was doing a great job of entertaining the gentleman, all of whom were still at the table. She was waving her hands in the air. "...and then I came down with a whoosh and landed flat on my back. When I opened my eyes, I was staring straight up at the bluest skies. At first, I thought I had died."

Gloria tapped her shoulder. Lucy swung around. "Oh, there you are."

One of the men eyed Gloria curiously. "Your friend here was telling us about her first skydiving adventure." He pointed to the men around the table. "We were just talking about trying it ourselves."

The man on the other side of the table spoke up. He looked to be the youngest of the bunch with only a smattering of gray in his hair. "You never can be too sure how long we'll be here on earth so we decided to try something adventurous."

"Lucy, here, is quite the daredevil." Gloria cleared her throat and changed the subject. "My sister lives over in Dreamwood. They have an interesting situation on their hands what with that Milt Tilton missing."

"Yeah, he's our morning coffee partner." The man paused. His eyes narrowed. "Say, you look familiar. He lifted an index finger and pointed it at Gloria. "I caught a glimpse of you on the evening news."

"Yeah." The guy seated next to Gloria nodded. "I saw her, too."

Gloria's face reddened. Lucy jumped in. "Some of the residents at Dreamwood asked Gloria here to see what she could find out about Milt's disappearance."

"Ahh." Several of the men nodded. Then they clammed up.

Gloria shifted her purse on her shoulder. "Did Milt say anything about odd occurrences or weird phone calls?"

All of them shook their head. No one spoke.

Gloria tried again. "What about people he may have known that didn't like him?"

Chirp. Chirp. There was only the sound of silence.

Gloria was striking out so Lucy tried to help. "Listen, your friend is missing. Aren't any of you concerned for his well-being?"

Finally, the man closest to Lucy spoke up. "Well, he did mention someone was peeping into his house days before he disappeared."

Gloria's brows formed a V. Clyde Ward had said the exact same thing. "Were there any business dealings that might have gone bad?"

"Naw." The young man in the back spoke up. "He did say some crazy lady was stalking him." He whacked the arm of the man next to him. "What was her name? Janet...Janice..."

The man on Lucy's left snapped his fingers. "Francine, I think."

Gloria shifted her foot. They were talking about Frances.

The men didn't seem to be able to offer any additional information. Gloria thanked them for what they did tell her and the girls headed toward the front entrance.

Lucy grabbed her keys and unlocked the doors of the jeep. She started to slide into the driver's seat.

"Excuse me."

Gloria spun around. One of the men that had been sitting at the table hurried over to the jeep. He stopped next to Lucy. "Most of the other guys didn't know this, but Milt, he had a few dealings on the side. You know...a small gambling habit."

The man turned to look behind him. "Between you and me, he mentioned owing some money and he didn't know how he was gonna come up with the cash."

Gloria dropped her purse on the passenger seat and stared over the top of the jeep. This was taking an interesting turn.

The man went on. "I gave him the name of a good quickie loan place." He shrugged. "Not sure if he took me up on it but he seemed pretty concerned about some mafia-types coming to track him down and break his legs – or worse."

"Do you recall the name of the place you suggested?" Gloria asked.

"Sure. Integrity Loans. They're up there in Lakeville." The man turned to Lucy. "Tell em Max sent ya. Max Field." He was giving Lucy googly eyes.

Gloria leaned against the passenger side of the jeep while Max leaned closer to Lucy. "Say, you wouldn't happen to wanna." He paused. "You know...maybe have breakfast sometime."

Lucy's face turned the same bright red shade as her hair. "I-I..." She looked at Gloria as if to say, "What do I do?"

Gloria was more than happy to oblige. "Why Lucy, here, would *love* to meet you for breakfast. Right, Lucy?"

Lucy swallowed hard and shook her head. "I-I..."

"How does Thursday sound?" Gloria was setting Lucy up on a date. "We live over in Belhaven and have a great restaurant in town. It's called Dot's Restaurant and it's on Main Street."

Max turned to Gloria and smiled. He was a fine looking fellow. She didn't see the harm in having him meet Lucy there for breakfast. That way, Gloria and girls could kind of "scope him out" so to speak.

Max cleared his throat. "Great. How does 9:00 o'clock Thursday morning sound?" He was talking to Lucy but asking Gloria.

Gloria grabbed the door handle. "Sounds perfect. She'll see you then."

Max gave Lucy a goofy smile and then sauntered off down the sidewalk. They watched as he climbed into a silver Audi convertible. He backed out of the parking spot and then drove past them, waving as he went.

Gloria slipped her sunglasses on and climbed into the jeep. "Will ya' look at that."

Lucy slid into the driver's side. "You just set me up on a date," Lucy huffed. "Wh-what if I don't want to go?"

Gloria lowered the visor and peered at her reflection in the mirror. "Oh, Lucy. It's just a little breakfast. What's the harm?" She glanced at her friend out of the corner of her eye. "He was kinda cute and he drives a nice sports car."

Lucy frowned and grabbed her sunglasses from the center console.

Gloria dropped her purse on the floor. "Don't worry. The girls and I will stick close by. Make sure things don't get out of hand."

Lucy pounded the steering wheel in frustration. "You set me up on this 'date' and now you're gonna *spy* on me?"

She stopped pounding and put the jeep in reverse. "He was kinda cute, huh," she agreed.

A small smile turned the corner of Gloria's lips. This was turning into a productive day. Not only did they have a lead, Lucy had a hot date.

Chapter 7

Lucy pulled up to the stop sign and looked first to the left then to the right. She glanced over at Gloria. "Do you want to run by that loan place tomorrow?"

The loan place was in Lakeville, on the opposite side of the county.

Gloria glanced down at the clock on the car radio. Paul would be by in a few hours. They wouldn't have time to go today. It would be cutting it too close. "Yeah, I think tomorrow would work out better."

The jeep rolled down Main Street, Belhaven. The small town was packed and they had trouble finding a parking place.

Lucy swung into a parking spot near the end of the block. The girls climbed out and headed to Dot's Restaurant. Since they had just eaten, the girls ordered a couple Diet Cokes and waited for Dot take a breather.

Dot set Lucy's Diet Coke in front of her. "What? No hot chocolate today?" she teased.

Lucy reached for her drink. "I just had some," she mumbled.

Dot placed Gloria's drink in front of her. "Let me guess. You're working on Frances' missing beau."

Lucy nodded. "Yeah. We have a few leads now, huh Gloria."

Gloria nodded. "We'll follow up on one tomorrow over in Lakeville."

"Well, lookie who we have here." The girls' friend, Margaret, wandered over to the table. She clasped her purse in front of her and folded her hands over the front. "I haven't seen either one of you in days now."

Gloria wiped the sweat from the bottom of her glass with her napkin. "I've been trying to do a little early fall cleaning."

Margaret pulled out a chair and plopped down. She looked at Dot. "I'll have a coffee but only when you get back around this way."

Margaret turned her attention to Lucy. "How you doin' Lucy?"

"Oh...fair," she answered vaguely.

Gloria held her tongue. She wasn't sure if the others knew that Bill and Lucy had split up.

Margaret dropped her chin in her fist. "How's Bill? I haven't seen his car around your place in a while now."

Lucy fidgeted in her seat. "We, uh, mutually agreed to part ways."

Margaret raised a brow but kept silent. Although no one had ever said nary a bad word about Bill, they all shared the same opinion. That it was mostly a one-sided relationship.

"Yeah," Lucy sighed. "I'm in a good place, though."

"Which reminds me," Gloria attempted to take a little heat off her friend. "Lucy and I were just discussing that cruise we've been talking about for ages. We need to pin down some dates."

Dot shoved her hands in the front pockets of her apron and nodded her head. "Man, I sure could use a vacation. I'm ready to go now."

"I bet you are," Gloria answered wryly. "My cousin, Millie, started working on a cruise line. I'll have to find out which one. Maybe we could try that one out."

"Sounds good to me," Margaret said. "Of course, I'm free whenever. The only one we'll have to check with is Ruth."

"My ears are burning," a voice behind them answered. Gloria swung around. Ruth, the postmaster, was bearing down on them. "What exactly are you checking on?"

"A cruise," Dot answered. "You know...the cruise Gloria and Lucy have been talking about forever."

Gloria watched as Ruth reached for the last empty chair. "We're ready to start looking at dates. What works for you?"

Ruth slid into the seat. "Any time before November 15th. That's when the holiday season kicks into high gear and I can't get any time off until after New Year's."

"Well," Gloria did a few mental calculations. "It's September now. That would only leave October and that might be too short of notice. How does January sound?"

"Sounds wonderful," Lucy exclaimed. "We can escape the gloomy Michigan winters, not to mention snow and ice."

"Ah. Warm sunshine, ocean breezes," Lucy murmured dreamily.

The girls all agreed January would work best, that they'd all need a nice, long vacation after muddling through the holidays with busy schedules and family get-togethers.

Gloria looked down at her watch. "I better get going. Paul's coming by later to pick me up for a dinner date."

Lucy slid out of her seat. "I'm ready."

"Are you gonna mention…" Gloria jerked her head at Lucy, who violently shook her head as if to say "absolutely not."

Gloria plowed ahead. "Lucy has a hot date here Thursday morning."

"I do not have a date," Lucy gritted through her teeth.

Gloria ignored her comment. "His name is Max. We met him this morning when we were working on Milt's case."

"We'll be sure to be here to scope him out," Margaret teased. "What time?"

"I don't need an audience," Lucy protested.

"9:00 a.m." Gloria answered.

Dot placed a light hand on Lucy's shoulder. "Lucy, we're just trying to watch out for you. We won't embarrass you in any way," she promised.

Lucy's shoulders drooped. "This is all Gloria's fault. She's the one that told him yes."

The girls all agreed they wouldn't put Lucy on the spot so Lucy relented. "I guess I might as well get this over with. After all, it's just breakfast."

"What if you really like him?" Ruth pointed out. She looked over at Gloria. "Gloria seems to think he shows promise."

"But I'm not sure I'm ready to date yet," Lucy argued.

"You just gotta get right back in the saddle," Margaret encouraged.

Lucy pulled a five from her pocket and handed it to Dot. "I guess I'll see you Thursday morning," she said.

Gloria winked at the girls and followed Lucy out the front door and they headed back to the farm.

Lucy pulled up next to the house and put the jeep in park. "What time you want to leave in the morning?"

Gloria grabbed the door handle and stopped. "Will right after lunch work?" She wanted to take a run by her friend, Andrea's place, in the morning. She hadn't heard from her in a few days, although she knew Andrea was hard at work, getting her Magnolia Tea Room ready to open for business.

Lucy nodded. "Sounds good."

Gloria pushed the door open and slid one leg out.

Lucy grabbed her arm. "Gloria."

Gloria twisted back around. "Hmm?"

"Thank you for being such a great friend. I don't know what I'd do without you."

Sudden tears sprung to the back of Gloria's eyes. She loved Lucy. Loved *all* of her friends. There wasn't anything she wouldn't do for them...including giving them the shirt off her back.

She leaned across the seat and hugged her friend. "Same here. That's what friends are for." When she pulled back, she could see Lucy's eyes brimming with unshed tears. "You alright?"

"Yes. Yes, I'm fine." Lucy waved her out. "Go on. Get out of here before both of us start bawling like babies."

Gloria stepped out and leaned her head in. "See you tomorrow then." She didn't wait for a reply. Instead, she softly closed the door and slowly walked to the house.

***

Gloria had a few minutes to kill before it was time to get ready for her date with Paul.

She wandered over to her computer and turned it on. Her cat, Puddles, had curled up on the computer chair, his favorite spot to hang out.

She picked him up and settled into the seat. She set him on her lap where he promptly began to purr.

It was time to do a little more Milt investigating. She logged into her Worldbook account and typed in "Milton Tilton."

Seconds later, a picture of Milt popped up. Much to Gloria's surprise, he had hundreds of friends, mostly women, she noted. Or maybe she wasn't surprised.

She read several of the messages posted on his page. Some of them nearly singed her eyebrows. She shook her head. This Milt was a real player.

She wondered if Frances was aware of all the female friends he had and all the racy posts they left on his page. She scrolled through his friends list to see if Frances and Milt were friends. She couldn't find her name anywhere.

A few of the women looked familiar and Gloria could only surmise that they were Dreamwood residents.

The last few posts were panicky women who wondered where Milt had gone and begged him to call them asap.

She almost clicked away when one message in particular caught her eye. It was from someone named "Raven Fair." Her text message read "Milt, baby. We need to get together again after you get back."

Gloria's eyes narrowed. She wished she knew who "Raven Fair" was. She clicked on Raven's profile. A picture of a black bird popped onto the screen. Did this "Raven Fair" know something that no one else did? Maybe that Milt had gone somewhere of his own free will?

Gloria wandered to the bath and drew a tub full of warm water. She poured several capfuls of her homemade rose scented oils in the water. Gloria stripped off her clothes and sank into the fragrant waters. She leaned her head back and closed her eyes.

Instead of a nice, relaxing soak in the tub, she spent the entire time bouncing between thoughts of Milt and Lucy.

Perhaps she had overstepped her boundaries when she set Lucy up on that date.

But what the heck. It was a harmless breakfast. The worst that could happen was that Lucy would end up with a new friend, someone to hang out with...or maybe it would turn into something more.

After all, the girls weren't spring chickens anymore. Life was too short to spend it pining over someone like Bill. On top of that, Lucy didn't seem all that upset. She even thanked Gloria for being such a good friend. That's what friends were for. Picking you up, dusting you off, setting you up on dates...

Satisfied that Lucy was on the right track, Gloria mulled over the Milt issue. The men at breakfast had mentioned a woman – Francine - that seemed to be a bit of a stalker. It was obvious they were talking about Frances. Maybe Milt was trying to escape Frances and the only way he knew how was to "disappear?"

The fact that Frances knew so many intimate details of Milt's daily schedule was disturbing. Who did stuff like that? Unless of course they were obsessed, which Gloria was beginning to think maybe Frances was a bit unbalanced. She made a mental note to discuss the possibility with Liz.

Then there was the small problem of Milt's gambling debts.

The bath water was beginning to cool. Gloria lifted her foot, flipped the dial and turned it all the way to hot.

Gloria still hadn't had a chance to question Trudy, who was supposedly one of the last people to talk to Milt before he vanished.

Her eyes narrowed. Something about Clyde Ward was bugging her. She got the feeling that maybe he was holding something back.

She wondered if Frances had tried to contact Milt's family, possibly his children, to see if maybe they had heard from him. Although she was almost 100% certain that Frances had tracked down every lead out there.

Gloria climbed out of the tub, relaxed and ready for her date with Paul. Her pulse quickened at the thought of seeing him. He had been working long hours and she hadn't seen him in several long, lonely days.

Gloria slipped into a pair of tan slacks and a white cotton blouse. The day was sunny and warm but the evening would be cool. She wasn't sure where they were going for dinner and Paul had told her it was a surprise.

Now all she had to do was wait.

Chapter 8

Paul was right on time. She watched as he eased his tall, athletic frame from the driver's side of his pickup. Gloria smiled at the sight of his truck. The truck meant he wasn't scheduled to work early the next morning.

Gloria noticed he was carrying a crimson-colored box as he stepped onto the porch. She looked down at the package in his hand. It was a box of her favorite Belgian chocolates.

He handed the box to her when he reached the top of the steps.

Gloria shook her head. "You are spoiling me rotten."

"Yep." He leaned forward and kissed her lips. "Just the way I like you – spoiled."

She led him inside, set the chocolates on the table and placed her hand on his arm. "Would you like to sit down?"

He jerked his head toward the door. "What about the porch?" The late afternoon was crisp and clear. Gloria nodded. She reached for her sweater hanging on the hook and followed behind as he headed back out to the porch.

Paul settled into the rocker and Gloria took the seat next to him. He reached for her hand. "How is the fall cleaning going?"

Gloria tapped her foot on the porch board and gave a gentle push. "Lucy came by to help. I don't have many clothes left," she groaned. "If I hadn't stopped her, I'd be running around in my birthday suit."

Paul raised his brows. "Now that I wouldn't mind seeing," he teased.

Gloria's face reddened. "You'd probably laugh your head off."

"Hm. I don't think so."

Mally wandered up to the porch and settled in on top of Paul's feet. He leaned down and patted her head. "You behaving yourself?"

Mally let out a low moan and closed her eyes.

"That's what I thought," he answered.

Gloria rubbed her hands together. "Where did you say you were taking me?"

"I didn't," Paul chuckled. "It's a surprise."

The two of them talked a few more minutes about kids, grandkids, the upcoming holidays and Lucy's date.

Paul frowned. "What happened to...Bill?"

Gloria explained the situation while Paul listened quietly, nodding once or twice. "I know you never cared for him that much."

"Yeah," Gloria admitted, "he wasn't my favorite."

Gloria went on to tell him about Frances and her missing boyfriend, Milt, and admitted she had agreed to look into his disappearance.

"Another mystery," he surmised.

She nodded. "What do you think?"

Paul clasped his hands together and placed them behind his head. He leaned back in the chair and stared thoughtfully at the barn across the street. "If this is out of character, there would be cause for concern. Has his family reported him missing?"

"That's something I don't know," she confessed. "I'm not sure if he even has family."

Paul rose to his feet. "I would start there."

Mally lifted herself from Paul's feet and waited by the back door. Gloria let her in, grabbed her keys and met Paul back out on the porch.

They rode in silence, each of them deep in their own thoughts.

Paul turned and headed toward the larger town of Rapid Creek, which was on the other side of Green Springs. Rapid Creek was halfway between Belhaven and Grand Rapids.

He made a few more turns and Gloria finally figured out they were heading toward Lake Harmony.

He parked the truck in the parking lot across the street from the lake. Gloria knew better than to try to climb out herself.

80

She obediently waited for Paul to come around to the passenger door and open it.

She slipped her hand into his and stepped out of the truck.

"Where..."

"You'll see soon enough," Paul assured her.

They walked down the small gravel path toward the boat launch. When they cleared the trees, Gloria saw the surprise. A long, wooden dock ran along the launch. Jutting out into the water was a large, two-story passenger boat. The bottom section was enclosed. An upper level sported an open, airy deck.

Paul and Gloria joined the line of people that were boarding. The man near the entrance took the tickets from Paul and they stepped inside.

A rich mahogany wood covered the interior walls. Antique lighting fixtures dotted the ceiling and intimate tables for two and four spread out around the cozy dining room. In the center of each table was a black taper candelabrum with three lit candles. At the base of the candelabra were pink and red roses, adorned with sprigs of baby's breath.

A waiter escorted them to their table. A placard with their names engraved in gold lettering sat off to the side of the gorgeous centerpiece. "You may be seated now but I suggest heading up one floor to order a cocktail and enjoy the breathtaking view during sail away."

Paul led Gloria to the stairs in the back and stepped to the side while she climbed the stairs ahead of him.

In the center of the upper deck was a large bar, built of the same magnificent mahogany as the lower level. Scattered across the deck were bistro tables. Several other guests were already standing at the edge of the railings, enjoying the view.

They made their way over to the bar where Paul ordered two glasses of tea. He handed one to Gloria and raised his glass. "A toast."

She raised her glass.

"A toast to dinner with the most beautiful woman in the world."

They tapped their glasses and Gloria lowered hers to hide the tinge of pink that colored her cheeks.

"Shall we?" Paul held out his arm.

Gloria slipped her arm through his as they made their way over to the side rail and watched as more passengers wandered down the dock.

Finally, the ship set sail. Gloria felt her tension slip away as the ship drifted from the shoreline.

Romantic music softly floated in the air as the boat circled the outer edges of Lake Harmony. They finished their glass of tea just in time to hear the captain announce dinner was about to be served. The two placed their empty glasses on the edge of the bar and descended the stairs.

Paul pulled out Gloria's chair and waited for her to slide in before taking the seat across from her. Water glasses sat nearby. A basket of bread and tin of butter were off to one side. Next to the basket of bread were two covered dishes. Gloria eyed them curiously.

Paul plucked a piece of crusty bread from the basket and set it on his plate. "You're dying to find out what's under there."

Gloria nodded. "I am," she confessed.

She gingerly reached over, lifted the lid and peeked underneath. She lifted it high enough to see herself but not for Paul to see. She set the lid back down and smiled.

He scooped a pat of butter on his knife and spread it across the bread. "Well?"

"Well what?" she asked innocently.

"What's underneath?"

Gloria sniffed. "Hm. Curiosity killed the cat."

Paul shrugged and smiled. "Touché."

The waiter arrived at their table. "What? Your salads – they no good?"

Paul reached for another piece of bread. "Salad. Huh."

"Have you looked at the menu?" The waiter turned to Gloria.

Gloria hadn't. She had been too busy trying to irritate Paul to notice them sitting on the edge of the table. "Not yet," she admitted.

"Take your time." He lowered into a small bow. "I'll be back."

Gloria settled on the salmon filet with new potatoes and a side of parmesan garlic green beans while Paul decided to try the prime rib, baked potato and steamed asparagus.

Their table sat facing a window. They gazed out the large, glass pane and watched as the sun dipped below the horizon. The twinkle of lights from the houses that dotted the shore cast a romantic glimmer across the water.

Their conversation flowed easily and bounced from missing Milt, to Lucy's hot date, to the holidays.

The waiter finally returned with their food. Gloria stabbed a bean with her fork and then nibbled the edge. "The food is delicious."

The interior lights had dimmed, giving off a warm glow. Soft violin music drifted in the air.

Paul sliced a piece of meat. "I hoped you would like it," he confessed.

Gloria set her fork on her plate. "Like it? This is one of the most romantic dinners I've ever had," she assured him.

They spent the rest of the meal chatting about Paul's job and his flip-flopping on retirement.

The waiter cleared their empty dinner plates and returned with two cups of coffee and two huge pieces of chocolate cake.

Gloria frowned at the large slice of cake. There was no way she could eat it. The waiter, noting her look of dismay, offered to box it up.

Finally, the romantic evening and cruise ended when the boat docked in the same spot where it had departed.

Paul held Gloria's sweater as she slipped her arms in the sleeves.

They wandered out of the dining room and onto the dock.

Gloria glanced back one more time and let out a wistful breath. "That was lovely." She grabbed Paul's hand and pulled him to her for a kiss.

A tingle ran down her spine when their lips met. The tingle started at the top of her head and raced all the way to the tip of her toes. Finally, they took a step back and Gloria worked to catch her breath.

Gloria sat quietly in the truck on the ride back. Paul was so thoughtful and loving. He was her perfect mate. A small sigh escaped her lips...maybe someday.

Her mind switched gears as she mulled over Milt's disappearance. She needed to call Frances and find out if any of Milt's family had reported him missing.

Then her thoughts wandered to Brian and the upcoming proposal. She felt a sliver of jealousy but quickly pushed it away. She was happy for them. Andrea was young and so was Brian. It would be fun to watch them have children and raise their family in Belhaven.

Paul pulled into the drive, shut off the truck and walked around to open Gloria's door. She slipped out of the seat and the two of them walked hand in hand up the steps.

Thankfully, she had remembered to leave the porch light on. She handed Paul her keys and waited while he unlocked the side door.

Gloria let Mally out and the two of them stood on the porch. They watched as she raced out to the barn, around the back of the shed and past the garden. She sniffed around her favorite spots and then patrolled the perimeter of the yard before she trotted up the steps and stopped on the porch.

Gloria tightened her sweater around her. "I love fall. I was thinking about having a little fall get-together this year. Maybe hook up the old wagon, throw a few bales of hay on it and have an old-fashioned wagon ride."

She gazed up at him and asked, "What do you think?"

Paul shoved his hands in his pockets. "I think it's a great idea. The kids would love it."

She went on. "We could have a bonfire and roast hot dogs and marshmallows after it's over. Invite all our friends and the kids – even yours."

He wrapped his arms around Gloria and pulled her close. "Sounds like a lot of fun. When were you thinking?"

She furrowed her brow. "Not this weekend." The boys were coming to finish the tree fort. Trying to do that plus organize a fall party would be too much. On top of that, she had the investigation. "I think the first weekend in October would be perfect."

That would give her time to do a little planning. She hoped Brian could wait that long.

Chapter 9

"Frances said Milt doesn't really have any family," Liz told her sister when Gloria called her the next morning. "I think there was a nephew he hadn't seen in several years that lives somewhere out west."

"So no one contacted the police to report him missing?"

Liz grunted. "No one, if you don't count Frances. I think she calls them every single day."

Gloria hung up the phone and headed to the washing machine.

She pulled her clothes from the washer, dumped them in the laundry basket and headed for the door. "C'mon Mally. Let's go hang some clothes out on the line."

Mally popped out of her doggy bed and waited for Gloria to open the door.

They stepped out onto the porch. It was shaping up to be a beautiful fall day. It was the perfect kind of day for hanging clothes on the line.

Gloria loved the smell of the fresh air and sunshine on clean clothes. It was something a dryer couldn't duplicate, no matter how many dryer sheet companies claimed their product smelled like fresh air.

It was sheet day and Gloria had already hung those to dry. She started on the next row, clipping clothespins to the edges of her slacks and watching them blow in the breeze. She had just finished hanging her last blouse when Lucy pulled in the drive.

Lucy wandered across the lawn. She stopped at the end of the clothesline pole. "You still hang your clothes out?"

Gloria's head whipped around. She shaded her eyes and stared at her friend. "You don't?"

Lucy shook her head. "Nope but maybe I should."

Gloria picked up the empty laundry basket and headed for the house. The laundry was the last chore on her list and she was ready to get the investigation under way.

She set the basket near the door, pulled her keys from the hook and grabbed her purse. "I'll drive since you drove yesterday."

Lucy waited until Gloria had pulled Annabelle from the garage before she climbed in the passenger side. They drove in silence for several long moments.

Gloria could see Lucy was a million miles away. "Are you alright?"

There was no answer.

"Earth to Lucy," Gloria teased.

"Huh?"

"I asked if you were alright."

Lucy nodded. "Yeah. Just thinking about..."

"Bill?"

Lucy nodded again. "Yeah. Not that I want him back or anything. Just wondering how he's doing."

"Why don't you give him a call?" Gloria suggested. She couldn't see the harm in that. They were both adults, after all.

Lucy tugged on the side of her seatbelt absentmindedly. "I might do that."

The town of Lakeville was larger than Belhaven and Gloria had a bit of trouble finding the quickie loan shop. They drove up and down the strip several times before Lucy finally spotted it. "I think it's right there," she pointed.

Gloria swung into an open spot and shifted the car into park.

The building was narrow and set back from the rest of the buildings that lined Main Street. Small, gold letters on the front of the glass window read: *Integrity Loans.* Below that in even smaller letters were the words: *Money in minutes.*

The girls got out of the car and walked to the door. Gloria grabbed the knob and pushed the door open. A small bell chimed.

The inside was even smaller than the outside. Two cheap, plastic chairs sat against one wall. Off to the other side was a dingy, artificial plant that obscured a small plywood desk.

An old, white ceiling fan hung above the entrance door. It was almost gray in color, whether from age or dirt, Gloria couldn't tell.

"Can I help you lovely ladies?"

A young man wearing several gold chains around his neck, sporting a large insignia ring and slicked back blonde hair leaned an elbow on the cheap counter and eyed them with interest.

Gloria shifted her purse on her arm and stepped to the counter. "Yes, we have a friend that appears to have come up missing. I." She looked at Lucy. "We think that you may have loaned him some money recently and wondered if maybe you could help us out."

His eyes narrowed. "What's his name?"

"Milton Tilton."

The man, *Johnny,* according to the tag on his shirt, drummed his fingers on the counter. "Lemme see...what does he look like?"

Gloria pulled her phone from her purse. She opened her Worldbook account and typed in Milton Tilton in the search bar. Milt's profile and picture popped up. Gloria turned the screen and tipped it so the man could see.

He studied the screen. "Yeah. Yeah. He was in here a few weeks ago lookin' for some real quick cash. I remember him cuz he seemed real desperate. So desperate that he used his fancy Caddy for collateral."

Gloria switched the phone off and shoved it back in her purse. "Did he mention who he might have owed the money to that he so desperately needed?"

"Yeah. He did mention a name." He snapped his fingers. "I know. It was Vinnie somebody." He nodded. "Yeah. I'm sure the guy's name was Vinnie. The only reason I remember is cuz I have a cousin named Vinnie."

Gloria leaned in. "Do you remember anything else?"

Johnny paused and stared up at the ceiling. "I asked him what Vinnie looked like. You never know. It mighta been my cousin, Vinnie."

"What did he say?" Lucy asked.

"That he had never met this Vinnie person and only dealt with a middle man."

Gloria lowered her purse. "Can I leave my number and if you remember anything else let me know?"

"Yeah. Sure."

The man scribbled Gloria's number on a piece of paper, shoved it in the drawer and pushed it shut. "Yeah. He was real nervous, that one."

"He's still on the hook for the $5k I loaned him." Johnny glanced at the calendar on the wall. "He has a couple of weeks left before the loan comes due. Otherwise..." The man leaned back and grinned. "I'm gonna have me a new ride."

The girls wandered out of the store and stopped out front. Lucy looked back. "Good luck finding Milt's car."

Gloria nodded. "Yeah. Hey. What do you think about me getting some business cards made and putting a company name on them? You know, something along the lines of Silver Sleuth Detective Agency or such."

Lucy nodded. That would be cool. It would make Gloria's investigative work more legit and it would save Gloria from having to scribble her name on scraps of paper.

"Are you gonna start charging a fee?"

Gloria blinked rapidly. It was a thought. She had built a reputation for her sleuthing. Perhaps there were people out there willing to pay for her services. At the very least, she could cover some of her expenses. Write them off: gas, dining out when under cover and maybe even buy some detective supplies.

"I need to track down my cousin, Millie. You know, the one that works on the cruise ship. She and her husband had a detective agency. Maybe she could give me some pointers on how to set up shop. I can ask her about booking a cruise at the same time."

She made a mental note to fire off an email to Millie.

"Do you have time to make a run by Dreamwood with me and see if Frances is around?" Gloria backed out of the parking space and headed out of town. "I have a few questions now that we're delving into this mystery."

Lucy buckled her belt and nodded. "Sure. I haven't seen your sister, Liz, in a while. Maybe we can all meet up and go over what we have so far."

Gloria stepped on the gas and they sped off down the road. "Say, I was thinking of having a fall party: a hayride, apple cider, bonfire, kind of thing the first weekend in October."

Lucy smiled. "That would be fun. Why, its been years since we had one. Not since the kids were all home."

The more Gloria thought about it, the more excited she became. It would be fun. She'd invite all the girls and their spouses. She gave Lucy a sideways glance. Maybe by then Lucy wouldn't be alone.

Not only that, but this would give Brian the perfect opportunity to pop the question to Andrea.

Gloria pulled into an empty visitor parking spot not far from Liz's place. Her car and Frances' car were both in the lot.

"Let's try Liz first." Gloria made her way across the manicured lawn to the back door. She peered in the window and tapped on the glass. Liz didn't answer. "She's not home."

The girls wandered across the grassy strip that separated Liz's building from the one that Frances lived in. She made her way under the small covered porch and lifted her hand to knock.

She could see Frances – and Liz – inside. They were sitting at the kitchen table.

94

Liz caught a glimpse of Gloria out of the corner of her eye. She waved her in.

Gloria opened the door and held it for Lucy.

"Were your ears burning?" Liz hopped out of her seat. "We were just talking about you."

Gloria plopped her purse on the table and pulled out a chair. "Good, I hope."

Frances eyed Lucy suspiciously. Her eyes narrowed. "You look familiar."

"This is my friend, Lucy. I think you've met her before," Gloria said.

Frances frowned. "Say, you weren't one of those loose women that Milt was running around with right before he disappeared..."

Gloria rolled her eyes. "Good heavens, Frances. Lucy's never even met Milt," she snapped.

She immediately regretted her sharp reply when Frances' eyes filled with tears.

Frances stared down at her hands. "I-I'm sorry. I didn't mean that. Of course you don't know Milt."

Lucy patted Frances' arm. "It's okay. I have one of those faces that look familiar. People get me confused all the time."

Gloria pulled a small pad of paper from her purse and slipped her reading glasses on. "Do you ever remember Milt mentioning a man named Vinnie?"

Both Liz and Frances shook their head "no."

"What about a guy named Johnny that owned a fast cash place called Integrity Loans?"

Again, they both shook their heads.

It was Frances' turn to ask questions. "Did you ever talk to Clyde Ward or Trudy over on Wisteria Way?"

Gloria tapped the end of her pen on the top of the table. "I talked to Clyde but Trudy wasn't home."

Frances slammed her fist on the table in frustration. "That woman is never, ever home. She's some sort of apparition."

"Maybe she's a vampire." Lucy muttered under her breath. "We could stakeout her place," she added.

Gloria's wheels were turning. Yeah, they could, but how could they do it without anyone seeing them?

Liz answered the question before Gloria had a chance to ask. "There is a small park that sits catty corner to her back yard. It has a small playground for the grandkids."

Gloria was intrigued. "How do we stay out of sight?"

Liz shrugged. "Simple. There's a small, cinder block bathroom. You could hide out in there."

Frances sprang to her feet. "We could go now. You know, four sets of eyes are better than one...or two."

Liz waved her down. "Frances, I know you're anxious but we need to leave this to the professionals," she advised.

Frances' face fell but she didn't press the matter.

Gloria didn't want to give Frances a chance to insist on tagging along. She grabbed Lucy's hand and they headed to the door. "I'll leave my purse here if that's alright."

Frances' chair scraped against the hard linoleum as she pushed the chair back and stood. "Wait. You'll need these."

She reached into the kitchen cabinet, pulled out a pair of large binoculars and handed them to Gloria.

Chapter 10

The girls picked up the pace as they hustled down the sidewalk toward Wisteria Way. They veered off on Paisley Place, the street right before Wisteria Way.

Gloria spied a small park at the end of the street. "This must be the one Liz was talking about."

The park was empty and the girls made a beeline for the women's restroom. Lucy stopped in front of the door. She shook her head. "This isn't gonna work."

"What do you mean it's not gonna work?"

Lucy pointed up. "Look. The women's restroom is facing the wrong direction."

She pointed to the men's side. "We're gonna have to spy on Trudy's house from the men's side."

Gloria looked around. "What if someone shows up and wants to use the men's room?"

Lucy shrugged. "Then we leave. I mean, it's not like anyone is going to recognize us."

Lucy had a point.

Gloria had the nagging sensation this was going to be a total waste of time. "Okay, let's roll." She sucked in a breath and barreled through the door. She squeezed her eyes shut, hoping that no one was in there taking care of business.

Much to her relief, it was empty. Her happiness was short-lived when she realized the window that overlooked Trudy's backyard was high - too high to look through unless you were standing on something.

Gloria lowered her gaze. Which happened to be the outer rim of the urinal...a filthy, dirty, disgusting urinal at that.

Lucy stuck her hand on her hip. "I'm not gonna stand on that," she announced. "I'll guard the door."

Gloria looped the binoculars around her neck, grabbed hold of the window ledge, placed one shoe, then the other on the rim of the urinal. She teetered back and forth for a second before gripping the windowsill to catch her balance.

From this position, she had a bird's-eye view of Trudy's backyard. It was tidy. A small flower garden sat near the corner. A white picket fence surrounded the perimeter of the yard. A covered porch ran the length of the rear of the house. A set of sliding glass doors took up one whole side.

Gloria lifted the binoculars to her eyes and adjusted the dial. The curtains were all drawn. "I can't see a darn thing," she grumbled.

She stood there for several long moments. Nothing was happening. The woman wasn't even home. Or, if she was, she wasn't spending time in the yard. Although she had to at some point, considering how tidy and meticulous the yard was.

Lucy, who had been guarding the door, stepped closer to Gloria. "See anything yet?"

99

Gloria shook her head. "Nope. Nada. Zip."

She remained perched on the urinal for what seemed like forever. Gloria's back began to ache. She handed Lucy the binoculars. "You wanna try?"

Lucy shook her head. "No way. I'd bust my butt in these shoes."

Gloria looked down at Lucy's feet. She was wearing a pair of flats. This was definitely more of a tennis shoe-type investigation.

"We can't stay here all day. I have stuff to do," Lucy pointed out.

Gloria's shoulders drooped. "Me, too. Unless Frances can give us a firmer timetable on this Trudy's coming and going, we're wasting our energy."

Gloria loosened her grip on the windowsill and took one foot off the side of the urinal. The narrow edge was slick and her foot began to slip. She started to fall backward, her arms flailing wildly in the air in large circles. "Whoa."

Lucy rushed over and caught her friend. The two of them stumbled backwards as Lucy wrapped both arms around Gloria's waist.

Lucy fell hard against the sink behind them.

"What is going on in here?" a stern, male voice called out from the doorway.

Gloria's eyes darted to the doorway. Her face turned bright red. Lucy's arms were still around her waist in what must look a whole lot like two women in a bit of an intimate embrace.

Lucy promptly released her grip on her friend. "It's not what you think."

The man raised a hand and shook his head. "I don't need an explanation on why two grown women are in a men's public restroom caught in a compromising embrace."

Gloria smoothed the front of her blouse and took a step forward. "You have it all wrong."

The man cut her off. "Get out before I call the police," he warned.

Gloria lowered her head and sidestepped the angry man.

Lucy scowled at him. "Jerk," she hissed under her breath.

The girls wandered out of the men's bathroom and across the park to the sidewalk out front. They made the trip back to Frances' apartment in silence.

When they reached the sidewalk in front of Frances' place, Gloria grabbed the door handle. "Let's pretend what just happened never did."

Lucy nodded. "I agree. That guy was a jack-."

"Lucy," Gloria cut her off.

The door swung open. Frances was on the other side. "Well? Didja see anything? Was Trudy home?"

Gloria shook her head. "No and no."

"We got a good look at the men's restroom," Lucy said.

Gloria handed Frances the binoculars. "You need to pinpoint Trudy's schedule so we can try to corner her – or spy on her – or maybe both." The fact that the woman was so evasive piqued Gloria's interest. It almost seemed as if she was hiding something.

All that sleuthing had made Gloria thirsty. "Can we swing by the restaurant and grab an iced tea before we head home?"

Lucy wiped her brow. "Yeah, I worked up a sweat."

The girls made their way to Dreamwood Eats and over to the soda fountain. Gloria filled her glass with ice and finished filling it with tea. The place was busy for early afternoon and the four of them squeezed into a small table near the front.

The girls chitchatted about everything except Milt. Honestly, Gloria was a little tired of hearing about him. After all, it was looking more and more as if he had intentionally gone missing and didn't care to be found.

"That's interesting," Liz commented.

"What?" Lucy wondered.

"Isn't that Vivian?" Liz answered Lucy's question with one of her own.

Gloria followed Liz's finger over to the small bakery counter off to one side. "Vivian there is ordering a box of those chocolate chip cookies that Milt likes."

Frances shrugged. "So? Those are one of the restaurant specialties and they always have them on sale. That's why Milt liked them."

"Yeah, but Vivian can't eat them. She's allergic to chocolate. I know that for a fact. She had a reaction here in the restaurant not too long ago when she bit down on a small chip mixed in with the "everything" muffins. She didn't notice it and when her throat started to close up, they had to call an ambulance."

Gloria's eyes narrowed. That was interesting. Why would a woman who was allergic to chocolate, order a big box of chocolate chip cookies? "What do you know about this Vivian?"

Liz and Frances stared at each other. "She moved in here about a year ago, after her husband died. I heard he was a high school principal at some school in Grand Rapids."

Vivian paid for her purchase and strolled across the dining area to the front door.

"What day is today?" Liz asked.

"Tuesday," Gloria answered. "Why?"

"Well, it's bridge day." Frances told them. "The ladies bridge club meets in the clubhouse every Tuesday and Thursday afternoon. She probably picked them up for the club."

Liz snapped her fingers. "Now that you mention it, I think that Trudy is part of the bridge club, too. I was in there talking to the manager one afternoon and a group of them were playing."

Gloria didn't have time to do a second stakeout today. "What time does it end?"

"It lasts a couple hours, I'm sure. Maybe three or so?" Liz wasn't 100% certain.

"I'll come back Thursday afternoon and we can check it out." Gloria reached for her purse. "For now, we should probably head out. I want to stop by Andrea's on the way home."

The girls made their way back to the car and climbed inside. Lucy slid her sunglasses on and glanced at Gloria. "What are you thinking?"

"That this case is tough to crack. It's easier when there are bodies."

***

Gloria pulled into Andrea's gravel drive and rounded the bend. Andrea's sports car was in the drive, parked off to the side.

A truck filled with tools and construction materials was right behind her car.

The girls climbed out of the car and headed to the front door.

Gloria rapped the lions head knocker and gazed out into the yard as she waited for Andrea to open the door. Something was different but she couldn't quite put her finger on what it was.

The door swung open. Andrea Malone grinned when she saw Gloria. "I thought you were coming by this morning."

"I was. I got bogged down finishing up a load of wash and then we went over to Dreamwood."

Gloria and Lucy stepped inside and Andrea shut the door behind them. "Isn't that where your sister, Liz, lives?"

Gloria nodded.

"Does she know that crazy lady that chained herself to the front of the restaurant?" Andrea laughed. "Man, she's obsessed with some guy..."

"Milton Tilton," Gloria told her.

Andrea's brow went up. "You know him?"

"You could say that," Lucy muttered.

Andrea's eyes widened. "Let me guess. You're *looking* for him."

"Bingo!" Lucy shouted.

The girls followed Andrea into the kitchen where Alice, Andrea's former housekeeper and new housemate, hovered over a hot stove. The aroma of cilantro, onion and garlic filled the air.

Alice wiped her hands on the front of her apron. "Ah, Miss Gloria. You're just in time for my firehouse fajitas."

Firehouse fajitas. The dish sounded delicious – and lethal. Although Gloria loved spicy foods, they didn't love her back. It was a recipe for disaster. She shook her head. "I'm sorry, Alice, I can't stay that long. I have to get Lucy home."

"But." Lucy started to protest. Gloria pinched her arm.

"Uh, yeah. Sorry Alice. I have to get home." She glared at Gloria.

"Oh, you can take them to go. I wrap them up for dinner."

Gloria protested. Alice insisted.

"While Alice finishes up, come check out the tea room." Andrea waved them into the hall.

Andrea had added a beautiful addition to the side of the house. A glass enclosed sunroom really and she had plans to turn it into a tea room. Gloria had a sneaking suspicion that part of the reason was so that Alice would have something to do.

Andrea and Gloria had stumbled upon a secret room inside Andrea's home that boasted a room full of beautiful paintings by the former owner and famous artist, Sofia Masson.

The girls trailed behind Andrea as they followed her down the hall and into the living room. They crossed the room as they made their way over to the set of French doors on the other side of the massive living room fireplace.

Andrea opened the leaded glass doors and the girls took a step down.

Gloria drew a deep breath and turned in a slow circle. The room was magnificent. Andrea had added a bit of her own personal touch with hanging plants and Persian rugs.

Off in one corner was a gurgling angel fountain. Several easels displayed a few of the famous artist's paintings. "It looks like you're almost ready to open for business."

Andrea nodded. "All I'm waiting on are the bistro tables, which should be here any day now." She looked back toward the living room. "I finally convinced Alice that we can't serve spicy all the time. We narrowed it down to Tuesday tacos in the tea room."

"Catchy name." Gloria nodded. "Good idea."

"The rest of the time will be light finger foods and bite size sandwiches." She eyed Lucy, the queen of sweets. "And there will be trays of tempting desserts."

Lucy grinned. "I'll be one of your first customers," she promised.

Andrea stopped in the middle of the room. Her brow furrowed. "You don't think Dot will be upset – like I'm competing against her?"

Gloria touched her arm. "No, dear. Dot thinks this place will be a wonderful addition to Belhaven," she reassured her.

Andrea ran a hand through her blonde locks. "That's a relief. I was worried."

She went on. "So what's up with this missing guy? From the news story, he just up and vanished."

Gloria nodded. "It's all very mysterious and not many leads so far. Although there are a couple."

She thought about the Vinnie guy that Johnny from the loan shop had mentioned.

"Milt was quite a ladies' man. He may have met with foul play if he was messing around with someone's girl or wife." Until that moment, Gloria hadn't considered that angle. At least not seriously. She would have to ask Liz who on the list might be suspect. She didn't dare ask Frances.

"There you are." Alice sidled over, a plastic grocery bag of goodies in each hand. She handed one to Lucy. "One for you." She handed the other one to Gloria, "and one for you."

Gloria gave Alice a hug. "Thank you, Alice. You are so sweet."

Lucy opened the bag and stuck her face in the bag. "This smells so good."

Andrea led them back out to the front entrance and opened the door. The four of them stepped out onto the large portico. "You notice anything different?"

"There is something different." Gloria's eyes searched the yard. "I can't quite put my finger on it."

Andrea pointed to the side yard. "The shed is gone."

The old garden shed had sat in the middle of the backyard for decades, long before Andrea purchased the large manor. It was inside the shed that the girls had discovered a body.

Gloria nodded. "Ah. You're right."

Andrea lifted a hand to shade her eyes. "I figured that place had enough bad history and I wanted it gone." She waved a hand to a spot on the other side of the gravel drive. "I'm putting in a two-car garage. It'll be done before the first snowflake hits the ground."

Andrea could use a garage, especially in Michigan where winters were sometimes long and brutal.

Once again, Gloria silently wondered what Andrea and Brian would do when they married. Both of them had sunk a great deal of money into each of their homes. It would be a tough decision.

Brian's home had belonged to his grandparents so Gloria wondered if it held some sentimental value.

On the other hand, she knew how attached Andrea was to her home...

Paul and Gloria would have to face a similar dilemma if they ever got married. That was a big "if."

"I think that's a wise decision," Gloria answered.

The girls climbed back in the car and headed to the farm.

"It's a wonder you have time to get any housework done," Lucy commented.

Gloria gave a half shrug. "Yeah, there are days when I wonder if I'm coming or going."

Back at the farm, she pulled in the drive and parked close to the house.

"I'm gonna head home," Lucy reached for her purse that was lying on the floor.

Gloria eased out of the car and came round to stand near the front. "Are you still going to call Bill?"

Lucy fiddled with the keys in her hand. "Yeah. I think I need some closure," she admitted. "We didn't really end with a fight but we didn't really end on the best of terms, either."

Gloria nodded. "Good luck. Call me if you need to talk later." She watched Lucy slide into the jeep and back out of the drive.

Gloria whispered a small prayer for her friend as she climbed the porch steps. She prayed that the Lord's will be done and that He protect Lucy's gentle heart.

Gloria's house phone was ringing when she stepped in the door. It was her daughter, Jill. "I waited until the boys were in school to call you," Jill told her. "Do you need any supplies to finish the tree fort? I don't want you having to buy anything else. You've already done enough."

"That's thoughtful of you, dear," Gloria replied. "I could use some small cans of paint and brushes so the boys can paint it once we have it together. Whatever color you think they would like except for black."

"Do you need anything else?"

Gloria shook her head. "No. I have the rest of the stuff here." Gloria stepped out onto the porch with Mally and the phone. "How do you think the boys would do using the cordless drill?"

Visions of Tyler drilling a long screw into the center of his brother's forehead popped into Gloria's head.

She remembered the last visit when Tyler went a little crazy driving the tractor and chased Mally across the yard. Perhaps she should give this a bit more thought.

Jill confirmed her decision. "I think I would be hands-on for that project. Tyler could get the bright idea to screw his brother to the planks."

Maybe she could get Paul or Brian to come by for the assembly part. That way, they could crawl up into the tree and supervise. "I'll work on it. Don't worry about them," she assured her daughter.

Gloria hung up the phone and headed to her computer. She put off calling Liz for a list of possible jealous boyfriends - or husbands – until she saw if Worldbook would give her some good leads.

She fired up the computer and headed to the kitchen to make a cup of hot tea.

When she got back, Puddles was in the chair, waiting for Gloria to pick him up. She settled him into her lap and reached for her glasses.

Gloria grabbed the mouse and spun the little black scrolling wheel as she scanned his list of friends. The list included Trudy Gromalski, the elusive woman. There was also another woman that looked familiar. Gloria inched closer to the screen. It was the woman from the restaurant. The one that bought the chocolate chip cookies. She clicked on her name. Vivian Coulter.

Gloria clicked back to the main page and scrolled through the comments. Several of the women had posted new messages, begging Milt to call them. "Raven Fair" caught her eye again. There was still no profile picture. Her last comment was unusual. "The mystical mystery of the missing Milt. If only he could tell you where he's at..."

Gloria scrunched her brow. It sure did sound like this person may have a good lead on Milt and that maybe they knew more than they were letting on. Or maybe this person was taunting the other posters who were concerned for his safety. A shiver inched down Gloria's spine.

She scrolled backwards through the screen - back to before Milt went missing.

There were several posts from men. Milt had his share of enemies. One post in particular seemed to be threatening. It was from an anonymous source.

"If I catch you hanging around Viv one more time, I'm gonna come over to your place and pound your pudgy pig face right into the ground."

Gloria leaned back. She wondered if this "Viv" was the Vivian that picked up the cookies in the restaurant. It was time to check out that bridge club Thursday afternoon.

She opened her few emails, which were mostly online bills, played a couple rounds of Solitaire and then shut it down.

Gloria grabbed her laundry basket and headed to the clothesline. The clothes had long since dried in the stiff autumn breeze. She worked her way down the line, as she folded each item and neatly stacked them inside the basket.

A rumble of thunder threatened in the distance as storm clouds gathered out behind the barn. She managed to get the clothes off the line just in time. Mally and Gloria dashed up the steps as the first large raindrop hit the ground.

They stood there and watched as the wind whipped the leaves on the trees and the skies opened up. Mally whimpered and backed closer to the door. She did not like storms.

The two of them stepped into the kitchen as a bolt of lightning hit on the other side of the tree and shook the ground.

Gloria looked down at Mally, who was shaking. "We cut that close."

She carried the laundry basket to her closet and hung what clothes she had left – the things that Lucy hadn't tossed out the other day – onto hangers before making her way to the bed.

Mally crawled under the bed to wait for the storm to pass. Gloria reached down and patted her reassuringly before returning to the task at hand.

She pulled the sheets from the basket and lifted them to her face. The sheets smelled so fresh, she could hardly wait to go to bed.

Back in the kitchen, Gloria opened the fridge. Front and center was the "Firehouse Fajita's" that Alice had given her. It was tempting – and lethal.

She quickly closed the door and opened the freezer. She reached for the frozen dinner that was closest, pulled it out of the box and popped it into the microwave. Tonight's dinner was going to be quick and easy.

Gloria mulled over the day's events as she nibbled on the drumstick.

It was nice to have a little peace and quiet for a change. She had no plans for tomorrow. Thursday was Lucy's breakfast date, followed by a trip to Dreamwood to spy on the bridge club. If she got lucky, she could corner the elusive "Trudy."

After dinner, Gloria sprawled out in the recliner and turned on the TV. She dozed off during the evening news and woke up in time to watch the beginning of her favorite TV show, Detective on the Side. It was a rerun but it was a good one. Actually, all of them were good ones.

Gloria climbed into bed after she watched two episodes. She snuggled down under the covers and pulled the sheet to her chin. It smelled wonderful.

As she drifted off to sleep, her brain cleared and she suddenly realized she had a good idea who the mysterious "Raven Fair" might be.

Chapter 11

"What do you mean Frances is now a suspect?" Liz asked in disbelief. That didn't make the least bit of sense to Liz.

It really didn't make much sense to Gloria, either. "Didn't you tell me that Frances had a small tattoo on her lower back?"

"Yeah. I always thought it was odd," Liz admitted.

"And why was it odd?" Gloria pressed.

"Because it was a black raven." Liz sighed. "And it's uglier than all get-out," she added.

"Go check out Milton's profile on Worldbook and you'll see why I added her to the list of suspects," Gloria told her sister.

Liz didn't want to believe her best friend could be involved in Milt's disappearance. If she was, wouldn't she want to sweep it under the rug instead of chain herself to the front of the restaurant and call the local news crew?

She hung up the phone and headed to her computer. Sure enough, Milt was friends with a mysterious Raven Fair, who seemed to be mocking other posters, alluding to the fact that she knew something about Milt's disappearance.

She promptly called Gloria back. "So should we confront Frances with our suspicions?"

"No. We don't want to tip our hand. Not yet, anyways. I want to check out the bridge club and investigate a few more people."

Gloria balanced the phone between her ear and shoulder as she poured herself a cup of coffee. She slid into the kitchen chair and unfolded the morning paper. "The more that I think about it, the more I'm convinced someone, somewhere – at Dreamwood – knows something about Milt's disappearance."

Gloria glanced at the clock. "I better get going. I haven't even showered yet." She assured Liz she'd be there around lunchtime tomorrow so they could "accidentally" bump into the bridge club and perhaps glean a few more clues into Milt's mysterious disappearance.

Gloria finished her coffee and morning paper and then Mally and she headed outside. A nice, brisk morning walk would get the sleuthing brain cells pumping. There was nothing like a long walk through the fields and back to the creek to clear the head.

Mally knew exactly where they were going. She darted off in front of Gloria, racing to the far edge of the field before turning around and running back. She did this two or three times before Gloria made it to the other end.

She was panting, her pink tongue hanging out of the side of her mouth as she looked up at Gloria.

Gloria shook her head. "You crazy dog. I wish I had half your energy."

The edge of the familiar woods was in sight. Gloria wove her way through the forest and settled onto her favorite resting spot – an old fallen tree log that sat not far from the edge of the creek. Mally splashed in the water and chased a few birds before she settled in at Gloria's feet.

Gloria absentmindedly scratched Mally's ear as she turned her attention to the trees. She studied the leaves. In a couple more weeks, the woods would be breathtaking shades of glorious gold and red. "What do you think Mally? You think Frances is involved in Milt's disappearance?"

Mally let out a low moan and closed her eyes. She wasn't at all interested in Frances' guilt or innocence.

Gloria stroked Mally's soft fur. Of course, it didn't make much sense that Frances was involved. Maybe she was bored with her life and this added a little excitement, a big mystery and a lot of attention.

If that was Frances's goal, boy, she was certainly getting that.

The fact that she seemed obsessed with Milt, his habits, his likes and dislikes. Maybe she had gone crazy and killed him, then buried his body and somehow mentally shut it out, her mind not able to deal with her obsession and the fact he was now gone. One of those "if I can't have you, no one can."

Gloria shivered...the thought creeped her out.

What about the threating message where someone told Milt to stay away from "Viv?" Then there was the mysterious Trudy and last but not least, Vinnie, the guy Milt owed money to.

That was four suspects. Four people Gloria needed to check out, and the sooner the better. The longer Milt was missing, the colder the trail became.

Gloria stood up and brushed the dirt from her pants. "C'mon girl. We better head home."

She stopped in the garage to assemble the fort building supplies. She plugged the battery for the cordless drill into the outlet to let it charge. Next, she placed a brand new box of wood screws on the table.

She would somehow have to figure out how to attach the boards for the railing. Gloria frowned. Better yet, she'd have to figure out *how* to build a railing...

Gloria didn't have a lot of experience with building things. She had always left those projects up to her husband, James. But James had been gone a long time now and it was up to Gloria to take care of these things.

She grabbed the kitchen phone from the wall and dialed Brian's number. "What are you doing Saturday?" she asked when he answered.

"Going on a hot date with you?" he teased.

Gloria snorted. "Yeah, right. No, I was wondering if you could spare a couple hours to come by and help my grandsons put the tree fort together."

"I thought you'd never ask," he replied.

Gloria let out a sigh of relief. "Oh, that reminds me. The fall party we talked about the other day..."

"The fall party?" Brian sounded confused. "You mean the engagement ring and your idea to surprise Andrea."

"Yeah, that's the one."

"Did you decide on a date?" he wondered.

"I was thinking the first weekend in October, or is that too late?"

"No, I think that would be perfect. You're going to invite all your, I mean our, friends?" he asked.

"Yes, of course. I picked up some nice little invitations the other day when I was out and about. I'll start addressing them if that Saturday works for you."

"Sounds great," Brian reassured her, "and I'll see you Saturday. I can swing by around 2:00."

"Perfect." Gloria hung up the phone and whispered a small prayer of thanks. It wasn't that she couldn't ask her son-in-law, Greg, or even Paul. The idea was for Jill and Greg to have a little time alone and Paul – well, she wasn't sure. He was always busy working.

Gloria grabbed the packet of invitations from the shopping bag. She pulled out the entire stack, set them on the table and picked up a pen. She made one out to each of the Garden Girls, along with Paul and his children. Then she addressed two more: one for her sister, Liz and one for Frances, if she wasn't in jail by then. Of course, there was Jill, Greg and the boys and last but not least, Andrea and Brian.

Gloria slid the invitations inside her purse and grabbed her keys. She wanted to get the invitations out as soon as possible.

She eased Annabelle into an empty spot in front of Dot's Restaurant and headed inside. The breakfast crowd was winding down. The only ones left were a few stragglers that stayed on for endless cups of coffee and socializing.

Gloria nodded to several of the diners and headed to the back. Dot was storing the leftovers in containers and putting them in the fridge. She did a double take when she saw Gloria. "Oh. Hi Gloria."

"Hey Dot. How's it going?"

Dot wiped her hands on the front of her apron. "Two visits in two days. So to what do I owe this honor?"

Gloria held out the invitation. "I'm inviting you and Ray to a fall party. It's the first Saturday in October."

Dot slipped on her glasses and lifted the flap on the envelope. She pulled it out and opened it. "Oh. This sounds like so much fun. A hay ride and bonfire." She looked up. "My goodness, it has been years."

Gloria nodded. "Way too long."

Dot tucked the invitation back inside the envelope. "Well, we will definitely be there. I'll bring the donuts."

Dot made the best donuts in all of Belhaven. Probably in all of Montbay County if truth be told. "Thanks, I hadn't even thought about that."

Next, Gloria headed across the street to the post office. Ruth was inside, waiting on Judith Arnett, another Belhaven resident.

Gloria and Judith had their share of differences and didn't always see eye to eye, but Judith had been instrumental in helping clear Ruth's name during a recent investigation, so Gloria had changed her opinion of Judith. She could still be a bit of a pain in the rear, but now she was tolerable.

Judith gave Gloria small smile as she exited the post office.

Ruth leaned an elbow on the counter. "I never thought I'd see the day when you and ole Judith buried the hatchet."

Gloria set her purse on the counter. She pulled out a small packet of banded invitations and dropped them in the outgoing mail slot. "Only because of you. Miracles are still alive and kicking in Belhaven," she joked.

"Ain't that the truth," Ruth replied. "So what brings you here to the post office two days in a row?"

Gloria frowned. It was apparent she needed to make an appearance more often. First Dot, now Ruth. She pulled Ruth's invitation from her purse and slid it across the counter. "I'm having a fall party the first Saturday in October."

Ruth picked up the invitation and turned it over. "Really? We haven't had a party since, well, since you had the cookout earlier this year."

"You're right," Gloria agreed. "Which reminds me. Still seeing Slick Steve?"

Ruth's face reddened.

Gloria nodded. "Ahh. You *are* still seeing Slick Steve." Slick Steve, aka Steve Colby, had moved to the small town of Belhaven over a year ago. He had dated several of the widowed women in town and left a trail of broken hearts, which is how he got his name, Slick Steve.

On impulse, Gloria had invited him to her backyard barbecue not long ago and he and Ruth had hit it off.

"We're just friends," Ruth mumbled.

Gloria didn't buy it but she didn't press it either. If – or when - Ruth wanted to talk about it, she would. "I'm doing the whole hayride and bonfire afterwards."

Gloria picked up her purse and turned to go.

"I can bring marshmallows, chocolate bars and graham crackers for s'mores," Ruth offered.

Gloria paused, her hand on the doorknob. "That would be great, Ruth." She turned the knob and opened the door. "You can bring Steve with you, too."

She quickly exited the post office and shut the door, not giving Ruth a chance to protest. A small smile lit the corners of her lips. She was happy to see Ruth finally had someone. Gloria shook her head...of all people, Slick Steve.

Her next stop was her friend, Margaret's, place. Margaret and her husband, Don, lived in a beautiful, sprawling ranch, perched on a small bank that overlooked Lake Terrace. It was one of the nicer homes in town. Don had recently retired as vice president of a local bank.

Out of all Gloria's dear friends, Margaret had been the hardest to get close to as far as friends went. That is, until Margaret volunteered to take a road trip with Gloria while she searched for her sister, Liz, who led them on a wild goose chase in the Smoky Mountains.

After that trip, the two had a special bond. The girls uncovered some old coins in Aunt Ethel's farmhouse. Along with Gloria's cousin, David, Ethel's son, they discovered the coins were worth a lot of money.

The government was fighting to claim ownership of the coins and the case continued to drag on in the courts. They were all waiting for a decision, which David kept promising would be soon. Although the coins could potentially make each of them rich beyond their dreams, Gloria was one of those "never count your chickens before they hatch" kind of people.

She would get excited if, and when, the coins were theirs to keep. In the meantime, she was taking the wait and see approach. Sometimes she even forgot about them. Life had a way of getting in the way.

Margaret's SUV was in the drive. Gloria pulled in behind it. She shut the car engine off and headed up the drive.

Margaret met her at the door. "Well, will you look at that. What brings you to this neck of the woods?"

Gloria rolled her eyes. "Good grief." She held out a hand. "From here on out, I am getting out more. You're the third person that has said almost the exact same thing to me."

She followed Margaret up the breezeway steps and into the kitchen. "Would you like a cup of coffee or tea?"

Gloria shook her head. "No thanks."

Margaret opened the back slider and the girls stepped out onto the expansive rear deck. "Have a seat."

Gloria eased into one of the padded patio chairs and gazed out at the calm, still waters of Lake Terrace. She took a deep breath and leaned her head back. "This is so peaceful. I could take a nap out here."

Margaret nodded. "Yeah. I sometimes do."

She pointed in the direction of the dock. "See my momma duck and her baby chicks?"

Gloria lifted her head and studied the water. "Oh, I do. How cute." She turned to Margaret. "Let me guess. You've named them all."

Margaret chuckled. "Yep. Chip, Skip and Flip." She crossed her arms and shifted her body to face her friend. "So what's the occasion?"

Gloria reached into her purse and pulled out the invitation addressed to Margaret and Don. "I'm having a fall party...on the first Saturday in October."

Margaret studied the front and turned it over. She lifted the flap. "Of course we'll be there. What can I bring?"

A slow smile beamed across Gloria's face. She had the best friends in the whole world. "Dot is bringing donuts; Ruth is bringing stuff for s'mores. I haven't talked to Lucy yet."

Margaret tapped the arms of her chair. "What would a fall bonfire be without apple cider? I'll bring that and some bags of chips."

Gloria grinned. "Between you girls, I'm not going to have to supply anything." They chatted for a few more minutes and then Gloria got to her feet.

Margaret opened the slider door. "I can't wait for the party. It sounds like fun."

Gloria had one more stop to make. Lucy's place. Not only did she want to drop off Lucy's invitation, she was curious to find out if Lucy had called Bill.

Chapter 12

Lucy's jeep was nowhere in sight and the garage door was closed. Gloria's heart sank. She parked the car and walked to the porch. Since Lucy wasn't home, she decided to tuck her invitation in the door.

Gloria opened the screen door and lifted her hand to shove the envelope inside when a movement inside caught her eye. Lucy *was* home. She was at the kitchen sink washing dishes.

Gloria tapped lightly on the glass. Lucy swung around. She lifted a sudsy hand and motioned her in.

"I thought you weren't home." Gloria slipped inside and closed the door behind her.

"Yeah, I was out earlier and decided to park in the garage. Might as well start now." She wiped her hands on a dishtowel and hung it on the handle of the stove. "You want a cup of coffee?"

"No. I wasn't gonna stay long. I wanted to invite you to a fall party I'm having first weekend in October." She set the invitation on the table and pulled out a chair.

Lucy picked it up but didn't open it. "Sounds like fun. What can I bring?"

Gloria went over the list of what the other girls were bringing. "You don't have to bring anything."

Lucy tapped the tip of the envelope on the table. "You sure? What about bales of hay?"

Gloria frowned. "Yes, that would be an important part of a hayride – hay."

"I have a bunch of bales stacked in the shed. They've been there awhile but I'm sure they would work just fine."

"That would be great." Gloria gazed out the window. "You still want to go with me to Dreamwood tomorrow?"

Lucy nodded. "Sure." She took a deep breath. "I am so nervous about that breakfast date you set up for tomorrow morning."

"You'll be fine. It's just breakfast," Gloria pointed out.

"I'm thinking of canceling," Lucy confessed.

"How you gonna do that?" Gloria argued. "You don't even have Max's phone number."

"True..." her voice trailed off. "Maybe he won't show."

"Oh, no. I saw the look in that man's eyes. He'll be there. Early probably," Gloria predicted.

Lucy smacked the palm of her hand to her forehead and shook it back and forth. "I don't know how I let you get me into these things," she groaned.

"Speaking of that, did you talk to Bill?" Gloria didn't want to pry, but she was curious.

Lucy lifted her head, placed the palm of her hand on the table and wiped at imaginary crumbs. "Yeah."

"And?"

"It went okay. We talked a little. He has a few things still here at the house that he's going to stop by and pick up but that's it," Lucy told her.

"How do you feel?" Gloria asked.

Lucy lifted her head and stared into Gloria's eyes. "I feel good. Like this was the right decision. He wasn't for me. I guess I knew that all along," she admitted. "Maybe I just didn't want to be alone."

"But you're not alone, Lucy," Gloria argued. "You have all of us. All of your friends."

Lucy nodded. "I know. Actually, I'm happier now than I've been in a long time."

"I'm glad," Gloria simply replied.

Lucy walked Gloria out to her car. "So you'll be at the restaurant at 9:00?"

Gloria grabbed the door handle and pulled. "With bells on."

Maybe this Max wouldn't turn out to be anything, but maybe it would. Either way, Lucy was on the right track.

***

By the time Gloria arrived at the restaurant the next morning, she wasn't sure who was more nervous – Lucy or her. Lucy was hanging out in the back, talking to Dot when Gloria made her way inside.

Dot was trying to calm Lucy's nerves. She stuck a cup of tea in her hand. "Here, I know chocolate is your drink of choice, but try this mint tea. It'll calm your nerves."

Lucy sipped the steaming tea and nodded. "I feel better already."

"He's here," Gloria whispered.

Sure enough, Max walked into the restaurant at 9:00 a.m. sharp. Gloria's eyes traveled from his head to his toes. He was sporting a nice pair of dress slacks and polo shirt. Not too overdressed, not too underdressed. He settled into a table and looked around.

He hadn't noticed the girls standing in the back.

Gloria gave Lucy a small shove in the middle of her back. "Get out there."

Lucy slapped at her hand and scowled. She straightened her shoulders, lifted her head and made her way over to the table.

Max jumped up, pulled her chair out and waited for her to sit before taking the seat across from her.

Dot and Gloria stepped off to the side and peeked at them through the wooden lattice that separated the eating area from the employee area.

Ray walked by with a pot of coffee. "What are you two up to?"

Dot waved her hand. "Shush. We're trying to spy on Lucy and her date."

Ray rolled his eyes and wandered over to Max and Lucy's table.

Gloria watched as Ray shook Max's hand while Ray pointed to the girls spying in the back. Gloria quickly ducked. "He just ratted us out." She started to giggle.

Gloria grabbed Dot's hand and the two of them made their way over to the table.

Max looked up. "Hi Gloria."

"Hi Max. How're you today?"

His eyes slid to the side as he gave Lucy a sly grin. "I'm having a wonderful day so far."

"Good." She turned to Dot. "This is my friend, Dot Jenkins. She and her husband, Ray, own this restaurant.

Max jumped to his feet. He shook Dot's hand. "Pleased to meet you."

Dot placed two menus on the table and patted the top. "Here are a couple menus. I'll be back to take your order." She took a step back. "No hurry. Take your time."

Gloria followed Dot to the back. "He looks like a very nice man," Dot decided.

"I think so, too," Gloria agreed.

Dot returned to their table a few minutes later to take their order while Gloria hung out in the back. She was torn. On the one hand, she was dying to know how the date was going. On the other, she wanted to respect their privacy.

An hour later, Dot wandered over to Gloria, still hanging out behind the lattice. "He's gone," she announced.

"Where's Lucy?" Gloria wondered.

"Still sitting by the window, gazing out like a love struck teenybopper," Dot answered.

Gloria jumped out of the chair and made a beeline for the table. She pulled out a chair – Max's chair – and plopped down. She leaned in. "Well? How did it go?"

Lucy was still staring dreamily out the window.

Gloria snapped her fingers in front of Lucy's face. "Hellooo Lucy."

Lucy jerked her head back. "Huh?"

"I asked how the date went."

Lucy turned a bright shade of red. Almost the same color as her hair. "It was nice," she answered vaguely.

Gloria crossed her arms. "It was more than nice. Your face is the shade of that bottle of Heinz catsup."

Lucy glanced at the bottle. She took a deep breath. "Okay. It was better than nice. He seems like a really great guy," she admitted.

"So?"

"So what?" Lucy replied.

"So are you going on another date?" Lucy was totally out of it. This Max guy had cast some sort of spell.

"Yeah," Lucy said. "I invited him to your fall party." Her eyes clouded over. "I hope that's okay."

Gloria nodded. "Of course it's okay. It'll give me – give us – a chance to get to know him better." *Run a background check, interrogate him...*

Dot swung by. She dropped a plate of scrambled eggs, bacon and toast in front of Gloria and then slid into an empty seat. "So you like him?"

Gloria picked up a slice of bacon and bit the end. "Like him? She's over here in la-la land."

Gloria grabbed her fork. "She invited him to my fall party."

Dot nodded. She was happy for Lucy. He seemed like a nice enough fellow. Course, she didn't want to see Lucy jumping into a new relationship too soon. "How long has it been since you and Bill broke up?"

"Oh, a month. Maybe a little longer," Lucy told her.

Gloria didn't see a problem with it. The girls weren't getting any younger. Of course, she didn't want Lucy in the same situation with Max as she had been with Bill.

After Gloria finished her breakfast, the two of them climbed into Gloria's car.

Lucy buckled her seat belt and stared out the window.

Gloria fastened her seatbelt and gazed over at her friend. It was going to be a quiet ride to Liz's place.

Chapter 13

Liz was pacing the floor when Gloria and Lucy arrived. She swung the door open and motioned them inside. "I've been thinking about what you said and it kept me up all night," Liz groaned. "What if my best friend is a killer?"

Lucy was out of her dream state and turned to Liz. "What do you mean?"

"She means that we think Frances is using the cover 'Raven Fair' on Worldbook to leave comments on Milt's page. Weird comments. As in, she may be involved in his disappearance comments."

Liz lifted the lid on her laptop and pointed to the screen. "Here."

Lucy leaned forward. She narrowed her eyes and studied the screen. "Well, I'll be darned." She scrolled through a few of the posts. "Whoever this Raven Fair is, the person does seem to be leaving some odd messages."

She stood up. "What makes you think this is Frances?"

Gloria held up a finger. "One, she doesn't have a profile on Worldbook." She held up a second finger. "Two, whoever Raven Fair is, seems obsessed with Milt, not unlike Frances."

She put her hand down. "Last but now least, Frances has a small tattoo of a raven on her lower back."

Lucy frowned. "That does seem like a lot of coincidences." She shook her head. "But why would she offer a reward, chain herself to the restaurant and call reporters?"

"Maybe we'll come up with something when we scope out the ladies' bridge club. Several of the women in the bridge club have also dated Milt in the past, including Trudy, Vivian and there's one other." Liz tapped the side of her computer thoughtfully. "I think her name is Carol something..."

Liz blew air through her lips. "Whew. Carol and Frances *really* got into it not long ago. Almost a knockdown, drag out fight right there in the parking lot."

Liz closed the lid on her laptop. "From what Frances told me, Carol and Milt were getting into his car while Frances was just coming back from the grocery store. When she saw the two of them together, she freaked out."

"Do you think Frances is unstable?" Gloria had to ask. She didn't want to believe Frances was capable of murder. Kidnapping, now that was another story..." She narrowed her eyes. *Kidnapping. Any of these women could be off their rocker and capable of...*

"I hate to even think about it," Liz grabbed her keys. "Ready to go?"

Lucy headed to the door. "What excuse are we going to use for being in the clubhouse?"

"Got it all figured out," Liz said. "I tell them I'll want to check dates to make reservations for a party."

136

"Which reminds me." Gloria reached into her purse and pulled out Liz's invitation. "I'm having a fall party the first Saturday in October," she told her sister.

Liz glanced at the invitation and set it on the counter. "Sounds like fun. Can I bring a – uh – date?"

"Al again?" Gloria teased.

Much to Gloria's surprise, she shook her head. "Nah. He wants to get serious and I don't. We kind of mutually agreed to take a break from going out."

Gloria lifted a brow. "Another beau?"

"Just a friend," Liz replied. She changed the subject. "Better get going."

The clubhouse was not far from Liz's place, which was in the front of the Dreamwood complex. There were several cars parked out front.

Gloria could see a group of women off in one corner as she grabbed the door handle and held it for the girls.

"That's them," Liz whispered in a low voice.

Gloria counted four women. She recognized a few of the faces from the Worldbook profiles. The women didn't pay the girls any mind as they talked amongst themselves.

The three of them headed to a small office in the rear. The gold sign on the door read: *manager*.

Liz twisted the knob and opened the door. It was a small space - only large enough to hold a desk and two cheap plastic chairs. The man behind the counter looked up as the girls stepped inside the cramped quarters.

"Hello Liz," the man said. "How can I help you?" He didn't give her a chance to reply. He tapped his pen on top of the notepad, lying open on the desk. "Let me guess, the lawn guys adjusted the sprinklers again and they're hitting your bedroom window."

Liz opened her mouth to speak.

"Or did someone dare to park in your favorite spot in the parking lot again? Wait."

Liz cut him off. "You make me sound like a big pain the rear, Ron."

"Now why would I do that?" He raised a brow and clasped his hands together. "If you're not here to voice a grievance, why *are* you here?"

She cleared her throat. "I wanted to check availability for the clubhouse the last week in October."

Ron reached behind him and grabbed a large, black book. He set it on the desk in front of him and opened the cover. He slipped his glasses on and flipped a few pages. "Hmm. Sunday afternoon is free. Sunday, October 30th."

"Pencil me in for that date," she told him.

The girls wandered back out into the main area. Liz closed the door behind them.

Gloria glanced back at the closed door. "You gonna have a party?" This was the first she'd heard of it...imagine having two parties in one month.

Liz jerked her head at the door. "Yeah. I'm gonna bring a bunch of my friends over here and trash the place. Serves the putz right."

The sound of laughter tinkled in the air.

Liz switched focus. "C'mon." She marched over to the women seated at the table in the corner. Lucy and Gloria trailed behind.

Liz went in for the kill. Her target? Trudy Gromalski.

She didn't bother with pleasantries, although she did pause long enough to nod at a couple of the other ladies.

Liz stuck a hand on her hip. "Trudy Gromalski. We have been trying to track you down for days now."

Gloria finally got a good look at her. Trudy sported a head of short, blonde hair. The frosted tips swirled up and shot out. Gloria liked the look. She patted her own unruly locks self-consciously.

The woman's gray eyes narrowed. She shifted the cards in her hand, pulling them close to her chest. "Why, whatever for?"

Liz didn't beat around the bush. "Milton Tilton is missing, has been for several days now."

Trudy nodded. "Yes, such a terrible situation."

Liz placed her hand on the back of Trudy's chair. "Clyde Ward said he saw you talking to Milt the night he disappeared."

Trudy's mouth drooped. She set her cards face down on the table and crossed her arms. "Are you accusing me of having something to do with Milt's disappearance?" Her voice rose shrilly. "Because if you are, I'm going to-to sue you for slander," she huffed.

Gloria studied the other women's faces as Liz and Trudy began to argue, which was even more interesting than the catfight that was ensuing.

Vivian Coulter smirked.

Carol Towers lifted her hand to her mouth to hide her laugh.

A woman that Gloria did not recognize looked as if she wished the ground would swallow her up.

Thank goodness the clubhouse was empty except for the bridge ladies and the three of them.

Gloria was so caught up in her observations that she had missed part of what the two women were saying to each other.

Suddenly, Trudy jumped out of her chair so fast, it fell backwards and hit the floor with a loud clatter. She shoved the sleeves of her blouse to her elbow and bowed up.

Gloria stepped between the two of them in the nick of time. Liz was making a grab for the front of Trudy's blouse.

She held her hands out to keep the women separated. "Now ladies." She stressed the word "ladies."

Gloria turned to Trudy first. "Liz was not accusing you of anything. We just wondered if perhaps you might be able to tell us if Milt had mentioned leaving town or given you some indication something was amiss," Gloria soothed.

Trudy softened her stance. "He did mention something about having to come up with some quick cash," she sniffed.

Lucy stepped forward. "Do you know what he needed the cash for?"

Trudy lowered her voice. "Some kind of gambling debt, I think. Course Milt was always vague," she confessed. "The last couple of weeks he kind of kept to himself." She shrugged. "I figured he found himself a new girl."

Tears filled the back of Trudy's eyes. She blinked them away. Even Liz felt bad. She held out a hand. "I'm sorry, Trudy. I had no idea."

Trudy lifted the back of her hand and wiped at the corner of her eye. "It's okay. I've been sick with worry." She turned to Gloria. "Rumor round here is that you're trying to help find him."

Gloria nodded. "Yes, I promised Liz – and Frances – that I'd look into it."

"That Frances is a lunatic," Vivian piped up. "Why, I caught her peeking in the windows at Milt's place. We were sitting on the couch, watching TV and I could feel someone stare at me." Vivian shivered. "You know, where your skin starts to crawl."

Vivian went on. "When I got up to look out the window, I could've sworn I saw Frances hightailing it across the lawn toward her apartment."

"So why are you convinced it was Frances peeking in?" Gloria wondered.

"Because the next morning, she cornered me on the sidewalk and told me to stay away from Milt or else," she answered.

"Or else what?" Liz prompted.

Vivian shrugged. "That's what I asked but she never answered. She just stomped off."

Gloria looked around the table. "Do any of the rest of you have something to add? Odd conversations, some sort of clue?"

Carol Towers had been silent the entire time. Up until that very moment. "Well, I saw a light on at his place night before last."

Chapter 14

Gloria leaned forward. "Did you tell anyone?"

Carol shook her head. "I guess I should have. I live in the unit next to his and I was coming home from a movie. It was dark out."

"What kind of light?" Lucy asked.

Carol shrugged. "It wasn't really like, you know, a lamp or anything." She tapped her finger on the table. "Now that I think about it, it was more like a bouncy light. Probably a flashlight if I had to guess."

No one seemed to be able to add any additional information. Gloria – and Liz – thanked them for their time and headed out the door and onto the sidewalk.

Lucy looked back. "What do you think?"

Gloria didn't know. It seemed as if one of the ladies knew more than they were letting on. She didn't have anything solid. It was just a hunch – a gut feeling.

"I think Frances needs counseling," Liz said.

Gloria nodded. That was true. The woman had an over-the-top obsession with Milt. It was a cause for concern that she was a peeping Tom, or in this case, a peeping Frances.

But just because she was peeking in his windows, making up a fake name on Worldbook to spy on him, chaining herself to the restaurant, didn't mean she was involved in his disappearance. Of course, it didn't mean that she wasn't either...

Gloria wasn't convinced that this mysterious debt was the reason he disappeared. Although, he could be hiding out, sneaking back into his apartment in the dead of the night to pick some stuff up.

Back inside Liz's apartment, Gloria paced the floor. She still believed the key to Milt's disappearance was in Dreamwood. "We need to organize a fact-finding mission." She stopped. "Liz, I need the addresses of Vivian and Carol. We already have Trudy."

She started to pace again. The last woman at the table had remained strangely silent the entire time. "Who was the other woman at the table, the one who didn't talk?"

Liz furrowed her brow. She shook her head. "I don't know but I'll find out," she promised.

Gloria and Lucy headed back to the car after Liz promised to find out the name of the mystery woman and her address. The girls decided to meet Sunday evening at dusk and do a little behind-the-scenes investigation of each of the women's homes.

Although Gloria was initially against it, they agreed a divide and conquer plan would work best. Each of them scoping out a different home, which meant that Frances would have to participate. They needed four people.

Gloria passed through downtown Belhaven. Main Street was like a ghost town.

"Do you think Frances will go over the edge if we include her in our spy mission?" Lucy asked the question that Gloria had already asked herself.

"Well, we don't really have a choice. Unless, of course, we ask one of the girls to help out." Gloria raised a brow. They *could* do that. Maybe Margaret, Dot or Ruth would be willing to help.

Gloria fumbled inside her purse and handed her phone to Lucy. "Give Liz a call and tell her to hold off asking Frances to be part of the investigation."

Liz's line rang and rang. Lucy was about to hang up when a breathless Liz answered.

"Oh, good. I'm glad I caught you," Lucy told her.

"Yeah, I was just sitting here talking to Frances. She's more than willing to help out with the fact finding operation."

Lucy frowned and glanced over at Gloria. "So Frances is with you and she's agreed to help out with the Sunday evening plan."

Gloria let out a low groan. They were stuck now. There was no way they could talk Frances out of this.

"Okay, well. We'll give you a call later." Lucy disconnected the line and dropped the phone into Gloria's open purse. "Too late. I could hear Frances in the background talking a mile a minute."

Gloria pulled in next to Lucy's jeep, still parked out in front of the restaurant. "What're you doing this weekend?"

Lucy grabbed the car door handle. "Well, I have a little canning to do. The apples are falling all over out in the backyard and I figured I could can them this year." She opened the door. "You need any?"

Gloria nodded. "Can you set some aside for the party?"

Lucy nodded. "Sure. I'll bring a bunch by Sunday before we head out. They'll stay fresh if you store them down in your root cellar."

"Ryan and Tyler are spending the night and we're gonna work on the tree fort Saturday. You're welcome to come by," Gloria offered.

She didn't want to think that poor Lucy was sitting home with nothing to do.

"Yeah, I might. I got some other stuff to do. What time do you think?" Lucy asked.

Gloria did some quick calculations. If the boys came after school, they could run by Dot's for dinner. She remembered Brian saying he would stop by around 2:00 on Saturday. "We'll probably eat dinner at Dot's Friday night and start on the fort around 2:00 Saturday. Brian is going to come by and help the boys assemble the fort."

"What? You're not going to crawl up there?" Lucy grinned.

Gloria shook her head. "No way. I mean, I suppose I could." She frowned. If Brian backed out, of course she'd have to. Otherwise, the boys would be heartbroken.

Lucy climbed out of the car and leaned back in. "Yeah, I don't want to miss this. Maybe I should stop by the hardware store and tell Brian not to bother coming by Saturday. That you and I can build the fort ourselves," she teased.

Gloria shook her finger at Lucy. "Don't you dare."

Lucy smirked and slammed the door shut. But Lucy didn't talk to Brian. Instead, she hopped in the jeep and headed toward home.

Gloria followed her out of town. She honked and gave a small wave as Lucy turned into her drive.

Gloria spent the rest of the evening puttering around the house. She pulled a leftover tuna noodle casserole from the freezer and popped in the microwave. Mally and she wandered out onto the porch to wait for it to cook.

There was a cool breeze in the evening air. Gloria stepped back inside to grab her sweater before returning to the porch. She slid into the rocking chair and absentmindedly watched as Mally made her rounds.

Mally had a set pattern for patrolling the perimeter of the farm. It cracked Gloria up each time she watched her.

Mally would start at the big barn on the other side of the driveway, careful to stay close to the barn since she knew Gloria didn't like her near the road.

She would disappear behind the barn and pop back out on the other side seconds later. The crazy dog would mark her territory when she stopped near the edge of the farm field. Next, she would make a sharp left and race along the backside of the yard, past the garden.

Gloria knew she would make another sharp left, run the perimeter behind the house, eventually taking a shortcut through the front yard, and end her run on the porch.

Gloria watched her pass the garden and waited for her to come around the back. When she didn't come back, Gloria scooted out of the chair and headed down the steps. She rounded the back corner of the house, in the direction that Mally had taken.

"Woof." Gloria heard her before she saw her. She recognized that "woof." It was one that meant Mally had found something – or gotten into something.

Gloria picked up the pace and jogged to the back.

Mally had crouched down on the edge of the field and was barking at something in the tall grass. Gloria could barely make out a black shape. Black and white. Striped. It was a skunk.

"Mally! No!" she shouted, but it was too late. The skunk turned around, lifted its tail and sprayed Mally. Thankfully,

Mally had just turned and the spray hit the side of Mally – not her face.

Mally let out a yelp and darted across the backyard– right toward Gloria. The smell of the skunk reached Gloria before Mally did. Gloria pinched her nose and took a step back. "Good grief," she cried.

Mally shook her body, trying to rid herself of the smell. Gloria tipped her head back. "It's gonna take more than that, girl."

"C'mon. We're gonna have to do something about that smell and fast."

Mally trotted along beside Gloria as they rounded the front of the house and made their way up the steps. She stopped Mally at the door. "Stay here."

Mally obediently sat on the porch while Gloria stepped inside and grabbed her leash from the hook on the wall. She made her way back outside, snapped the leash to Mally's collar and then hooked that to one of the spindles on the porch rail. "You wait here until I figure out how to get rid of that smell."

Mally sank to the floor, dropped her head on her front paw and looked at Gloria as if she'd been sentenced to some terrible punishment.

Gloria made a beeline for the computer, switched it on and pulled up the search page. "Get rid of skunk smell." The homemade recipes were her best bet: a mixture of hydrogen peroxide, baking soda and dish soap. Thankfully, they were all common household items Gloria knew she had on hand.

She quickly whipped up a double batch and carried it to the bathroom. She left the container next to the tub before going out to the porch to get Mally. The smell was even stronger now and hung heavy in the air. Gloria waved a hand over her face, sucked in a deep breath and reached down to unhook Mally's leash.

She led her inside, careful to keep a firm grip on her collar.

Puddles was standing inside the door, wondering what in the world was going on. When his sniffer got a whiff of the skunk, he backed up and darted out of the room.

Despite the gravity of the situation, Gloria burst out laughing. She wished she could make a run for it, too, but unfortunately, she didn't have much of a choice.

Gloria and Mally hustled into the bath. "Hop in," she told her dog.

Mally loved taking a bath and promptly jumped in the tub, which was a bit of a luxury. Her baths were usually in her own special tub and using the garden hose.

Gloria shoved the plug in the drain and turned the water on warm as Mally patiently waited for the tub to fill.

She leaned over to start scrubbing and noticed she was wearing one of her few nice outfits. Gloria pushed herself to her feet. "Stay right there," she commanded Mally.

In the bedroom, Gloria slipped out of her blouse and peeled off her slacks. She pulled an old t-shirt over her head and yanked on a pair of garden shorts.

Mally was right where she left her.

Gloria reached up, unlatched the locks on the bathroom window, shoved the pane all the way up and took a deep breath.

Gloria poured a healthy dose of the concoction along Mally's backside, added some water and began to scrub. There were a few times Gloria stood up, leaned over the open window and gulped fresh breaths of air.

When the last of the mixture was gone and Gloria had rinsed Mally so many times, her fur gleamed, she emptied the tub and grabbed a towel from the bathroom cabinet.

Gloria dried her as best she could and then opened the bathroom door to let her out into the dining room. Puddles was in the far corner, hiding under the computer desk. His eyes glittered in the dark as he warily watched Mally and Gloria.

Mally did a doggie shake to get rid of the excess water, spraying the hutch and table with droplets of water. She followed Gloria into the kitchen and promptly crawled into her bed.

Gloria filled her food dish, then filled Puddles' dish before she reached inside the microwave to check on her casserole. It had not only unthawed and warmed up, but it was cold again. She pressed the warmer button to turn it back on and settled into the chair.

She glanced up at the clock on the wall. It was already 7:30. So much for a relaxing evening, she thought to herself.

Puddles wandered into the kitchen and slunk along the outer wall, careful to stay as far away from Mally possible as he headed to his food dish.

Mally didn't move. "Aren't you going to eat?" Gloria asked her.

Mally shifted in the bed and closed her eyes, clearly depressed by the turn of events.

Gloria pulled her dinner from the microwave, set it on the table and unfolded the morning paper she hadn't had time to read. She grabbed her reading glasses and slipped them on.

There, on the front page, was a picture of Milt. The caption underneath read:

"Have you seen this man? Police are investigating the mysterious disappearance of Milton Tilton, a longtime resident of Dreamwood Retirement Community in nearby Green Springs, Michigan.

Mr. Tilton was last seen the evening of Friday, September 2nd. Several key witnesses told authorities that Mr. Tilton had been talking to a man driving a dark blue, four-door sedan, possibly a late model Ford Taurus, near the entrance to Dreamwood.

Police would like to talk to the man driving this sedan. If you have any information about the whereabouts of Milton Tilton, Montbay County Sheriff's Department is asking you to contact them at 229-1627."

Gloria pulled her glasses off and set them on top of the paper. This might throw a wrench into the investigation now that the police were involved.

Gloria ate her casserole, rinsed the dishes and slid them into the dishwasher. She wondered what Liz and Frances thought now that police were involved. She didn't have to wonder long.

Her home phone started to ring. It was Liz. "Did you see this morning's paper?"

"I just read the front page about Milt and the police opening an investigation."

Liz let out an exaggerated sigh. "Someone tipped the police off that Frances had been lurking around Milt's place just before his disappearance. She's down at the police station in Langstone being questioned."

"Vivian."

"Bingo," Liz said. "Remember when she said Milt and she caught Frances peeking in the windows? She must've told the police."

Poor Frances. She wondered if Paul was involved in the investigation since it was at the precinct he worked at in Langstone.

Gloria hung up the phone. She was tired. It had been a long day and tomorrow was shaping up to be a repeat of today. She glanced down at Mally, who looked up at her with sorrowful eyes. She thrust a hand on her hip. "I'd love to let you sleep in the bedroom but you're still wet."

Mally's ears sank low, she shifted her body and turned to face the wall. Gloria felt bad but there wasn't much she could do.

"I have an idea." She reached down and tapped Mally. "Here, you can sleep in the bedroom. You just won't be able to jump up on the bed."

Gloria grabbed Mally's bed. Mally followed her into the bedroom. She settled her into the corner and returned to the bathroom to brush her teeth and change into her pajamas.

Puddles had already curled up near the pillows. Gloria pulled back the covers and climbed in.

She closed her eyes and prayed. "Dear Lord, my heart is heavy for poor Frances tonight. I don't believe that she is involved in Milt's disappearance, but if she is, please let her confess and tell the police what she knows."

She finished her prayers for her family and friends before pulling the covers to her chin. She was out before she had time to worry about one more thing.

Chapter 15

Gloria's eyes flew open. It was still dark outside. She leaned over and glanced at the clock: 6:48 a.m. It was a bit early for her. She settled back under the covers and closed her eyes, hoping for a few more minutes rest.

Her mind had other ideas. It began a mental checklist of everything that needed to happen before Ryan and Tyler arrived. Then it wandered over to Frances. She wondered what had transpired the night before.

Then she thought about her friend, Lucy. She made a mental note to give her a call before she gave up on trying to go back to sleep.

Gloria threw back the covers and shoved her feet into her slippers. Her bathrobe was on the end of the bed. She grabbed that and headed for the door.

Mally was in her doggie bed, curled up in a ball. She opened one eye and stared at Gloria as if she wondered what in the world she was doing.

Gloria shuffled to the kitchen and over to the coffee pot. She switched it to on and made her way to the porch door. The sun was barely peeking up over the back of the yard. She stepped outside and gazed at the glorious sunrise.

Mally had followed Gloria to the kitchen and pawed at the door. Gloria opened it far enough for Mally to slip out. "Changed your mind, huh?"

Mally took a tentative step down and looked around. "Are you looking for the mean old skunk?"

Satisfied there was no black and white menace in the vicinity, Mally trotted out into the yard.

Gloria cupped her hands together. "Go get the paper."

Mally trotted out to the end of the drive, picked the morning paper up with her teeth and headed back to Gloria. She dropped the paper at Gloria's feet and looked up, her tail wagging.

"Good girl." She patted her head and reached behind her to open the plastic container she had installed on the wall. Inside the container were special treats for Mally. She reached her hand inside and pulled one out.

Mally licked her hand and grabbed the treat. Gloria stepped inside the kitchen, dropped the paper on the table and reached for her Bible. She poured a fresh cup of coffee and wandered back out onto the porch.

The stillness of the morning made Gloria appreciate the farm and all her blessings. Gloria read her Bible each morning and then spent time in prayer before she started her day, something she had done for as long as she could remember.

When James was alive, they would read at the kitchen table together. After he died, she continued to read by herself. She opened to her bookmark, slipped on her glasses and pulled the Bible a bit closer.

"Not everyone who says to me, 'Lord, Lord,' will enter the kingdom of heaven, but only the one who does the will of my Father who is in heaven." Matthew 7:21 (NIV)

Gloria looked up from the Bible. The sun was out now, warming the air. She tilted her head back and let the beams of light shine down on her face.

Gloria often wondered about heaven. After James died, she read all the books she could get her hands on – the ones where people had near death experiences or had actually died and come back to life.

Looking back, if not for the presence of her Lord and Savior, she wasn't sure how she would have made it through. There were long days of loneliness, where she shut herself away from her family and friends while she mourned.

During that time, she poured herself into her prayers and studying her Bible.

One night, she had a dream, or a maybe it was a vision, that the Lord had given her. It was of James. He was much younger in her dream, closer to the age he had been when they first met and married. He was smiling. He was happy.

When she awoke that next morning, she knew that the Lord was telling her to mourn no more. That James was happy. That he was in his eternal home.

From that morning on, Gloria forced herself back into the land of the living. She knew it wasn't her time to go home. She would remain on the earth as long as she was supposed to be there and not a moment longer.

A few months after that, she prayed again for purpose in her life. Not long after, she met her young friend, Andrea Malone, when she solved the murder of Andrea's husband. Paul was in charge of Daniel Malone's investigation and that's how Gloria met him.

Ever since that time, her life was full. She had purpose again. No, God wasn't done with her yet, but when He was, she would be ready. Until then, she had stuff to do.

Gloria closed her Bible and headed inside. It was time to shift her day into high gear.

***

Gloria was waiting out on the porch when Jill pulled into the drive. She had called Gloria before she left the house, warning her they were on the way. Gloria could hear the boys in the background chattering loudly.

"Can you tell they're excited?" Jill asked.

Gloria didn't have time to answer.

"Hey Grams, you got everything for the tree fort?" It was her oldest grandson, Tyler.

"Yes, of course, Tyler. Ready and waiting for you out in the barn."

"Okay. We're on our way."

The line disconnected. Gloria grinned and replaced the receiver. She could just envision the boys driving Jill crazy until they left. Which was why she was on the porch waiting. The countdown had begun. The boys would arrive in 20 minutes or less.

Gloria had it pegged within five minutes.

Jill hadn't even turned the engine off before both rear doors of the sedan flung open and the boys raced across the yard and up to the porch.

Gloria wrapped an arm around each of them and leaned in for a welcome hug.

Ryan pulled back first. "Can we start working on the fort?"

She shook her head. "No. Brian is coming by tomorrow to help, but you can check out what it will look like. She pointed to the barn. "It's in there."

Tyler and Ryan raced each other to the barn. Gloria had unlocked the door before they arrived, certain they would want to see what Brian had built for them.

Jill and Gloria followed the boys. "Thanks for taking them tonight."

"Whew," she added. "I'm glad I didn't tell them until they got out of school that they were coming over. They have been driving me nuts."

The boys held the corners of the boards together to get a glimpse of how it would look. "This is cool, Grams. Way cooler than I even thought it would be," Tyler said.

If the boys were this excited and it wasn't together, she wondered how it would be once it was all done. "Can we stay tomorrow night and sleep in it?" Ryan begged.

The original plan had been for only one night. Gloria didn't mind. She turned to her daughter.

Jill studied her boys. "It's up to you, Mom."

"I'm fine with it if you are."

Jill and Gloria left the boys in the barn and wandered back to the house. Jill stopped in her tracks. "Are you going to sleep in it?"

Gloria shook her head. "I don't think so. It'll be a tight fit for those two." She glanced out at the front porch. "No. Mally and I can sleep on the porch and keep an eye out from down below."

She remembered the stakeout Sunday evening. "I do have plans for Sunday evening."

"And I'm sure church on Sunday morning," Jill added.

"Of course."

"The boys don't have church clothes, so how about if I pick them up Sunday morning?"

Gloria nodded. "It's a deal."

Jill dropped the boys' backpacks on the porch and handed Gloria a shopping bag. "What's this?"

"Paint," Jill replied, "which reminds me. There's a set of old play clothes for each of them. Make sure they put them on before they start on the tree house."

Gloria gave a mock salute. "Will do."

Jill cupped her hands to her mouth. "Boys, I'm leaving now."

They turned and gave Jill a small wave.

Gloria took a step toward the barn. "Get over here and tell your mom goodbye," she hollered across the yard.

The boys obediently dropped what they were doing and walked over to the car. She gave each of them a hug. "Both of you. Behave."

"We will," they answered in unison.

After Jill left, Gloria shut the barn door and clicked the lock into place.

Back in the kitchen, she glanced at the row of keys hanging from the hook. The key to the tractor was hanging right where she had left it. Now that the boys knew how to drive the tractor, she kept the key inside. Just in case they were tempted to take it out, say in the middle of the night...while Gloria was asleep.

The boys were wound up like tops so Gloria decided to take them for a walk down by the creek. They wandered out of the yard and between two of the fields.

Ryan reached down and picked up what he thought was a rock...but it was mushy. He squished it in his hands. "What's this?"

Gloria wrinkled her nose. It had a distinct smell. "Rotting potato?"

Ryan nodded and tossed it back on top of the dirt.

Tyler picked one up and while his brother wasn't looking, hit him smack dab between his shoulder blades.

"Ouch!" Ryan swung around. "Hey."

In response, Ryan picked another up and returned fire with fire, which was an open invitation to his brother.

Gloria held up her hands. "Oh no you don't. Drop them now or no tree fort," she threatened.

The boys promptly dropped the potatoes and continued to shuffle along the narrow strip of grass.

When they reached the edge of the woods, they raced ahead with Mally to the creek nearby. "Don't get wet," she hollered.

It was too late. When she got there, their shoes and the bottoms of their pant legs were soaked.

She gave up. Instead, she sat down on her favorite log and watched. They reminded her so much of Ben and Eddie when they were younger. She smiled as she thought about the upcoming visit.

Ryan waded out of the creek and over to Gloria. "Mally smells funny."

Tyler joined him. "Yeah, like a dead skunk," he added.

Mally slunk over to the log and sat down. "She had a run in with a skunk last night, which reminds me, if you see him out in the yard, stay clear. He has a pretty potent sprayer."

When they got back to the house, it was close to dinnertime. She picked up her cell phone and called Lucy. "The boys are here. We're eating at Dot's tonight. You wanna come?"

"Nah. I think I'll pass," Lucy told her. "I just finished building a few explosives and then I'm gonna get my gun out and fire a few rounds."

"You still doing that?"

"Yeah. These are a little bit bigger than the ones you saw, though."

Gloria shook her head. "What about tomorrow?"

"We're still on for 2:00?" Lucy asked.

"Yep. I'll throw some hot dogs and hamburgers on the grill after the fort is done."

Gloria hung up the phone and grabbed her purse. "Let's head to Dot's."

Chapter 16

Gloria and the boys beat the dinner crowd. They had their pick of tables with the boys deciding on a booth in the rear.

Dot rounded the corner and smiled when she saw the boys. She headed to the back and returned with two root beer floats. She set one in front of each of them.

Gloria shook her head. "You're spoiling them."

"Not any more than you do."

Ryan grabbed a spoon and scooped a chunk of ice cream. "We're building a tree fort," he announced.

Dot nodded. "I heard."

"And Grams is going to let us sleep in it tomorrow night," Tyler added.

Dot chuckled. "Is she going to sleep in it, too?"

Gloria snorted. "I don't think so. I'm going to sleep on the front porch – on the futon."

"Sounds like fun," Dot told the boys.

Ray stopped by with a glass of Diet Coke and set it in front of Gloria. "Well, look who we have here…haven't seen you two fellas in a while."

Ryan nodded. "We're spending the weekend with Grams." He eyed his grandmother. "I wish I could live with her *all* the time."

Tyler sipped his float. "Me, too. We have the most fun ever at Grams."

Gloria's heart melted. She wished she could freeze this moment in time. Just for a little while, so she could savor it for a quiet time, when she was all alone.

Instead, she tucked it into her heart, vowing to remember it later, when they were older and Grams wasn't as much fun.

Dot pulled her notepad and pen from her pocket. "Do you boys know what you want?"

"A cheeseburger," Tyler said, "with lots of catsup."

"We're having those tomorrow," Gloria reminded him.

"Okay. What else you got?"

Dot's brow furrowed and she tapped her pen against her lower lip. "How about having liver and onions?"

"Yuck." Ryan shook his head violently.

"I would throw up," Tyler predicted.

Dot laughed. "Maybe you could settle for a couple plates of spaghetti and meatballs."

"That's more like it," Gloria replied. "We'll take three."

Their dinner arrived at the same time Andrea and Brian strolled in the front door. They headed to Gloria's booth. "We still on for tomorrow?" Brian asked.

"Can we do it tonight?" Ryan asked hopefully.

"No, Ryan. We need to wait until daylight. It's going to be dark soon," his grandmother reminded him.

Ryan's face fell.

Brian smiled. "I'll be there before you know it, bud," he assured him.

"I'm grilling hot dogs and hamburgers after the fort is done." Gloria turned to Andrea. "You can come over too, if you like, dear."

Gloria remembered Alice. "Bring Alice with you."

The couple left and headed to a table near the window.

After Gloria and the boys finished their plates of pasta, she paid the tab and the three of them headed down to the corner grocery store. She let the boys each pick out a candy bar while she grabbed hamburgers, hotdogs, buns, a large container of potato salad and some coleslaw. Normally, she would make her own but she knew she wouldn't have time, not with the boys here.

Back at the farm, she let them horse around in the yard with Mally and then finally called them in for the night.

Between the walk in the woods and playing in the yard, she must've worn them out. Neither of them argued when she told them it was time for bed.

She tucked them in and listened to their prayers before slowly closing the bedroom door. Mally settled on the rug in front of the bed, it was her favorite place to sleep when the boys were over.

Gloria checked the doors, brushed her teeth and pulled on her pajamas. Puddles was already in the bed. Gloria settled in and turned on the small TV she kept on top of the dresser.

The late night news was on. She managed to stay awake until the weather was over before she dozed off and woke to an infomercial.

Gloria switched off the TV and rolled over. There was no need to set the alarm. The boys would take care of that.

***

"Grams! Grams! Come quick!"

Gloria bolted upright in bed. Her eyes frantically darted around the room. Tyler was standing in the open doorway. "What? What's wrong?"

He motioned her out. "We caught it."

She flung the covers back, grabbed her robe and headed for the door. Her brain was still half-asleep. "Caught what?"

"The skunk," Tyler answered.

She shook her head. "You caught the skunk?"

"Yeah, come and see."

168

Visions of Tyler and Ryan soaking in a tub of peroxide, soap and baking soda filled her head. Gloria reached forward, grabbed the edge of Tyler's pajamas and lifted it to her nose. He didn't smell like skunk.

The back porch door was wide open. Ryan and Mally were nowhere in sight. Nowhere, that is, until she gazed out at the other side of Annabelle where she could see the tippy-top of Ryan's head.

She pulled her bathrobe tight and shuffled over to the car.

"Peppy is in there," Ryan pointed at the passenger side window.

She narrowed her eyes. "Peppy?"

"Yeah, we named the skunk Peppy," Tyler said.

Her horrified gaze shifted to her car window. She swallowed hard and squeezed her eyes shut, praying that Ryan did not mean that the skunk was INSIDE her car.

When she opened them, she leaned forward and peered in the window. There, wandering around, appearing extremely agitated, was a large skunk.

"Can we keep him?" Tyler asked.

Gloria hadn't heard a word that he said. She was too busy calculating how long it would take to get the smell of skunk out of her car and where on earth she'd be able to find new seats to replace the ones that more than likely smelled so very, very bad.

Ryan tugged on her hand. "Can we keep Peppy?"

Gloria decided to pass the buck on this one. "If your dad says you can keep Peppy, then by all means, take him home."

The boys raced up the steps and into the house to phone home. When Gloria got inside, she could tell by the looks on their faces it was a definite "no."

"Go turn on the computer and see if you can find an animal or critter control to come pick up Peppy," she instructed. "Pronto," she added.

She pulled pancake mix from the pantry and the griddle from the cabinet. It was going to be a long day. It was time for a lumberjack breakfast.

The boys found several area critter people and she put Tyler in charge of flipping pancakes while she worked her way down the list. The first two Gloria called informed her they did not pick up skunks. The third finally agreed – when she begged him – at a cost of $50.

Gloria glanced out the window at poor Annabelle. "Really - $50?"

Ryan tugged on her arm. "Hey Grams. We can take Peppy out somewhere and let him go and we won't even charge you," Ryan whispered.

As much as Gloria would love to save the $50, visions of Ryan, of all of them, getting sprayed and spending the day trying to get rid of the smell, ran through her head. Although it was probably already too late for her poor car...

She covered the receiver. "We want to work on the fort instead, right?"

Ryan nodded. "Yeah, you're right."

The man on the other end told her he would stop by before noon, which gave Gloria and the boys plenty of time to eat and clean up.

The boys set the table while Gloria put the pancakes, along with some bacon and home fries in the center. She slid into a chair across from the boys and bowed her head. "Dear Lord, thank you for this food. Please bless this food."

She went on. "Thank you for my grandsons, Tyler and Ryan. And thank you that they caught the skunk but didn't get sprayed," she added. "Please, please, PLEASE save Annabelle from getting sprayed," she begged.

"Amen." The three of them ended the prayer in agreement.

The boys ate in record time. She put them in charge of cleaning the kitchen and loading the dishwasher while she showered and dressed.

When they had finished, Gloria turned the dishwasher on and the boys headed to the porch to wait for the pest control to arrive. A young man showed up a short time later.

The marked truck, "Montbay County Pest," pulled in the drive, right behind Gloria's car. A young fellow sprung out of the

171

driver's seat. Young to Gloria, anyways. The boys ran out to greet him. "Peppy is over here," Ryan pointed.

The man grinned. "Peppy, huh? You sure you don't want to keep him for a pet?"

Tyler's shoulders sagged. "My dad said no."

The man stepped to the driver's side of the car and peered in. The boys stood on either side of him. Gloria decided the safest spot was on the porch. Mally started down the stairs and Gloria grabbed her collar. "Oh no, you don't."

The man returned to his truck. He pulled a large cage from the bed of the truck, reached in the passenger side and pulled out a bag of marshmallows. He dropped a few jumbo marshmallows inside the cage and made his way back to the car.

"Step back," he warned the boys.

The boys took a step back. The man took a step forward. He slowly opened the driver's side door and gently placed the cage against the front seat. Next, he dropped a marshmallow in front of the cage door.

From her perch on the porch, Gloria could barely make out the skunk as he eyed the man warily. The tempting marshmallow was too much and the skunk took a small step forward. He ate the marshmallow and took a step inside the cage, over to the far side where the rest of the marshmallows had rolled.

The man slowly lowered the cage to the ground and dropped the lid, clicking the lock in place.

Gloria was surprised at how close the skunk let him get without spraying him.

He kneeled down and studied Peppy. "Well you're pretty lucky," he observed.

Gloria and Mally stepped onto the sidewalk. "Why is that?"

"Peppy is a girl and she's gonna have a litter of babies."

Tyler's head swung around. His eyes grew wide. "Cool."

The man gingerly carried the cage to the back of his truck. He set the cage inside the back and turned to Gloria, who had bravely made her way down the sidewalk.

"How did the skunk get inside the car?" the man wondered.

Tyler tapped the tip of his tennis shoe on the ground. "It was easy." He made a sweeping motion with his arm. "Ryan just opened the door and the skunk climbed right inside."

The man shook his head in awe. "I never heard of a skunk willingly climbing into a vehicle."

Gloria and Mally joined the trio near the front of the truck. The man reached inside, grabbed his clipboard and scribbled some notes on the front. He handed the clipboard and pen to Gloria. "Sign here, please."

Gloria didn't have her glasses on and couldn't read the board but signed anyways. She was just relieved to have the skunk and soon-to-be-babies – gone.

She reached into her pocket, pulled out a check, and handed it to the young man. "That was the best $50 I've spent in a long time."

The man glanced at the check and slipped it under the clip on top of the board. "Yeah, skunks can be pesky – and hard to get rid of." He nodded toward Mally. "You're lucky your dog didn't get sprayed."

Gloria frowned. "Oh, she did...yesterday."

The three of them watched as the man climbed into his truck and drove off.

Now that the skunk was gone, Gloria turned her attention to Annabelle. Her steps dragged as she approached the driver's side door. She grabbed the door handle, took a deep breath and jerked it open. She stuck her head inside and took a cautious breath. It smelled – like a car.

"Thank you, God." She felt like bursting into tears, knowing that the inside of her car was skunk-free.

Chapter 17

Lucy pulled in the drive at 2:00 p.m. sharp. Brian pulled in right behind her. He climbed out, walked over to the passenger side, reached in and grabbed his toolbox.

Ryan hopped up and down on one foot. "Finally. We've been waiting *forever*."

"Or at least a couple hours," Gloria teased.

Lucy and Gloria headed inside while Brian and the boys headed to the barn. Gloria watched them go. Brian was going to make a wonderful father.

Inside the kitchen, Gloria poured a glass of lemonade for Lucy and slid a box of cookies to the side.

Lucy peeked inside. "Oatmeal raisin. One of my favorites." She lifted a cookie from the box and took a bite.

Gloria told Lucy about the skunk. Then she told her how the police had taken Frances down to the station for questioning and that someone had reported seeing Frances peeking inside Milt's windows.

Lucy rolled her eyes. "That woman." She made a twirling motion with her finger near her forehead. "Cuckoo. Cuckoo."

Gloria couldn't argue with that. She wondered how it turned out. Maybe she'd get a chance to call Paul later to see what happened.

Lucy sipped her lemonade. "Still on for tomorrow night?"

Gloria nodded. "Yeah. We need to crack this case."

"What do you think of the guy that was talking to Milt the night he disappeared?"

Gloria's brow formed a "V." She wondered if the police had tracked the man down and if his name was Vinnie.

The tree fort took up most of the afternoon. Every once in a while one of the boys would pop in, asking for this or that.

Halfway through, Gloria and Lucy brought them some bottled water and granola bars. "How's it going?"

"Great." Ryan told them. He looked at Brian, admiration shining in his eyes. "Brian is the bestest builder ever," he declared.

Brian sipped his water and winked at Gloria. "I'm just practicing for someday."

Gloria picked up the empty water bottles and wrappers and the girls headed back inside. She threw the trash in the can and the girls wandered out to the porch to enjoy an almost perfect, nearly fall day.

"We need to decide who investigates which house," Gloria told her friend. She lifted a finger. "First, there's Trudy. Then we have Vivian. Next is Carol Towers. Last but not least is the mystery woman. Hopefully Liz was able to figure out who she was."

Lucy shrugged her shoulders. "I guess it doesn't matter, except for whoever we assign to Frances. It should be the person she'd be least likely to have a run in with."

Lucy was right. They would have to pick carefully – for Frances, anyways. Maybe even Liz.

Lucy snapped her fingers. "That reminds me. I have those walkie-talkies. You want me to bring them?"

Gloria nodded. "Great idea."

Tyler tore around the corner of the house and skidded to a stop in front of the porch. "It's done," he announced.

The girls followed him to the tree in the front yard. Sure enough, the fort was finished. Well, all except for paint, which the boys could work on later.

Ryan and Tyler stepped out onto the deck, complete with a nice, large balcony. "Hi Grams. Are you gonna come up and see?"

Gloria shook her head. "I'm afraid not. I'll give you my camera, though, so you can take pictures and show me," she told him.

Lucy rolled up her sleeves. "Well, I'll go up," she declared.

The boys had built a swinging ladder and hooked it to the back side of the deck. Lucy hoisted herself onto the first step and then quickly scrambled up the rest. "Pretty cool," she hollered down. "You sure you don't want to come up?"

Gloria was sure. 100%. She shook her head. "No thanks." Brian and Lucy made their way down while the boys started to paint.

It was getting late. Gloria was getting hungry. She looked at Brian. "If you want to go ahead and wash up, I'll start the grill."

By the time Brian emerged from the house wearing clean clothes and his damp hair slicked back, the burgers were almost ready. Gloria emptied a package of hot dogs on the top rack and closed the lid.

Brian settled into a chair at the little patio table. "Andrea is on her way. She's bringing some chips."

While Gloria grilled, Lucy busied herself, setting the table and pouring drinks. Brian loaded the meat on a large platter as Andrea pulled in the drive. He handed the tray to Gloria and made his way out to Andrea's car to meet her.

Andrea hopped out of the car, popped up on her tippy toes and planted a sweet kiss on his lips.

A twinge of jealousy shot through Gloria. Andrea was a lucky girl. Even better, Brian was a lucky man. The two would have a wonderful life together. Someday, maybe, it would be her turn.

The rest of the afternoon flew by and dusk settled in. Gloria enjoyed spending time with her friends and grandsons.

By now, Gloria was feeling worn out. The boys had been hounding her all afternoon about sleeping in the fort. She had already decided there was no way she could tell them no.

She waved to Lucy, the last to leave, and headed to the front porch. Gloria had already set a couple sleeping bags and extra pillows on the futon – Gloria's bed for the night.

She let the boys pull other camping supplies from the cupboard: a couple heavy-duty flashlights, some insect repellant wipes and a canteen that Gloria had no idea where it had come from but the boys declared a necessity for the fort.

By the time they were done, the boys had amassed a small stockpile of treasures to take with them.

Gloria stuck her hand on her hip. "I'm not sure if all this stuff and the two of you are going to fit."

"It will, Grams. Don't worry." Tyler was convinced.

Now all they had to do was wait for nighttime.

They headed across the porch toward the dining room. Ryan stopped. "What's this Grams?" He patted the top of the old TV console.

Gloria wandered back to the TV. She leaned down in front of the screen. Although she hadn't used the old TV in years, she couldn't bear the thought of parting with it. There had been many nights where Gloria, James and the kids had gathered around that TV in the living room to watch TV as a family.

Of course, back then, there was no such thing as cable and if you were real lucky, you could get three stations to come in. Four was like hitting a jackpot.

"It's a television set," she told him.

Tyler grabbed a knob on the front and twisted. "Does it work?"

"Hm. Let's see." Gloria reached behind the back, grabbed the plug and stuck the end in the outlet. She switched the button to "on" and waited. The screen was fuzzy at first but then it cleared up enough for Gloria to be able to make out some murky shadows.

There was an old set of rabbit ears perched on top. "I'll be right back."

She wandered into the kitchen and returned with a box of tin foil. She ripped two strips off and crinkled the first strip around one of the antennas.

"Let me try." Tyler snatched the other sheet and began wrapping it around the second antenna.

She let Ryan fiddle with the other antenna and took a step back. She directed the boys to move the antennas until the reception was pretty darn good - for a TV that was over forty years old.

A rush of emotion filled Gloria – along with tears she blinked back. "How 'bout Grams pops us some popcorn? We can sit out here and watch TV until you're ready to head up to your new tree fort."

Ryan turned an eager, young face to his beloved Grams. "Can we?"

The three of them headed to the kitchen. She popped two bags of popcorn. One for now and one for the boys to take with them, in case they got hungry later. She poured three glasses of caffeine free pop and they headed back to the porch.

Gloria settled in the center and one boy climbed in on either side.

Ryan shoved a handful of popcorn in his mouth. "Where's the remote?"

Gloria snorted. "There is no remote. This TV is back from the good ole days...before remote."

"You mean we have to turn it by hand?" Tyler was shocked.

Gloria handed him her popcorn bowl and shuffled over to the TV. "Just like this." She grabbed the dial and turned. Most of the channels were fuzzy. Only two stations were clear enough to watch and she immediately vetoed one of them. The other was an old western. It looked vaguely familiar but it seemed to hold the boys' interest.

The three of them sat there, munching on popcorn, watching the old western. The moment took Gloria back decades, when Jill and the boys were young. She closed her eyes and tried to burn this moment in her heart, so she could pull it back out later.

The movie ended and Gloria helped them carry their treasures to the base of the tree.

Tyler had found some old rope. He tied the end of the rope to a bucket and then scampered up the tree. He lowered the bucket to Gloria, who was waiting below. "Throw the stuff in here."

Gloria loaded the supplies inside. "How clever, Tyler."

After everything was up and the boys had settled in, Gloria headed to the porch. "If you need anything. Anything at all, I'll be right inside on the porch with the windows open."

The boys' heads popped out. Ryan nodded. "We'll holler just like this." He let out a loud scream.

"That'll work."

Gloria opened the porch door and waited for Mally to go inside first. She tucked a sheet around the outside of the futon and pulled a couple blankets over the top. Gloria decided early on that it would be best if she sleep in some old sweat pants and t-shirt. Just in case she had to run outdoors in a hurry.

She lay down on the futon. Mally curled up on the floor, keeping one eye on the tree and one eye on Gloria. Gloria patted her head. "Good girl. Keep an eye out," she told her.

Gloria whispered her prayers and closed her eyes. Much to her surprise, she was out like a light.

Chapter 18

Gloria opened one eye, then the other. It took a few minutes for the fog to clear and for her to remember she was sleeping on the porch. She rolled over on the makeshift bed then sat up. Mally was gone.

The tree fort was quiet. Gloria was certain the boys were up by now.

She wandered to the kitchen and smiled at the sight that greeted her. There, sitting at the table, quiet as church mice, were her grandsons. They had managed to fix two bowls of cereal without waking her.

Ryan turned, his spoonful of cereal midair. "We fed Mally and Puddles for you, Grams." Gloria reached down and hugged him. "Why thank you, Ryan...how sweet."

"Me too," Tyler chimed in.

Gloria leaned over and hugged her eldest grandson. "I have the best boys in the whole world," she declared. She glanced up at the clock. Jill would be there any minute to pick them up.

Tyler slid out of his chair. "That is the awesomest tree fort in the whole world," he declared.

"Yeah," Ryan added. "Can we come back and sleep in it again?"

Gloria nodded. "Of course, but for now, your mom is probably on her way. Can you go run out to the fort and bring everything back down?"

The boys dashed off, with Mally in hot pursuit.

Gloria unloaded the dishwasher from the day before, then loaded the cereal bowls and spoons inside and closed the door. She could hear the boys chatter through the front windows and she smiled.

It would be quiet – once again – after they left.

Today was going to be a busy one. After church, the girls would make their rounds to the shut-ins. Later, she and Lucy would head over to Dreamwood for their fact-finding mission. She hoped they would finally be able to get closer to solving the mystery of Milt's disappearance.

Gloria had just enough time to get ready for church after the boys left. She remembered to close and lock the front porch windows on her way out.

Gloria reached the doorway to the dining room and turned back. Her eyes wandered to the old TV and futon couch as she remembered the night before. It had been a wonderful weekend and Gloria thanked the Lord for all her blessings.

The church was packed and Pastor Nate's message was a powerful one. It was Jesus' promise of heaven:

"In my Father's house are many mansions if it were not so, I would have told you. I go to prepare a place for you." John 14:2 King James Bible.

The Garden Girls met in the usual spot, right outside the front door, after the service. Dot focused on Lucy. "Any new dates with Max?" she asked.

Lucy reddened. "Maybe," she answered noncommittally.

"What's this about a date?" Ruth demanded. "You already have a new beau?"

Gloria lifted a hand. "Now, Ruth. Lucy and Max have only gone out once."

"It was not a date," Lucy gritted through her teeth. "I mean, not a dinner date. It was breakfast."

"A date is a date," Margaret decided.

Dot could see Lucy was getting flustered. "Let's let it be girls." She gave them a hard look.

Ruth quickly changed the subject. She didn't want them starting in on her about Steve Colby. "How's the investigation going?"

"We're meeting Liz this afternoon. We planned a little fact-finding mission over at Dreamwood."

"You have a suspect?" Dot asked.

"Several. We're doing a simultaneous investigation," Gloria told them. She turned to Ruth. "Who's on the list for visits today?"

Ruth patted down a stray hair. "Eleanor Whittaker is the only one."

Gloria frowned at Ruth. "Oh no. What happened?"

Dot answered. "She took a little spill in the kitchen, but she's going to be okay."

The last time Gloria had visited with Eleanor was during her investigation into the body Andrea had found in her dumpster. That was a few weeks ago and at the time she'd vowed to put Eleanor on the list of weekly Garden Girls' visits.

Although Eleanor seemed to be in good health, she was on the frail side. Gloria was disappointed in herself for forgetting. "I meant to add Eleanor to the list for weekly visits but completely forgot," Gloria said. "Shame on me."

Margaret touched Gloria's arm. "Don't be so hard on yourself. You've got your hands full."

Lucy glanced down at her watch. "I better go. I won't be able to make the rounds today. I have a few errands to run before we head over to Dreamwood." She didn't wait for a reply and turned on her heel as she headed to the jeep. The rest of the girls watched her go.

"We need to cut her some slack," Dot wisely suggested.

Gloria reached in her purse and grabbed her car keys. "I agree. I think she's still trying to sort everything out."

The girls parked in front of Dot's Restaurant and Dot headed inside. The lunch crowd would soon follow. Most Sundays, Dot wasn't able to visit the shut-ins with the rest of the girls because she had to work.

Gloria watched her friend disappear in the front door. "That woman is in serious need of a vacation."

Ruth, Gloria and Margaret climbed into Ruth's van and headed across town to Eleanor's place. Eleanor answered the front door on the first ring.

She eased the door open and stepped to the side. "Why. What a pleasant surprise." Her face lit up like a Christmas tree. "I haven't had company in days now."

Gloria's heart sank. This was all her fault. She was turning into such a scatterbrain. "We'd like to start visiting every Sunday after church, if you don't mind."

"Mind?" Eleanor's shaky hand reached out to grasp Gloria's arm. "I would love the company."

The girls followed her into the kitchen and Eleanor insisted on making her specialty tea. She also insisted that they eat one of the cookies she'd just taken from the oven.

The girls visited for a good hour before Gloria glanced at her watch. She had some cleaning up around the house to do before heading to Lucy's to pick her up.

"I'm sorry, Eleanor," Gloria said, "I have some things to take care of but we'll be back next Sunday."

Eleanor's face drooped but she quickly recovered and a bright smile replaced the sad look. "Yes. Of course. I'll bake a cake next week," she promised.

"Oh. I almost forgot." Ruth set a bag of apples and a small box of donuts on the table. "These are for you."

Eleanor lifted the bag and peered inside. "Thank you. You girls are so thoughtful."

Back outside, Gloria opened the door on the side of the van and climbed in the back. She plopped down in the seat and fastened the buckle. "She is such a sweet little lady."

Ruth climbed in the driver's seat and Margaret into the passenger side. Ruth peered at Gloria through the rearview mirror. "I hope someday when we're older and can't get out, someone will take the time to visit us."

Back on Main Street, Ruth pulled the van next to Gloria's car and placed it in park. "Good luck on your investigation."

Gloria thanked her before she climbed into Annabelle and headed home. She called Paul on her cell phone on the way. "How did it go with Frances Crabtree?"

"How did...?" He paused. Of course, Liz told her. "Fine. She was a bit evasive." He sighed. "She finally admitted to peeking in Milt's windows but swears she had nothing to do with his disappearance."

"Do you know she has the poor man's entire routine memorized?" he asked.

Gloria did know that. She had Frances' notes.

"What about the man that was spotted with Milt the night of his disappearance?"

"Vincent Tolino?" Paul replied. "He's not a suspect."

Gloria pulled in front of the farm, careened into the drive and came to an abrupt stop. "Why not?"

"He has an airtight alibi for most of that evening and for several days after that," Paul told her.

"And how's that?"

"He was in jail," Paul answered.

Well, at least that narrowed the pool of suspects. There was the man that was going to pound Milt's pudgy face and the rest were women. All of them on the list to scope out – or as Gloria preferred to call it – a part of her fact-finding mission.

***

Gloria swung by Lucy's on her way out of town. She didn't bother getting out of the car. Instead, she honked the horn and waited and waited.

189

She finally gave up and reached for the door handle when she spotted Lucy bouncing down the steps, backpack in hand.

Lucy opened the back door and dropped the bag on the seat. It landed on the cushion with a loud *THUD*. Lucy climbed into the passenger seat and reached for her seat belt.

Gloria stared at the backpack in the rearview mirror. "What on earth is in there? That thing sounds like it weighs a ton."

Lucy fastened the clasp and leaned back in the seat. "Well, I wasn't sure what all might come in handy." She tapped her finger on the door handle. "Walkie-talkies. Luckily I have four. Binoculars and a monocular." She looked at Gloria. "Just like the one I bought you."

Gloria had remembered to bring hers. It had been useful during the last stakeout that she and Andrea had done. "I've got mine, too."

"Good." Lucy paused. "And some snacks...and water."

Gloria was convinced her friend had a tapeworm that was only happy when Lucy fed it sweets. Lots and lots of sweets.

Liz and Frances were inside Frances' place when Gloria and Lucy tapped on the door. It swung open. Frances peeked her head around the side before grabbing Lucy's arm and jerking her in. "Hurry up. I don't want anyone to see you."

The girls rushed in. Frances slammed the door and pulled the shade.

Gloria shook her head. Frances had always acted a bit odd but this took the cake.

Liz rolled her eyes. "Frances is convinced the police are watching her place."

Gloria leaned forward, peeking through the edge of the window and shade. That wouldn't be too far off, especially if they considered her a prime suspect.

Frances pulled out a chair and plopped down. "What's the plan?"

Lucy dropped her backpack on the chair and unloaded the contents onto the table. It was quite an impressive array. There were things even Gloria hadn't thought of. Night vision goggles, black gloves and caps. A Ziploc bag loaded with snacks.

Last but not least, Lucy pulled out something Gloria could only describe as a Halloween costume one would wear if you were dressing up as Big Foot. It was gray-green in color and covered with a combination of fur and feathers. It reminded her of an ugly brown bush.

Gloria lifted the edge. "What is this?"

"Camo outfit. You know, so I can blend in with the landscape."

"We aren't in the middle of the woods." Liz pointed out. She lifted one of the sleeves. "Now this I gotta see."

Lucy wrinkled her nose. "Laugh all you want. At least I won't stand out like a sore thumb."

191

Frances fingered the sleeve. "I'll wear it if you don't want to," she told Lucy.

Gloria turned to Liz. "Did you have any luck finding out who the fourth person at the bridge game was? The one who was mysteriously silent?"

Gloria's detective antenna went up when she thought about the woman. There was something about her...

Liz nodded. She opened her purse and pulled out a photo. She pointed at the woman, the same one they had seen the other day. "Her name is Stella White and she's 75 years old. She's originally from Indianapolis, her husband died two years ago and she lives on Catalina Court."

Frances opened her mouth. "I'll..."

Gloria held up a hand. "Frances, you take Carol Towers, Liz, you take Trudy Gromalski." She turned to Lucy. "Lucy takes Vivian Coulter and I'll take Stella White."

"How come I have to hang out in the men's bathroom?" Liz whined.

"You?" Frances screeched. "I have Carol Towers. She has a bulldog."

Gloria crossed her arms and tapped her foot on the floor. "We don't have to do this," she threatened.

Frances clamped her mouth shut.

Liz shook her head.

Lucy laughed. "That quieted 'em down."

Since Liz's stakeout was in the back of the complex, they agreed she would drop the others off, then park the car out in front of the park. Frances was first. Liz handed her a pair of binoculars and a walkie-talkie.

Frances reached out to grab the items. Liz pulled her hand back. "Under no circumstances are you to approach the suspect. Got that?"

Frances nodded and exited the car. She lowered her body and crept across the manicured grass to the edge of the shed. She gave a thumbs up and Liz drove on.

Lucy was next. Instead of binoculars, she grabbed her monocular, her snacks and a walkie-talkie. Lucy had a different strategy. She bolted across the lawn, slammed her body to the ground when she reached the mulch bed and then slithered behind a bush.

"She's pretty agile," Liz observed.

Gloria was in awe. "Yeah. If I tried that, I'd have busted my behind."

Catalina Court and Stella White were next. Gloria patted her pocket to make sure she had her cell phone. She grabbed her monocular, wrapped the binoculars around her neck, just in case, and picked up the walkie-talkie.

She opened the rear passenger door. "Good luck," she whispered as she slunk out of the seat and hurriedly strolled to the side of the fence that divided Stella White's house from the neighbors next door.

Gloria shook her head as she gazed down the side of the fence that seemed to continue on indefinitely. These people were really into their fencing.

Liz parked in her spot and headed to the men's room, praying there was no one inside.

Chapter 19

Milton Tilton was sporting a massive headache. He groggily opened his eyes and lifted his head. A sharp pain shot through his skull.

The room came into focus and he realized he was in a bathtub. He reached out to grasp the sides of the tub when he noticed a handcuff on his wrist. Attached to the handcuff was a long length of chain. At the other end of the chain, fastened to a safety bar inside the shower was another handcuff.

Milt lifted himself from the tub. The length of the chain allowed him to reach all the way over to the sink but it wasn't long enough to reach the bathroom door handle.

Milt rubbed his wrist and glanced down at his clothes. At least he still had his clothes on. "Is anybody here?"

He waited. "Hello?"

Silence. The only sound he could hear was the ticking of the clock on the wall. It was 3:30 in the afternoon.

Milt lowered the lid to the toilet seat and sat down. The last thing he remembered was eating dinner. He was eating dinner at someone's house and he began to feel groggy so he decided to lie down. That was the last coherent thought he had...until now.

Had someone drugged him and chained him to the bathroom wall?

Milt's mouth was parched – as if he'd just swallowed an entire bag of cotton balls in the middle of the Sahara desert under the noonday sun.

A small glass cup sat on the counter next to the bathroom sink. Milt grabbed the cup and filled it with water. He downed the cup and filled it again. He drank glass after glass until his stomach started to churn.

He wiped the last bit of water from his lips with the back of his hand and realized he was still wearing his watch. He glanced down at the face. His eyes widened when he noticed the day. It was Sunday. He shook the cobwebs from his brain. It couldn't be Sunday.

It all came rushing back. He'd golfed a few rounds with the guys and then headed home to clean up. After that, he had a dinner date. His eyes narrowed.

"Milt, my love. Are you awake yet?" The door swung open and Milton Tilton faced his abductor.

***

Gloria took a deep breath, sucked in her stomach and squeezed between the lamppost that stood at the edge of the property and the tall, white vinyl fence. She stooped over and tip toed the length of the fence before arriving at the back corner of Stella White's property.

A thick, low hedge ran a straight line across the back yard until it ended at a tall, concrete wall on the other side.

This lady has more perimeter borders than Lowe's, Gloria decided. She darted across the back of the property and came to a sudden stop halfway in. There was a small gap in the hedge. She vaulted over the low bush and skidded to a halt on the other side.

A dog barked in the distance and Gloria's eyes widened. She hadn't thought about that. What if Stella had a dog? A big one that didn't like strangers in the yard.

Gloria dropped down on all fours and crawled across the back lawn until she reached the side of the house.

"Gloria, do you copy?"

The radio in Gloria's front pocket squawked. She fumbled with the button and quickly twisted it between her fingertips. She had forgotten to turn it down.

She pulled the small radio from her pocket and pressed it to her lips. "I'm here, Lucy," she mumbled. "What've you got?"

"Nothing. No one's home," Lucy answered. "What about you?"

Gloria stared down the side of the house before she lifted her eyes. "This place is lit up like the 4th of July," she whispered. "Just hang out. Maybe Vivian will come home soon."

Gloria shoved the walkie-talkie into her pocket, pressed her back against the wall and inched her way around the corner.

There were two low windows and a smaller, higher one in the middle. Must be a bath, Gloria thought.

She eased up to the edge of the first window and peeked inside. The curtains were open, the lights on but no one was around.

Gloria ducked her head and eased past the window. She could see a faint shadow move back and forth through the glass of the bathroom window but nothing more. The window was too high and on top of that, the glass was frosted.

She crept past the bathroom window and stopped at the window on the other side. More curtains and the lights were on. It was another bedroom. This one looked to be the master. She could see a door off to the right. If her calculations were correct, the door connected the master bedroom with the bath.

"Gloria, do you copy?"

Gloria's pocket was going off again. This time it was Liz. She pulled the radio from her pocket and pressed the button. "Go ahead."

"I'm in the backyard. The curtains are drawn and I can't see a doggone thing," she complained.

"Circle around the side," Gloria instructed. "Don't call me back until you've made it around the entire perimeter," she barked into the radio. She was beginning to regret having given each of the women a radio.

Gloria moved on to the front and to a large picture window that faced the street. A semi-sheer curtain obscured the view.

Gloria could see a little of the inside, mainly the table lamps. She noted that the TV was on.

There were two men duking it out inside a boxing ring. "Great, hopefully this Stella lady isn't into boxing," she mumbled under her breath.

Her eyes scanned the room as she searched for clues. Something that screamed Milt's name – or maybe even Milt himself. Nothing looked even remotely suspicious.

Gloria tiptoed past the front door and over to the other side of the house. There was another window. This one higher. From her vantage point, Gloria could see the tippy top of a refrigerator. It was the kitchen. A shadow moved back and forth.

Stella was home.

Gloria leaned around the side of the corner of the house. There was a long, paved drive leading back to a one-stall garage. This side of the house was windowless. There was a door near the back.

She stepped back behind a tall, thin juniper tree that decorated the front corner.

Gloria was torn. Should she make her way toward the garage or circle back? She decided to head back to the living room window to try to catch a glimpse of Stella inside.

Staying close to the wall, she slunk back to the living room window and stood silently staring inside.

Gloria impatiently shifted back and forth on her feet. The woman was taking *forever* in the kitchen.

Finally, Stella wandered into the living room with a plate of food. It looked like pizza. Gloria's stomach growled.

Stella paused for a second as she switched the TV channel to a car race before she continued into the bedroom. She shut the door behind her.

The radio beeped again. It was Lucy. "Yeah, I think I'm onto something over here. There's a bottle of men's cologne on the kitchen counter and some sort of men's hair goop right next to it."

That sounded promising. "I'll be right there."

Gloria didn't dare pass by the bedroom window since Stella had gone into the room. Instead, she stuck to the edge of the fence and stepped out onto the sidewalk.

Gloria spotted Lucy one block over, crouched down and hidden behind the bushes.

Lucy motioned her over to look in the window. Sure enough, there was a bottle of men's cologne and a box of *Just for Men*. "See? Vivian is a widow, too. What's she doing with men's stuff?"

Good point. "Good eye," Gloria complimented her friend.

Gloria's radio squawked again. It was Liz. "Gloria, we need to rendezvous stat."

Gloria rolled her eyes. She could hardly wait to find out what kind of pickle Liz had gotten herself into now.

"The cops just picked up Frances."

***

"Frances had just radioed to say Carol Towers was clean and I was on my way over there to pick her up," Liz blurted out. "When I rounded the corner, the cops had Frances handcuffed and were putting her in the back of the cop car."

"Was it a Montbay Sheriff?" On the one hand, Gloria hoped it was since she could talk to Paul and straighten this whole thing out.

On the other hand, she hoped it wasn't the Montbay Sheriff for the exact same reason.

Liz nodded. "Yep. Sure was."

"Well, we better get down to the sheriff's station and try to spring Frances," Gloria told them.

Chapter 20

Paul's squad car was in front of the station when Liz pulled up. The girls climbed out of the car and up the front steps.

Gloria recognized the girl behind the counter but for the life of her, she couldn't remember her name. She smiled brightly. "How are you this evening?"

The girl returned the smile. "Just fine, Mrs. Rutherford." She tapped her pen on the counter. "Are you here to see Paul?"

"Yes, dear. If it wouldn't be too much trouble, I need to speak with him for a moment."

"I'm sure he'll be happy to see you." The girl turned, headed through the door and into the back.

"I don't know about the happy part," Liz muttered under her breath.

Gloria took a deep breath and waited. Paul rounded the corner and made his way over to where they were standing. "I'd like to say I'm surprised to see you but I'm not."

He waved them down the hall and into his office. "Have a seat."

Gloria let Liz and Lucy sit closer to the wall. She sat near the door.

He propped his feet up on his desk. "Well? What happened?"

"You see, we-uh," Gloria tried to form the most reasonable explanation.

Liz went for a total cover up. "This is clearly a mistake. Frances was out for a walk with..."

Paul held up a hand to stop her. "Don't dig the hole, Liz. Frances was caught with a set of binoculars and a walkie-talkie, peeping into a resident's window."

He pointed to the walkie-talkie sticking out of Gloria's pocket. "And it looks just like that one. Start again."

Gloria spilled her guts, explaining to him how the girls had decided to do a little investigative work in hopes of either finding Milt or finding some clues.

"And?"

Gloria averted her gaze and studied her hands.

"You have something, don't you?"

Liz and Lucy leaned back as Paul focused his gaze on his girlfriend. "Well-uh," Gloria stuttered.

"We found some men's toiletry items in Vivian Coulter's house." Lucy clarified. "We saw them through the window. We didn't break in or anything..." she trailed off.

"Vivian is definitely single," Liz added.

He clasped his hands together. "We'll bring her in for questioning but just because someone has men's grooming products in their house doesn't mean they had something to do with Milton Tilton's disappearance. For all you know, he could be dead."

Paul was right. He could be dead. But why – and who – was in his house the other night? Gloria had a gut feeling he was alive and well.

"Maybe he doesn't want to be found," Paul pointed out.

"I had that same thought," Gloria admitted.

Paul stood. "I'll spring your friend but you have to promise me you're going to let this go."

Lucy and Liz nodded. Gloria didn't like to make promises she couldn't keep. "I'll try" was all she would say.

Gloria was silent on the ride back to Liz's place. Liz could almost see the wheels spinning in Gloria's mind. "What? I know you're onto something," she prodded.

Gloria was thinking about the day's events. It looked as if Vivian Coulter might be suspect but there was something else.

It was floating around the back of her mind, just out of reach. A clue. "I'm missing something. I know I am." She climbed out of Liz's car and reached for her purse. "I'll have to think about it. Mull it over."

She turned to Frances. "I'm sorry you ended up in the slammer," she told her apologetically.

Frances patted Gloria's arm. "Don't worry about it. I know you're trying to find Milt and I appreciate it," Frances reassured her.

Gloria shuffled to the car and unlocked the doors. Lucy dropped her backpack on the back seat and climbed in next to her friend. "I'm sure you'll figure it out." Lucy sounded more confident than Gloria felt. "Maybe he is dead or wanted to disappear."

Lucy frowned. "True, but what about the lights on in his house? Someone was in there," she pointed out.

"I guess I just can't understand why someone would up and leave without telling anyone." That's what stuck in Gloria's craw. It didn't make one bit of sense.

She dropped Lucy off at her house and headed home. The house was dark. The porch was dark. How nice would it be to come home to someone again?

Gloria dropped her purse on the table and hung her keys on the hook while Mally waited patiently for Gloria to finish before she nudged her hand.

Gloria bent down and wrapped her arms around Mally's neck. "I shouldn't feel sorry for myself. I'm the luckiest person in the world. I have you."

The next morning, Gloria rambled around the farm, puttering at this or that, her mind half on her chores and half trying to figure out what clue was just out of reach.

She finally gave up. Dinner that evening consisted of a leftover burger from the cookout and a bag of potato chips.

Gloria carried her plate into the living room and settled into the recliner. Mally laid at her feet while Puddles jumped up on her lap.

She turned the TV to the local news just in time to catch a small clip about Milt. They flashed a quick shot of his face. It was looking at Milt's face, his shiny, cue ball head that Gloria had her "aha" moment.

Vivian Coulter was not the suspect in the disappearance of one Milton Tilton. She scrambled out of the chair and raced to the phone to call Paul. "I think Stella White, one of Dreamwood's residents over on Catalina Court, has something to do with Milt's disappearance and here's why."

Paul listened to Gloria's explanation. It was a bit of a stretch but worth looking into. His girl had a nose for sniffing out the clues. "I'll bring her in in the morning."

Gloria could hardly wait for Paul to call her back. He promised to stop by Stella White's house early the next morning, catch her off guard and try to get inside. Inside the house where Gloria believed the woman was keeping Milt against his will.

Gloria scrubbed her house from top to bottom. She mopped floors, cleaned out the refrigerator, and dusted the inside of all the curio cabinets.

Finally, the call came. "She confessed. We found Milt inside her bathroom, handcuffed to the handicap bar in the bathtub."

"I knew it," she exclaimed. After she hung up, the first call she made was to Liz. "I have some great news. I'll be right over."

She swung by and picked up Lucy on her way. Lucy tried every which way to wrangle the story out of Gloria, but Gloria clamped her lips shut and shook her head. "No. I'll explain it to everyone at the same time."

Frances was pacing the sidewalk when the girls pulled up. "They found Milt. Alive."

Gloria nodded. "I know. Stella White abducted him."

The girls headed inside Frances' house. They all slid into the kitchen chairs and stared at Gloria, waiting for her to explain.

She told how when the girls confronted the women at the clubhouse during their bridge game, everyone talked. Everyone that is, except for Stella White, who was strangely silent, something Gloria found interesting.

"That's why I wanted to check out her place."

Then she explained how she surveyed the perimeter of Stella's house. How she looked in a bedroom window. Nothing. She walked past the frosted bathroom window to the other side and peeked inside the master bedroom, still nothing.

Into the living room where the lights were on but no one was around. When she got to the kitchen, she saw Stella's shadow standing there. How she moved back and forth. Just like Gloria noticed a shadow moving back and forth through the frosted glass in the bathroom. Which meant Stella could not be in two places at once: in the bathroom and in the kitchen.

The final clue was when Stella carried her plate of pizza to the bedroom and closed the door. "Why would someone who had the living room TV, the lights, everything on, go into the bedroom and close the door?"

Lucy was lost. "Why?"

"Because Milt was in that bathroom and she was taking food to him."

"I ruled Vivian out last night," Gloria added.

"That's what I don't understand," Frances said. "She had the men's grooming stuff on her counter. You saw it yourself."

Gloria snapped her fingers. "Right, I saw men's cologne *and* a box of JustForMen hair color. Milt is bald. He has no facial hair."

"Ahhh," Frances nodded.

Gloria tapped the side of her head. "Gotta always be thinking."

"So when Paul got there and asked Stella if he could come in, she slammed the door in his face."

"And?" Lucy asked.

"He went back to the office and got an expedited probable cause search warrant. When he showed up on her doorstep a second time, warrant in hand, she had to let him in. Paul found him handcuffed to the safety bar in the shower."

Liz shook her head. "Well, I'll be."

Lucy shook her head. "But why?"

Gloria took a deep breath. "Believe it or not, she thought she was helping him. That by keeping him prisoner in her home, the men he owed money to wouldn't be able to track him down. The police just found his car in the Meijer grocery store parking lot."

Liz pushed back her chair. "I assume he's going to press charges."

Gloria slowly shook her head. "Believe it or not, Milt told Paul he didn't want to press charges – at least not yet."

Frances jumped to her feet. "I hate to rush you all out of here but I just saw Milt's car pass by and I want to go check on him."

She rushed out the door and down the sidewalk. Milt was unlocking his front door when Frances got there. He opened the door and he and Frances disappeared inside.

Gloria watched until Frances was out of sight. "That lady is gaga over him."

Liz groaned. "A little too much, I suspect."

Chapter 21

The next couple of weeks were a whirlwind for Gloria, between working on the fall party and finishing her around-the-house projects. Eddie and his wife, Karen, would be there for a visit soon and Gloria was thrilled to spend time with them.

The day of the party, Gloria was nervous as a tic. She wondered how Andrea would react when Brian proposed and if she'd be upset that he'd done it in front of all of their friends.

Gloria had worked hard making sure everything was just right for the big day. She had consulted with Brian several times asking him what he thought and such. He seemed content to let Gloria plan it all but she figured that was just a guy thing. Leave all the party planning to the girls. Although she was anxious that she might mess something up for them.

The fire pit was clean and the wagon loaded down with bales of hay that Lucy had so generously donated. Each of the girls had called during the day to make sure Gloria didn't need anything else.

Her grandsons, Ryan and Tyler, had gone on a hayride years ago when James was still alive. They were so young at the time, they didn't remember. Jill had called earlier to say they were bouncing off the walls and couldn't wait.

Gloria's son-in-law, Greg, offered to drive the tractor and Gloria gratefully accepted. Paul had offered, too, but when he found out Greg had asked first, he seemed relieved.

Storm clouds had threatened early in the day but when evening rolled around, the sky was clear and the air was cool and crisp.

After all of the guests had arrived, Ryan and Tyler insisted that everyone check out their new tree fort. Gloria and Paul found a ladder in the garage and carried it to the front yard. Paul propped the ladder against the side of the fancy new deck and he and Gloria watched as several of the guests made their way up the ladder to admire the fort.

The last one to tour the fort was Paul. He and the boys were up there for several long moments. Finally, Tyler, then Ryan emerged and scrambled down the swinging ladder, not bothering to use the sturdier one. Last, but not least, Paul eased his way back down the ladder.

Ryan darted over to Gloria and tugged on her hand. "Grams. Paul is gonna take us fishing next time we come over."

Gloria looked down at the eager young face and ruffled his hair. "He is?"

"We're gonna catch a fish this big," Tyler added, holding his hands a good three feet apart.

Gloria put her arm around his shoulder. "Then you can bring him home and we'll fry him up in the pan and eat him for supper."

The boys darted off to tell their parents they were going fishing.

Paul came up behind her. He wiped his hands on his pants. "Why didn't you ask me to help build the tree fort?"

Gloria turned to look at Paul. His expression was somber and Gloria's heart plummeted.

"Well. I-I just figured you were busy with work and all..." her voice trailed off.

"Next time, I'd like a chance to help," he said quietly. "At least ask."

Gloria wished the ground would open up and swallow her. She never asked because she didn't want to bother him. Looking back, she should have. "I'm sorry. Next time the boys have a project, I'll check with you first," she promised.

Paul nodded, a sly smile turning the corners of his mouth. "Just for that, you have to go fishing with us."

Gloria hadn't been fishing in years. It looked like she was "on the hook" for this one. Maybe it wouldn't be as boring as she remembered...

"It's a deal." Gloria slipped her hand into Paul's and they wandered over to the wagon. Paul lifted Mally first, then helped Gloria hop on.

Andrea was the straggler and the last one on as she stood back and took several pictures of the wagon and the riders.

"All clear," Gloria hollered to Greg. The tractor and wagon lurched forward and Greg headed through the field to the dirt road on the other side.

Paul and Gloria settled in against the backboard and watched as the boys shoved hay down each other's shirts. Brian decided that looked like fun as he lifted Andrea's hat and filled it with straw.

"What a great idea," Paul told Gloria.

She snuggled closer. "We should do this more often."

The tractor chugged along. Dusk had set and the stars began to shine. Too soon, the wagon turned around and they headed back to the farm.

Gloria kept glancing at Brian, wondering when he was going to pop the question. Finally, she couldn't stand it any longer. She crawled over to him and whispered in his ear. "Did you chicken out?"

Brian chuckled. "No, I didn't get cold feet. I decided to wait until everyone gathers around the campfire."

Gloria raised a brow. Smart thinking. That way, everyone could watch. "Good idea." She nodded and crawled back under the blanket with Paul.

Greg unhooked the wagon and backed the tractor into the barn then closed the door. By the time the girls brought out the hotdogs and s'mores, the bonfire was burning nicely, and everyone circled the fire.

Paul let go of Gloria's hand and cupped his hands to his mouth. "Can I have everyone's attention?" Everyone grew quiet. Everyone that is, except for the boys. Jill tapped Tyler's arm. "Shush."

The boys quieted.

Paul took a step forward. "Today is a special day and I want to thank each of you for being here."

He turned to Gloria, bent down on one knee and pulled a box from his pocket. A very familiar jewelry box. He opened the cover and the beautiful princess diamond that Gloria had admired so much was twinkling up at her. "Gloria Rutherford, would you do me the honor of becoming my wife?"

Tears streamed down Gloria's cheeks as she stared at the ring, then at Paul's face, then back at the ring. "I..."

Paul lifted the ring from the box. "I'm taking that as a yes." He slipped the ring on her finger and rose to his feet.

Gloria blinked back the tears as Paul wrapped his arms around her waist and kissed her slowly at first and then it deepened, promising her so much more.

Breathless, they finally took a step back to catcalls and whistles.

The rest of the evening was a blur as everyone hugged Gloria and shook Paul's hand. She was in a daze. It was a wonderful moment of pure happiness.

Lucy was the only one to ask the question that was nagging every one of the Garden Girls' minds: Dot, Margaret, Ruth and Lucy.

Lucy hugged Gloria and turned to Paul, a serious look on her face. "This doesn't mean you're going to take Gloria from us, are you?"

Paul gazed lovingly at his bride-to-be and turned a solemn face to answer Lucy's serious question. "Absolutely not and I doubt there is any way on this earth that Gloria would allow that to happen."

A slow smile spread across his face. "No, I'm afraid that all of you will now be stuck with *me*."

Ray overhead the exchange. He slapped Paul on the back and grabbed his hand. "Welcome to the family, my friend."

The group began cleaning up around the campfire when Gloria spied Brian setting out some of the lawn chairs. She pulled him aside. "You tricked me," she said.

Brian grinned. "Paul wanted everything to be perfect so we hatched a plan to let *you* plan your own engagement party. He was so nervous, that he had me show you the ring to make sure you were going to like it."

Andrea spoke up. "I swear, I knew nothing about this," she promised.

Gloria hugged Brian and then Andrea. "I have to keep an eye on you two."

Finally, after the hotdogs and s'mores were all gone and the last guest headed home, Paul turned to his bride-to-be. "I hope this night meant as much to you as it has to me."

Gloria looked down at the beautiful diamond ring and back up at Paul. Her throat closed and the tears began to flow. She was at a loss for words.

Paul wrapped his arms around the woman that he loved and let the tears of joy flow.

They sat on the porch for a long time after everyone had left as they talked about the future. They made some very important decisions. One decision they made was to keep both farms, at least for now, and split their time between the two.

Paul would keep working, maybe for another year...maybe less.

Last but not least, they set the wedding date. They would marry when all of Gloria's children would be home for the holidays.

Home for the holidays. Home for a wedding.

Finally, in the wee hours of the morning, Paul got to his feet. "I should go." He kissed Gloria one more time and stepped off the porch and to his truck.

Gloria quietly stood by the back door and watched as his taillights disappeared from the drive. She stepped inside, turned off the porch light and locked the door.

Today. This day had been the best day ever.

The end.

Layered Cream Cheese Pumpkin Pie Recipe

<u>Ingredients</u>:
Baked pie crust OR graham cracker crust

<u>For cream cheese, white chocolate layer</u>:
¾ - 1 Cup white chocolate chips
8 oz. cream cheese, softened
2 Tbsp heavy cream

<u>For no bake pumpkin layer</u>:
1/3 Cup light brown sugar
4 Tbsp corn starch
¼ tsp nutmeg
2 Cups milk (whole milk works best)
½ Cup pumpkin puree
1 Tbsp butter
1 Tbsp vanilla extract
1 Teaspoon pumpkin spice
¼ Teaspoon salt

<u>To prepare white chocolate cream cheese layer</u>:

-Beat the cream cheese with an electric mixer on medium/high speed until light and fluffy.

-In medium bowl, mix chocolate chips and heavy cream. Microwave on 50% power until chocolate has melted. Be careful not to let it get too hot or it will clump. (If that happens, add a little more cream and whisk until smooth.)

-With the mixer running, add the melted white chocolate a spoonful at a time to the cream cheese and beat until fluffy. Cover and place in refrigerator until ready to assemble pie.

To prepare pumpkin layer:

-Using a heavy-duty saucepan, mix the brown sugar and cornstarch together. Add 1/3 cup of the milk and whisk until smooth. Add the rest of the milk.

-Cook on medium heat, stirring constantly until the mixture comes to a boil. Let cook for another minute. Continue whisking.

-Remove from heat and whisk in the pumpkin puree, vanilla, pumpkin pie spice and salt. Blend until smooth.

-Place in large glass bowl. Press plastic wrap on the surface of the pudding to prevent a skin from forming. Let the pudding cool completely.

To assemble:

-Spread the white chocolate-cream cheese mixture evenly over the baked piecrust (or graham cracker crust). Spoon the chilled pudding over the cream layer.

-Chill for 3 hours. Serve with whipped cream or white chocolate shavings – or both!

Bully in the 'Burbs – Book 8

Garden Girls
Cozy Mystery Series

Hope Callaghan

hopecallaghan.com

_____

Visit my website for new releases and special offers: hopecallaghan.com

Thank you, Peggy Hyndman and Wanda Downs, for taking the time to preview *Bully in the Burbs,* for the extra sets of eyes and for catching all my mistakes.

Chapter 1

The tick-tock of the wall clock was about to drive Gloria insane. She stared at the minute hand as it slowly inched along, second by agonizingly slow second. She sucked in a deep breath and then slowly let it out. "Whew..."

Liz, Gloria's older sister, slammed her open palm on the kitchen table. "Will you *please* stop doing that? I'm already nervous as a tick."

Margaret, Gloria's friend, jumped in. "Both of you, we need to exercise a little patience. David should be calling any minute now."

Three sets of eyes turned to stare at the clock again.

Liz pushed her chair back and jumped to her feet. Her eyes narrowed as she studied the dime store rooster clock that hung on the bulkhead above Gloria's sink. "Is that what I think it is?"

Gloria started to giggle, which turned into a belly laugh. The stress of waiting for David to call was causing her to crack under the pressure.

Liz, Margaret and Gloria had unearthed some rare coins at Aunt Ethel's family farm in the Smoky Mountains several months ago. Liz had done some preliminary research on the coins and discovered they were worth money – a lot of money.

The coins had been evenly divided: two for David, Ethel's son, two for Liz, two for Margaret, two for Gloria and last, but not least, two for Sandy McGee, who may or may not have had a legal right to the coins, but to avoid future hassles, they had all unanimously decided to include her in the split.

The State of Tennessee claimed they owned the rare coins and there had been a fierce battle waging in the courts for months now between the five of them and the state.

David had phoned Gloria yesterday and asked her to round up Liz and Margaret for a 10:00 a.m. conference call. The courts had reached a decision.

Gloria had tried to weasel the verdict out of David but he flat out refused, explaining it was best to give them the news at the same time, which is why they were sitting in Gloria's kitchen at 9:58 a.m., waiting with baited breath for his call.

Gloria had hidden her two coins in plain sight and that was what Liz had just noticed. She had stuck the coins inside her kitchen clock. One coin was on 12 and the other on the six.

Gloria plucked the cordless phone from its base and set the phone on the table between the three of them. The group stared at the silent phone, each of them lost in their own thoughts.

Gloria saw this as a blessing and a curse. Her life was almost perfect. She had all that she needed – her family and her friends. She and Paul, the man of her dreams, were now engaged. To her, this windfall might very well be the worst thing that could ever happen. Money changed people, changed attitudes. What would happen when word got out that they had all this money?

No, it would surely upset the applecart. She was certain the others at the table had the exact same thoughts.

She glanced at Margaret out of the corner of her eye. Margaret would probably fare best. Her husband was a retired banker, although the fact that she'd known there was the possibility of inheriting a windfall and had not mentioned it to Don, her husband, could pose problems for her friend.

Next, she glanced at Liz. At least Liz didn't have to explain herself to anyone, but Liz was single. Gloria could just envision both married and unmarried men coming out of the woodwork to court her. How could she ever find true love? If she were Liz, she would always wonder if the man loved her for who she was or loved her for her money.

This was turning into a real pickle.

Liz slammed her fist on the tabletop in frustration, which caused Gloria to jump. "You're going to give me a heart attack."

Briing. All three women reached for the phone that sat in the middle of the table. Gloria got to it first. "Hello?"

"Yes. Hi David. You don't say." Gloria was messing with the other two. David had just asked her to put him on speaker.

Liz yanked the phone from Gloria's hand and gave her hard look. She jammed her thumb on the speaker button and set the phone in the middle of the table.

"Go ahead, David. We're all listening now." Liz glared at her sister.

Gloria stuck her tongue out at Liz who promptly gave her the bird.

"Stop bickering this instant," Margaret hissed. "We're ready," she told David.

"Great." His deep voice boomed through the fuzzy line. "I have some good news and some bad news."

"Start with the good news." Margaret wanted to savor at least a moment of happiness.

"The court ruled in our favor. The coins are ours to keep."

Liz shrieked.

Margaret clutched at her chest.

Gloria twisted her brand spanking new princess-cut diamond engagement ring around her finger. The first person who came to mind was Paul, her fiancé. Her second thought was of her children.

The girl's joyous moment was short-lived. "So what's the bad news?" Liz asked.

"Inheritance tax. The government is going to get their share, one way or another," he said.

"How much is the inheritance tax?" Liz wondered aloud.

"Forty percent," David and Margaret answered in unison. Margaret had already done preliminary research.

Gloria was shocked. "You mean if the coins are worth, say $2 million, the government gets $800k of that right off the top?"

The girls could hear David's laborious sigh over the phone line. "Yep. The good news is you don't live in Japan where the inheritance tax is a whopping 55%."

That did little to make the girls feel better. Still, they would each end up with a cool million, minimum.

Gloria's head was spinning. She missed part of what David said. "...the auction house in New York."

Gloria tried to focus. "I'm sorry, David, I missed what you just said."

"That's okay, Gloria. I'm sure this is a lot to absorb at once. I said that Heritage Auctions in New York is your best bet to get the most bang for your buck if you sell the coins."

All eyes turned to Liz, who had been in charge of locating auction companies. "I've got it covered," she winked, "I've already set up an account."

The conversation ended with the girls thanking David for all of the hard work he'd put into winning the case.

"We need to do something extra nice for him," Margaret said, after the line disconnected.

The room grew silent, each of the girls in deep thought.

Liz spoke first. "I say we wait 24-hours before we breathe a word, so that we can give it time to sink in." She slid out of the kitchen chair and headed for the door with Margaret and Gloria trailing behind.

"Good idea," Gloria agreed.

Gloria and Mally stood on the porch and watched as Margaret and Liz climbed into their vehicles and pulled out onto the main road.

Deep down, Gloria had always thought this day would never come, that somehow the government would find a way to claim ownership of the coins.

Liz had told them before she left that the last quote the auction house had given her was a flat 12% commission for selling the coins. The representative also said that the coins could go for as low as $1.8 million and as high as a cool $2.5 million for two coins.

Gloria wandered over to her desk in the corner of the dining room and pulled out the chair. Sound asleep on top of the chair was Gloria's cat, Puddles. She lifted her cat and settled him on her lap. He opened one eye for a quick glance before he closed it again and fell back asleep.

Gloria did some quick calculations on her desktop calculator and at $1.8 million after the auction house's commission and the government's inheritance tax, she would end up with less than a million bucks.

Almost half the money would go to pay taxes and commissions. Gloria still had a hard time swallowing the amount of taxes she would have to pay.

She spent the rest of the afternoon mulling over how to divide the windfall. After contemplating several different scenarios, she decided to split half amongst her three children, with a stipulation that a percentage of the money go into college funds for all four of her grandchildren.

The other half would be for Paul and her to keep since they planned to marry later that year. Now it was time for her to break the news.

Chapter 2

Gloria paced the kitchen floor of her old farmhouse nervously. She glanced at the clock every few minutes. The girls had sold the coins a few days earlier and after taxes and commissions paid to the auction house; she had netted a cool $1.1 million. One million, one hundred seventy-five thousand, three hundred sixty dollars and twelve cents to be exact.

She had told her children and Paul about the coins and the money, and then explained to each of them her plan to divide the windfall. She was proud that there was nary a gripe or groan from any of them. They all took it quite calmly, even calmer than Gloria herself had hoped.

If Gloria's announcement had surprised Paul, he had done an excellent job of hiding it. He told her whatever she felt was best was what she should do. They had almost $600k to invest, to take care of much-needed repairs around the farms – both his farm and hers - and to take a nice long honeymoon...

That left $196k for each of her children. Gloria had wired Ben's money to an account that he and his wife, Kelly, shared. She also wired money to her son, Eddie, and his wife, Karen's, account.

That left her daughter, Jill, and her husband, Greg. They were on their way over.

Gloria stopped wearing a hole in her kitchen linoleum and Mally and she wandered out to the back porch to wait.

Fall had come early and there was a brisk chill in the air. She gazed at the thick carpet of leaves that covered the ground. Perhaps she could have her grandsons, Tyler and Ryan, over for the weekend to help rake the leaves...

The sound of gravel crunching on the drive caught her attention and she watched the familiar dark sedan pull into the drive. Four doors popped open. Her grandsons raced across the yard to reach their beloved Grams first, while Greg and Jill brought up the rear.

The boys hugged Gloria, and then ran off to check on the tree fort they had built during their last overnight visit. Tyler and Ryan scampered up the ladder and disappeared inside.

Gloria opened the porch door and waited while her daughter and son-in-law stepped into the kitchen.

The check was on the kitchen table, under the glass sugar bowl sitting in the center. Gloria plucked the check from under the bowl and handed it to Jill.

Gloria hadn't told Jill the exact amount and she had asked her sons to keep it quiet. She wanted it to be a surprise and it was, judging by the look on Jill's face.

Her daughter swallowed hard and handed the check to Greg. The color drained from his face and his hand started to shake. He looked up at Gloria. "Are you sure? I mean, this is a lot of money..."

Gloria nodded. "Yes. One hundred percent sure. This is for you to use as you see fit. The only thing I ask is that you set aside some of the money for each of the boys' college funds."

It finally began to sink in. Jill's eye lit. "Greg. We can move. We can finally move into a bigger house."

Gloria smiled. Greg and Jill had outgrown their small two bedroom bungalow years ago, but money had been tight and with the downturn in the economy, Greg's company had all but eliminated overtime hours, which meant no extra income. The couple was able to make ends meet but there wasn't much left over at the end of the month and certainly not enough money to buy a larger, more expensive home.

"I think that's a wonderful idea," Gloria agreed.

The boys stampeded up the steps and burst through the kitchen door. "We're hungry."

Gloria reached for Tyler and hugged him tight. "I'm hungry, too," she declared. "Let's head down to Dot's. My treat."

"Dot's" was Dot's Restaurant, the only restaurant in the small town of Belhaven. Dot Jenkins, Gloria's close friend, and her husband, Ray, had owned the restaurant for decades.

The five of them climbed into Greg and Jill's car. Gloria squeezed in the backseat, smack dab in the middle of her grandsons. The drive to town was short and she didn't mind being squished between two of her favorite people.

It was just shy of 5 o'clock and the dinner onslaught had not yet begun. The five of them wandered in the front entrance and made their way to the back.

Dot spied the group and after a quick stop in the kitchen, made a beeline for the booth, water glasses in hand. She also had two chocolate milkshakes – one for Tyler and one for Ryan.

"Thank you, Mrs. Jenkins," Tyler said.

"Yeah, thanks." Ryan reached for his milkshake, grabbed the straw and then took a big sip. "We're rich," he informed Dot.

Dot chuckled. She tucked the empty tray under her arm. "You're rich? Can I borrow some money?" she teased.

Ryan nodded. "Yep. You can borrow some from Grams, too."

Dot winked at Gloria. She knew all about the money. The whole town of Belhaven was talking about the girls' newfound wealth. Heck, all of Montbay County was abuzz.

Dot was happy for her friends. If anyone deserved to have fortune smile down on them, it was Gloria.

"We're gonna buy a new house," Tyler said.

Gloria raised a brow. She didn't think the boys had listened to their conversation. She remembered a saying her mom liked to quote, "*Little pitchers have big ears.*"

"That sounds wonderful," Dot said.

"I'm starving," Tyler stuck the bottom of the menu in his mouth and chewed the corner.

"Stop that." Jill grabbed the menu and yanked it out of his hands.

Dot covered her mouth to hide her grin. "Our special today is all-you-can-eat-tacos."

"Sounds perfect." Gloria hadn't bothered looking at the menu. She knew the entire menu by heart.

"I'll have tacos, too," Ryan piped up. "I can eat at least seventeen," he predicted.

Gloria tapped the tabletop with her fingernails. "Are you sure that's all? You said you were starving."

Ryan ran his hand over his cropped locks. "Yeah...make that twenty."

"Got it," Dot nodded solemnly and winked at Gloria. "Tacos for everyone?"

Gloria wondered if Dot was using Alice's spicy recipe that she had shared with her not long ago.

Alice was her friend, Andrea's, former housekeeper and new roommate. She made some mean Mexican dishes that Gloria adored but that didn't adore Gloria quite as much.

She decided to splurge and try them anyway. After all, they were tacos. How deadly could lettuce, tomato, cheese and a little meat be?

Dot jotted down their order and headed to the back. Gloria turned to Jill. "Will you stay in Green Springs?" Jill had mentioned several times that they would like to move to the larger town of nearby Rapid Creek.

Greg and Jill exchanged a glance

"I'm sure you need to talk it over," Gloria said.

"I don't wanna move," Ryan whined as he kicked the bottom of the booth.

Tyler lifted his shake and took a big gulp that left a chocolate moustache on his upper lip. He wiped it away with the back of his hand. "Me either. I want to live in our house forever."

"We'll discuss this later." Jill gave the boys one of those "don't-mess-with-mom" looks and the boys grew silent.

Gloria frowned. She had hoped the money would be a blessing, not divide their family.

Thankfully, the food arrived and they got off the subject of a new house and onto Paul and Gloria's upcoming wedding. She had already decided that her youngest grandson, Ryan, would be ring bearer while her two older grandsons, Tyler and Oliver, would be ushers.

Ariel, Gloria's only granddaughter, would be the flower girl.

233

Although she didn't plan to have a large wedding – just family and friends – she wanted her grandchildren to be part of it and feel important.

Jill spooned hot sauce on her taco and lifted it to her mouth. "Have you decided on a location?"

Gloria frowned. She hadn't gotten that far in the planning stage. She could have Pastor Nate marry them at her church, the Church of God in Belhaven. They had planned a winter wedding, over the holidays, when all of Gloria's children would be in town.

She had two months to work out the details and in the meantime, make room for Paul to move in. They had decided to divide their time between Paul's farm a few miles away and Gloria's farm, just outside the small town of Belhaven.

With the money from the sale of the coins, she had decided to take care of some much-needed repairs on her old place, including a fresh coat of paint and new flooring. The farmhouse's electrical and wiring had never been updated. James, Gloria's first husband, had said years ago that he was concerned that the old wiring was a fire hazard.

Paul's family farm was in similar condition and she had offered to do some updates on his place, as well.

Other than that and a nice honeymoon, she wasn't sure how to spend the rest of the money. Maybe she could set it aside for a rainy day or an emergency.

"I'm not sure where the wedding will take place," Gloria confessed, "I guess we should decide soon."

Jill waved a hand. "Oh, you've got plenty of time, Mom. You have a whole ten weeks or so," she teased.

Beads of sweat formed on Gloria's brow. Ten weeks? That was it?

Jill recognized the look on her mother's face. She reached over and squeezed her hand. "Don't worry, Mom. I'll help out."

Dot was back and had overhead the tail end of the conversation. "We'll all help, Gloria. Don't stress yourself out over this."

They were right. Gloria's close-knit group of friends would give her a hand.

Dot lifted the dirty plates and piled them on her tray. "Why don't you have it at Andrea's place?"

Gloria's eyes widened. Why hadn't she thought of that? Andrea had a lovely tearoom inside her newly remodeled home. It would be perfect for a winter wedding.

After dinner, the five of them wandered to the car and Greg drove back to the farm. During the short drive home, the boys begged Gloria to let them spend the night but Jill was firm. Tomorrow was a school day and they needed to be in their own beds.

"How about a week from Saturday night? I need someone to help rake all those leaves in the yard. I'll even pay you."

Tyler shot as far forward in his seat as his seatbelt would allow and grabbed his mom's shoulder. "Can we, Mom? Can we stay at Grams?"

Jill glanced at her mother. "If she wants you to."

The matter was settled. The boys would spend the night and help rake the yard, burn leaves and still have plenty of time to play in the tree fort. It would work out perfectly since it might be the last chance Gloria had time to spend with them before the holidays and life got too hectic.

Gloria hugged each of her grandsons before she climbed out of the car. She watched the car disappear from sight before she headed to the back porch.

It was still early evening but already dark. The days were growing shorter and although she welcomed the changing season and looked forward to the months ahead, she wished the daylight hours lasted a little longer.

Gloria prayed for her children as she locked the porch door behind her. She prayed that God would find them the perfect house.

Change was hard, particularly for young boys who would have to move away from friends and everything familiar.

Chapter 3

The days flew by as Gloria arranged for electricians to inspect both Paul's farm and her farm. She brought in several local companies to give her quotes to replace the worn linoleum in the kitchen and bath and to put down new wood floors in the dining room.

Greg and Jill had previewed several homes in Rapid Creek and her daughter had called her mother the day before yesterday to let Gloria know that the offer on the home they had fallen in love with had been accepted.

Jill was excited to have her mom look at the home and Gloria couldn't wait to see it. Even the boys started to get excited after they saw the place. They would each have their own room instead of sharing a room.

Gloria pulled Annabelle into Jill's drive and parked off to the side. It was the middle of the week and the boys were in school. The plan was for Gloria and her daughter to look at the house then have lunch together to discuss the upcoming move.

The closing date on the house was exactly one week before Thanksgiving. A lot needed to happen in a short amount of time and Gloria had offered to do whatever it took to help her family.

A harried Jill met Gloria at the door.

Gloria peeked over her shoulder. The house was in shambles. Boxes filled every inch of available space, leaving only a small path from the door, through the kitchen and beyond.

"You don't want to go in there," Jill warned.

Gloria believed her. She herself hadn't moved in years but she had helped plenty of friends and moving was one of Gloria's least favorite things to do. That and paint.

Her plan was to live on the farm until she breathed her last. The kids would have to worry about the rest.

Jill grabbed her car keys and she followed her mother to the car. Green Springs, where Jill currently lived, was a short ten-minute drive to the new house in Rapid Creek.

The town of Rapid Creek was both charming and historical. Many of the town's original structures remained. A small, touristy area lined the side of the creek and at the end of the shops was an old flourmill a local had turned into a popular restaurant and bakery, The Old Mill.

In the summer, a small livery rented canoes, kayaks and inner tubes to area residents who were brave enough to plunge into the icy waters of the clear, cool creek.

When Gloria was young, such a place didn't exist. Instead, they made do with old tire tubes that they would drag to the edge of the water and then hop in from the banks of the river.

They drove past Main Street, crossed over the river and headed up the hill to the other side of town where several small neighborhoods had sprouted up in recent years.

Jill steered the car to the right and into one of the neighborhoods, "Highland Park."

"I still can't believe the deal we got on this place," Jill chattered excitedly, "four bedrooms, two full baths and even a half bath, plus a two car garage. The lot is almost a quarter acre and the house is less than ten years old."

Jill turned down a side street, "Pine Place."

"It even has a stone fireplace in the living room."

They pulled into a drive near the end of the cul-de-sac. "Here it is."

The front of the house was brick.

The first thing Gloria noticed was the large picture window in front, covered by an expansive porch, perfect for a pair of rocking chairs.

Jill reached for the door handle. "I can't wait to show you the inside."

Gloria hoped they were spending the money wisely. "How much did you say this house cost?"

"Only $125,000. Can you believe it? Houses in this neighborhood are selling for closer to $200,000."

Gloria had prayed about finding the right place. It appeared as if God had answered her prayers.

The real estate agent had given Jill the code to unlock the lockbox that hung on the front door knob. She punched in the code, pulled out the key and unlocked the front door.

A small foyer opened up into a large living room with vaulted ceilings. Tall, cherry-stained bookshelves flanked a large, stone fireplace.

Light oak covered the floors and continued into the kitchen and dining room, all open and within view of the living room. It was a popular, modern floor plan and a good fit for Jill and the boys. Her daughter could keep a close eye on them from the main living area.

On the other side of the kitchen was a small hall that led out to the garage. A laundry room was off to the left of the kitchen and a small half bath to the right.

Jill pointed to the bath. "This will be perfect to keep the boys from running through the house with dirty shoes."

Gloria nodded to the laundry room. "You can strip 'em down at the door."

They wandered back into the kitchen. Gloria ran her hand lightly across the dark granite counters. They were beautiful. The kitchen was an ample size and sported a large center island with enough room for several barstools.

The kitchen appliances were all stainless steel and looked almost new.

Gloria spun around. "I love this kitchen." She touched the counters again, "especially these countertops."

"You should put them in your kitchen," Jill told her.

It was a thought. The granite was beautiful. The counters she had now worked just fine but James had put them in back in the 70's and they were apricot orange. Through the years and the kids, they had accumulated several chips and scuffs, and many memories along the way... "Perhaps I don't need new ones after all," she decided.

They started to pass by the kitchen on their way to the bedrooms in the back when something on the back counter caught Gloria's eye. It was a sheet of paper, folded in half. "What's that?"

Jill shook her head. "I don't know. What is it?"

Jill stepped to the counter and picked up the paper. She opened it up. Gloria peeked over her shoulder.

"Beware. This house is cursed. Death awaits."

Jill released her grip on the note and it fluttered to the floor. "What in the world?"

Gloria slipped her reading glasses on, bent down and picked up the note. "Someone is trying to scare you."

"Someone that has been in this house." Jill glanced around nervously.

Gloria didn't reply. She walked over to the service door that connected the garage to the kitchen and twisted the knob. The door was locked.

Next, she stepped into the laundry room and pushed up on the window sash. Locked.

She moved from room-to-room, checking each window and door. The entire upper floor was secure; the girls descended the center staircase to the lower level, and stepped into the walkout basement.

Gloria flicked the lights on and gazed around the room. It was an enormous, open area, perfect for her grandsons to play and roughhouse without breaking anything.

Gloria's ears burned at the thought that someone was trying to scare her family from buying the house. She marched across the room and down a long hall. At the end of the hall was a large bedroom. She stomped over to the window, grabbed the sash and yanked. The window easily lifted. Cool, fall air rushed in.

Jill eased in behind her.

Gloria turned. "See? Someone snuck in and left that note, hoping to frighten you."

Jill shivered and rubbed her upper arms. "They did a good job."

Gloria pulled the window closed and clicked the lock in place. They checked the rest of the windows then headed back up the stairs.

Jill led her mom through the garage and service door into the back yard. Two large, oak trees sat near the back. Off to one side were the remnants of a garden. A tiered wooden deck that looked brand new covered the back of the house.

They wandered back through the garage and into the kitchen. "Do not let this scare you, Jill."

Jill frowned at the note, still on the counter. "I'm going to call the real estate agent as soon as I get home. Maybe she knows something about this house or neighborhood."

She folded the note and shoved it into her purse. "I knew it was too good to be true."

The girls stopped at The Old Mill to grab a bite to eat. Jill picked at her food. Gloria knew the note bothered her daughter. She tried to reason with her but once Jill got something in her head that was it. She would agree or go along with what you said, but all the time her plan was to do the complete opposite.

The entire trip back to Jill's place, Gloria tried to convince her daughter it was nothing.

Gloria followed Jill into the house. "Call the agent so you can clear this up and quit worrying."

Jill dialed the number and put the phone on speaker. Luckily, the agent was in the office and it was a short time before her agent, Sue Camp, picked up the line. "Hello Jill," a cheery voice greeted them.

"Hi Sue. I have you on speaker. My mom and I just came back from the house."

"Oh good. I'm sure your mother approves of the lovely home."

"She does," Jill agreed, "but now I'm not sure anymore."

The cheer turned to alarm. "You're kidding. Why not?"

Jill explained how they found the note on the counter. She told the real estate agent what the note said and that they discovered an unlocked window on the lower level.

Gloria jumped in. "Gloria, here. This house has been on the market for a long time. At that price and as nice as it is, someone should have snatched it up long ago. Is there something we should know?"

There was a long pause on the other end, so long that Gloria thought the line had disconnected.

"Hello? Are you still there?"

"Yes, I'm still here. There has been an issue with this particular home," Sue Camp admitted.

Chapter 4

Jill tugged on a loose strand of hair. "Wh-what kind of issue?"

"Several other buyers have gone to contract on this house, only to back out days later."

"Because?" Gloria asked. Getting this woman to talk was like pulling teeth.

"Oh, threatening notes and other small nitpicky things."

"Such as?" Gloria prompted – again.

"Desumbap." Unintelligible reply.

"What did you say?"

There was a heavy sigh on the other end. "I said some dead, rotting animals keep popping up on the porch."

There was more - Gloria just knew it. "Anywhere else?"

"The deck out back and in the garage."

Gloria had never met Sue Camp, but the woman was starting to get on Gloria's last nerve. "Surely a couple dead animals and threatening notes have not scared buyers to the point that they cancelled." Gloria had another thought. "How many buyers have walked?"

"Seven."

Jill had started to recover from her shock. "Seven buyers in seven months, including us?"

"No. In addition to you."

"I-I'm not sure I want to buy this house," Jill told the woman.

"You'll lose your deposit," the real estate agent warned her.

"She'll call you back." Gloria grabbed the phone and disconnected the line.

Gloria turned to her daughter. "How much was the deposit?"

Jill swallowed hard. "Almost seven thousand dollars."

"Seven thousand dollars – for a deposit?" Gloria had never purchased real estate. Her farm had passed down through the family for generations.

She had friends who had purchased real estate, though, and she knew that an earnest money deposit was small – maybe a thousand or two.

"They wanted to make sure we were serious," Jill whispered in a small voice.

Gloria grabbed her daughter's hand. "C'mon. We're going back to that house for a closer look."

They drove back to the house in silence. Jill was mulling over how she could get out of the contract. Her mother, on the other side of the car, was trying to figure out how to get to the bottom of this.

Jill pulled into the drive and the women climbed out of the car. Jill hung her head and slowly made her way up the sidewalk.

It broke Gloria's heart to see her daughter so despondent. She had been so excited about the place and now the thrill was gone, replaced by dread, which caused Gloria to be even more determined. Someone was trying to scare them off and she was not going to have any of it.

Gloria stepped inside the front door and right into detective mode. She grabbed her reading glasses from her purse and slipped them on. She studied the walls, the windows and she even pulled the grate from the fireplace and peered inside.

The women made their way into the garage. Gloria opened the cabinets, got down on her hands and knees and looked under the shelves. Her gaze wandered up to the ceiling and to the yellow string attached to the attic ladder.

Gloria grasped the string and pulled. She unfolded the steps and started up. It was dark except for a small amount of light that filtered in through the round louver centered above the garage door.

Nothing appeared to be out of place. Gloria backed down the stairs, folded the steps and pushed the ladder back in place. She dusted her hands and rubbed them on the front of her jeans.

Jill watched in silence, unable to muster enough enthusiasm to help her mother search for clues.

247

The laundry room was clean. The half bath was clean. Gloria pulled open the cupboard door nearest to the stove. She inspected every drawer and every cupboard in search of something, anything.

Finally, Jill joined her mother and started on the other end of the kitchen. It was a lovely kitchen, bright and beautiful with a large bay window above the stainless steel sink that overlooked the garden and backyard.

Gloria turned her attention to the open dining room on the other side of the kitchen island. A bright beam of sunlight reflected off the freshly painted wall on the far side.

Gloria noticed a faint outline on the wall. "Do you see that?"

"See what?" Jill asked.

Gloria walked over to the wall. She followed the outline with her hand. She took a step back and then stepped to the side. The outline was much clearer from that angle. It was an inverted pentagram.

Gloria had a sneaking suspicion the real estate agent knew all about the pentagram and had kept mum, probably hoping she could finally unload the house and collect her commission.

Gloria felt the steam roll out of her ears. She held out her hand. "Give me your phone. I'm calling Sue Camp."

Jill did as her mother requested. She recognized that look and the tone of her mother's voice and she almost felt sorry for her real estate agent. Almost.

"I'd like to speak with Sue Camp, please," Gloria told the receptionist in a firm voice...a voice that said, "don't even try to tell me she's unavailable."

Sue's calm voice answered. "Hello?"

"Gloria Rutherford, here. I'm Jill Adams' mother. We're back at the house. Were you aware someone has drawn a pentagram on the dining room wall?"

Jill couldn't hear Sue's answer but she cringed anyway.

Gloria responded "Yes" three times in a clipped tone. "Jill will call you back."

No, "Have a nice day." No, "Thank you for your time."

She handed the phone back to her daughter. "That woman knows more than she lets on."

Mother and daughter wandered out the front door. Jill locked the door behind them. "Good-bye house."

"Jill Rutherford Adams, you are not a quitter."

"I don't want to live in a haunted house." Jill knew she sounded whiney but she couldn't help it. She wouldn't sleep one wink in that house if she thought for even a second that it was haunted.

Gloria grabbed her daughter's arm. "Let's go meet the neighbors."

She dragged her reluctant daughter across the lawn to the house next door.

Gloria sucked in a breath and pressed the doorbell. She could hear the faint chime within. No one answered. She tried a second time then gave up.

They tried the house on the other side. No one answered there either.

"We'll be back," Gloria vowed as they made their way to the car. Neighbors always knew each other's business. If anyone knew the history of the house, it would be the people next door.

Gloria climbed in the passenger seat and fastened her seatbelt. Jill closed the driver's side door and slid the key in the ignition. She looked as if she was about to burst into tears. All she could think about was that her dream home was slipping away and she had just wasted over seven thousand dollars – on nothing.

"Give me seven days," Gloria bargained. "Do not cancel your contract for seven days."

Jill didn't have a choice but to agree to give it a week. After all, she wouldn't have even had a shot at a new home if not for her mother's generosity. "Okay," she relented.

Gloria reached over and patted her hand. "In the meantime, find a new real estate agent and start looking at other homes. That way, if this one doesn't work out, which I am almost 100% certain it will because I'll get to the bottom of this," Gloria vowed, "you'll have a head start."

"Okay?"

Jill had nothing to lose. She quickly agreed. "You have yourself a deal," she said. They drove back to Jill's house in silence. Jill eased into the drive and put the car in park. "Just promise me one thing."

"What's that?" Gloria asked.

"That you won't do anything foolish...like stake out a haunted house in the middle of the night by yourself."

"I won't," Gloria promised. No way would she be brave enough to tackle that alone. Now if she had someone with her? Maybe.

Chapter 5

Gloria left Jill's place and headed home. Downtown Belhaven was packed. Gloria swerved into the post office parking lot and squeezed into the last open spot. She scooted out of the car and made a beeline for the front door.

Gloria's friend and Head Postmaster, Ruth Carpenter, was behind the counter helping a customer.

Gloria wandered over to the wall covered with flyers, showing pictures of missing persons. She was glad that Milton Tilton's mug was not one of the pictures.

Gloria and her friends had recently helped solve the case and had rescued poor Milt, which reminded her that she needed to call her sister, Liz.

Liz was a spendthrift and Gloria thought that maybe she could give her sister a few pointers on investing her money.

Ruth finished the transaction and the customer headed toward the exit. It was Patti Palmer. Patti scowled at Gloria, stuck her nose in the air and walked right past her without uttering a word.

Gloria watched as she exited the post office and slammed the door behind her.

"Yeah. I think she's still a little miffed," Ruth observed.

Gloria sniffed and shrugged her shoulders. "It's not my fault her son is a criminal."

She changed the subject. "Jill is in a pickle." She went on to explain the dilemma. "Something is rotten in Denmark and I plan to get to the bottom of it," Gloria vowed.

Ruth, always willing to offer a helping hand since Gloria had gotten her out of some tight spots, not the least of which was drug trafficking charges. "I'd love to help but haunted houses freak me out."

"Supposedly haunted," Gloria corrected. "I have my doubts."

Ruth tapped her fingernails on the counter top. "Let me know if I can help in some other way." She shivered. "The place is already giving me the creeps and I haven't even been there."

"Thanks for the offer." Gloria headed for the door. "Say, what do you think about Paul and me getting married over at Andrea's place?"

"In her new tearoom?" Ruth smiled. "That would be the perfect spot."

Gloria nodded. "That's what I thought." She stepped out of the post office and quietly closed the door.

She hopped into Annabelle and fired up the engine.

Gloria headed out of town. She started to pass by her best friend, Lucy's, place and made a last minute decision to stop in.

Lucy's bright yellow jeep was in the drive. Behind her jeep was another car – one that looked vaguely familiar but that Gloria couldn't quite place.

Gloria pulled the car behind the jeep and shut the engine off.

She climbed out of the car and stepped onto the sidewalk.

Wham.

Gloria recognized the sound. It was the sound of explosives. Lucy was at it again.

She stepped off the sidewalk and made her way toward the shed in the back of the yard.

"No. You gotta stand like this, with your feet apart, so you can keep your balance. Otherwise, the gun is gonna kick back and knock you on your rear."

Lucy, in full camo gear, wearing eye goggles and earplugs, demonstrated her stance to the man standing next to her – Lucy's new boyfriend, Max Field.

Max nodded. He followed Lucy's example and did as she told him. Max lifted the gun.

Gloria covered her ears.

Boom!

Max lowered the gun. Lucy patted him on the back. "Much better," she told him.

Gloria started to clap. "Bravo. Bravo."

Lucy and Max whirled around. The gun in Max's hand pointed right at Gloria.

Gloria's threw both hands in the air. "Don't shoot."

Max cringed. He lowered the gun. "Sorry Gloria."

With the gun safely at Max's side, Gloria stepped closer. "Is Lucy teaching you how to blow stuff up?"

Lucy was an adrenaline junkie. If she wasn't jumping out of planes, she was racing across her field on her four-wheeler. She had recently taken a hankering to building small explosives and then using them for target practice.

She tried several times to get Gloria to join in the "fun" but Gloria drew the line at blowing stuff up.

Gloria kept a small handgun in her dresser drawer. Thanks to Lucy, Gloria had become a good shot. If an intruder broke into her house and threatened her, she was confident she would be able to protect herself.

Max set the gun on top of the tree trunk next to him before he removed the safety goggles and earplugs. "Yeah. I guess I am getting better. This time I didn't shoot out her window."

He nodded to a small window frame at the corner of the shed...one without glass. "Thank goodness I found someone who is able to come by here on Monday to fix it."

Lucy picked up the earplugs and goggles and set them on the workbench inside the shed before she returned. "You didn't have to do that, Max. I could have just as easily boarded it up. That way, if you accidentally hit it again, it won't matter."

He nodded. She had a point...although he was getting better with his aim. Max glanced at his watch. "I better take off. I'm meeting the guys for a round of golf over in Green Springs."

Lucy walked Max to his car while Gloria waited by the shed. She watched as they disappeared around the old oak tree and out of sight.

Gloria liked Max. He seemed a much better fit than Bill, Lucy's ex-boyfriend. Lucy met Max during their last case, when Milton Tilton had come up missing. Max and Milt were friends.

Max's sport car pulled out onto the road and Lucy met her friend in the rear yard. Gloria waited while Lucy put the gun and explosives in the shed.

Gloria followed her inside and watched as Lucy stood in front of a small sink and washed her hands.

"You put a sink in the shed?"

Lucy squeezed a glob of dish soap on her hands and rubbed them together. "Yeah. I decided it was best if I got the gunpowder residue off my hands before going in the house. Don't want to blow up the inside of my house."

She dried her hands on a towel nearby then closed the door to the shed. "What brings you to my neck of the woods?"

Gloria explained the situation with Jill's house as they wandered up the back porch steps and into the kitchen. "Something fishy is going on over there at Highland Park. Someone is trying to scare Jill away from that house and they're doing a darn good job."

Lucy reached for a box of peanut brittle sitting on top of the fridge. She lifted the lid and held it out. "Want some?"

Gloria shook her head. "No thanks, although it looks delicious."

Lucy grabbed a piece and closed the lid. "Did you say Highland Park?"

"Yeah. The house is in Rapid Creek. In a neighborhood called Highland Park."

Lucy crunched on a chunk of the hard candy. "I think RJ and his wife, Carol, live there."

"Really?"

RJ was Randall, Jr., Dot and Ray Jenkins', nephew. RJ was almost like a son to them. He was about the same age as Gloria's children and growing up, the kids had all been close.

"I'll give her a call later to see if I can get RJ's number. Maybe he knows of odd occurrences that have happened in the neighborhood or that house."

Gloria eyed the box of peanut brittle.

Lucy grinned and slid the box toward her. "Changed your mind, huh?"

Gloria lifted the lid and took a small piece. She bit the end. It was delicious and almost melted in Gloria's mouth. "Did I tell you Liz is moving to Florida?"

"Nope." If the news surprised Lucy, it didn't show. Of course, everyone knew Liz was impulsive so it probably wasn't a surprise. "She's taking all that money and hitting the road."

Gloria eyed the box of peanut brittle, her small piece long gone. She swept a hand across her extra tummy roll. If she was going to lose a few pounds before the wedding, she needed to stop eating all the goodies.

What Gloria said next, did surprise Lucy. "Frances is going with her."

Lucy lifted a brow. "Is she taking Milt?" Lucy had been part of Milt's search and rescue mission. She knew all about Frances' extreme obsession with the man.

"Nope. Milt ran off to Vegas and got married."

Lucy's jaw dropped. "No way."

"Yes way. I haven't seen Frances," Gloria shook her head, "but I can just imagine she's fit to be tied."

"You'll never guess who he married." Gloria was about to tell Lucy but her phone chirped. Gloria opened her purse and stuck her hand in. She turned the front so that it faced her and squinted at the screen. It was Jill.

"Hello?"

There was no one there. Gloria had just missed the call.

She started to dial her back when she noticed that Jill had left a message.

Gloria punched in the access code and turned it to speaker. "Hi Mom. I wanted to let you know that Greg and I found another house that we like. I told Sue that I needed to talk to you before I put in an offer."

The rest of the message was brief. Gloria frowned and dropped the phone inside her purse. She didn't want to see Jill lose all that money and the house of her dreams.

"I guess you better get cracking on the case," Lucy said.

Gloria shoved the kitchen chair back and jumped to her feet. "Yeah and the sooner the better. I guess I need to head back into town and talk to Dot."

Lucy followed her to her car. "Let me know if you need help with the investigation," Lucy offered.

Gloria thanked her, climbed into the car and backed out of the driveway.

She pulled Annabelle into an open spot and turned the car off before calling her daughter back. "Tomorrow. Give me until noon tomorrow," she bargained. "Stall the agent, whatever you have to do."

Jill finally relented and Gloria knew she needed to get a move on.

Gloria stepped inside the restaurant and scanned the room. Dot was nowhere around.

Ray, Dot's husband, who had just poured coffee at a nearby table, walked across the dining room. "Dot had a doctor's appointment earlier."

He shifted the coffee carafe to his other hand. "You can check the house. She's probably back by now."

Gloria thanked him and headed back out the door.

Ray and Dot lived a few short blocks from the restaurant, which was a good thing since they spent most of their waking hours working.

Dot's dark blue van was in the drive. Gloria pulled in behind her and wandered up the steps to the front door.

She rang the front bell and waited. The curtain rustled and Dot peeked out before she opened the door.

Gloria took one look at her friend's face and knew something was wrong. "What is it?"

"Uh..." Dot shook her head but the look was still plastered across her face.

Gloria adjusted her purse and crossed her arms in front of her. "Something is wrong, Dot Jenkins. It's written all over your face."

Dot's face turned red. She closed her eyes and swayed back, as if she might go over.

Gloria grabbed her arm to steady her. "Are you okay?"

Dot shook her head. "I don't know."

That was all Gloria needed to hear. She placed a protective arm around her friend's shoulder and led her into the living room.

"Come on. Let's go to the kitchen," she urged.

Gloria led her into the kitchen. She pulled out a chair and Dot settled in. She promptly dropped her face in her hands.

Gloria's heart sunk. She had never seen Dot so discombobulated, unless she counted the time that someone died at the restaurant after eating Dot's dumplings.

Dot was the most levelheaded, analytical, and thoughtful one of their group of friends. Her feathers were rarely ruffled. It was always smooth sailing in Dot's world.

"Coffee. I'll make some coffee." Gloria was as familiar with Dot's kitchen as she was her own. She reached into the cupboard, pulled down a Tupperware container full of freshly ground coffee along with a stack of filters.

Gloria filled the empty glass pot with water. After she dropped a filter in the top, she dumped a scoop of coffee on top. She turned the switch to "on" and whirled around to face her friend.

Dot was in the same position: her head in her hands and her shoulders slumped.

"Dot," Gloria kneeled next to Dot's chair, "talk to me."

Dot lifted her head. Her face was pale, her lips pinched and her expression blank. "The doctor..."

Her voice trailed off.

Gloria remembered Ray telling her that Dot had gone to the doctor earlier.

Call it a sixth sense. Call it a premonition, or call it a knowing your friend so well that somehow Gloria knew what was coming next.

Dot took a deep breath. "I have cancer."

Chapter 6

The words hung heavy in the air. It was as if, for a moment, time stood still. Gloria's mind went blank. She was having trouble wrapping her head around the word cancer.

Finally, she found her voice. "Does…"

Dot slowly shook her head. "No. Ray doesn't know. He didn't even know I had gone in for a biopsy. I didn't want to worry him. I figured it was nothing."

Gloria's mouth flapped open and shut as she tried to digest the news. "Why didn't you…"

"…ask one of you to go with me?" Dot shrugged. "Same reason. I thought it was nothing and I didn't want anyone to worry."

The coffee had finished brewing. Gloria jerked forward like a robot. Her body went through the motions but her mind was a jumble of emotions.

Cancer. Gloria's mother had cancer. It had taken her slowly, sucking the life out of her one day at a time until there was nothing left. Nothing left but death.

Tears stung the back of Gloria's eyes as she tried desperately to blink them away while she fixed them both a cup of coffee.

She needed to be strong for Dot, for Ray and for herself.

She dumped a packet of creamer and packet of sugar in Dot's cup before she picked it up and carried both cups to the table.

She plastered a smile on her face and set the cup in front of Dot. "You're a fighter, Dot. You're gonna kick this thing's butt."

Dot smiled hollowly as she faced her dear friend. "Yes, I am." Whether she felt it yet, she wasn't certain, but just saying it aloud made her feel better.

Gloria slid into the kitchen chair and cradled her cup as she listened to Dot pour out her story. She told Gloria as much as she could remember and ended with the doctor wanting to meet with both Dot and Ray the next day to go over her treatment.

After she finished, her eyes dropped to the half-empty cup of coffee.

Gloria grabbed Dot's hand. "Let's pray." She didn't wait for an answer as she bowed her head and poured her heart out to the only one who could help.

"Dear Heavenly Father. Our hearts are heavy this afternoon as we learn about Dot's diagnosis. Lord, we know You are the great physician and we pray that You heal Dot completely. Heal her body and let her be a testament to Your Glory. Amen."

Gloria lifted her head and quoted the first scripture that came to mind.

"Therefore confess your sins to each other and pray for each other so that you may be healed. The prayer of a righteous person is powerful and effective." James 5:16 NIV

Dot reached for a Kleenex to wipe her eyes. "Thank you, Gloria."

Gloria picked up her empty coffee cup, along with Dot's cup and carried them to the sink. She washed the cups, dried them with the towel and placed them back inside the cupboard.

"Now, I'm going to head back to the restaurant and send Ray home. He needs to be with you right now and you two need to talk," Gloria said.

"But..."

Gloria shook her finger at her friend. "No ifs, ands or buts. Holly and I can handle the restaurant," she said. Holly was a part-time employee at the restaurant and Gloria had seen her earlier when she had stopped by to track Dot down.

Gloria wasn't 100% certain she was up to the task but somehow, some way, she was going to help her friend. She grabbed her purse and headed for the front door.

Dot trailed behind.

Gloria impulsively spun around and hugged her friend tightly. She squeezed her eyes shut and willed herself not to burst into tears. "I'll talk to you tomorrow."

She hurried out of the house, afraid she might lose it right then and there.

Dot quietly closed the door behind her.

Inside Dot's restaurant, Gloria charged right down the center aisle and made a beeline for the back. Holly and Ray were in the kitchen.

She dropped her purse on the chair near the door and grabbed an apron from the hook.

Ray pulled a basket of fries from the fryer and hung it on the hook to drain. "You're back. Dot wasn't home?"

Gloria nodded. She reached around to tie the strings in the back. "Yes. She needs you to come home. I'm taking over."

Ray shook his head, confused. "Who will..."

Gloria pointed to Holly. "Holly and I can handle this," she said.

Ray started to argue. Gloria lifted her hand. "Please. Ray. Go home."

The tone of Gloria's voice and the expression on her face finally sunk in. Something was wrong. Terribly wrong.

Ray nodded. He quickly removed his apron and without another word, headed out the rear door.

She watched as he backed his compact car out of the dirt parking lot behind the restaurant and eased the car down the alley. Gloria closed her eyes and prayed for them both.

Holly wedged her fist on her hip. "You think we can pull this off?" she asked doubtfully. "Dinner crunch starts in half an hour."

Gloria reached for her purse – and her cell phone. "It's time to call in the troops."

Gloria went right down the line as she called each of the Garden Girls. She started with Ruth, who was across the street working at the post office. "I'll be over in half an hour, as soon as I lock up here," she promised.

Lucy was next. She could tell by the tone in Gloria's voice she needed help. "I'm on my way," she said.

Last, but not least, was Margaret. For a minute, Gloria thought she wasn't home but she finally picked up. She sounded out of breath. "Sorry, I was out filling the bird feeders."

When Gloria told her there was a slight crisis and she needed help covering for Dot and Ray at the restaurant, Margaret cut her off. "Be there in less than five minutes." She hung up before Gloria could even thank her.

Holly listened to Gloria as she called each of her friends. "I wish I had friends like that," she said wistfully.

The front doorbell tinkled. A few customers had trickled in. Holly held up a finger. "Be right back."

Gloria watched her retreating back and for the first time since she had arrived at the restaurant, she actually began to believe they would survive the day.

When all of the girls arrived at the restaurant minutes later, Gloria herded them into the back. "I can't tell you what is going on; only that Dot and Ray need us right now. We have to run the restaurant tonight and maybe even tomorrow."

None of the girls, other than Holly, had experience working in a restaurant, other than pitching in here or there when Dot was in a pinch and only under her direct supervision. "We've gotta fake it until we can make it," Gloria told them.

The dinner rush had begun and the girls spent the rest of the evening racing around the restaurant, putting out fires, one even literally when Margaret accidentally put the frying pan oil too close to a roll of paper towels and it caught fire. Thankfully, she was able to put it out before it spread.

Hours later, after the last customer walked out the door, the last dish washed and put away; they breathed a collective sigh of relief.

The girls had even managed to do some prep for the next morning's breakfast crowd.

Ray had called earlier to check in and ask how they were doing. Gloria calmly told him they had it under control, although that was not quite all of it. They were running around like chickens with their heads cut off.

Gloria was more than a little relieved when Ray told her his brother, Randall, and his family would open the restaurant the next morning. Randall owned a restaurant up north. The restaurant was only open during the summer months and they had just closed for the season. Randall was also RJ's dad.

In another month, Randall and his wife would head to Florida for the winter.

After she hung up the phone, the girls each grabbed a plate of leftover chicken pot pie and settled into a table near the back.

Lucy was the last to take a seat and the first to speak. "How is Dot?"

Gloria had asked Ray if it was okay for her to tell the other girls about Dot and he said he thought it was a great idea and that it would take a little pressure off Dot.

Gloria explained the situation and when she said the word "cancer," the group gasped, each of them having a reaction similar to hers.

When the news sunk in, they all vowed to do whatever they could to help their dear friend, Dot.

Gloria and Lucy were the last to leave. Gloria locked the back door and followed Lucy down the alley and around front, where they had parked their cars.

Lucy fiddled with her keys, twirling the ring around her finger. "When will we know what the doctor has to say?" she asked Gloria.

"Ray said he would let me know tomorrow. As soon as I know, I'll call everyone," she promised.

Lucy impulsively reached over and hugged Gloria. Dot's unexpected news made her – made them all – cherish their friendships now more than ever.

Back at the farm, Gloria wearily climbed out of Annabelle and wandered up the porch steps. Mally, who was ready to go out, greeted Gloria at the door.

She followed Mally back out to the porch and waited while she raced around the yard, tromped through the garden, visited her favorite tree and wandered back to the porch.

Gloria settled into the rocking chair. Soon, she would have to store the chairs in the barn – before the first snowfall.

Small piles of fallen leaves danced in the yard, taunting her. She knew she needed to rake and burn the leaves but once again, she had so much going on. Between Jill's haunted house and Dot's cancer, she would have her hands full.

Her eyes wandered to the front yard. She could see the branches from the tree out front, the one that was home to her grandsons' tree fort, sticking out. Maybe she could have them over for the afternoon to play in the fort and help rake the leaves.

The tree reminded her that she needed to call Jill back. So much had happened.

Jill picked up on the first ring. "We put an offer in on that other house," Jill told her.

"Did you put down a deposit?" Gloria asked.

"No. The real estate agent said we could wait until the sellers accepted the offer. This deposit would only be $1000."

"So you've given up on the other house?"

Jill sighed deeply. "I love that first house and it kills me to think we're going to lose all that money."

"You know RJ and his wife live in Highland Park," Gloria said. "Maybe I can ask them about the house."

"If you think it would help," Jill said doubtfully, "go ahead."

It certainly couldn't hurt. On top of that, RJ would more than likely be at Dot's Restaurant in the morning. She could ask him then. "Good. I'll ask tomorrow."

If Jill put down another deposit and decided to go with house #1 after all, at least she would only lose $1000 on the second house. The other way around, losing house #1, would be a lot more costly. Of course, Gloria didn't want to see her lose a single penny.

Gloria hung up the phone, turned off the kitchen light and headed to the bathroom to brush her teeth. Tomorrow was shaping up to be a busy day and she was whupped.

Chapter 7

The next morning, Dot's Restaurant was a beehive of activity. Gloria drove around the block twice before she gave up on finding an open spot and pulled into the post office parking lot.

She dashed across the busy street and glanced in the front window. Her heart sank when she realized she wouldn't see her friend's familiar figure dart back and forth through the window.

Instead, she saw a tall, lanky man doing the darting. It was Randall.

He caught Gloria's eye when she stepped in the front door and gave a small wave. Gloria made a beeline for the back, nodding to a few of the diners she recognized.

Stacy, Randall's wife, was standing in front of the flat top, cooking pancakes. She turned her attention for a brief moment and smiled. "Hello Gloria."

Gloria returned the smile and glanced around the kitchen. Her eyes settled on RJ, bent over the kitchen sink, up to his elbows in sudsy water.

He caught Gloria's eye. "Ah. I heard you were looking for me."

He turned on the cold tap water and rinsed the bubbles from his arms. "I heard that Jill is thinking of moving to Highland Park. It's a great area," he assured her.

"I'm glad to hear that but she may not move there after all." Gloria explained the situation briefly.

"Have you heard anything about Pine Place that would cause Jill concern about buying that house?"

RJ rubbed the faint stubble on his chin. "What is the address?"

Gloria couldn't remember. She was lucky if she could remember what day of the week it was. She slipped on her glasses, lifted her cell phone and scanned her text messages until she got to the one Jill had sent her with the address. "726 Pine Place."

RJ's eyes widened. "Oh yeah. Now that you mention it, there was a big ruckus over there about six months ago."

RJ went on to explain that the owners of the place Jill and Greg had put an offer on had been running a puppy mill. Some of the neighbors had tipped off local authorities who swooped in and shut it down.

"I think their last name was Acosta." RJ continued. "They got mad and promptly put the house up for sale and now I guess it has been on the market for a while."

Gloria's brow furrowed. Did the owners have something to do with the notes and pentagram painting? Wouldn't they just want to unload the house and move on? Not if they kept collecting huge earnest money deposits from potential buyers.

Gloria remembered that Sue Camp had mentioned that the house had gone pending several times already. Each deal had fallen apart. Seven thousand dollars several times over was a tidy profit.

She made a mental note to do a little more research into the previous owners.

Gloria thanked RJ for his time. She needed to get back over to Highland Park to talk to the neighbors, although it may already be too late and Jill and Greg would move forward with this other house.

Gloria wandered out of the restaurant and headed back to the farm.

She spent the rest of the afternoon on "busy work," which was not much of anything. She couldn't concentrate. All she could think about was poor Dot.

Gloria had just settled in at the kitchen table with a plate of leftover tuna noodle casserole and a small tossed salad when the house phone rang. She paused for a moment, deciding whether to pick up. Maybe it was Dot or Ray...

"Hello?"

"Hi Gloria. I hope I'm not bothering you." It was Dot.

Mally's sniffer honed in on the goodies near the edge of the kitchen table. Gloria reached over and slid the plate to the center. She wagged her finger at her pooch, who slunk off and crawled into her doggie bed near the dining room door.

"What happened?"

She could hear Dot suck in a breath. "It's good news and bad news."

Gloria squeezed her eyes shut. She prayed the good news outweighed the bad.

"The good news is the doctors said they caught the cancer early."

Gloria stepped over to the kitchen window and peered out into the yard. "And the bad?"

"The surgery is scheduled for week after next and I'm terrified," Dot admitted.

"We'll start a prayer chain today," Gloria said. "Pastor Nate can add you to Sunday's prayer list."

Dot's voice grew thick. "I couldn't even sleep last night. All I could think about was dying."

Gloria's heart sunk. It was moments like this that you just had to hand it all over to the Lord. "Pray about it, Dot. Ask the Lord for peace."

Dot went on. "Anyways, Ray refuses to let me go back to work at the restaurant for the next few days. He thinks it would be too hard on me."

Gloria had to agree. News of Dot's cancer would spread through their small town like wildfire, if it hadn't already. "He's right," she simply said.

Gloria could hear muffled sounds on the other end. Dot was on the move.

"I talked to RJ a little while ago. He told me about the house Jill is trying to buy over in Rapid Creek. It sounds like something fishy is going on."

Gloria didn't want to burden Dot with Jill's crisis but she briefly explained what had happened.

"Are you going to stand by and let her lose that money?" If it had been Dot's daughter, she would have tried to get to the bottom of it. Dot knew that Gloria would not simply throw in the towel, so to speak.

"Not if I can help it," Gloria declared. "I'm going over there in the morning and pound on some doors." It would be the perfect day. Saturday morning. People would be home from work...

"Can I go with you?" Dot asked. "I mean, I can't go to the restaurant. What else am I gonna do?"

Gloria frowned. Dot had enough on her mind, but then again, maybe what she needed was to take her mind off the upcoming surgery. "Sure, Dot. If that's what you want to do."

She glanced at the wall clock. If they got there around ten, most people should be up and about. "I can swing by around 9:30 tomorrow morning and pick you up."

"Thanks, Gloria. I'd like that."

Gloria's cell phone chirped. Someone was trying to call but Gloria didn't want to cut Dot off so she let it ring. Whoever was trying to call could leave a message.

The girls chatted for a few more minutes. "I better go. Ray is hovering over me now," Dot laughed.

After Gloria hung up, she grabbed her cell phone off the table and plopped her reading glasses on her nose. Paul had called.

She hadn't talked to Paul since the day before. It seemed as if so much had happened since then.

She called him back and he picked up right away. She explained the situation with Jill's offer on the house. When she tried to tell him about Dot, she could barely form a coherent sentence.

Finally, she burst into tears and began to sob. Paul tried his best to soothe his soon-to-be-bride over the phone and vowed that he needed to be around more and work less. Maybe it was time to set a firm retirement date.

Life was too short. What if Gloria had called to tell him she had cancer? Paul vowed that when he hung up, he would put in his notice. His last day would be December 31st.

It was time to start a new life with his new wife.

Gloria's sobs eventually turned to sniffles. She blew her nose loudly. "I'm sorry. I didn't mean to fall apart."

Paul assured Gloria she could cry anytime she needed to, as long as he wasn't the reason for her tears. "At least you got it out of your system before you see her tomorrow," he pointed out.

True. Gloria hadn't thought about that. She needed to show a brave face for her friend.

"It sounds as if your morning is booked," he said. "What if I come over on my next night off and we can talk more about the wedding."

So far, Paul had been content to leave all the planning to Gloria. His main priority was to make sure the two of them made it to the altar. Gloria and her friends could handle the rest.

"That sounds perfect," Gloria said. "I'll cook something special." She had no idea what that would be, but she had all evening to decide.

"No, I'll take you to dinner," he insisted, "somewhere nice."

After Gloria hung up the phone, she slid into the chair and pulled her lukewarm meal toward her. She picked up her fork and toyed with the food, her mind was a million miles away and her appetite had vanished.

Gloria managed to eat half of what was on her plate. She cut the rest of the meat into small pieces, and split it between Mally and Puddles.

Gloria watched a little TV and then headed to bathroom to get ready for bed. Her body went through the motions as she brushed her teeth and washed her face.

She turned off the light and ambled to the bedroom. If she herself felt this awful about Dot's cancer, she couldn't even begin to imagine how her friend felt.

Chapter 8

Gloria's eyes popped open bright and early the next morning. It had taken a long time before she was finally able to drift off to sleep. When she did, she had jumbled dreams. In one of them, Dot was sprawled out on a stretcher, her hair tucked under a surgical cap as nurses wheeled her down a long hospital corridor.

Gloria chased after the stretcher and begged the nurses not to take her away, certain that she would never see her friend again.

There had been other dreams, but nothing as frightening as the one she remembered.

Mally was waiting at the door when Gloria wandered into the kitchen. She patiently stood by the door as Gloria fixed a pot of coffee. The coffee started to brew while she stepped out onto the porch.

A light frost covered the ground. The air was crisp and she watched as puffs of warm air escaped her lips. "Winter is right around the corner, girl," she told Mally.

Mally didn't care about winter – or snow. She was more concerned about patrolling the perimeter of the yard.

Thanksgiving was a few short weeks away. Gloria had been so focused on the upcoming visit from all of her children, not to mention the wedding; she hadn't had time to think about Turkey Day.

The coffee finished brewing. Gloria headed back inside to grab a cup from the cupboard and fill it.

Gloria grabbed her Bible and settled into a chair at the kitchen table. Morning Prayer and Bible reading was Gloria's favorite time of the day. The peace and quiet of the morning helped her to focus on the Word of God.

Not today, though. Her mind wandered. The ticking of the kitchen clock echoed in the room and the house creaked even more than usual, at least in Gloria's mind.

She made it through Psalm 104 and then closed her Bible. She meditated on the words and pushed back the chair from the table. It was time to get ready. It was time to solve the mystery of the house at 726 Pine Place.

***

Gloria pulled in Dot's drive and parked behind her van. She hadn't even had time to honk the horn when Dot sprang through the front door and down the cement steps.

Gloria studied her friend's face through the car window as she made her way to the passenger side. She looked...well, she looked at peace.

Dot pulled the door open and climbed in. She dropped her purse on the floor and reached for her seat belt. "I was up half the night."

Gloria reached over and patted Dot's arm. "I'm sorry, Dot. I had hoped you were able to get more rest than the night before."

Dot buckled the belt and adjusted the strap. "Believe it or not, I wasn't awake worrying about the you-know-what. I was thinking about Jill's house."

Gloria backed out of the drive and onto the road. "And?"

Two heads were better than one. Maybe Dot remembered something RJ had said that he forgot to mention to Gloria.

"Well, it seems to me that if the sellers keep insisting on large deposits and after they get the deposit, strange things start to happen, maybe it's a racket. You know, they keep making money on the place."

Gloria pulled to the stop sign and looked in both directions. "I was thinking the exact same thing. I mean, these aren't stellar, upstanding citizens in the first place, what with running a puppy mill."

"Maybe you could have Paul run a background check on them," Dot suggested.

Gloria raised a brow. "Great idea. I'll look into that."

The girls chatted about the restaurant, the upcoming holidays and Gloria's wedding. Gloria was careful to avoid mentioning doctors and surgery.

If, and when, Dot wanted to talk about it, she would.

Gloria pulled into the Highland Park neighborhood and turned onto Pine Place. The *For Sale* sign was still in the front yard. The real estate agent had taken down the top section, the part of the sign that read, *pending*.

She frowned. As far as she knew, it was still technically pending as long as the contract hadn't been cancelled.

Gloria shut off the engine and the girls climbed out of the car. She had gotten the access code for the lockbox from Jill. She punched in the code and removed the box cover.

The key fit the top lock. Gloria pushed the door open and waited for Dot to step inside. Dot followed Gloria through the living room and into the kitchen.

There was an odd odor in the house. Dot noticed it, too. She sniffed the air. "You smell that?" She wrinkled her nose.

Gloria waved a hand across her face. "Yuck. It smells like something died."

They walked through the house, checking cupboards and opening closet doors.

Gloria opened the dining room slider and the girls stepped onto the deck. "I don't get it. Unless the smell is coming from the attic."

After they cleared their lungs, they stepped back inside and Gloria closed and locked the slider. The girls checked each of the rooms and the lower level. The smell was definitely coming from somewhere upstairs.

They climbed the steps and walked back through the living room as they headed out the front door.

Dot grabbed Gloria's arm. She pointed to the living room fireplace. "We didn't check that."

They walked over to the beautiful, fieldstone fireplace. The odor grew stronger the closer they got to the mantle.

Dot pinched her nose and took short shallow breaths through her mouth. "It has to be coming from there."

Gloria was almost afraid to move the fireplace screen. Jill's sad face swam in front of her eyes. She was doing this for Jill, she reminded herself.

Gloria stuck her hand on the top of the decorative screen and lifted it up.

Dot gasped.

Gloria took a step back.

Curled up in a ball on top of the grate was a small, white bunny rabbit, its neck slashed. As much as Gloria wanted to drop the screen and run away, she took a step closer. She noticed several fresh puddles of blood...the rabbit hadn't been there long.

Whoever killed the poor thing had done it recently. Brown streaks covered the fireplace insert, which Gloria surmised, was where the foul odor was coming from. The rabbit had not begun to smell. Whatever was in the insert smelled horrible.

Gloria fumbled inside her purse and pulled out her cell phone. She turned the screen to camera mode and snapped several pictures.

She replaced the metal screen and the girls made their way outside. "Should you tell the agent?"

Gloria nodded. "Yes, but we need to try to talk to the neighbors first."

Her head swung around as she looked at the neighbor's house on the left. A car was in the drive. There were also cars parked in the drive of the neighbor on the other side and the one across the street.

Gloria nodded to the right. "Let's start there."

She marched across the lawn and up the front steps of the house next door. Dot pushed the doorbell and the girls waited.

Moments later, the door slowly opened and a woman's face peered out. "Hi."

"Hello. My daughter has put an offer on the house next door and I wondered if I could ask you a couple questions." There was no need to beat around the bush.

The door opened wider. The woman, appearing to be in her early 30's with straight brown hair and sharp green eyes peered at them. "I wouldn't live in that house."

Dot leaned in. "Why not?"

"Because it's haunted."

Chapter 9

Gloria felt a momentary burst of disappointment. If Jill heard even a whisper of the word "haunted" there was no way she would live in the house. "Why do you think it's haunted?"

"The Acostas had a heck of a time...odd phone calls in the middle of the night, creaking noises coming from the attic, not to mention dead animals showing up on the doorstep." The woman shivered. "The last straw was when they came home one day and someone had drawn a pentagram on the dining room wall."

"I wouldn't live there, either," Dot declared. She turned to Gloria. "Maybe this isn't such a good idea."

Gloria frowned. Someone had scared the Acostas off...maybe even a neighbor.

"How long did the Acostas live in the house?" Gloria was curious.

The woman tapped the side of her cheek with her index finger. "Let me see. It had to have been a couple years. They moved in not long after my husband and I bought this place."

Dot knew where Gloria's questioning was headed. "They stayed in the house for two years even though it was haunted?"

The woman shook her head. "No. It was only the last few months that strange things started to happen."

Gloria thanked the woman for her time and Dot and she headed across the lawn. They stopped behind Annabelle.

Dot nodded at the place. "What do you think?"

"That it's mighty suspicious the house 'suddenly' became haunted."

Dot finished the sentence. "After having lived there for at least a year."

Gloria grabbed her arm. "C'mon. Let's talk to the people across the street."

They started down the drive at the same time the garage door on the house across the street opened. The occupant spotted the girls headed his way. It looked as if he planned to dart back in the house, the door half open. Gloria could hear a dog bark from somewhere inside.

Instead, he changed his mind as he shut the door and waited while they walked up the drive. "You the new neighbors? I heard they finally sold the house across the street."

Gloria shook her head. "My daughter and son-in-law have a contract on the house."

The man, short and thick with a few sparse hairs sticking out from under a ball cap, nodded. "The place has been empty for a while now. Is she sure she wants to live there?"

"The home is a good deal," Gloria pressed. "One of the neighbors said strange things started happening not long ago."

"True," he admitted. "Good riddance to the Acostas. They were an odd bunch."

He shoved his hands in his pockets. "They ran a puppy mill over there."

"So you didn't know them that well?" Dot piped up.

The man shook his head. "Nope. Only what the Holts told me." He pointed to the house Dot and Gloria had just left.

"Did the Acostas put the house up for sale and then odd things began to happen?"

"Not sure. Like I said, I wasn't real friendly with them." He rocked back on his heels. "I do know it wasn't long after the fire."

Gloria's eyes widened. "There was a fire?" Sue Camp had never mentioned a fire. Could it be the Acostas tried to burn the place down and collect on the insurance?

He shrugged. "Guess it was a small one. Fire department had it under control right away. Not a day or two later, the for-sale sign went up in the yard. The Acostas moved out quick. One day they lived there, the next day they were gone. I never saw a moving truck or anything."

The door leading into the house opened and a head popped out. "Ron, you've got a call."

The man excused himself. "I need to go. Sorry I couldn't be of more help." He turned on his heel and started up the steps.

The girls watched him go. "Maybe Jill doesn't want this house," Gloria said.

They had one more house to visit – the one on the other side. It was a large two-story with a spacious, covered porch.

Gloria admired the white wicker rocking chairs as they made their way to the front door. Maybe once her remodeling projects were over, she would splurge and get new porch chairs.

The *thump, thump* of loud music echoed through the closed door. Gloria pressed the doorbell and waited. No one answered.

She tried again but there was still no answer.

"Maybe they can't hear the doorbell," Dot pointed out.

That was probably true. As loud as the music was through the closed door, Gloria could just imagine how much louder it was inside.

The girls finally gave up and headed back to the car. Gloria climbed into the driver's seat and slipped the key in the ignition. She was torn on whether or not she should call the real estate agent. She wasn't sure how happy Sue Camp would be if she found out Gloria had been inside the house.

She decided not to call. Sue Camp would find the poor, unfortunate bunny rabbit soon enough.

The girls rode for several long moments in silence. Before Gloria had left that morning, she had gotten the Acostas current address from Jill. The address was on the first page of the offer to buy the house.

She turned to Dot. "Do you have time to make a drive by the Acosta's new residence?"

"You thought of everything." Dot grinned. "Yeah. Sure. I have all day."

Gloria entered the address in her GPS and the girls were on their way. The address was still Rapid Creek but it wasn't in town. They drove past downtown and headed out into the country.

They passed several large farms before they reached their destination – a ramshackle, wood framed house with peeling paint and a sagging front porch. The house suffered from severe neglect. Several cars sat parked in the rutted drive. One car, minus the wheels, was sitting on carjacks and next to a long, narrow shed.

Gloria slowed the car but didn't stop.

Dot pointed out the window. "I see a dog run out back."

Gloria drove a mile down the road before she turned around for a second drive by. She was able to see a dog run and a dog kennel. "You think they're still selling dogs?"

Dot frowned. "It looks like it."

Short of stopping in the drive and knocking on the door, there wasn't much else to see. The house that the Acostas had moved out of was a lot nicer than the house they now lived in.

If they were trying to swindle potential buyers out of their earnest money deposits, they certainly weren't spending the money on the house they currently lived in.

Gloria's heart sank. There wasn't much else to do except go home. Unless...

She jerked the wheel and careened into the driveway. "I have an idea."

Dot took a deep breath. "Oh no," she muttered. When Gloria had an idea, it could be a good thing...or it could be leading them right into a sticky situation. Based on the look on Gloria's face, Dot was leaning toward the sticky situation.

Gloria put the car in park, hopped out of the car and waded through the weed-infested lawn.

Not wanting to leave her friend in the lurch, Dot took a deep breath and opened the passenger side door. *Dear God, please protect us from whatever Gloria is about to get us into.*

By the time Dot caught up with Gloria, she had already knocked on the side door. "Just go along with whatever I say," Gloria mumbled under her breath.

"Got it."

The door creaked open a crack and a young face peered through the small opening. "Yes, ma'am."

"Hi...Uh...my friend and I," Gloria motioned to Dot, "heard that you might have some puppies for sale."

The door opened further, which was a good sign.

"I live alone and I'm looking for a new companion," Gloria blurted out. Mally would be thrilled – not.

The door swung open. The young woman, who couldn't have been more than sixteen years old, faced them. She wore a pair of ragged bib overalls and stained t-shirt. Her feet were bare. She eyed them with suspicion. "How'd you hear that we have puppies?" she asked.

"Uh..."

Dot weaseled her way closer. "Over at the post office in Belhaven." She scratched the side of her cheek. "There was a small sign on the bulletin board."

The petite brunette shoved her hands into her front pockets and frowned. "My mom and dad aren't home. I can show you what we have..."

Gloria clasped her hands together. "Perfect. Can we take the puppy home?"

The girl slipped her feet into a pair of ratty tennis shoes and grabbed a sweater from the back of the kitchen chair. "Maybe," she answered noncommittally.

Gloria and Dot followed the girl out to the backyard and behind a large, gray shed. Chunks of red paint had flaked off and dotted the weeds that surrounded the structure.

Woof! Woof! The barking of excited dogs wafted from inside the shed.

They rounded the corner and peeked inside the open door. Gloria's heart plummeted at the sight.

Stacked in metal crates three and four high were puppies, some of them so small Gloria could barely see them.

Tears stung the back of her eyes at the sight.

Next to her, Dot drew a ragged breath.

Gloria squeezed her eyes shut. She wanted to take every one of the dogs home today. *Pull yourself together, Gloria. You can't help these poor animals if you lose it now.*

She opened her eyes and steeled a closer look at the cages. One in particular caught her eye. Inside the cage was a scrawny little puppy, curled up in the back corner. He looked at her with drooping eyes but never made a move. He let out a sigh and buried his head under his paw.

Gloria stepped closer.

"That's Jasper. He's part lab and part mutt so we're having a hard time finding a home. Most people want purebred."

Gloria slipped her index finger through the bars. The inside of the cage was filthy and smelled horrible. She wrinkled her nose. "Hey, Jasper," she coaxed.

Jasper opened an eye, gazed at Gloria and then closed his eye again, clearly depressed.

"I'd like to take Jasper." She spun around and faced the girl. "How much?" Not that it mattered.

The girl's eyes darted to the cage. She could tell that Gloria wanted the dog. She could probably name her price and the woman wouldn't bat an eye. Jessica couldn't do that, though. Jasper had a special place in her heart, too, and she knew this woman was Jasper's best shot at a better life.

She threw out the first number that came to mind. "Ninety five dollars."

"Sold." Gloria reached inside her purse. Luckily, she had enough cash on hand. She handed the girl a hundred dollar bill and waited while she unlocked the cage. Jessica slid her hand under the pup and pulled him out.

Dot was on the other side of the cramped shed, peering into a lower cage. "What about this one?" She pointed to a larger dog, bursting at the seams, his fur pressed tight against the cage that was two sizes too small for a large dog as large as he was.

The girl placed Jasper in Gloria's open arms. He barely stirred. Gloria hoped it wasn't too late, that the dog was just sad and not about to die. It would break Gloria's heart.

"That's Odie." The girl unlocked the cage and Odie burst out. Or maybe it was more like exploded. He hit the cement floor with a thud, landing on all fours.

The girl shoved her hands in her back pockets. "He's a handful," she warned.

Dot bent down to pat Odie's head.

Jessica continued. "I found him wandering on the side of the road last week. My parents were mad when I brought him home."

Jessica bent forward and stroked Odie's back. "They told me that we can't keep him and that if someone didn't take him this week, he would have to go."

Gloria and Jasper stepped closer. "Go where?"

Jessica's eyes met Gloria's eyes and then lowered. "Not sure," Jessica mumbled.

Dot shot to her feet. "That settles it then. I'll take Odie home with me."

Jessica scuffed the tip of her shoe on the bare concrete floor. "My parents will be furious if I don't charge you," she said.

Dot opened the clasp of her purse. "How much?"

The girl shrugged, unsure how much a stray she picked up off the side of the road was worth. "Twenty five dollars?" She lifted her brow and gazed into Dot's eyes.

Dot fumbled inside her purse and pulled out a twenty and ten. She shoved the bills into the girl's open hand. "Keep the change."

Before the girl could change her mind, Dot and Gloria stepped out of the "kennel" for lack of a better word, and headed toward the car.

Gloria took one final glance behind her at all of the sad faces of animals that she couldn't rescue, at least not today.

Dot and Gloria gave the dogs a few moments to take a potty break and then gently set them both on the back seat.

At least Gloria gently placed Jasper on the back seat. Odie tromped back and forth across the seat as he tried to look out the rear windows.

Gloria slid into the driver's seat and turned to Dot. "You sure you can handle that one?"

Dot waved a hand dismissively. "Yeah. Piece of cake."

She snaked a hand behind her and patted Odie's head. "Ray won't mind. He'll probably be happy that I have something to take my mind off the other."

Gloria had been so caught up in the puppy mill, she had completely forgotten about Dot's cancer – and her daughter's house dilemma.

Gloria backed out of the drive and pulled onto the road. She glanced in the rearview mirror. "We have to do something about those poor animals."

Dot agreed. "I was thinking the same thing." She adjusted the seatbelt across her lap. "Do you think those people and the dogs have something to do with the strange messages and someone scaring off potential buyers from the house?"

Gloria had been wondering the same thing. It didn't make sense that the people would kill their own deal so-to-speak,

296

although they were collecting large non-refundable deposits as soon as they had the signed paperwork.

Gloria narrowed her eyes. *What if the real estate agent, Sue Camp, was involved?* She wondered how much Sue Camp stood to gain each time a buyer cancelled a contract. If she didn't make any money off the canceled contract, what benefit would it be to her for the property to remain on the market?

Looking back, the woman had seemed in an awful big hurry to cancel the contract instead of trying to work it out so that Jill and Greg would follow through with the purchase of the home.

If she had more time, she would swing by the agent's office and question her face-to-face. She glanced in the rearview mirror. Right now, she had a more pressing matter. Getting her new pooch home and welcomed into the family.

Chapter 10

Gloria dropped Dot and Odie off first. Ray was already home, waiting for his wife, when Gloria pulled in the drive. If he was surprised that they had a new family member, he did a great job of hiding it.

He greeted Odie as if they'd been together forever. Gloria grinned as she watched the three of them disappear inside the house.

Dot turned back for a second, gave her friend a "thumbs up" and then closed the door behind her. Odie might be the best medicine for Dot...far better than doctors or surgery, at least as far as lifting her spirits and giving her something to focus on other than the "c" word.

Back at the farm, Gloria pulled Annabelle into the garage and made her way to the rear passenger door.

Jasper lifted an ear and opened one eye when Gloria reached for him. "C'mon Jasper. We're home. Your new home. It's time to meet Mally and Puddles," she cajoled.

Jasper rose up on wobbly legs and tottered toward Gloria. Could it be the poor thing had spent so much time inside the cage that his legs weren't strong? Gloria felt a surge of heat rush through her.

She lifted Jasper from the backseat and then carried him over to the grass. He stood still for a long moment as he looked around. Gloria tried to see the farm through his eyes.

It must look foreign and so very different from anything he'd ever seen before.

Jasper lifted his head and sniffed the cool, fall air. He took a step forward and then stopped. His whole body shook, as if overwhelmed by it all.

Gloria dropped to her knees and patted his back. "Don't worry Jasper. You're safe now." She ran her hand down his legs. As soon as they were in the house, she was going to call the vet and make an appointment.

Jasper, feeling a little more confident with Gloria next to him, took a few tentative steps as he tottered over to the big oak tree. Mally's favorite tree.

Gloria's eyes darted to the back door. She could see Mally's face pressed tight against the window. How would Mally react to Jasper?

Jasper and she wandered around the yard. The more Jasper explored, the more confident he became. He explored the front yard and sniffed around the edge of the garden before he came back to Gloria and settled in at her feet.

Apparently, he had enough exploring for now.

She lifted Jasper and tucked him into the crook of her arm. It was time for Jasper to meet the rest of the family.

Gloria unlocked the door and let herself into the kitchen, keeping a firm grip on Jasper. He began to tremble when he caught sight of Mally, who was ten times larger.

Mally paced back and forth, trying to get close to Jasper.

Gloria held the door. "Want to go out, girl?"

Mally hesitated, looking from the door to Jasper, then back to the door. The outdoors won out. Mally raced across the porch and over to her favorite tree.

While Mally was outside, Gloria set Jasper on the floor of the guest bedroom. "I'll be back in a minute," she promised. She quietly closed the door behind her.

Gloria stepped out onto the porch and watched as Mally stretched her legs and darted around the yard. She disappeared on the far side of the garden – or what was left of it – and returned to the porch, an ear of corn clenched between her teeth.

She dropped it on the floor near Gloria's feet and looked up with pleading eyes, as if to say, "I can keep this, right?"

Gloria patted her head. "Yeah, you can keep it...finders keepers, I guess."

Mally picked the ear of corn back up and made her way to the porch door.

Gloria opened the door and waited for Mally to wander back inside. She watched as Mally dropped the ear of corn in her box of toys and trotted right into the dining room.

Gloria knew she was looking for Jasper.

Puddles was already at the bedroom door, his nose sniffing the perimeter. He flopped down on the floor and playfully stuck his paw under the frame, as if waiting for Jasper to join in.

Gloria lowered her head and peeked through the crack. She could see two small paws and the tip of Jasper's nose.

Mally whined and lowered down. Now both of her pets were trying to get in. They didn't seem agitated, just curious.

Gloria's cell phone chirped. She left the pets at the door and grabbed her phone off the table. It was Lucy. "How did it go?"

"How did what go?" So much had happened; she wasn't sure what Lucy wanted to know.

"Did you find anything interesting in the house?"

Gloria placed the palm of her hand on her forehead and closed her eyes. "Did we ever." She eyed the bedroom door.

Mally was trying to nudge the door open with her nose.

Puddles was using his back feet to kick at the door.

"Are you busy?" she asked Lucy.

Her friend yawned. "Nope," she said.

"Can you come down? I might need a second set of hands," Gloria told her.

"Sure." Lucy didn't probe. It was hard telling what exactly Gloria had gotten herself into, but knowing her friend, if she said she needed an extra hand, it had to be good.

Lucy grabbed her keys off the hook by the door and her purse from the chair. "I'm on my way."

Gloria kept one eye on the bedroom door and the other on the driveway. Lucy made it in record time and Gloria held the door while she stepped inside.

Lucy took one look at Gloria's face and frowned. "Uh-oh. Something big happened." She dropped her purse on the table and shoved her keys in the side pocket. "Why do I always miss the good stuff?" she groaned.

"Woof!"

Jasper had finally found his voice, although it was more of a yap and less of a bark.

Lucy tilted her head and peeked into the dining room. "That wasn't Mally, unless she lost her voice."

"Nope." Gloria shook her head. "That was Jasper," Gloria said.

"Jasper?" Lucy started for the dining room. "You didn't..."

Gloria was right on her heels. "Oh, I did and so did Dot."

Lucy tiptoed past Gloria's pets, still firmly planted in front of the door. "Jasper is in here?" She tapped the outside of the bedroom door.

"Yep. Somehow, we need to get Puddles, Mally and Jasper acquainted. I figured it would be easier if I had a little help."

Lucy snorted. "Whatever possessed you to get another dog?" She held up her hand. "Wait. I'm sure this will involve more than a couple minutes explanation. We should wait 'til the current crisis is over."

Gloria sucked in a breath and nodded. "Good idea."

She reached for Mally's collar and led her out to the kitchen. Lucy picked Puddles up and they trailed behind.

Gloria placed the doggie gate in the doorway that separated the kitchen from the dining room. Next, Lucy and she headed back to the guest bedroom.

Gloria opened the door and peeked around the corner. Jasper sat on the floor nearby. His ears drooped as he looked at Gloria then Lucy.

"Oh. How adorable." Lucy reached out to pet his black fur.

He shrank back and began to quiver.

Lucy pulled her hand away. "He's terrified."

Normally, Lucy was afraid of dogs. The only two dogs that her friend wasn't afraid to be around were Mally and Andrea's dog, Brutus. When Lucy was young, a dog had attacked her on her way home from school. She had ended up in the emergency room with several stitches on both of her arms and legs.

She had a fear of dogs...not the other way around. Lucy's heart melted. She dropped to the floor and crossed her legs. She patted the floor. "C'mere Jasper." She looked at Gloria. "Where did you get him?"

"It's a long story. A puppy mill."

Lucy shot her a look of surprise. It wasn't like Gloria to shop for a dog at a known puppy mill.

Gloria sighed. "Let's just say that I rescued Jasper and Dot rescued another dog, Odie."

Jasper tiptoed toward Lucy's outstretched hand then rubbed the top of his head on the palm of her hand.

"He likes you," Gloria said.

Lucy didn't move a muscle as Jasper sniffed her hand and then licked her thumb. After giving her the once-over, Jasper climbed onto Lucy's lap and curled into a ball.

Gloria clasped her hands together. "That dog belongs with you."

Lucy stroked the top of Jasper's head. "I never thought I would say this, but I think you're right. He just stole my heart."

She rubbed his ear. "He's still trembling - just a little."

Her head shot up. "But you picked him out."

Gloria grinned. "I may have picked *him* out, but he most definitely picked *you* out."

She knew right then and there that the matter was settled. Lucy, for the first time in her life, had a pet.

"Woof!" That bark belonged to Mally and Gloria could tell from the tone that her beloved pooch was getting anxious.

Lucy snuggled Jasper to her chest and carried him out of the bedroom.

Gloria stepped into the kitchen first. She bent down to Mally-level. "Don't you dare scare poor Jasper," she warned her. She turned to Puddles. "You, either."

Lucy stepped over the gate. Jasper eyed Mally, a look of sheer terror on his small face. "Maybe we should save the introductions for another day."

"I agree." Gloria opened the back door and Lucy and Jasper stepped onto the porch.

Mally attempted to follow behind but Gloria stopped her. "Maybe next time, girl." Mally hadn't shown any sign of aggression but Jasper was too skittish and she didn't want the poor dog, who had probably already gone through so much, to be traumatized.

Lucy eased into the porch chair and settled Jasper onto her lap while Gloria slid into the other rocker. She explained everything that had happened up until the moment she called Lucy and asked her to come over.

Lucy rubbed Jasper's chin thoughtfully. "You mean there are more dogs, just like Jasper?"

Gloria nodded grimly. "A lot more. Somehow, some way, those poor animals need to be rescued."

Chapter 11

Gloria packed a bag of goodies for Jasper, including some of Mally's favorite doggie treats. She gave Lucy the name and phone number of Mally and Puddles' vet, Andy Cohen, and then watched as Lucy loaded her new best bud in the front of the jeep and drove off.

Gloria couldn't have picked a better dog for her best friend if she tried.

She turned back to catch a glimpse of Mally's forlorn face in the window. She looked disappointed that Jasper was gone.

The Lord sure knew how to work things. Gloria already had her plate full, what with trying to plan the wedding, prepare for her kids holiday homecoming, solve the mystery surrounding Jill's house and now figure out how to rescue those poor pooches, not to mention deal with Dot's cancer.

Just the thought of all of that made her head spin. She glanced up at the skies. Clouds had started to gather but there were still several hours of daylight left. A nice, long walk back to the woods would do wonders and it would definitely cheer Mally.

She opened the kitchen door and stuck her head inside. "Want to go for a walk?"

Mally thumped her tail against the door and pushed past Gloria as she trotted out onto the porch.

Gloria grabbed her cell phone, a lightweight jacket from the hook and her house keys. She locked the door behind her but left all the lights on.

Mally darted ahead of Gloria, the path so familiar the two of them could probably make it back there with their eyes closed.

She stepped off the porch and glanced across the street at the small farm. The farm had once belonged to James and his family. James' grandparents had lived there for many years.

When they passed on, James' brother, who had never married, lived there for years until one day, he up and moved away after having met some woman on the internet. The last time Gloria had talked to him; he had married the woman and was now living somewhere in Minnesota.

The house sat vacant for several years before James finally sold it. He split the money from the sale evenly amongst the siblings. Local farmers had purchased the property, but only for the farmland. No one had ever moved into the house.

The empty house hadn't bothered Gloria. She rather liked the fact there was no one directly across the street. It appeared that was all about to change. Over the last few days, Gloria had noticed strange cars parked in the drive. She had even caught a glimpse of a young couple with a baby.

Gloria had a sneaking suspicion that the farmers had sold the house, which meant that soon she would have new neighbors.

For now, the house was empty, except for a dim light that shone through the front window, which is what caught Gloria's attention. There hadn't been any lights on in that house for years. Maybe whoever had bought it had left an interior light on by accident.

She shrugged her shoulders and turned her attention to more pressing things.

Halfway across the backfield, Gloria's cell phone rang. It was Paul. "How's my girl?"

"Overwhelmed," Gloria admitted. The cell reception was good and Paul was coming in loud and clear.

"Did you find anything out about Jill's place?" he asked.

Gloria told him how her day had gone and ended with Lucy taking Jasper home with her. "So I dodged another dog?" he teased.

"So far," Gloria admitted. "There are more that need to be rescued."

She knew there was no way she could take all of those dogs. Even if she convinced every single one of her friends to adopt one of the dogs, there would still be too many. She couldn't just set them free. That was irresponsible.

On top of that, what would stop the Acostas from going out and getting more to replace the ones they had sold?

No. There had to be another plan...a better one. She needed to find out more about the people who ran the mill –

Jessica's parents. She could send someone else over there to sort of scope the place out, maybe glean a little more information into the Acosta's background and in the process find out more about Jill's place.

"...so we could honeymoon on Mackinac Island."

Paul was talking. Gloria hadn't heard a word he had said, although she caught the tail end. "That would be lovely," she replied.

Paul snorted. "You didn't hear a word I said, did you?"

"Only the part about Mackinac Island," she admitted. "I love that place."

"We can't honeymoon there in the middle of winter, unless you plan on getting there by snowmobile," he pointed out.

That was true. The island was somewhat remote, accessible only by boat or small plane. In the winter, the only way to get there was by snowmobile. Visions of Gloria in an elegant, lacy dress wearing snowmobile boots, snow pants and a ski jacket filled her head.

"Maybe we should go somewhere warm and save that for next summer," she suggested.

She changed the subject. "About that puppy mill. Aren't those illegal?" she asked.

Paul paused. "Not that I know of...at least not if they're registered."

"Can you find out?" she asked.

"I'll see what I can do," he promised. "Are you too busy with all of your dilemmas to have dinner with your betrothed?" he teased.

She was in the woods now and had settled onto her favorite log. "Of course not."

"Good. I can't make it tomorrow but I have the next night off. Maybe we can have dinner at that Italian place you investigated not long ago over in Lakeville...what was the name?"

"Pasta Amore." Gloria was surprised she remembered, what with all the stuff running through her head.

"Yes, dinner at Pasta Amore," he agreed.

After Gloria finished talking to Paul, she wandered over to the edge of the creek. The water level had dropped. Fall had been dry but winter was on the way and it would fill back up during the winter season and when the snow melted in the spring.

She glanced around the woods that she loved. The place had brought her many hours of quiet reflection when she needed to be by herself and clear her mind. She wondered if this would be her last visit before Paul and she married and if Paul would come here with her, too.

On the one hand, she wanted to share it with him, but on the other, it was her own secret hideaway. She guessed she would have to start sharing some things.

Mally had finished splashing in the creek and raced over to Gloria. "Ready to head back, Mally?"

Mally circled her several times and then raced ahead to the edge of the woods.

The light on her answering machine was blinking when Gloria stepped back inside the kitchen. She hung her jacket on the hook near the door, stepped to the kitchen counter and pressed the button on the machine. It was Jill.

"Hey Mom. It's me." She let out a heavy sigh. "I called to find out if you came up with anything on the house. It looks like we didn't get the house we put an offer in on yesterday. The owners went with another offer so we are once again homeless."

Gloria could hear the frustration in her daughter's voice. "Anyways, call me back. Thanks."

Gloria promptly dialed her daughter's number. Tyler answered. "Hi Grams. Mom said we might be moving in with you."

A stab of sheer something ran through Gloria. She had offered to let Jill, Greg and the boys live with her if they needed to, but she hadn't seriously pondered the idea.

If Gloria couldn't figure out who was trying to stop them from purchasing the house on Pine Place, they may very well have to move in with Gloria – lock, stock and barrel.

She had visions of Paul, her kids and her grandkids all living under one roof. She wondered if perhaps she could just run away.

She grinned as she envisioned dragging her suitcase out of the house...peeling out of the driveway in Annabelle as if the devil himself were on her heels.

He went on. "Ryan and I already decided that we're gonna live in the tree fort." Well, that solved some of the crowding issues.

Gloria swallowed the lump in her throat. "That's quite a thought, Tyler," she said. "Is your mom there?"

Tyler handed the phone to his mother.

"Sorry Mom. You know that would be a last resort," she assured her. "Did you find anything out about the house?"

"Not much...yet," Gloria admitted. "I'm still working through some of the clues and will be on it first thing in the morning," she vowed. *With a vengeance,* she silently added.

"We have a couple houses to look at tonight, but I can already tell that they won't work. They're either in the wrong school district, the yard is too small or the price is too high."

Perhaps Gloria could add a little more cash for the purchase. Desperate times called for desperate measures. "I may be able to give you more money if you're close on price," Gloria told her.

Jill stopped her. "No. We aren't going to do that. First of all, it wouldn't be fair to give me more money than Eddie and Ben got and second of all, you've already been far too generous."

Jill had a point. If Gloria gave her daughter more money, it would only be right to give her sons more, too. "Well, don't give up on that house yet, Jill. I haven't failed to crack a case yet."

Jill sighed. "True. If ever there was a time I needed you to get to the bottom of something, now is it."

Gloria reassured her daughter it was a top priority and hung up the phone. She stared at the silent phone in her hand and closed her eyes. "Dear God. Please help me figure out who is trying to stop Jill from buying that home."

She lifted her head and gazed out the window. Gloria needed help and fast. There was only one place to go.

She grabbed her purse from the table, the keys from the hook by the door and headed to Dot's Restaurant.

She swung by Lucy's place on the way. Lucy met her at the door. "Where are you going?"

"Dot's Restaurant. I need some help on Jill's house." She told her about her conversation with Jill.

Lucy scrunched her nose. "Wow. Yeah, this is a 911 emergency, for sure. Let me get my purse."

Gloria stood at the door and waited. Jasper wandered over, his tail wagging. He looked different, somehow...happy. She bent down and kissed his head. He smelled fresh, like lemons.

Lucy was back.

Gloria looked up. "Did you give Jasper a bath already?"

Lucy laughed. "Yep. He loves baths. He had a ball."

Jasper turned adoring eyes to Lucy.

"I'll be back before you know it," she promised her pooch.

Two sad, brown eyes bore into Lucy's own. "Ugh. Don't look at me like that."

Gloria grinned. "Better get used to it. I call it the pitiful play. Don't worry, he'll be thrilled when you return and completely forget that you left him at home."

Lucy glanced down at Jasper one final time. "I hope you're right," she fretted.

The girls discussed the house on the way to Dot's place. This one had Gloria stumped, something that had never had happen before. She always had an idea on how to solve a mystery, but this time her mind was blank.

"Maybe you have too much going on," Lucy pointed out.

Wasn't that the truth. The house, Dot's cancer, the puppy mill, the wedding and the holidays was so much. Her head was spinning just trying to organize the events. Now she had to wonder if Jill and her family were going to have to move in.

Soon, she would be ready for the nut house. It wasn't that she didn't love them all to pieces, but there was only so much one person could take.

"You can come stay with me," Lucy offered.

Gloria pulled Annabelle into an open spot in front of the restaurant and shut the engine off. "I may take you up on that...seriously."

Dot's Restaurant was busy but not packed. Gloria caught a glimpse of Margaret and her husband, Don, in a booth in the back.

Dot was standing near their table, coffee pot in hand.

Gloria pointed at the pot. "You're not supposed to be here," she accused her friend.

Dot lifted a hand. "I can't help it. What am I supposed to do? Sit home and twiddle my thumbs, worrying that the cancer cells are multiplying?"

True. Dot had a point. If Gloria were in the same position, she wasn't sure that she would be able to sit still.

She changed the subject. "How is Odie adjusting?"

Dot pointed a finger toward the kitchen. "He's great. He's in the back, helping Ray." She leaned forward. "He loves that dog."

Gloria was relieved. She felt responsible for dragging Dot along to the puppy mill in the first place.

"How is Jasper?" Dot asked.

Lucy settled into the chair next to Margaret. "He's adjusting quite nicely."

Dot raised a brow. "Really?"

"Lucy came over to help me with the dogs and Jasper took a liking to her," Gloria explained.

"Huh." Dot shoved a hand on her hip. "Lucy has a dog. Miracles never cease."

"What miracle?" Ruth had come up behind Gloria and now stood near the table. She shrugged out of her jacket and dropped it on the back of the chair.

"Lucy has a dog," Dot explained.

Ruth raised a brow. "Lucy? Our Lucy?"

"We can tease Lucy later." Gloria changed the subject. "I need all of your help and fast."

Chapter 12

Gloria outlined her dilemma. The girls clucked in sympathy when she got to the part where she feared her entire family would be moving in, lock stock and barrel. "So I need to figure out what in the world is going on at that house and fast," she finished.

Dot had returned with several cups of coffee and a small pot of hot water and packet of hot chocolate for Lucy.

Lucy dumped the packet in the bottom of the empty cup then poured hot water over the top. She stirred the mix and took a sip. Her face puckered. "I think they stopped putting sugar in this stuff."

She reached for several sugar packets, tore the ends off three and dumped them into her cup. She stirred the contents and took a sip. "Much better," she decided.

Her gaze turned to Gloria. "What about another stakeout?"

"But what would we stake out? The house is empty," Ruth pointed out.

Margaret snapped her fingers. "What about the real estate agent? She must know something more that she hasn't shared."

Gloria suspected the same...that Sue Camp knew more than she was letting on. "I'll track her down in the morning."

Dot returned. "Follow the money." She refilled the girls' cups and set the carafe on the edge of the table.

Gloria looked up. Her eyes narrowed. "Follow the money and find out who cashed in the previous earnest money deposits."

She patted Dot's hand. "Great idea. Why didn't I think of that?"

"Love has clouded your head," Lucy joked.

"That, or fear," Ruth added.

After Gloria and Lucy finished eating, they climbed back in the car. Lucy was carrying a small folded napkin.

Gloria pointed at her lap. "Whatcha got in there?"

Lucy's eyes fell to her lap. "Just a little snack for Jasper."

"Hm." Gloria smiled knowingly. Yep. The dog had officially taken over and now controlled Lucy's life. She hoped that Max liked dogs...

Back at Lucy's ranch, Gloria waited for her friend to make her way inside before she pulled out of the driveway and headed home. She would need to get a good night's rest. She wanted to be up early the next morning to corner Sue Camp in her office.

***

Gloria, feeling guilty that she had left Mally at home the last few trips from the farm, decided to bring her sidekick along. Mally was happy as a clam to be in the car and going somewhere – anywhere.

Green Springs Premier Realty's parking lot was almost empty, except for two cars. She hoped that one of the cars belonged to Sue Camp.

Gloria slid out of the driver's seat. "I'll be right back," she told Mally. She wasn't sure if they allowed dogs in the office and she didn't want to give Sue Camp a single excuse for not talking to her.

The front office door was unlocked. Gloria turned the knob and stepped inside. A young woman sat at the front desk, filing her fingernails. She looked up when Gloria closed the door behind her.

"Can I help you?"

"Yes, I'm looking for Sue Camp."

The girl's eyes darted to the back of the building. "Let me see if she's in."

Gloria smiled. "Thank you."

The girl slid out of the seat and scurried down the hall and out of sight.

The girl returned a few moments later. "She is here and will be right with you."

Gloria nodded, then turned her attention to the bulletin board, chock full of houses for sale.

Moments later, a surprised Sue Camp wandered into the reception area. "Oh. Hello Mrs. Rutherford. What brings you to my office bright and early this morning? Looking for a new home?"

Sue Camp had heard the gossip. She knew that her client's mother had given her money to purchase a new home.

"I'm sure that my daughter, Jill, told you that as of right now, they are still moving forward on the purchase of 726 Pine Place."

The woman rested her hip against the counter. "Are you sure? I mean, that house has her a little rattled what with the mysterious notes and such."

Gloria pulled her purse in front of her and leveled her gaze. "Why do you think those things are happening, Ms. Camp?"

The woman shrugged. "I wouldn't have the slightest idea."

Gloria took a step forward. "None whatsoever?"

The woman was nervous. Gloria could smell it from a mile away. "Who keeps the deposit money when a deal falls through?"

"Not me," she answered.

"The sellers?" Gloria probed.

"I don't know where you're going with all these questions." The woman's eyes narrowed. "Look. I have no idea who is trying to drive off buyers. All I know is that it's not me."

She turned on her heel and stomped into the back office, slamming the door behind her.

The girl behind the counter gasped. Her mouth fell open, then quickly closed. She promptly clamped it shut and picked up her nail file.

Gloria turned on her heel and slowly stepped out the front door. Something was going on and Gloria was determined to find out what.

She climbed behind the wheel of her car and headed to Rapid Creek. There was still one neighbor Gloria hadn't talked to; now was as good a time as any.

She pulled in the drive at 726 Pine Place and climbed out of the car. Still prominently displayed in the front yard was the "for sale" sign, minus the "pending" part.

Gloria stepped to the end of the drive and turned left, toward the two-story house next door. Once again, she heard the loud thump of rock music before she reached the door.

Someone had tossed a newspaper into the grass out front. Out of habit, Gloria reached over to pick it up. The yard was full of land mines. Big land mines. Whoever lived inside this house had a large dog - or two.

When she reached the front door, the music abruptly stopped. She raised her hand to ring the bell when the door swung open.

Behind the screen door stood a tall, gangly teen with ear buds draped around his neck. He had a tight grip on the collar of a large German shepherd that looked none too happy to see Gloria. He bared his teeth, lowered his ears and let out a low warning growl.

Gloria glanced at the flimsy screen that separated them. If the dog wanted to, he could burst through the screen as if it wasn't even there.

"H-hi. My name is Gloria Rutherford and my daughter is buying the house next door." Gloria pointed to the house. "I was wondering if you could tell me about the neighbors...the Acostas who recently moved out."

The dog leaned forward and gave another warning growl.

She glanced at the dog. Maybe it wasn't such a good idea for Jill and the boys to move next door. What if the dog got loose and attacked one of her grandsons?

The first thing they would need was a fence. She made a mental note to discuss the matter with her daughter.

From a distance, somewhere in the back of the house, Gloria heard another bark. She could tell from the bark that it was a much smaller dog.

The boy shrugged. "Yeah, they moved out kinda fast. Like overnight. They had a ton of dogs out back."

"Did you ever see the dogs?" Gloria was curious.

"Yep. My mom and dad bought one before they moved."

The house phone began to ring. "I gotta go."

Before Gloria had a chance to reply, the boy closed the door in her face. She heard the lock turn. The large dog barked until Gloria was off the porch and back on the sidewalk.

She wandered around the side of the empty house and into the back yard. She hadn't noticed before, but the rear yard was partially fenced. Well, maybe partially wasn't quite accurate. There was a haphazard fence. Several boards were missing and it tilted at a precarious angle, as if a good, strong wind would knock it over.

She glanced over the top of the rickety fence and into the neighbor's yard. There was nothing to prevent the puppy mill dogs and the neighbor's dogs from wandering into each other's yards.

Obviously, the neighbors got along if what the boy said was true, that they had purchased a dog from the Acostas. What if they had purchased a dog and it had died?

Gloria needed to get someone back inside the puppy farm, to try to glean more information out of the owners and check on the dogs...

She also needed to set up some sort of surveillance at the house. Gloria stepped onto the back deck. She shaded her eyes and peered into the rear slider. She needed someone who could loan her some sort of surveillance equipment for a day or two...

Gloria took a step back. She knew just who to ask.

Chapter 13

Ruth Carpenter clicked the end of the ballpoint pen and studied Gloria. "So you need me to loan you my surveillance equipment?"

Gloria nodded. "It will only be for a couple days. I promise."

Ruth turned her gaze to the SP5500 Series spy camera she had recently purchased with the garage sale money she had made at Gloria's house. It was her prized possession...her baby. She used it every night after work.

Since the drug bust at the post office, things had been quiet, but Ruth knew that could change at any moment and nothing was ever gonna get by her again. Not on her watch.

"Okay, you can borrow it but only for a day or two," Ruth relented. "How soon?"

"Now?" Gloria knew Ruth wasn't big on having surprises sprung on her, especially when it involved her spy equipment.

Ruth frowned.

"I have a better idea." Gloria changed her mind. "Why don't we head over there after work tonight?"

It sounded perfect until Gloria remembered her date with Paul. "I mean, tomorrow night after work and you can help me set it up. You know, make sure it's installed correctly."

Gloria knew that would pacify Ruth somewhat, to know that no one would be handling the equipment except her.

"Okay. We can do that," Ruth agreed.

Gloria told Ruth she would pick her up at 5 o'clock sharp the next afternoon and then headed out of the post office.

Next on her list was finding someone to make a trip out to the Acosta's new place, pretending to be interested in a puppy. She had just the person for the job.

Gloria headed up the hill to Magnolia Mansion and Andrea's place.

***

Gloria pulled in the drive and rounded the small bend. Andrea's luxurious Mercedes sports car wasn't in the drive. In its place was a four-wheel drive pick-up truck. It looked new.

Gloria slid out of the car and slowly closed the car door.

Behind her, a construction crew was hard at work on the walls of Andrea's new detached garage.

Andrea had told her she wanted to have the garage finished before the first snowflake hit the ground. It looked like she was going to make that deadline.

Gloria eased past the pick-up truck. On closer inspection, the truck was a beautiful metallic dark blue color. From what she could tell, it was a roomy four door.

"Checking out my new ride?" Andrea called from the doorway. She didn't wait for Gloria to answer as she shoved her feet into a pair of clogs that sat just outside the door and hurried to the truck.

Andrea pressed the button on the clicker in her hand and unlocked the driver's side door. She grabbed the handle and swung the door open. "Hop in."

Gloria had, on and off, thought about buying a pick-up truck. It would come in handy during the winter months when snow blew across the flat farm fields creating large snowdrifts on the roads. There were days it was nearly impossible to get around during a snowstorm, not that Gloria liked to drive around in snowstorms in the first place.

She climbed into the driver seat and wiggled around on the leather seat. She reached over and rubbed the gray strip of cloth that covered the spacious center console.

Andrea smiled. "You can see pretty good from up there, huh?"

Andrea was right. Gloria could see a lot more in the truck than she could when she was behind the wheel of Annabelle. The seats were large and, for a truck, luxurious. This was no cheap run-of-the-mill truck. Gloria was certain Andrea had paid a pretty penny for it.

Gloria could afford to buy a new vehicle with her windfall, although it didn't seem like a necessity. Still, it would be nice to have something that got around in the winter better than her car.

She closed her eyes and breathed deeply. The smell of brand new vehicle filled her nose. It had been years since she'd been inside a new vehicle, let alone driven one.

Gloria eased out of the driver's seat and slid to the ground. "I'm sure this set you back a pretty penny."

Andrea nodded and then closed the driver's side door. "Yep." She shrugged. "The Mercedes wasn't practical, at least not living out here."

The girls made their way to the house. "You should think about getting one," she added.

Gloria grinned. She stopped in her tracks and turned back. "Nah, I can just call you to come pull me out of the ditch now," she teased.

The girls wandered inside. Alice, Andrea's new housemate and former housekeeper, met them in the hall. "You like Miss Andrea's new truck?"

Gloria smiled at the petite woman. "Yes. Are you going to drive it?" Now that Gloria thought about it, she wasn't sure if Alice knew how to drive.

Alice waved her hands in front of her. "No! No! Not me!"

Andrea patted Alice's arm. "Alice would like to learn how to drive but I'm afraid now that I have the truck, she thinks it's too big."

Gloria adjusted the purse on her shoulder. "Do you think Annabelle – my car- would be too big?"

Alice glanced uneasily over Gloria's shoulder, past Andrea's new truck at Gloria's car. "Well..."

"I-I think..." Alice said nervously.

Gloria interrupted. "Great. It's settled. We can start your first driving lesson today."

Gloria had enough on her plate, but what if there was an emergency and Andrea wasn't home – or worse yet – something happened and Alice needed to drive somewhere? At the very least, she should be able to get help.

Gloria could tell from the look on Alice's face that she was starting to waffle. "Go grab your purse."

Alice opened her mouth and then closed it. She turned on her heel and headed up the steps.

Andrea and Gloria watched until she disappeared from sight.

Andrea turned to Gloria, her eyes wide. "You're going to teach her to drive? I've been trying for weeks now to get her behind the wheel and she keeps coming up with excuses."

Gloria grinned. "No time like the present."

Alice returned a few moments later. The first thing Gloria noticed was her olive complexion was pale...just a tad. The second thing she noticed was that Alice's hand trembled as she nervously shifted the small handbag in her hand.

Gloria swung her arm around her shoulder. "You'll do fine."

The girls marched out the front door and over to Annabelle. Gloria clicked the key fob to unlock the doors and then opened the driver's side door. She waved her hand at Alice to slide into the driver's seat. "We'll start slow," she promised.

Alice swallowed the lump in her throat and nodded, too terrified to speak.

Andrea climbed in the back seat while Gloria made her way to the passenger side. When the women were safely inside the car, she told Alice to start the engine.

Two terror-filled eyes gazed at Gloria. "Now?"

Gloria nodded. "Yes. Now," she urged.

Alice started the car. She made a cross sign using her hand. "Protect us, Jesus."

Slowly, step-by-step, Gloria instructed Alice on how to back the car out of the drive. Alice took a very wide turn and only one of the construction workers had to dive for cover when she panicked and pressed the gas pedal instead of the brake.

They crept out onto the road. "Turn right," Gloria told her when they reached the end of the long, gravel drive.

The car, as if in slow motion, turned onto the road and started down the steep hill. It was a dead end road and it ended near a small public access beach and boat launch.

Alice turned the steering wheel and made a large swooping circle. The front bumper grazed one of the metal guardrails that lined the edge of the road as the car careened to the side.

Alice turned terrified eyes to Gloria. "I'm sorry."

"Don't worry about it," Gloria assured her, "Annabelle is tough."

After the car was back in the drive, safely parked behind Andrea's new truck, Alice shut the engine off and dropped her forehead on the steering wheel.

Gloria patted Alice's back. "Great job, Alice."

The woman lifted her head. "You think so, Miss Gloria?"

Andrea unbuckled her seatbelt and leaned forward in the seat. "Yes. Next time we can drive into downtown."

Alice groaned and Gloria grinned.

The girls headed back inside the house. Brutus, Andrea's dog, waited by the door, as if wondering why he hadn't been invited for a ride. Gloria reached down and patted his head. "I'm sorry, Brutus. I plum forgot about you."

The girls wandered into the kitchen. Andrea stepped over to the back counter and grabbed a coffee cup from the cupboard. "Coffee?"

Gloria nodded. "Yes, thanks."

Andrea poured a cup and set it in front of Gloria. "So what brings you by?"

Gloria wasn't one to show up unannounced, unless, of course, she had a specific reason. Andrea knew her friend well enough to know there was a reason.

"I have a favor to ask." She went on to explain everything that had happened and ended with: "Can you take a run by the Acosta's place and scope out the puppy mill?"

Gloria had done so much for Andrea, her friend could ask her to fly to the moon and she would tell her yes. "Of course," she replied.

Alice, who had settled in at the bar, sat silent.

Gloria turned to her. "Would you mind going with her?" she asked.

Alice brightened. So far, she had never been involved in one of Gloria's investigations. "Yes."

Gloria slapped the palm of her hand on the gleaming counter. "Great. It's settled."

Andrea jotted down the address and Gloria gave them instructions on where the puppy mill was located. She looked up from the notepad and frowned. "What do I say if they ask how I found them?"

Gloria gazed out the window thoughtfully. "Well, you can tell them that your friend came by the other day and Jessica helped them purchase two of the dogs. Maybe they will think they have another easy sale." Not that Andrea needed another dog...

"You don't have to take one of the dogs," Gloria went on, "tell them that you have to think about it."

Andrea nodded. "Sounds good." She changed the subject. "A little birdie told me you were thinking about having your wedding here at the house."

Gloria had almost forgotten. "Yeah. One of the girls suggested it."

Alice piped up. "Yes, Miss Gloria. That would be beautiful. I can prepare some of my famous Mexican dishes for the reception."

Gloria loved Alice's spicy dishes but they didn't love her back. The last thing she needed to do was eat a bunch of spicy food on her wedding day. "Uh..."

Alice's firehouse fajitas + Gloria's wedding night = recipe for disaster.

Andrea patted Gloria's shoulder. "We will definitely have Alice's world famous fajitas but probably some other dishes to go along with them." She winked at Gloria who breathed a sigh of relief.

The last thing she wanted to do was to hurt Alice's feelings. "Great. Maybe we can go over some sort of menu."

"The wedding will be here before you know it," Andrea pointed out.

The way Gloria's life was going, ten weeks would fly right out the window and before she knew it, she would be walking down the aisle, or in the case, across the sunroom. "We can do a tentative menu now, if you want."

Andrea grabbed a notepad from the back counter and a pen from a small penholder nearby. The three women came up with the perfect menu. Not only would they have Alice's firehouse fajitas, they would include some dishes from Dot's restaurant: stick-to-your-ribs foods like baked chicken, sliced beef, mashed potatoes and macaroni and cheese.

"This won't be too much work for you?" Gloria asked.

Alice interrupted. "No, Miss Gloria. Andrea and I already talked about having my sister from Texas come help." She pronounced "sister" as "seestar" and Gloria smiled. "We will take care of everything."

Gloria tipped her head back and swallowed the last of her coffee. "When you come up with an estimate of how much it will cost, let me know and I'll write a check," she said gratefully.

She suddenly remembered Dot's cancer. What if Dot wasn't up to catering a wedding? They would need a back-up plan.

As Gloria explained Dot's situation, Andrea teared up. She reached for a Kleenex and dabbed her eyes. "Oh…I had no idea."

Gloria hadn't meant to upset Andrea. "We have to believe that the Lord is going to heal Dot."

Andrea nodded. "I'll add her to my prayers."

"Me too," Alice whispered. She didn't know Dot as well as some of the others, but any friend of Andrea's was a friend of hers.

Alice and Andrea walked Gloria to the front door. "We'll head over to the Acosta's place as soon as I shower," Andrea promised.

Gloria hugged them both and headed to her car. Things were falling into place.

Gloria's wheels were spinning on the way home. She needed to convince Jill to move forward with that house. Whoever was trying to scare them off would make another move soon and Gloria hoped to catch them in the act.

Now all she had to do was convince Jill.

Chapter 14

"Are you one hundred percent *sure*?" Jill asked.

"Yes, I am." Gloria had finally convinced her daughter to move forward on the ranch house at 726 Pine Place. "If something happens and you have to back out, I will replace the lost deposit AND you, Greg and the kids can stay at the farm until you find another house."

"I need you to call Sue Camp and tell her that you're bringing a home inspector through the house," Gloria added.

Gloria hung up the phone and twisted the engagement ring around her finger nervously. The pressure was on. If ever there was motivation to solve a mystery, this was it.

She spent the rest of the afternoon cleaning house. There were two bedrooms upstairs that the boys could use and then the guest bedroom downstairs where Greg and Jill could sleep.

Ben, Gloria's middle child, his wife Kelly and their twins, Ariel and Oliver, would be here a few days before Christmas. Their flight home was the day after Christmas.

Gloria's oldest child, her son, Eddie, and his wife, Karen, planned to come for the same days, but it was only the two of them.

Gloria mentally counted eleven people shacked up in a four-bedroom house. The adults could get the bedrooms and she could turn the living room into a huge sleepover for her grandchildren. The boys would outnumber poor Ariel. Gloria hadn't seen her granddaughter in almost a year now.

It would only be for a few days, she tried to convince herself. A few days to house her entire family, marry Paul and celebrate Christmas. The idea of getting married when everyone was in town had seemed like a brilliant plan at the time. Now she wasn't so sure.

Remain positive, she told herself. *We need to get Jill in that house, safe and sound.*

The afternoon flew by and Gloria had just enough time to take a bath and change into a clean outfit before Paul arrived.

Mally saw Paul first, her excited bark announcing his arrival. Gloria opened the door as he reached the top step. He was holding a bouquet of beautiful fall flowers. Gloria reached for the flowers and lifted up on her tippy toes at the same time for a kiss.

She closed her eyes and breathed in his cologne. Gloria loved the musky, masculine scent. For a moment, all was right in her world. Gone were thoughts of puppy mills and haunted houses.

Paul wrapped his arms around his bride-to-be and drew her close. "I've been waiting for this all day."

Gloria laid her cheek on his chest and soaked it in, the flowers still clutched in her grip.

Finally, Paul backed up. "You are more beautiful each time I see you," he said.

Gloria blushed. "I bet you say that to all the girls," she shot back.

Paul bent down for a second kiss. "Only my girl," he promised.

Moments later, Gloria reluctantly stepped away as she headed to the cupboard. She reached inside and pulled out a large, glass vase. She filled the vase with water and set the flowers inside.

With a little arranging, the blooms filled the vase and spilled over the sides. "You're spoiling me," she said as she set the vase in the center of the kitchen table.

Paul pulled out a chair and sat down. "This is just the beginning," he assured her.

Paul was Gloria's perfect mate. He was her anchor. He had the patience of a saint...never annoyed with her when she got herself into a pickle, which she'd done on more than one occasion.

On top of all that, he was easygoing, which she chalked up to working as a police officer for decades. One would have to have a lot of patience for that line of work.

Gloria worried about him, though. He still patrolled the streets some nights. At least there wasn't a ton of serious crimes in Montbay County.

The last murder investigation had been the one that involved Andrea's place and the body they had stumbled upon had been decades old.

No, the crimes in the area were more along the lines of missing persons, drug activity... Now that Gloria thought about it, she had been involved in several of those as well.

Still, she would be relieved when he retired, which would bring on a completely new set of worries. If he retired, would they get on each other's nerves? They would be newlyweds and with Gloria's windfall, maybe they could do a little traveling, find a new hobby that didn't involve dead bodies...

"Earth to Gloria," Paul said.

Gloria snapped to attention. "I'm sorry. I guess my mind had wandered."

"Let me guess. Your new investigation," he said.

"Kind of." She didn't want to admit she was nervous about married life. Instead, she told him the status of Jill's house.

He frowned. "You think there's a chance that they might have to move in with you?" Gloria was good at juggling a lot of different things at once, but all of this might be too much, especially with the wedding. The last thing he needed was for her to become overwhelmed and get cold feet.

"If that happens, some of them can come stay at my place," he offered.

Gloria smiled at the generous offer. She didn't want to impose but it was a thought, especially if it got as crowded as she envisioned. "Thank you, but hopefully it doesn't come to that."

Paul didn't dare mention that his son, Jeff, and daughter-in-law, Tina, were having trouble paying their rent and had hinted at moving back in with him.

He glanced at the clock. "Ready to hit the road?" He stood, lifted his arms over his head and stretched his back. It had been a long week and this was the first chance he'd had to relax.

The restaurant, Pasta Amore, was in the nearby town of Lakeville. Gloria had eaten there a couple times. One time was with Paul and another time with the Garden Girls when they were investigating the deadly poisoning at Dot's Restaurant.

She couldn't remember much about the place, other than the food was delicious, but not as good as the food that Dot served.

During the drive, Gloria told him about the wedding plans and the menu that Andrea and she had discussed. He told her he would leave all of that up to her. All he needed to know was what time he had to be there.

Gloria was a "take charge" person and the fact that he left those details up to her suited her just fine.

Paul parked his truck in an empty space in front of the restaurant and climbed out of the driver's seat. Gloria knew date night meant she had to wait until he came around the other side and opened her door.

She put her hand in his and slid out of the truck. The last special date night had been when he had taken her on the dinner cruise over at Lake Harmony. If they had planned a summer wedding, Lake Harmony would have been the perfect spot to marry.

Paul held the door and Gloria stepped inside the dimly lit restaurant. It looked different from the last time she had been there. The setting was more intimate. Red-checkered tablecloths covered the tables. A small, flickering candle sat in the center of each of the tables.

The hostess stepped forward. "Table for two?"

Paul nodded. "Give us the most romantic one you've got."

"Of course." She led them to a corner table.

After they sat down, Paul ordered two glasses of tea. Gloria sipped the tea when it arrived but didn't lift the menu. He glanced up. "You know what you're going to have?"

She shook her head. "You decide for me." This evening was all about relaxing. She didn't even want to have to decide what to eat.

"Okay," he warned, "but don't blame me if you don't like it."

When the waiter returned, Paul ordered two of the dinner specials: tossed salad and baked lasagna with a side of garlic bread.

"Perfect," she assured him.

The conversation turned to the children, to the investigation, to the puppy mill and last, but not least, Dot's cancer.

Paul lifted his glass and sipped his tea. He eyed her over the rim of the glass. "You're worried."

Gloria sighed. "Very much." She couldn't imagine anything happening to her dear friend – to any of her friends. It seemed the worry had been sitting in the back of her mind, always there.

She knew that Pastor Nate had already talked to Dot and Ray and that he had added them to many prayer chains in the community and in the Town of Belhaven itself.

The meal arrived and it was delicious. The serving was twice what Gloria was accustomed to eating so they boxed the leftovers and headed to the truck.

Paul closed the door after Gloria slid into the passenger seat, walked around the truck and climbed into the driver's side. The air had a definite chill and Gloria pulled her jacket tighter as Paul turned the heat on "high."

"I'm thinking about buying a truck," she blurted out.

Paul shot her a sideways glance. That was the first time she had mentioned buying a truck. "You're going to get rid of Annabelle?"

She shook her head. Gloria would never part with Annabelle. She had already decided that if – and when - Annabelle finally stopped running, she would store her in the barn. No, Annabelle would be around as long as Gloria still had breath in her lungs. "I'll never get rid of Annabelle but I was thinking that maybe I could get a truck to drive around in the winter. Something that's dependable."

Paul nodded. It was a good idea. "Okay. Let me know when you want to start looking and I'll go with you," he promised.

Paul pulled the truck into the drive and made his way to the passenger side. He glanced across the street as he opened the passenger door.

"Is someone moving in over there?" A light was on. The same light Gloria had noticed the night before.

Gloria grabbed his hand and slid out of the truck. "Something is going on. I've seen several cars over there but no moving truck." Of course, Gloria was gone a lot. Someone could have moved in and she just hadn't noticed.

Paul unlocked the kitchen door and opened it wide to let Mally out. She greeted them both and then raced across the yard to start her patrol.

Inside the house, Gloria stepped over to the kitchen counter. "Coffee?"

Paul shook his head. "I have to work in the morning."

Gloria's heart sank. What he meant was he had to work in a few hours. Morning to Paul was a shift that started at 4:00 a.m. "So you can't stay?"

"I'm afraid not." He reached over and pulled her close. "But don't worry. Soon enough you'll be stuck with me all the time and will be itching to get rid of me."

Gloria wrapped her arms around his neck. "I don't think so."

Paul leaned down and kissed her lips. It was a slow, tender, there's-so-much-more-to-come kiss that left Gloria breathless.

When he released his grip, she lifted a hand to her throat. "My goodness."

"There's more where that came from," he teased.

For once, Gloria was at a loss for words. She fiddled with the edge of her blouse as she followed him out onto the porch.

He gave her one final quick kiss and a warm hug before he turned and reluctantly made his way to the truck. It was getting harder and harder for Gloria to watch him go. Maybe because she knew soon, she wouldn't have to.

She waited until his taillights disappeared into the night before Mally and she headed back indoors.

Chapter 15

The drive to the Acosta's home in the country was about half an hour from Belhaven. Andrea had never technically worked on one of Gloria's investigations by herself. This one was important and Andrea was nervous that she might mess it up.

Alice could see Andrea was anxious. "We must make it sound good for Miss Gloria," Alice said.

Andrea tapped the steering wheel. "I know. The only problem is that I don't need another dog." Brutus was a handful. He was a good dog and Andrea loved him dearly but two dogs in the house, even a house as large as hers, was out of the question.

Alice adjusted her seatbelt. "No worries. We will figure it out."

Andrea pulled her shiny new pick-up truck into the drive and shut the engine off. She grabbed the door handle and turned to the woman who was like a second mother. She hoped they weren't walking into real danger. She would feel terrible if something went awry. "Ready for this?"

Alice nodded firmly. "Yes."

The women exited the pick-up truck and made their way across the weed-infested yard. Off in the distance, they could hear what sounded like a thousand barking dogs.

They made it as far as the edge of the yard when the side door opened and a tall man with a long black beard and piercing gray eyes met them at the top of the steps. "Can I help you?" The tone of his voice wasn't mean, but it was firm.

"I-I..." Andrea trailed off.

Alice stepped closer. "Yes, our friend told us she was here the other day and bought a puppy. We were wondering if you have any others for sale."

The man stepped off the porch. He narrowed his eyes and glanced at Andrea first. Then he turned to Alice. "You speak Spanish?" He had noticed her accent.

"Si," she replied.

The man smiled wide and began speaking in Spanish, talking 90 miles an hour. Andrea caught a word here or there. Words she had picked up over the years from Alice, but the conversation was flowing so fast that she couldn't keep up.

The man had relaxed his stance as he shoved his hands in his pockets and rocked back on his heels.

Andrea peeked at Alice out of the corner of her eye. Alice was enjoying the exchange. No one in the Town of Belhaven knew how to speak Spanish, as least as far as she knew.

Andrea caught the word "perro" a few times and knew that meant dog. Moments later, the man motioned them to follow him.

As they made their way along the side of the building and toward the back, the barks grew louder. Andrea wondered how many dogs were inside the place.

A combination lock secured the entrance door. The man twisted the dial back and forth and finally pulled down on the bottom. He unhooked the lock and pushed the door open.

Andrea took a deep breath and followed him inside. The first thing that struck her was the smell. A strong urine odor caught in her throat and she started to gag. She quickly clamped her hand over her mouth.

The man appeared not to notice.

Alice had a stronger stomach and the smell did not even faze her. She continued talking to the man in Spanish as they made their way down the long row of cages to the rear of the building.

The farther they walked, the darker the shed became...and the stronger the stench. There was zero air circulation in the back.

Andrea's heart sank at the sight of all of the poor creatures caged inside the building. Some of them pressed against the small cages, desperate for even an ounce of attention.

Others cowered in the back or curled up in a ball, barely moving at the sight of the three visitors.

Tears stung the back of Andrea's eyes. She closed them, willing the scene before her to disappear, but she knew in her heart what she was seeing would be with her for a very long time. No wonder Gloria had been distraught. This place was not fit for any living creature.

The man seemed proud of his animals as he wandered from cage-to-cage, pointing at various dogs and describing them in Spanish to Alice. She nodded several times. "Si."

When they finished their tour, the man stopped near the shed door. He pointed behind him.

"Usted quiere comprar un perro?"

Alice tilted her head toward Andrea. "He wants to know if we want to buy a dog."

"There are so many to choose from," Andrea said. "Can I talk it over with Alice and come back later?"

The man nodded. He said something else in Spanish and motioned them out of the building. He pulled the door closed and slid the lock through the slot. He snapped it shut and tugged on the bottom, making sure it was secure.

He held up a finger and headed back inside the house. "He's going to give us his telephone number," Alice explained.

He returned a moment later and handed a small slip of paper to Alice. After a few more exchanges, the women turned to go.

Safely inside the truck, and back on the road, Andrea spoke. "You have to tell me everything he said."

On the ride back to the house, Alice repeated the entire conversation.

***

The ringing of Gloria's phone awoke her the next morning. She leaned over and glanced at the clock beside her bed. It was already 8:30.

She flung back the covers, slipped her feet into her slippers and moseyed to the kitchen. By the time she got there, the phone had stopped ringing. It was Andrea and she could hear her voice as she left a message on the answering machine.

"Hi Gloria. I meant to call you last night. Alice and I went to the Acosta's farm yesterday and I wanted to report back."

Gloria grabbed her coffee tin from the back of the counter. She scooped a heaping spoonful into the top of the coffee maker, filled the carafe with water and dumped it into the back. She slid the carafe under the drip and turned it on.

While the coffee brewed, she picked up her house phone and dialed Andrea's cell phone.

"I hope I didn't wake you," Andrea fretted.

"It was time for me to get up," Gloria assured her.

She relayed the story of the visit to the puppy mill and that the owner spoke Spanish. "He took a liking to Alice and I think she enjoyed speaking to someone in her native tongue."

"The place was so sad, though," Andrea continued. "When I close my eyes, I can still see those poor animals in the cages. It makes me want to bawl every time I think about it."

She went on. "Alice seems to think that he doesn't see anything wrong with the living conditions of those dogs. He is proud of his business. He believes that he is helping those poor animals, not hurting them."

How anyone could believe that the conditions of that puppy mill were acceptable was beyond Gloria's comprehension.

"She seems to think with a little guidance, that place could be turned into a thriving dog business...one that was good for the animals, not harmful."

Gloria could hear a second voice in the background.

"Hang on." Andrea covered the mouthpiece with her hand.

Moments later, she was back. "If you think about it, Alice does have a point. I mean, that huge old farm is a great place for dogs. Wouldn't it be something if they were able to turn it into some sort of training center, one that trained Seeing Eye dogs and companion dogs?"

Alice had taken the phone from Andrea. "Yes, Miss Gloria. The Acostas, they care for the animals but they have little money. I think with some guidance, they could turn that puppy mill into something good. Good for the dogs and the owners."

Gloria frowned. She had tossed around the idea of using some of her money for a worthy cause...something to help others. Perhaps the Lord was pointing her in the right direction.

Andrea had said several times that Alice rambled around the house and that she didn't have enough to keep her busy. What if, with a little of Gloria's money and Alice's help, they turned the Acosta's puppy mill into something completely different?

"I have an idea, Alice. Can you put the phone on speaker so that Andrea can hear?"

The girls spent several minutes brainstorming how Alice could approach the Acostas about turning the puppy mill into a thriving business – one that would help others AND the dogs. The more they talked, the more excited Gloria became.

She could invest some cash and Alice could invest her time. Before they hung up, Alice promised to do some on-line research on how to start a dog training service.

"I start now," Alice declared.

Andrea was back. "Hey…" There was a long pause.

"Oh my gosh. I've never seen Alice so excited," Andrea whispered into the phone. "She's already in the office starting her research."

Gloria was excited, too. Alice would not only help those poor animals, she would have purpose again AND help the disabled to boot. The whole project could be a win-win for everyone.

After she hung up the phone, she let Mally back in from her morning run.

She poured a cup of coffee and settled into the kitchen with her Bible. She turned to the concordance in the back and searched for the perfect verse:

"Do not be anxious about anything, but in every situation, by prayer and petition, with thanksgiving, present your requests to God." Philippians 4: 6-7 NIV

Gloria bowed her head and prayed for peace – and strength – for not only Dot but for herself, her family and friends, and for guidance with the dogs, which weighed heavy on her mind.

When she lifted her head, she felt better…better prepared to handle the upcoming days and weeks. She closed her Bible and slid it back onto the curio cabinet shelf.

Gloria shoved the kitchen chair across the floor and headed to the bathroom. It was time to start her day.

Chapter 16

By the time she finished showering and dressing, she had two more messages on her answering machine. One was from Jill and the other from Ruth. Both had asked her to call them back.

Gloria started with Jill, hoping that her daughter had followed through with her promise to call the real estate agent to let her know that they definitely wanted to move forward with the purchase of 726 Pine Place and to tell her they had scheduled an inspection for the following day.

Jill picked up on the first ring. "I did it. I told Sue Camp we were moving forward with the home purchase," she said triumphantly.

"Good."

Jill went on. "Guess what? We *are* going to move forward with that house. Greg and I prayed about it together last night and feel that the Lord wants us to have that house."

Praise the Lord! The God of all miracles was at work in the Rutherford household.

"I'm so glad, Jill. You were meant to have that house." Now, the neighbors, Gloria wasn't quite so sure about that. She remembered the big dog and the broken fence in the backyard...

"I called an inspection company and we're going to do the inspection day after tomorrow," Jill told her.

"Why not…"

"Because, if what you said was true - that someone is going to sabotage the house tonight thinking that we're going to have an inspection *tomorrow,* then we want to get in there before the inspector does, just to make sure things are ship shape."

Gloria grinned. She hadn't thought of that. Jill was right. "That's my girl," Gloria said proudly.

After she hung up the phone, she thanked the Lord for her kids…all of her kids. So far the day was shaping up to be perfect. Now if they could only get a good report on Dot's cancer…

Instead of calling Ruth back, Gloria decided that Mally and she would make a trip into town. She could kill two birds with one stone so-to-speak: check on Dot and stop by the post office to go over the plan for later that evening.

Gloria hadn't mentioned to Paul that they were setting up surveillance equipment in the house. She knew he would not approve of the plan and didn't want him to have to tell her not to do it when she knew that she would.

By the time Gloria made it into Belhaven, Dot's place was in between the breakfast and dinner rush. She pulled into the post office parking lot and wandered across the street.

Through the big picture window, she could see Dot as she darted back and forth behind the lattice that separated the back of the restaurant from the seating area.

The bell chimed when Gloria stepped inside and Dot paused, pot of coffee in hand. Gloria made her way to the back and waited while Dot set the coffee pot on the warmer. "How is Odie?"

Dot rolled her eyes. "Good heavens. That dog has taken over the Jenkins' household."

Gloria laughed. It sounded like her own house.

Dot placed her hands on her hips. "Can you believe that Ray lets that crazy dog sit at the kitchen table while we eat breakfast and even gives him his own plate?"

That did surprise Gloria a little. Ray was a neat freak. Everything had a place and he made sure that it stayed there. Of course, running your own business, one would almost have to be organized to some extent. Dot smoothed a stray strand of hair back in place. "They're in the back now."

Gloria shifted her purse to her shoulder. "When is the next doctor's appointment?" she asked.

The smile left Dot's face and Gloria was sorry she had mentioned it.

"We have an appointment Friday. They ran some more tests and the results will be back so the doctor wanted to go over them in person," Dot explained.

Gloria nodded. "I'll be praying."

She stopped in the kitchen to say hello to Ray and Odie before she gave Dot a quick hug and headed for the door.

Dot stopped her. "How is the investigation going?"

"Good," Gloria said. "Ruth is helping me with it later today."

Dot raised a brow. "Ruth. Don't tell me..." She waved a hand. "Nope. I don't want to know. I'm sure you have it all under control."

Gloria wasn't certain about that. She was a fly-by-the-seat-of-your-pants kind of sleuth. So far, it always seemed to work for her. One of these days, it would probably blow up in her face. She hoped that today wasn't one of them.

Gloria turned to go and then stopped. She lowered her voice. "Andrea and Alice visited the farm yesterday." She gave her a dark look.

"The farm? Oh. You mean the place out in the country." Dot caught on.

"Yep. Those two have a great plan. You won't believe what they came up with."

Dot shoved her hands in her apron pockets. "Hopefully something that will help those poor animals."

"Uh-huh." A couple entered the restaurant and settled into a booth near the front.

"I'll tell you later." Gloria headed out the door and across the street.

Ruth was inside, waiting on Sally Keane, one of the locals. The two leaned over the counter, their heads close together. Their conversation abruptly ended when Gloria stepped inside. Sally's eyes darted to Gloria. "I better go." The woman grabbed her purse and made a beeline for the door.

She looked guilty as all get out and from the look on Ruth's face; Gloria must have been the topic of conversation. She dropped her purse on the counter and turned to Ruth. There was no point in beating around the bush. "What was that all about?"

Ruth's eyes dropped. She rubbed an imaginary spot off the counter with her thumb. "Oh...nothing much."

"C'mon, Ruth. I know you better than that," Gloria cajoled.

Ruth sighed. "We were just talking about how lucky you girls were to come into that pile of money."

Gloria's brows formed a "V." Good ole Sally Keane was stirring the pot.

Ruth had seemed happy for the girls...all of them had. The last thing they needed was for someone – namely Sally Keane - to start making a fuss, jealous over something that Gloria, Margaret and Liz had no control over. They just happened to be in the right place at the right time.

Gloria frowned. "Let me guess. Sally thinks I should donate all the money to charity."

Ruth shrugged. "Something like that," she mumbled and lifted her gaze. "Listen. I think it's wonderful and you are not a selfish person by any means, Gloria, so whatever you do with that money is your business."

In Ruth's mind, the subject was closed. She grabbed a sheet of clean paper and set it on the counter. Next, she grabbed a pen from the holder and slid it forward. "I need a diagram of the house," she whispered, "so I can figure out the best place to put the you-know-what."

Gloria grabbed the piece of paper. "Why didn't I think of that?" She picked up the pen and began to sketch the layout of the house. When she finished, she slid it back across the counter.

Ruth slipped her reading glasses on and studied the paper. "Hmm." She looked up. "You're going to pick me up here at five?"

Gloria nodded. "On the dot." She turned to go. "Thanks for doing this for me. I know how much your spy equipment means to you."

Ruth shrugged. "You know I would do anything for you...for any of my friends."

Gloria smiled. "I know and I appreciate it." Without saying another word, Gloria slipped out of the post office and wandered back to her car.

She had one more stop: Margaret's place.

Chapter 17

Margaret's SUV was in the drive but when Gloria rang the bell, no one answered.

She made her way around the side of the garage and into the backyard. When she got to the back of the house, she found her friend settled into a patio chair with a cup of coffee and her Bible.

Gloria wandered onto the deck. "You read in the morning too."

Margaret slipped off her reading glasses. "Until the snow flies, I like to come out here in the morning." She gazed at the lake. "It's peaceful."

Mally made her way over to say "hi" and Margaret patted her head. "What brings you out this morning?" Gloria wasn't one to show up unannounced, but after running into Sally Keane in the post office this morning, something had stuck in Gloria's craw.

She settled into a chair across from Margaret while Mally darted toward the edge of the water to chase the ducks. "Have you heard any scuttlebutt about the money?"

Margaret closed her Bible, placed her hand on the top and sighed heavily. "You too?"

Gloria frowned. "Yeah. Apparently, Sally Keane is making her rounds, stirring up trouble. I caught her in the post office with Ruth. At first Ruth tried to deny it but she admitted that Sally had mentioned the money."

"Huh." Margaret didn't seem as concerned about the gossip as Gloria. Of course, Margaret's husband had retired a couple years back as vice president of a local bank and they already had money. Now they had more. "So you're feeling guilty."

"Somewhat," Gloria admitted.

"What do you propose we do?" Margaret asked.

"I have some ideas," Gloria said.

They talked for quite some time as they discussed how they could best help each of their friends. Gloria clapped her hands excitedly and jumped to her feet. "So we have a plan?"

The two of them had come up with good ideas: wonderful surprises for each of their friends. Now all Gloria needed to do was keep it secret long enough to put it all together.

Margaret walked Mally and Gloria to the car and waited while her friend climbed in the driver's seat. Gloria rolled down the window. "I'm thinking of buying a truck for the winter."

Margaret frowned. "You're going to get rid of Annabelle?"

Gloria shook her head. "Nope. I'll always have Annabelle but I was thinking a truck might be nice to get around in the winter on the snowy roads."

"You need one." Margaret had to agree. Out of all the friends, Gloria was the one that lived the farthest from town and there were days Gloria was stuck at home because the roads were impassable, at least for Annabelle.

Back in the day, Margaret used to worry about her friend driving on the treacherous roads but since cell phones came along, she didn't worry as much. If Gloria ended up in the ditch, she could call Gus, a Belhaven local, who owned a towing and automotive shop. Still, a truck would come in handy.

"You'll probably need it once you and Paul marry, what with moving furniture back and forth."

Gloria scratched her chin thoughtfully. *Would they* be moving furniture back and forth? So many details hadn't been settled yet.

Just take one day at a time, Gloria.

Back at the farm, Gloria rummaged around in the fridge for some lunchmeat and cheddar cheese. She grabbed two slices of bread from the package and stuck the rest in the refrigerator so it wouldn't go bad. Perhaps after Paul and she married, she would do a better job of stocking groceries. For the past several years, her diet consisted of sandwiches and frozen dinners. It made no sense to cook a big meal for just one person.

She placed the sandwich on a plate along with a small bag of chips and headed to the living room for the noon news.

Now that the weather was starting to change, she liked to keep an eye on the forecast.

The weather looked clear and the news uneventful. Gloria finished her sandwich and carried the plate back to the kitchen. She was restless. She was always restless when it was detective day and today was an important one. Gloria's sanity was at stake.

She wondered if Ruth had finished mapping out the location of the spy equipment.

Gloria opened the dishwasher and placed the dirty plate on the bottom rack. She closed the door and turned to Mally. "Let's head to the barn."

It had been weeks since Gloria had been in her barn, not since her grandsons had come over for the weekend to work on their tree fort. Gloria turned her gaze to the front yard. She smiled at the color the boys had decided to paint the outside of the fort – florescent green.

Tyler and Ryan had come by the week before to finish the tree fort project. It was during that visit they decided to paint the exterior. She tried to talk them out of the bright green, but finally gave up. The three of them had gone to Nails and Knobs, the local hardware store, to purchase the paint the boys couldn't live without.

The bright color would fade through the long winter and by spring would turn into a nice shade of green that would blend in with the leaves on the tree.

Mally raced Gloria to the barn and stood outside the door, waiting for her to unlock the padlock and push the heavy door aside.

Gloria pulled it to the side, just enough to peek through the crack. Ever since the time she had discovered someone hiding out in her barn, she was leery to go in when she was at the farm all by herself.

The coast was clear and she tugged the door the rest of the way open. Mally went in first and began sniffing around. She trotted off to the milking parlor while Gloria stood in the doorway and surveyed the contents.

There was plenty of room inside. She'd had a garage sale not long ago and sold a bunch of stuff she no longer needed and that the kids didn't seem interested in inheriting.

She looked up at the old Massey Ferguson tractor and grinned as she remembered teaching Tyler and Ryan how to drive it.

Mally had finished her inspection and plopped down next to Gloria's feet. Mally had never been inside the tractor, let alone ridden in it.

Gloria bent down and patted her head, still staring at the bulky machinery. "You want to go for a spin?"

Mally wagged her tail.

The decision made, Gloria headed back to the house. She grabbed the tractor keys and her jacket, and Mally and she went back into the barn.

Gloria looked from Mally to the tractor. Her pooch had to weigh nearly fifty pounds. How on earth was she going to carry her dog up the steep steps to the cab of the tractor?

"Wait here." She climbed up the side and opened the door before she made her way back to the barn floor.

"This ought to be fun," she muttered. "Here goes nothing."

Gloria shoved the keys in her front pocket and lifted Mally. At first Mally wouldn't stop wiggling, which made it difficult for Gloria to hang onto her. "Settle down or no ride," she warned.

Mally immediately stopped moving and Gloria shifted her thick frame so that Mally's paws hung over her shoulder and Gloria had a firm grip on her backside.

Slowly, she made her way up the side steps. When she got to the top, she stopped. "Okay. Climb in."

Mally twisted at an angle then half hopped, half jumped into the cab, which sent Gloria reeling backward from the force of Mally's leap.

If not for the ironclad hold she had on the side handle, Gloria would have fallen off the tractor and tumbled backwards onto the concrete floor.

She nudged Mally to the side so they could share the seat and then pulled the door shut. "You better enjoy the ride because I don't think I can do this again," she warned, "not without breaking a few bones."

Gloria inserted the key in the ignition and turned it. The tractor fired on the first try.

She eased her foot off the clutch and pressed the gas. The tractor lurched forward and bumped off the curb.

They coasted around the drive a couple times. Mally seemed to have so much fun that Gloria decided to take the tractor for a spin out back.

She eased the clunky piece of farm equipment through the center of the empty fields, all the way to the edge of the property line.

They were on their final turn when something caught Gloria's eye. "Look, Mally. Deer."

At the edge of the fence line, nibbling on withered stalks of corn were several deer, including a doe. Deer were a common sight around the farm and sometimes a nuisance when they went after Gloria's garden.

She kept deer repellant on hand and regularly sprayed the perimeter of the garden to keep them out. It worked like a charm and Gloria rarely had a problem with them eating her fruits and vegetables. It also kept the wild rabbits out, another pesky critter that loved the goodies in Gloria's garden.

The deer were brave to be out right now. Bow season had just ended and gun season would start up in a couple weeks.

Mally leaned across the armrest, pressed her nose to the window and kept a close eye on the animals until they were out of sight.

Gloria backed the tractor into the barn, shut off the engine and opened the door. Getting Mally out of the tractor was going to be as tricky as getting her in.

Her eyes scanned the interior of the barn and stopped when she found something that might work to get Mally out without Gloria having to carry her.

Several years ago when they had chickens and a chicken coop, James had built an old ramp. "Wait here."

Gloria scrambled out of the tractor. She dragged the ramp over to the tractor, leaned one end of the ramp against the door and placed the other end on the cement floor. "Can you come down?"

Mally looked at the ramp, placed one paw on the ramp and then pulled it back.

Gloria lifted her end of ramp until it was level with the other end, which rested on the floor of the cab. "C'mon girl," she coaxed.

Mally put one paw, then another on the ramp as she tentatively crept along the wooden walkway. The closer she got to Gloria, the lower Gloria moved the ramp. By the time

Mally got to the end, it was resting on the cement floor. They had done it.

"Good girl."

"Ruff." Mally licked her hand and pranced around.

Gloria crawled back inside the tractor, pulled the keys from the ignition and closed the door. She waited until Mally was out of the barn before securing the barn door and snapping the padlock in place.

Gloria was halfway to the house when something across the street caught her attention. There were cars in the drive and she could see someone standing next to one of the vehicles. "Shall we go meet the new neighbors?"

She didn't wait for a reply and the two of them headed across the road.

Chapter 18

Parked in the drive was a new sedan. Standing next to the car was a young couple. They turned as Gloria approached. "Hello, I'm Gloria Rutherford. I live across the street."

The woman smiled, her long dark hair falling forward, covering a bright blue eye. She shifted the baby she was holding in her arms. "Hello. I'm Melody Fowler and this is my husband, Chris."

Gloria smiled at them as she patted Mally's head. "This is Mally."

The woman reached her hand forward so Mally could sniff. Mally licked her palm...the Mally seal of approval.

The man stuck his hand out and Mally did the same. "Hello Mally. What a beautiful dog."

Gloria knew her dog was a good judge of character so if Mally liked them, she was sure she would. "Are you moving in?"

The man, Chris, shook his head. "Not yet. We're doing some renovations first."

Gloria glanced at the house. "This farm once belonged to my husband's family. He sold it to one of the local farmers years ago, but I don't believe anyone ever moved into the house."

"It needs updating," the young woman admitted.

They exchanged a few pleasantries and Gloria turned to go. "I better get going. I'm sure you have work to do. Let me know if I can help," she called out as she wandered back across the street.

It would be nice to have neighbors again. They seemed like a friendly couple and the baby was cuter than a button.

She had wondered what kind of renovations they planned but didn't want to seem nosy. It had been years since Gloria had been inside the house.

She couldn't date the house but knew it was at least a hundred years old and a lot of the house was original: the plumbing, electrical, mechanicals, not to mention old wallpaper, paneling and carpet.

Now that she thought about it, it could probably use a major overhaul. She hoped they got a good deal.

The rest of the afternoon crawled by. When 4:30 rolled around, Gloria changed into dark slacks and a navy blue sweater – the perfect attire for an undercover operation. Although this wasn't an undercover operation, it was a habit to wear dark clothes. Sleuthing and dark clothing just seemed to go together.

Gloria steered Annabelle to the back of the post office parking lot and pulled in next to Ruth's car to wait.

At 5:01, Ruth exited the rear of the post office carrying a large cardboard box. She opened the rear passenger door and slid the box onto the seat before she climbed into the passenger side. She pulled the seatbelt across her lap and fastened the buckle. "I'm nervous as a tic."

Gloria grinned and started the car. "If you're nervous now, just wait."

On the drive to Rapid Creek, Ruth outlined her strategy. She patted her pocket. "I have the drawing with me...just in case. I was able to do a little research online and found a rough blueprint for this house. It was built by a local company."

Gloria snorted. "You're kidding."

"No." Ruth's expression grew serious. "Mechanicals are very important when installing surveillance equipment."

Gloria hadn't considered that. "Will you need electricity?" She couldn't remember if the power had been shut off.

Ruth shook her head. "Nope. The surveillance equipment runs on electricity and has a battery backup but it will only last a day or so."

Gloria turned Annabelle onto the main road and pressed down on the gas pedal. "We're going to pick the equipment up tomorrow so that shouldn't be a problem."

Gloria had already given some thought as to how they should enter the house. They could pull in the driveway but if the neighbors spotted them...

She was torn. On one hand, she could come up with an excuse for being there. On the other, she didn't want the suspect - or suspects - to see them enter the house, carrying a large box. She erred on the side of caution and decided to park one street over, directly behind the property.

They pulled onto the side street and climbed out of the car. Ruth reached into the back of the car and pulled out her box of surveillance equipment.

Gloria frowned. She wished she had thought to bring a backpack or something that was less conspicuous. Lucy would have definitely thought of that.

It was too late now. "This way." She waved Ruth to follow as they walked between two houses and made their way to the back yard.

A rickety fence ran along both sides of the property but the back perimeter was wide open. They stepped into the backyard and something squished under Gloria's sneaker. She lifted her foot to inspect the bottom of her shoe. Whatever it was, was dark brown and mushy.

"I think I just stepped on a landmine," she groaned.

Ruth leaned forward for a closer look. "Yep. That is definitely dog doo."

She began to gag when she got a good whiff of the brown squishy stuff on Gloria's shoe. "Oh no." Ruth covered her mouth and turned away, all the while still making the gagging noises.

"Shush. You're going to blow our cover," Gloria whispered fiercely as she scraped her foot along the grass to remove as much of the poo as possible.

Ruth sucked in a breath of fresh air. "I'm sorry. I've always had an overactive gag reflex."

"Don't ever get a pet," Gloria warned.

"Let's get this over with." She motioned Ruth along and the women tiptoed through the rest of the yard as they made their way to the rear slider.

Gloria tugged on the handle. The door was locked.

She remembered that the basement door had been unlocked last time she was there. Then she remembered that Jill and she had locked it before they left.

Still, it was worth a try. "Wait here," she told Ruth.

She wandered to the side window and stuck her finger on the ledge. It didn't budge.

Gloria's heart sank. That meant she would have to go to the front of the house and enter through the front door.

Gloria closed her eyes and whispered a quick prayer that she would make it inside undetected.

She walked around the side of the house and picked up the pace as she headed to the front porch. She twisted the knob on the combination lock and then yanked on the base.

The key dropped into her hand. She inserted the key, opened the door and stepped inside. Safely inside, she peeked out the front window. No one was in sight.

Ruth peered at Gloria through the rear slider. She waited while her friend scooted across the dining room floor, flipped the lever lock and slid the door open.

Ruth stepped inside and looked around. "Just as I envisioned." She set the box on the kitchen counter and began pulling equipment from the box and placing it on the counter.

"What can I do to help?" Gloria reached for the box. The sooner they could get the spy gear set up, the sooner they could get out of there.

Ruth shook her head. "Nothing. It would take too long to explain."

Gloria pulled her hand back. "Okay. No problem."

While Ruth worked on the installation, Gloria headed to the front door and replaced the key in the container then put the lockbox back on the door. She closed the front door and tugged on the handle to make sure it had locked.

She stood off to one side and watched Ruth work, impressed by her speed and efficiency. Ruth had it down to a science.

Ruth had almost finished her installation when Gloria had a thought. Perhaps she should unlock the basement window again to give the would-be perpetrator a way to get in.

"Almost done," Ruth announced.

"I'll be right back." Gloria hustled down the basement steps and to the bedroom in the back. She unlatched the window and headed back up the stairs.

Ruth was waiting at the top, the empty box tucked under her arm. "Mission accomplished."

Gloria didn't want to leave using the front door, not with Ruth holding a large brown box. She opened the rear slider. "Wait for me out here."

Ruth stepped onto the back deck.

Gloria pulled the door shut and locked the door behind her. If her goal was to avoid detection, there was only one way out.

Gloria headed back down the basement steps to the window she had just unlocked. She lifted the window and grimaced. "Here goes nothing."

She hoisted herself up onto the window frame, her legs dangling in the air behind her as she desperately tried to pull her body through the opening.

A rustling on the other side of the fence caught her attention.

Gloria tipped her head to peer through a small gap between two of the boards. Her eyes widened in horror. There, on the other side of the fence was a large black eye and sharp canine teeth.

Chapter 19

Gloria put a finger to her lips. "Shhh, puppy. I'm almost out of here," her raspy voice giving way to her fear. Trying to soothe the dog seemed to have the opposite effect and make him even more agitated. The mutt began to bark his fool head off.

"Woof! Woof-Woof!"

Gloria dragged one knee onto the frame and pulled herself across the metal barrier.

The dog, focused on Gloria's every move, began to ram his head against the wooden panel as he tried to get to Gloria.

"What in the world are you doing?"

Shiny black shoes stepped into Gloria's range of vision. Her eyes traveled from the shoes and up the pant legs to the top of a uniform...a police uniform. A very *familiar* police uniform.

Paul knelt on the ground. He blew a puff of air through thinned lips. "I would offer to help but it looks like you have it all under control."

Paul stood upright, grabbed his radio and unclipped it from his belt. "Yes, this is Officer Kennedy. Disregard the 10-14."

He clipped the radio to his belt and grimaced as his fiancé rose to her feet and brushed the dirt from her dark slacks. "A neighbor reported a suspicious person prowling around the house."

The dog, still on the other side of the fence, began to growl. Paul glanced across the fence. "Let's move to the back so the dog will stop barking."

Gloria nodded. She lowered the window frame and followed him to the back yard where Ruth was waiting on the rear deck.

"This just keeps getting better and better," Paul muttered under his breath.

He tipped his hat to Ruth. "Hello Ruth."

Ruth shifted the box in her hands. "Hello Paul. Nice to see you."

Gloria gave her a hard stare.

Ruth swallowed hard and lowered her gaze. "Or maybe not."

He turned his attention to Gloria. "Do you want to explain to me why you were sneaking out of this house and why Ruth is carrying an empty box, looking guiltier than a fox in a hen house?"

"Well..."

Paul lifted a hand. "Let me guess." He waved his hand toward the house. "This is the house that Jill intends to buy."

Gloria nodded. It was best not to say too much. She knew he had caught her red-handed but hoped he wouldn't force them remove the spy equipment...

He pointed to the box Ruth was holding. "I don't even want to know what that is for."

Gloria let out a sigh of relief. "It's probably best."

He jerked his head to the house next door, the one with the barking dog. "The neighbor next door appears to be keeping an eye on this place," he warned.

"Thanks for the tip," Ruth piped up.

Gloria gave her a warning look. She turned to Paul. "We'll be on our way now."

Paul followed the women through the backyard and over to Gloria's car. He waited for Gloria to slide into the driver's seat and roll down the window. "Please don't make me come back here again," he said.

Gloria nodded. She couldn't promise him anything. After all, they had to come back tomorrow to retrieve Ruth's equipment. "We'll do our best." She smiled brightly.

Paul rolled his eyes. "That's what I was afraid you would say."

The girls pulled out of the neighborhood and Gloria followed Paul's police car out onto the main road. "That went off fairly well," Ruth observed.

Despite the minor snag of running into Paul, Gloria had to agree. "Yes. As well as can be expected."

On her way out of the neighborhood, they passed a familiar car. Gloria glanced in her rearview mirror. "That car looks just like the one Sue Camp, Jill's real estate agent, drives."

The car turned onto Pine Place and disappeared from sight.

Annabelle drifted toward the center of the road. "Watch where you're going," Ruth yelled.

Gloria yanked the car back into her lane. "Sorry about that."

On the drive back to Belhaven, Ruth explained that the equipment was motion activated so she wouldn't have to watch the screen constantly, like she had done when she set up the surveillance equipment at Gloria's house a few months back. "It gives off a warning beep to let me know the camera picked up movement."

Gloria frowned. "You leave it on all the time – day and night?"

Ruth set her purse on the floor. "Yeah. I'm used to it, though. I leave it on at the post office all night."

"Doesn't it have a recorder? What if it goes off while you're sleeping?"

"I like to catch the action live. It's loud enough to wake me." Ruth shrugged. "I just get up and check the monitor then go back to bed."

Gloria glanced at her friend out of the corner of her eye. She knew Ruth was obsessed with her surveillance equipment but this was taking it to the extreme.

Gloria pulled her car next to Ruth's van and waited while her friend pulled the empty box from the backseat. "A backpack might work better. You know, so it's not quite so obvious," Gloria hinted.

Ruth nodded. "Yeah, you're right. I never thought of that..."

Ruth closed the back door and leaned her head in the front window. "I'll text you if I catch anything on the camera."

She pulled the van door open, tossed the box in the passenger seat and climbed in the driver's seat. She gave Gloria a small wave and backed out of her parking spot.

Gloria waited until the van had turned onto Main Street before she pulled out onto the road and headed home, all the while praying that they would finally get a break in the case.

Chapter 20

Gloria waited for Paul's evening phone call with a hint of dread. She wondered if he would mention the incident from earlier and was relieved when he didn't. The only thing he said was he hoped for her sake that Jill got the house.

She kept her cell phone close by in the hopes that Ruth's surveillance equipment would do the trick and they would catch someone breaking into the house.

She stayed up until after the 11:00 news. Ruth never called. Gloria finally gave up and fell asleep in the recliner. The cuckoo clock chimed midnight and Gloria woke.

Mally was sprawled across Gloria's lap. She opened one eye and stared a Gloria.

Gloria shifted her legs. "C'mon, girl. It's time for bed."

Mally eased out of the recliner, straightened her paws out in front of her and stretched her long limbs.

By the time Gloria brushed her teeth and washed her face, Puddles had already curled up in her favorite spot on the pillow and Mally was asleep at the end of the bed.

Gloria sandwiched herself between her two pets and promptly drifted off to sleep.

***

Chirp...chirp...chirp.

Bright sunlight streamed through the bedroom window. Gloria had forgotten to close the curtains before she crawled into bed. She groggily glanced at the clock on the nightstand. It was 6:30 a.m.

Chirp.

Gloria flung the covers aside when she realized it was her cell phone. She made her way to the dresser and picked up the phone. There were several text messages. Gloria carried the phone to the kitchen, slipped on her reading glasses and stared at the screen.

All of the messages were from Ruth. The first one read: "I just saw something." The time stamp was 2:48 a.m.

She scrolled to the second message. "You are not gonna believe what just happened." That message arrived at 3:12 a.m.

Ruth sent the third and final message at 3:22 a.m. "Stop by the post office ASAP in the morning."

The post office opened at 8:00 a.m., although she knew that Ruth was at work earlier than 8:00 a.m. Kenny Webber, the rural route carrier, and she arrived early to sort mail and get ready for the day.

She threw on the first thing she found in her closet, grabbed her keys and headed out the door. It was mornings like that she wished the small town had a fast food restaurant with a drive-thru or even a coffee shop.

It was 7:22 a.m. according to Gloria's dashboard when she pulled in the post office parking lot. Dot's place was already busy with early morning diners. Many of the local farmers showed up as soon as she unlocked the doors, having already milked the cows and tended to their livestock.

She wandered around the back and tapped on the employee entrance. Kenny opened the door a crack. He smiled when he saw Gloria. "Ruth said you were stopping by." He swung the door open and Gloria stepped inside.

Ruth, her back to Gloria, shoved an envelope into one of the mailboxes and then set the rest of the stack on the sorting table. She waved Gloria to the small desk in the back. "Wait 'til you see this."

Gloria gave Kenny a quick glance.

"Kenny knows all about the surveillance. He noticed my equipment was missing this morning."

Gloria grinned. Kenny was a good guy and Ruth's right hand man. She was sure that Kenny had many stories he could tell about the goings on inside that little post office. He probably knew more about Gloria than she knew about herself.

She stepped over to the computer screen and slipped on her reading glasses. The screen was dark. Gloria watched closely, waiting for something to happen. *Was she missing something?* "What am I looking at?"

"Just wait," Ruth replied.

Seconds later, a small light beamed onto the screen. Gloria could tell from the angle that it was coming up the basement steps. The beam flashed around the room like a light show on steroids before it settled on the kitchen.

The intruder set the flashlight on the counter so that the light illuminated the ceiling. There were several long moments of silence followed by several loud whacks.

"What in the world..."

It was hard to see through the dark grainy computer screen, but the sound was loud and clear. After what seemed like an eternity, the whacking stopped.

The person picked up the flashlight and turned the light to the kitchen cabinets. Gloria realized with horror what the whacking noise was. The intruder had smashed some of the fronts on the lower kitchen cabinets while others appeared to be completely missing. Splintered chunks of wood scattered the floor. "Oh no."

Her heart plummeted. What would possess someone to destroy a home like that?

"Can we watch it again?" she asked.

Ruth glanced at the clock. It was 7:50 a.m. "Yeah, I have a few minutes before I have to unlock the front doors."

She fiddled with the mouse and set the surveillance video back to the beginning. Gloria leaned forward, searching for a

384

clue...anything that might help them figure out who this person might be.

She couldn't come up with anything. She waited until the flashlight and dark figure disappeared down the stairs before she turned to Ruth. "Was that it?"

Ruth nodded. "Yep."

Gloria stood upright and gazed out the front window. "We have two problems now," she said.

Ruth lowered the laptop cover. "What's that?"

Gloria lifted a finger. "One, we don't know who that was." She lifted a second finger. "Two, as far as anyone knows, we were the last two people inside that house."

There was the possibility they could be charged with destruction of property, theft, breaking and entering, unlawful use of surveillance equipment...although she wasn't certain of that.

Ruth shook her head. "No. We are down to just one problem. There was a big clue and I'm surprised that you missed it."

Chapter 21

Gloria frowned. "What clue?"

Ruth let out a dramatic sigh and lifted the top of the computer. "Gloria, Gloria, Gloria, are you losing your touch?" she teased.

"I'll cover the front," Kenny offered.

Ruth acknowledged him briefly. "Thanks, Kenny."

She turned back to the screen and started the video from the beginning.

The light bounced up the stairs and started across the room.

"Close your eyes and just listen," Ruth urged.

Gloria closed her eyes and focused on the sounds. This time, she heard it: a faint scraping sound, as if the person was dragging something across the tile floor. "Yeah, I hear it."

Ruth crossed her arms. "Whoever was in that house either dragged the sledgehammer OR what I think, is that they walked with a limp."

"Hmm." It was a stretch.

Ruth fast-forwarded to the end. "You can hear it again."

Sure enough, toward the end of the video, they heard the distinct sound of something dragging.

It was a good clue, but how in the world could they figure out who it was? It could be anyone. For all they knew, the person could have driven their car from the other side of the state and snuck in, just like Gloria and Ruth had done.

The fact that the intruder had destroyed the kitchen cabinets and stolen the rest was scary. Leaving a dead animal or two was bad enough...

Ding. A customer had walked into the post office. "Be right back."

Ruth headed to the counter to help the customer while Gloria stared out the window. All she could visualize was Jill, Greg, Ryan, Tyler, Eddie, Karen, Ben, Kelly, Oliver and Ariel, along with Gloria and Paul all trying to cram into her house.

Ruth returned. "I think it's one of the neighbors."

She had Gloria's undivided attention and pressed on. "Think about it. Who else could it be? I doubt it's the homeowners, especially now that whoever it was destroyed the kitchen cabinets. It's one thing to try to drive away buyers so you can keep collecting the deposit, but it's a completely different story when they start destroying stuff. I mean, those homeowners will have to pay to have the cabinets repaired and the missing ones replaced."

True. Ruth had a valid point. It would be completely counterproductive. On top of that, Gloria had seen the house the Acostas lived in. If they were collecting deposits for cash flow, they weren't using the money to improve their current living conditions.

"Plus, whoever it is knows the comings and goings of that place, which would point right to a neighbor, someone who can watch the place."

Gloria thought about the neighbors she had met. On one side, the people had seemed quite friendly and informative. Gloria didn't get the impression that they had hard feelings toward the Acostas. In fact, it seemed quite the opposite.

There was the nice woman on one side, although she had been the one who had called the police on Ruth and her.

Then there was the older couple across the street, the ones who had pets of their own.

Last, but not least, there were the noisy neighbors on the other side. The ones with the big dogs and the flimsy fence that separated their property from the one Jill and Greg intended to buy. She had never met the people who lived in that house, only the boy who had come to the door.

"So we're looking for someone with a limp. What do you suggest that we do? Go door-to-door asking the neighbors if they walk with a limp?"

Ruth shook her head. "Nope. I've been giving this some thought." She held out her hand. "Be right back."

Gloria watched her disappear in the back room. Kenny watched her go. "Wait 'til you see this," he said.

Gloria could hardly wait.

Ruth returned with a large, shiny, plastic copter. "This is a DR650, able to fly up to 250 feet. It has a 720 x 240 resolution that can take 3MP photos and video tape for a full five minutes."

Gloria stared at the contraption in confusion.

Kenny touched one of the propellers with his index finger and gave it a spin. "It's a drone."

"A drone?" Gloria had seen drones on the local news in recent weeks. They were a nuisance for airplanes at the Grand Rapids Airport. Pilots had reported several near misses with drones when they accidentally wandered into the planes' flight paths.

From what little she knew, Gloria considered them a dangerous toy. She could tell from the look on Ruth's face that Ruth did not consider her drone to be a toy.

Ruth carefully placed the drone on the counter. "We can use this to film aerial footage of the neighbors. They won't even know it's there."

Gloria stared at the drone. An idea began to form in her head. "So we come up with some kind of lure to draw the neighbors out of their houses. The drone is overhead, capturing their movements on camera. Whoever shows up on video with a visible limp..."

Ruth snapped her fingers. "Voila. We have our man. Or woman." she added.

The bell chimed again. Gloria waited while Ruth took care of the customers. She nodded to Judith Arnett, who was one of them.

When Sally Keane walked in, Gloria glared at her then turned her back. She was the last person Gloria wanted to see.

Sally made a quick exit after checking her mailbox.

Kenny had finished sorting his mail, organizing it in the large plastic bins and then loading the bins into his mail truck. He came back to grab his keys.

Gloria stepped to the side, out of view of the lobby.

Kenny walked over and whispered in Gloria's ear. "I've got a few 4th of July fireworks left over if you want to use them." He winked and then turned on his heel, whistling a catchy tune as he exited the post office and climbed into the mail truck.

Ruth caught the tail end of the conversation. "We might want to take him up on that."

Gloria slowly nodded. They would need something to draw the suspects out into the open. She turned to Ruth. "Can you forward a copy of that videotape to me?"

"Of course." Ruth settled into the desk chair. She clicked a few buttons and turned to Gloria. "Done. I emailed a copy to you."

"Thanks." Gloria reached for the door handle. "When do you want to pick up the spy equipment?"

She remembered Jill telling her that she had scheduled an inspection of the house for the following day. "Maybe we can run by there before Jill's inspection. How long do you think it will take?"

Ruth stared at the ceiling. "I'm guessing no more than 20 minutes. Tops."

Gloria stared at the back door thoughtfully. They could pick up the spy equipment and implement their plan to flush out the perpetrator at the same time.

She opened the door. "Yeah. We can do it tomorrow morning." That would be perfect. "Ask Kenny to drop off the fireworks, just in case."

Ruth nodded. "Got it covered. Want to swing by my house say around 10?"

Gloria pulled her keys from her purse. "Yeah, that'll work. I'll see you in the morning."

Gloria climbed into her car and started the engine. Her next stop was Montbay County Sheriff's office to visit Paul.

Gloria settled into the chair across from her betrothed. He leaned his elbows on the desk and clasped his hands in front of him. Gloria wasn't one to drop by for a casual social visit, not while he was at work. He was certain the reason she was there had something to do with Jill and the house.

Paul got right to the point. "Something happened," he stated bluntly.

Gloria rubbed the palms of her hands on the front of her slacks. "Yeah. The box that Ruth had yesterday... You got a minute for me to show you something on the computer?"

Paul nodded. "Sure."

Gloria inched her way around the desk and leaned over Paul's keyboard. "Do you mind if I log into my email account?"

"Be my guest."

Gloria opened her email and scrolled through the messages until she got to the one Ruth had sent her. She opened the message and clicked on the attachment. "Watch this."

Gloria pressed the "play" button and stepped back.

Paul leaned forward. He watched the video in silence and then pressed the stop button. "This is what you and Ruth were doing yesterday? Installing surveillance equipment?"

Gloria cringed inwardly and nodded. "Did you notice anything about the person?"

Paul played the video again. "Whoever it was walked with a limp."

"Right. Do you think you can question the neighbors?" Gloria would love to hand it over to Paul. It wasn't that she didn't want to be involved, but the fact that they had been inside the house right before it had been broken into and vandalized would make Ruth and her prime suspects.

Paul forwarded the video to his own email then clicked out of hers. He shook his head. "Unfortunately, our hands are tied, unless, of course, the homeowners file a report."

She frowned. Maybe they would. Maybe they wouldn't, although if they were to file an insurance claim, they would have to file a police report. She wasn't sure how long that would take. It could take weeks. Gloria didn't have weeks - she had hours.

Her shoulders drooped. "It was worth a try."

Paul knew Gloria was not going to let this go. "What are you going to do now?"

"We think it's a neighbor." She shrugged. "We only have one choice...flush the perpetrator out."

"How do you propose to do that?" He paused. "Never mind. I don't think I want to know."

Paul got out of his chair and followed Gloria down the hall and out to the main lobby. "Please be careful. When do you plan to 'flush them out?'" If he knew "when," at least he could be on the alert in case she needed help.

"Tomorrow morning, right after we pick up the surveillance equipment."

Paul gave Gloria a quick kiss and held the door. He shook his head and slowly closed the door behind her. She sure did know how to keep him on his toes.

Chapter 22

Gloria made a pit stop at Lucy's on her way home. Lucy, the closest to an explosives expert that Gloria could come up with, might have an idea on how to attract attention without blowing – say – a hand or other body part - off in the process.

She parked Annabelle behind Lucy's jeep and started down the sidewalk.

Brrrup!

Gloria stopped in her tracks.

Brrrup!

That noise. It was coming from the direction of the shed.

She could see that the shed door was open.

Brrrup!

It had to be Lucy.

Gloria wandered around the corner and spotted her friend, bent over her workbench. Lucy was wearing a metal welding mask. Gloria burst out laughing at the sight of the mask. Protruding out of both sides of the mask were two deer antlers – one on each side.

Lucy dropped the welding gun and jumped back. "You scared the crap out of me."

She lifted the mask and clutched her chest. "I almost had a heart attack."

Gloria patted her arm. "I'm sorry, Lucy," she apologized. She pointed at the antlers. "Don't tell me those are from a deer that you shot."

Lucy ran her hand along one of the antlers. "Yep," she said proudly. "A four point buck."

"Are you going hunting this year?"

Gun season ran from mid-November until the end of November. Last year, Lucy had gone hunting with her ex-boyfriend, Bill. They had broken up not long ago, right after Lucy told him she didn't want to go bow hunting, but instead wanted to hang out with the girls.

Bill had never been one of Gloria's favorite people and she always thought that Lucy always went along with whatever Bill wanted but he would never do anything that she wanted to do. It was a one-sided relationship, not that she had ever admitted that to her friend.

Lucy wrinkled her nose. "I'm not sure. I don't want to go alone and Max doesn't sound too enthused about it."

Her eyes sparked. "Hey. Why don't you go with me?"

Gloria shook her head. "Oh no. I don't…"

Lucy clasped her hands together. "Please," she begged. "You need more shooting practice and I need someone to go with me. It'll be fun."

Gloria sucked in a deep breath. Lucy had always been a good sport about helping Gloria out with her investigations and had asked for little in return. In fact, this was the first time Gloria could remember her ever asking for a favor…

"Well, maybe," she conceded.

Lucy bounced on her toes. "Oh, thank you, Gloria. It's going to be so much fun," she gushed.

Gloria slowly shook her head, certain she would rue the day this day. Deep down, Gloria knew she would go if it meant that much to her friend.

She pointed at pieces of metal sitting on top of the workbench. "Whatcha building?"

Lucy lifted two bars she had just welded together. "Wait 'til you see what I'm making."

She stepped over to the wall and dragged two pieces of barn wood to the center of the floor. "It's going to be a small table. I'm going to put it out on the porch. Since this is my first welding project, I thought I'd start small," Lucy explained.

Gloria wrinkled her nose. A table didn't sound small. Wall art or jewelry holder - that was small.

"When I'm done with this, I want to build a fire pit out of old tire rims. I found a picture of one on the internet and I've already got the rims."

"Sounds cool, Lucy. I can't wait to see it," Gloria said.

"Yeah, I kinda need a hobby. I was thinking I could start making some stuff and selling it at the flea market during the summer months."

"Do you need some money?" Gloria had never heard her friend mention money being tight and Gloria had never asked.

"Nah." Lucy shrugged. "I need something to keep me busy during the winter." She pointed to a cast iron wood stove in the corner. "I can come out here and work when it's nasty outside."

Jasper tromped into the garage, his paws covered in a thick coat of fresh mud.

Lucy stuck her hand on her hip. "Jasper. What did you get into this time?"

Jasper hung his head and looked up at Lucy guiltily.

Gloria reached over and patted his head. "There's so much fun stuff to get into living out here in the country, huh?"

She looked up at Lucy. "Don't worry. The newness will wear off and he'll settle down. Just tell him no and soon he'll understand what he can and can't get into. Labs are smart dogs."

Jasper slumped into a heap at Lucy's feet and let out a sigh. "He sure does wear himself out."

She changed the subject. "So what brings you by?"

The women stepped out of the garage. Lucy shut off the lights and closed the door, locking it behind her. Jasper led the way as the three of them headed to the house.

Inside the kitchen, Lucy pulled a plate from the microwave and set it on the table. "Monster cookie? I made them this morning."

Gloria plucked a candy-coated cookie from the plate and took a bite. "I love cookies with nuts. These are delicious. What's in them?"

Lucy pulled a large cookie from the plate and nibbled the edge. "My grandmother's secret recipe," she said.

Gloria wasn't nearly as fond of sweets as Lucy, but these were delicious. She reached for another one.

Lucy grinned. "Wow. You must like them."

"Either that or I'm starving." She eyed the cookie before breaking a chunk off and popping it into her mouth.

Lucy reached for another cookie. "So what's going on?"

Lucy listened while Gloria explained everything that had happened. She started with the surveillance equipment Ruth had installed yesterday and ended with her visit to the police station and how there was nothing Paul could do until the homeowner filed a report.

"So you're going to take matters into your own hands to try and flush out the perpetrator," Lucy surmised.

"Exactly and since you're an explosives expert, I thought I would get your professional opinion," Gloria said.

Lucy drummed her fingers on the tabletop thoughtfully. "The plan is to have the drone circle over the top of the neighbors' houses and then set off some kind of bait to lure them out."

She gazed out the window. "The only problem is, once you ignite one set of explosives, how are you going to sneak into the neighbor's yard across the street and do the same thing? I mean, it will be loud and everyone is going to hear it."

Gloria rubbed her temple. True. She hadn't thought of that. Maybe they could set the explosive off in the middle of the street and all of the neighbors would come running out to see what was going on.

"What about putting a trash can in the middle of the street and blowing it up?" Gloria was thinking aloud.

"Nope. Someone might see you and then you risk getting arrested."

The dilemma had Lucy and Gloria stumped. Gloria needed a plan and she needed it by morning. "Maybe I'll go home and sleep on it," she said.

Lucy and Jasper walked Gloria to her car. "If I come up with an idea, I'll let you know," Lucy promised as she waited for Gloria to climb in the car.

Lucy brightened. "You want me to go with you?"

Gloria started the car and rolled the window down before she shut the door. Lucy looked so excited; Gloria didn't have the heart to tell her no. "Sure. The more the merrier."

"I'll pick you up around ten," she added.

"Great." Lucy gave a small wave and then headed back inside.

Gloria pulled out of the drive and onto the road. *Please, God. Help us come up with some sort of idea on how to flush out the culprit.*

She turned into her drive and pulled into the garage. Maybe if she watched a couple episodes of *Detective on the Side,* she might come up with an idea or two.

Chapter 23

Gloria finally came up with a plan but she didn't get it from her favorite detective show. She got her brilliant idea while she was on the back porch waiting for Mally to fetch the newspaper from the drive. It was when a school bus drove by the house.

Gloria took the paper from Mally and exchanged it for a doggie treat.

When they got indoors, she promptly called the local high school to ask what time the bus dropped students off at the Highland Park subdivision. After she had that information, she called the girls to change the pick-up time to 2:45 p.m. They would arrive at Highland Park just in time for the bus to drop the neighborhood students off.

Ruth's work schedule ended at five but Kenny said he could make it back in time to cover for her.

Ruth was the designated driver, and the women arrived at the neighborhood a little ahead of schedule. She pulled her van to the end of the street and parked near the entrance.

The women waited patiently for the familiar bright yellow and black striped bus.

When it rounded the corner and stopped at the end of the cul-de-sac, Gloria unhooked her seatbelt and reached for the door handle. "Wait here." She didn't want to raise suspicion by having them all get out and on top of that, she wasn't even certain who she was looking for.

She stepped around the front of the van and waited on the sidewalk as high schoolers exited the bus and began to wander down the sidewalk.

A young blonde wearing ear buds and staring at the ground stepped off. Gloria studied her briefly and scratched her from the list. *She wasn't at all observant.*

Next were a boy and girl, who started to quarrel as soon as they hit the pavement. *Brother and sister, plus I don't have enough cash.* Scratch #2.

A teenager darted off the bus and ran full speed ahead down the sidewalk, racing past all of the other teenagers. *He's too fast. I'll never catch him.*

Finally, Gloria saw him: the one. A towhead moseyed off the bus, in no particular hurry. He moseyed down the sidewalk with a skateboard in hand. He set the skateboard on the sidewalk and hopped on.

Gloria hurried over. "Excuse me." The young man, whose hair was too long for Gloria's taste, turned dark green eyes on her. "Huh?"

Gloria pointed down the street. "You live here?"

"Uh-huh."

"Do you know most of the people who live on this street?" Maybe he was one of those nice young men that mowed lawns for extra cash in the summer...

He eyed her suspiciously. "What's it to you? You some kind of undercover cop?"

"No, I'm not, but I need your help." She fished inside her purse and pulled out a five-dollar bill. "I'm looking for someone – possibly a male – that lives in the neighborhood and walks with a limp."

The boy stared at the money.

"Here, take it," she urged.

The boy grabbed the five and shoved it in his back pocket. "Maybe." He eyed her open purse, waiting for more.

Gloria sucked in a deep breath and pulled out another five.

The teenage boy reached for it.

Gloria pulled it back, just as his fingers touched the edge. "Is there or isn't there?"

He eyed her thoughtfully as he rolled the skateboard back and forth with his foot. "Yeah, but I'm not sure of the name." He grabbed the second five and shoved it in his pocket.

"Is it a man or woman and can you point to the house?" she asked. Maybe she was finally getting somewhere.

"Who are you - Angela Lansbury?" he smirked.

Gloria gave him a dark look. "Don't get smart with me, young man. I have underwear older than you."

The boy grinned. "Okay, just kidding. You don't have to get all turned up."

She raised a brow.

The boy rolled his eyes. "You know, worked up."

Gloria didn't know, nor did she care.

He jerked his head toward the row of houses. "Over there. The dude in that house has a limp. Most of the time, he walks with a cane."

Gloria followed his gaze. "The white house with black shutters?"

He nodded. "That's the one."

Finally. They had it narrowed it down.

Gloria grabbed a ten, the final bill she had tucked into the side of her purse and slapped it into his outstretched hand. "Thank you. You've been quite helpful."

The boy grinned, shoved the money in his pocket and adjusted his backpack. "You're welcome, granny."

She watched as he coasted down the sidewalk, eventually swerving into a driveway at the end of the street.

He picked up the board, tucked it under his arm and disappeared inside the house.

Gloria returned to the van and slid into the passenger seat. "We got a lead."

Ruth twisted in her seat. "Can I use the drone now?"

Gloria furrowed a brow. Although she believed the young man was telling the truth, it wouldn't hurt for her to see for herself that the man walked with a limp. She nodded. "Somehow, we need to get him outdoors."

Lucy leaned forward from the backseat. "That shouldn't be too difficult." She patted Ruth on the shoulder. "Ruth is dying to use her drone. Why don't we let her fly it down the street or something?"

Gloria studied Ruth's face. She could see the eager look in her friend's eyes. On top of that, Gloria had asked her bring it for a reason. "Fly away."

Ruth was never one to look a gift horse in the mouth and not wanting Gloria to change her mind and come up with a "Plan B," scrambled out of the van and scurried to the rear cargo door. She carefully pulled her drone from the back and carried it to the front of the van.

Gloria climbed out of the van. She, herself, was curious to see how the drone operated.

Ruth placed the drone on the cement sidewalk and pulled the controller from her purse.

Gloria glanced at her friend's face. She'd never seen her so excited, except maybe the time she had glued herself to her computer screen to spy on the post office. Yeah, the look was about the same.

"I think you missed your calling in life, Ruth," Gloria told her.

Ruth half-turned, her attention honed in on her precious piece of surveillance equipment. "Huh?"

"Never mind," Gloria mumbled.

Lucy climbed out of the van and stood next to Gloria.

Ruth took a step back, the controller gripped tightly in both hands.

"*Whirr.*" Small propellers, located on the four corners of the small machine, began to spin and the drone slowly lifted off the ground.

Ruth's face contorted as she concentrated on maneuvering the flying craft up into the air. Ruth steered it back and forth across the street as she practiced moving it along.

It lifted high in the air and then suddenly shot forward like a speeding bullet.

Ruth began to run as she tried to keep pace with her runaway machine.

Lucy cupped her hands to her mouth. "Pull back on the throttle," she yelled.

Ruth must have heard Lucy's advice as the drone suddenly slowed and began to hover over the center of the street.

Gloria and Lucy darted down the sidewalk to catch up with their friend.

The drone hovered about ten feet above them. "Time to move it into position," Ruth said.

Gloria frowned. "How much practice have you had with this?"

"I've only had it out once," Ruth admitted.

Gloria closed her eyes and offered a quick prayer that Ruth and her new toy wouldn't get them into trouble.

Lucy and Gloria followed close behind Ruth as she made her way across the street. She positioned herself off to the side, out of view of the suspect's house.

The women stepped off the sidewalk and slipped behind a cluster of tall juniper bushes at the edge of the property.

Off in the distance, Gloria could hear the faint "whirr" of the drone's propellers as it soared over the top of the six-foot privacy fence that separated the front of the yard from the rear.

Ruth shot out of the edge of the bush as she tried to keep a visual on her drone.

"Is it filming anything?" Lucy hissed.

Ruth shrugged. "I won't know for sure until I take a look at the memory card." She puckered her lips and narrowed her eyes. "I better bring it in. The battery is probably getting low."

Whoop. A faint "whooshing" sound came from behind the other side of the fence. "Uh-oh." Ruth's face fell.

"What?" Gloria whispered.

"I think the drone went down behind enemy lines." Ruth shoved the controls into Lucy's hands and darted across the yard.

Gloria cupped her hands to her lips. "What are you doing?" she hissed at Ruth.

"Going for the drone," she shot back, never slowing her pace.

Ruth grabbed the top of the dog-ear fence panel with both hands and hoisted herself onto the top of the panel. She teetered there for a long moment, half-in, half-out, her feet swinging wildly as she tried in vain to gain enough momentum to pull herself the rest of the way over.

"Help me," she pleaded.

Gloria bolted across the lawn. She gave Ruth's feet one good shove and then they disappeared from sight.

"Umf."

Gloria peered through the crack in the wooden boards and caught sight of Ruth sprawled out, face down on the grass. "Hurry UP," Gloria urged.

Ruth pulled herself up onto all fours and began to crawl across the yard. Her drone was a good eight feet away.

She had almost made contact with the drone when around the corner of the house, a pair of boots appeared.

"What is going on back here?" a male voice demanded.

Ruth's hand reached for the drone while her eyes traveled upwards. "I lost control of my drone," she explained breathlessly.

The man planted his feet apart, hands on hips. "You're trespassing," he growled.

"I am so sorry," Ruth apologized.

Lucy leaned over Gloria's shoulder as they watched in horror. "We need a distraction. Fast."

She darted out into the street, her eyes searching frantically for a diversion. Her eyes fell upon a street drain. Lucy dropped to pavement and wedged her right foot between the top of the drain and metal grate.

Lucy sucked in a deep breath and screamed at the top of her lungs.

Gloria nearly jumped out of her skin. She spun around, her eyes falling on Lucy's small frame, sprawled out in the street.

She started to run over to help Lucy when Lucy frantically waved her away. "No."

Gloria realized that Lucy had created a diversion, sprinted along the edge of the property line and disappeared behind the bushes.

The man looked down at Ruth and then toward the front of the house. He paused for a brief moment then disappeared inside, leaving Ruth and the drone behind.

He bolted out of his front door and made his way over to where Lucy, who was doing an excellent job of appearing to be in a dire situation, shrieked helplessly.

If the situation hadn't been so serious, Gloria would have burst out laughing. Lucy and helpless were two words Gloria would never use in the same sentence.

"I twisted my ankle and now my foot is wedged in the drain," she moaned.

She reached down and tugged on her calf. "Ahhhh! I think something is nibbling on my ankle."

The man bent down and peered into the sewer. "I don't see anything. Hold still."

While his attention was on Lucy, Ruth grabbed her drone and ran to the rear of the yard. She caught a glimpse of Gloria as she ran along the other side. "Take the drone."

Before Gloria could answer, Ruth tossed the drone over the fence. Gloria lifted her hands above her head and grabbed onto the drone's propeller.

Ruth vaulted over the corner fence. Thankfully, the fence in the back was lower than the one that faced the front.

When Ruth was safely on the other side, Gloria hunched over and grabbed her friend's arm. "Let's get out of here."

They scurried across the rear neighbor's yard and onto the adjacent street. When they reached the safety of the street, Gloria let out a sigh of relief.

Meanwhile, Lucy, who still had the homeowner distracted, had one eye on the drain and one eye on Ruth's van parked at the front of the cul-de-sac.

"Just relax your leg," the man advised.

Lucy had tightened her calf muscle in attempt to make it seem as if her foot was truly stuck. She caught a glimpse of Ruth and Gloria as they opened the van doors and slipped inside.

She rubbed the side of her lower leg. "I think it's starting to come loose."

The man, using both hands, gently tipped her leg to the side and slowly pulled. Her foot "miraculously" freed itself from the inner drain and slid out.

Lucy blinked her eyes rapidly. "Oh thank you Mr. ..."

"Hendricks. Ron Hendricks."

"Mr. Hendricks," Lucy repeated. She lifted her pant leg and inspected her bare ankle. "Huh. I could've sworn something was gnawing on my flesh."

She rolled over to her knees and slowly stood. She brushed her hands on the top of her pants and held out a hand. "Thank you so much."

"You're welcome." He pointed at the drain. "What in the world were you doing?"

Lucy waved dramatically. "I was searching for my dog, not paying attention to where I was going and my foot caught on something slippery. Next thing I know, I'm on the ground and my foot was wedged inside."

She went on. "When I felt something on my ankle, I panicked and when I tried to jerk my foot out, it wedged even tighter." She shuddered. "If you hadn't helped me, I would probably have rabies right now."

He glanced down the street. "You live around here?"

Lucy shook her head. "No...I live in B-." She corrected herself. "I live a few miles away and my dog seems to have wandered off so I'm checking all the neighborhoods."

"I haven't noticed any stray dogs," he said.

Before the man could ask more questions, Lucy turned to go. "I better keep looking."

She limped along the street, turning back once to watch Mr. Hendricks, whose limp was worse than Lucy's limp, make his way down the drive and back inside his house.

Lucy slid into the backseat, right next to Ruth, who had set up a small command post with her computer. She studied the screen. "I got some great footage of the suspect's backyard."

"Ron Hendricks," Lucy corrected.

Gloria grinned. "You got his name?"

Lucy nodded triumphantly. "Yep. Did you see his limp?"

Gloria gazed down the street. "Yes, I did. It's time to visit Paul with our evidence."

Chapter 24

After Ruth picked up the spy equipment from the house at 726 Pine Place, the women headed straight to the Montbay Sherriff station.

Luckily, Paul was at the station. He watched the drone footage in silence. "This is a good lead but it doesn't prove that he was the one that broke into the house and caused the damage."

He placed his reading glasses on the desk and leaned back in the chair. "What's his motive?"

Gloria frowned. True. The man lacked motive. He had opportunity and fit what little clues they had about the intruder.

Ruth closed her laptop and slid it back into her computer bag. "I wish I had been able to help crack the case," she said.

Gloria rose to her feet. "Do you mind if I borrow the card and take it home to study the footage?"

Ruth shrugged. "Sure. I have a spare at home."

She pulled the small memory card from a side pocket and placed it in Gloria's outstretched hand.

They rode back to Belhaven in silence. Gloria mulled over the clues they had. Why *would* someone intentionally sabotage a neighbor's home sale – unless it was an enemy?

From what the other neighbors had said, they had all been amicable, if not friends.

Back at the farm, she waited on the porch while Mally did her customary inspection of the yard and barns. Her eyes fell on the house across the street. It was a buzz of activity. Construction vans, electrical vans. It reminded her of Andrea's place.

When Mally finished, Gloria and she went inside. Her stomach grumbled. She opened the refrigerator door and peered inside. She had everything needed to make a sandwich but it seemed like she had been eating a lot of those lately.

She pulled out a small plastic grocery bag and untied the top. Inside was Alice's firehouse fajita. "Here goes nothing," she muttered under her breath.

She placed the fajita on a glass plate and then stuck the plate inside the microwave. Mally sat and watched the microwave intently. Gloria glanced down. "You will not like that," she told her.

Mally let out a low whine and flopped down onto the linoleum. "Alright," Gloria caved, "I'll give you a treat."

She pulled the packet of deli meat from the fridge and placed two slices on a paper plate. She tore a third piece into small bits and put those in Puddles' food dish. "I know you're not sick of ham," she said.

Mally and Puddles gulped their treats. After those were gone, they continued to watch Gloria's food cook. After the microwave turned off, she slid the plate from the oven and placed it on the table.

The scent of cilantro and Chile peppers drifted up, taunting Gloria. She eyed the piping hot fajita then headed back to the fridge where she grabbed a half gallon of milk. She poured a tall glass before she settled in at the table. "Maybe this will help offset the heat," she muttered under her breath.

The food was delicious and Gloria ate every single bite. She placed the dirty plate in the dishwasher and closed the door. The only plan she had for the rest of the evening was to go over what the drone had captured on camera earlier.

She made her way over to the computer and settled into the chair. Puddles waited for Gloria to settle in before he jumped onto her lap for a catnap.

Gloria fumbled around for several moments as she tried to remember where the small disk went. Finally, after she put her reading glasses on, she figured it out.

The file popped on the screen and Gloria clicked the tab. The first seconds of footage made Gloria dizzy as Ruth attempted to smooth out the drone's flight. There was no sound, just the recording.

When the video zoomed in then abruptly dropped close to the ground Gloria closed her eyes. She began to feel nauseous.

Gloria opened her eyes. The video had smoothed out. She was able to make out the suspect's backyard quite clearly. The drone zoomed haphazardly across the space before it plunked onto the grass when it ran out of battery power.

Mere seconds before it plunked to the ground and the screen went blank; Gloria caught a glimpse of something...something important.

She rewound the footage and played it again. She paused when she got to what she had noticed before. There it was. In plain sight...the link between Mr. Hendricks' house and the house across the street.

She darted to the kitchen for her cell phone. Gloria dialed her daughter's number, praying that she would answer and that she was with the home inspector.

"Hello?"

"Hi Jill. Are you still at the new house?" Gloria blurted out.

"Yeah." Jill covered the mouthpiece.

"Hello?"

Jill was back. "The inspector said he should be done in about 45 minutes," she explained. "You'll never guess who I ran into."

Gloria had no idea. "Who?"

"Sue Camp. She was showing another couple this house. Can you believe it?"

Somehow, Gloria could believe it. "Stay there. I think I have a break in the case." Before Jill could respond, Gloria disconnected the line and dialed Paul.

"I can link the intruder at 726 Pine Place to the neighbor across the street," Gloria told Paul. "Can you meet me at the house?"

"I'll call you right back."

Gloria paced the kitchen floor and waited. She needed Paul to be onboard, to show him the evidence. Otherwise, the suspect might get away and Jill would have a new neighbor who had no qualms about breaking into neighbors' homes.

The phone chirped. "So can you?" Gloria skipped the pleasantries.

"I'll be there in 30 minutes," he told her.

Gloria was halfway to the car when she remembered her laptop and the small disk. She placed both on the passenger seat, started the car and roared off down the road.

Paul was there when Gloria pulled in the drive. Jill's car was parked out front, along with another vehicle Gloria didn't recognize.

She grabbed her computer bag, slid out of the car and hurried up the steps. Paul met her at the front door. "I just got here."

He held the door while Gloria stepped inside. She could hear Jill's voice from somewhere in the back.

Gloria waved him to the dining room. "Take a look at this first."

She led him to the kitchen where she showed him the smashed cabinets and pointed to the gaping holes where the doors were missing.

Gloria placed her laptop bag on the kitchen counter, unzipped the cover and pulled it out. She switched it on and clicked the icon for the video recording. "Watch the very end," she told him.

Paul leaned in and studied the video closely. At the end of the video footage, he noticed several cabinet doors, propped up against a wall inside a small storage area. The doors looked similar to the ones that were missing from 726 Pine Place. He hit the pause button. "I see them."

From where they were standing, they could look out the front picture window and had an unobstructed view of the house across the street. "I'll go have a chat with the neighbor." He looked at Gloria. "What's his name?"

"Ron Hendricks."

Paul nodded and then walked out the front door and across the street.

Gloria closed the lid on the computer and slid it into the bag as her daughter, Jill, and the inspector appeared from the hall.

She walked into the kitchen and hugged her mom. "I thought I heard your voice. What's up? Where did Paul go?"

Gloria nodded through the window. "He's having a chat with the neighbor."

The inspector interrupted. "I'll be in the basement checking mechanicals." He disappeared down the stairs.

"You're onto something," Jill said. "Please tell me you found something."

"We shall see," Gloria's eyes twinkled. The spark disappeared as she gazed at the gaping holes where cabinet doors were either missing or the intruder had smashed them.

Jill followed her mother into the kitchen. "Sue Camp said the owner's insurance is going to have all new kitchen cabinets installed before we move in and I get to pick them out."

"So you get a new kitchen?"

Jill clasped her hands together and spun around. "I know, right?"

Gloria shifted the computer bag on her shoulder. "You mentioned Sue Camp was here showing the house to buyers?"

Jill crossed her arms. "Yes, and when I asked her what she was doing, she blew it off and said that if we backed out of the contract, she had several other backup offers."

"What a lovely woman," Gloria muttered.

Gloria caught a movement through the front window out of the corner of her eye. She stepped into the living room and watched as Paul lifted his radio to his lips. He stood in the drive across the street for several moments before he escorted Ron Hendricks down the drive and placed him in the back of his squad car.

Gloria and Jill waited at the door for Paul to return. "I'm taking Mr. Hendricks to the station for questioning. I need that disc," he told his fiancé.

Gloria pulled the small disk from the computer bag and dropped it into his hand.

"Thank you," he said.

She leaned forward and gave him a quick peck on the lips. "Thanks for being my knight in shining armor and coming to my rescue."

He grinned and winked. "Anything for my damsel in distress," he teased.

Jill rolled her eyes. "Oh brother."

She turned to her mom. "That video...it has something to do with the guy across the street?"

"It's a long story, but Ruth was able to spy on the neighbor's backyard. The video she taped showed a stack of cabinet doors, identical to the ones missing from this kitchen, propped up in an open storage area behind his garage."

"On top of that, the footage of the break-in that Ruth's spy equipment recorded, tipped us off that the intruder had a limp, similar to Mr. Hendricks' limp."

Jill placed a hand on each side of her head. "But why? Why this house?"

Gloria tapped her foot on the floor. "That, my dear, is the million dollar question."

Chapter 25

Gloria was on pins and needles the rest of the day as she waited for Paul to let her know how Ron Hendricks' questioning had gone.

Gloria's number one priority was that Jill and her family move forward on the purchase of a new home.

Gloria was certain beyond a shadow of a doubt that the perpetrator had been uncovered and her daughter could safely move into the new home without worrying about someone breaking in.

She even offered to help Jill do a little painting before they moved although, in Gloria's book, painting was right up there with moving.

On her drive back to Belhaven, she noticed that Margaret had sent her a text message. When she got into town, she pulled off to the side of the road to read it.

"Stop by my place. Stat."

Gloria groaned inwardly. "Please, Lord. No more excitement, at least for a couple of days," she pleaded.

Instead of turning right at the stop sign on Main Street, she drove straight through town and up the hill toward Lake Terrace and Margaret's place.

Margaret's SUV was the only car in the drive and Gloria pulled Annabelle in behind it.

Margaret met her at the door. "It's here. It's *all* here."

Gloria frowned as Margaret grabbed her hand and dragged her into the garage.

She flipped the light on. There, in the center of Margaret's garage, were several large boxes.

Gloria stepped forward. "What is all this?"

"Our surprises for the girls," Margaret exclaimed. "Remember? We decided to buy something special for each of them with our windfall?"

Gloria had been so wrapped up in Jill's house and the puppy mill; she had forgotten they were going to buy each of their close friends a special gift. Margaret hadn't forgotten.

"Bless your heart." Gloria impulsively reached over and hugged her friend. "You are the best," she gushed.

Margaret blushed. "I tried. I know you have your hands full." She brightened. "So when do we get to surprise them?"

Now that Gloria had Jill's fiasco behind her, her mind began to clear. "The sooner the better." She snapped her fingers. "How about an afternoon tea at Magnolia Mansion? We can have Andrea and Alice put on our first shindig."

"Brilliant," Margaret agreed. "I'm so excited." She rubbed her hands together.

"Remind me what we picked out again," Gloria said.

Margaret ticked off each of the surprises and it all came back to Gloria.

They had picked out the perfect gifts. There was only one problem. "What about Andrea?"

Margaret's mouth formed an "O" as she realized that they hadn't purchased anything for their young friend.

Andrea didn't "need" anything. When Andrea's husband, Daniel, had died, she collected a large amount of money from a hefty life insurance policy. On top of that, she had recently sold the insurance agency so that she could focus on the Magnolia Mansion Tearoom.

Their young friend had also started dabbling in interior design, which Gloria decided was the perfect fit for Andrea.

If Andrea wanted something, she could just go out and buy it.

Gloria stared at the tower of gifts in Margaret's garage. There were special gifts for each of the Garden Girls. It suddenly dawned on Gloria – the perfect gift for Andrea. "I've got it."

She explained her idea to Margaret, who nodded eagerly. "That's perfect. Hers will be the best gift of all," Margaret predicted.

Gloria promptly called Andrea. "Yes, dear. I'm here with Margaret and we would like to plan a special afternoon at the tea room...a private party for the Garden Girls."

After she hung up the phone, she grinned at Margaret. "All set for this Sunday afternoon. All we need now is to get everyone rounded up at the same time."

Margaret interrupted. "You work on Andrea's gift and I'll take care of the other."

Paul called just as Gloria was getting back into her car. "What happened?" She couldn't wait to find out.

"Ron Hendricks confessed," Paul told her. "With a little strong arm," he added.

"But why? Why target that house?" That was the big question.

Paul went on to explain that Ron Hendricks and Marco Acosta had had a falling out. It all started when Mr. Hendricks purchased a puppy – a purebred Labrador retriever – from Acosta. When the dog became ill and Hendricks had to spend hundreds of dollars, only to have the dog die, hard feelings surfaced.

One day, not long after the dog died, Hendricks chased one of his other dogs across the street and into Acosta's yard where he fell into a deep hole. His ankle broke in several spots and after numerous painful surgeries, the doctors told him he would never walk again without a noticeable limp.

Paul switched the phone to his other ear. "He believed that Acosta had intentionally booby-trapped his backyard so that Hendricks would get hurt. The Acosta family moved shortly after the accident and that was when Hendricks hatched a plan for revenge."

"Wow, talk about bad blood," Gloria said.

"Yes. It's up to Marco Acosta if he wants to pursue legal action," Paul told her. "Too bad he didn't get to keep all that deposit money when the potential homebuyers backed out of the deal. I'm sure he could use it."

"What happened to all that money?" Gloria asked.

"The real estate agent's broker got to keep it," Paul replied.

After Gloria hung up the phone, she backed Annabelle out of Margaret's drive and headed through town, in the opposite direction of the farm and home.

She had two stops to make for Andrea's special gift. The first one was Trinkets and Treasures, the oddities shop in nearby Green Springs. She was certain they would have just what she was looking for.

Chapter 26

The rest of the week flew by and before Gloria knew it, Sunday morning had arrived. She woke up early, anxious to hear Pastor Nate's message, a continuation of a series he had recently started on the Book of Revelation and the tribulation. Today was also the day that Margaret and she planned to surprise the girls with their gifts.

Gloria stepped inside the sanctuary and started down the center aisle. She stopped to hug her friend, Ruth, who had been instrumental in solving the intruder mystery.

Then she stopped to hug Dot, who said she had some good news from the doctors and would share it later when they all met at Andrea's for the party.

Andrea and Alice scooched across the bench seat to make room for Gloria. She had just settled into her seat when the choir began to sing and she stood back up.

Some Sunday mornings the music was upbeat and cheerful. Other Sundays, it was more solemn worship music. Today was the slower, more reverent hymns of praise.

Gloria blinked back sudden tears as the music touched her heart. Andrea must have felt the same. She reached over and squeezed her friend's hand.

Pastor Nate's message was both stirring and thought provoking. Gloria made a mental note to study the key scripture from Revelation:

"Truly I tell you, this generation will certainly not pass away until all these things have happened. Heaven and earth will pass away, but my words will never pass away.

But about that day or hour no one knows, not even the angels in heaven, nor the Son, but only the Father. Be on guard. Be alert. You do not know when that time will come. Mark 13: 30 – 33. NIV

After the service ended, the girls wandered outdoors to their usual meeting spot. Gloria shivered as a brisk November wind tugged at the collar of her shirt and gave her a taste of what was to come.

Andrea felt it too, as she stomped her shiny, black designer shoe on the cement. "Brr."

The meeting was brief since the girls would be gathering at Andrea's place in a few short hours. Gloria caught Margaret's eye and winked.

Lucy and Ruth offered to visit the shut-ins since Andrea had to prep for the party, Dot had to cover at the restaurant for a few hours before the girls met, and Gloria and Margaret had to gather all their goodies and take them to Andrea's place.

Andrea had a hunch the girls were up to something but she wasn't about to spoil the fun so she kept mum about what little she did know.

Gloria and Margaret met at Andrea's place right after lunch.

When they stepped inside the sunroom, Gloria gasped. Tiny twinkling lights illuminated the large, towering trees Andrea had strategically placed about the room.

Several small bistro tables, covered with an array of pastel-colored cloths, sat clustered together in one section. Andrea had put them together so that all of the girls could sit next to one another.

Margaret and Gloria carried the boxes of goodies into the room and set them off in the corner. Andrea raised a brow when she saw the huge stack.

Alice slid in front of Andrea and clucked. "What is this? Christmas?"

Margaret rubbed her hands together. Not wanting to leave Alice out, Margaret had managed to find a special gift for her, too.

After the girls finished unloading the boxes, they wandered into the kitchen. Lined up on the counter were several rows of mouth-watering, tempting morsels.

"Try one," Andrea urged.

Gloria plucked one from the plate and nibbled the edge. Tangy Dijon mustard tickled her tongue. She pulled it back to inspect the contents. It was a slice of French bread and on top of the bread was a piece of salty ham and brie cheese.

Margaret selected watercress. It was the perfect finger food. "This is delicious," she exclaimed.

Andrea smiled. "Are you sure?"

"Absolutely," Gloria reassured her friend.

Alice pulled a smaller side tray to the front. "Now you must try this," she declared.

The tray was loaded with bite-size tortilla chips. Gloria lifted a small chip, shaped like a cup and studied the mixture inside.

Alice rattled off the ingredients. "Black beans, salsa, cream cheese and green onion."

Gloria gobbled the tasty morsel and grabbed a paper napkin to wipe her lips. "This is so good. By the way, I ate my firehouse fajita yesterday for lunch and it was delicious."

Alice beamed with pride. "You like? I make you more."

Andrea held up a hand to stop her. "But not today. We have our hands full," she reminded her.

"Si," Alice agreed.

Finally, the hour arrived and the rest of the Garden Girls straggled in, hanging their coats on a beautiful antique coat rack that Gloria hadn't noticed before. It was beautiful and looked old.

"Where did you get this?" Gloria asked.

Andrea ran her hand down the smooth, solid oak coat rack. "I've been rummaging around estate sales. You should go with me sometime. They have lots of cool stuff."

Gloria grinned and shook her head. "I'm sure it's a lot of fun but I'm trying to get *rid* of my things, not accumulate more," she pointed out.

"True," Andrea agreed.

The girls oohed and aahed over the tasty treats that Alice and Andrea had worked so hard to create. They gushed at the beautiful decorations and Andrea beamed like the proud manor owner that she now was.

Finally, the goodies consumed, everyone turned their attention to Dot. Gloria spoke first. "First and foremost, how are you Dot?"

All eyes turned to their friend.

Dot's eyes traveled around the room as she focused on each of her dear friends. Tears threatened to spill as she thought about how they had pitched in to help and how much they all meant to her. "I-I'm going to be fine. They caught the cancer early and with a little treatment after the surgery, I should be cancer-free before you know it."

A collective sigh of relief filled the room. The women impulsively joined hands as Gloria prayed. "Thank you, Dear God, for Dot's good news. We pray for continued healing in her life as she moves through treatment and thank You for answering our prayers."

A unanimous AMEN erupted and Alice ran out to grab a fresh pot of hot water. She moved quickly since she couldn't wait to find out what kind of goodies the girls had brought to surprise their friends.

Margaret and Gloria made their way around the cluster of tables and stood near the divider that hid the gifts from sight.

The room grew quiet as the rest of the girls wondered what they were doing. Gloria nodded to Margaret.

"As you know, Gloria and I were fortunate enough to stumble on those rare coins in the mountains when we were chasing after Liz." She glanced around the room. "Gloria and I decided that there was no one else in the world we would rather share our unexpected gift with – than you – our dearest friends."

She paused and Gloria picked up. "So, without further ado, we have something special for each of you."

Margaret and Gloria slid the partition to the side to reveal the tall stack of boxes.

The girls gasped in surprise.

"Ruth first," Margaret said.

Ruth paused for just a moment before she jumped out of her chair and crossed the room.

Gloria grabbed one box and Margaret reached for a second.

Gloria held out her box. "Inside this box is the ultimate spy package. It includes a spy pen with audio recording, a set of GPS tracking devices in case you need more than one and an

433

amplifier to hook up to the surveillance you already have so you don't have to use ear buds."

Ruth's eye lit up and Gloria could tell she was ready to rip the box open. "We're not done."

Margaret held out the larger box. "This is the deluxe Phantom II drone with longer range, a battery that can last up to an hour and more camera time."

Ruth clutched her chest. "Really? Oh my gosh. How did you know I wanted the Phantom II?"

"Kenny," Gloria explained. "He told us you wanted it but it was out of your price range."

Ruth impulsively kissed Gloria's cheek first and then Margaret's.

"Thank you, Ruth, for letting me use your drone to crack Jill's case," Gloria added gratefully.

Ruth floated back to her seat, the larger of the two boxes securely in her grasp.

Gloria placed her other box off to the side. "Don't forget this later."

Ruth shook her head. "Are you kidding me?"

Margaret snapped her fingers. "Oh, and one more thing. Inside that box is the name and number of a company in Grand Rapids that retrofits vehicles with special equipment.

We've already paid to have your van equipped with state-of-the-art spy equipment for mobile use."

Ruth placed her hands on both sides of her cheeks. "I think I just died and went to heaven."

The group of friends giggled at Ruth's reaction. Truly, Margaret and Gloria had given her the perfect gift.

"Dot, you're next," Gloria waved her to the front.

Dot strode to the front of the room.

Gloria reached for her hand. "The best gift ever is the good news from the doctors." A tear slid down Dot's cheek, then Margaret's cheek. Soon, all of the women were crying and Andrea darted out of the room in search of Kleenex as she wiped at her wet eyes.

Gloria cleared her throat and smiled through her tears. "We know that the old stove in your restaurant has been on the fritz for a while now so," she turned to Margaret, "so we bought you the best commercial grade oven and stove we could find." She thrust a stack of papers in Dot's hand. "All you have to do is call the number on the sheet and they will schedule the delivery."

"I-I." Dot closed her mouth, afraid she would become unglued and then they would all be bawling again.

"You're welcome." The women all got out of their chairs and surrounded their friend.

Finally, when the hugs and the tears subsided, Dot sat back down and Gloria pointed to Lucy. "You're next."

Lucy grinned and jumped to her feet.

When Lucy got close, Margaret began to speak. "We tried to get you a lifetime supply of sweets but no one could handle the order."

The girls giggled and Lucy frowned.

"We hope you like what we came up with instead," Gloria told her. She handed her a box. "We bought you a lifetime supply of ammo for your guns."

Margaret held out an envelope, "And we arranged for a company to come out and build you your own custom shooting range."

Lucy grinned from ear-to-ear. "Are you kidding me?" She spun around and faced Andrea, who also liked to target practice at Lucy's place in her free time. "Did you hear that? We're getting a new shooting range?" She grabbed the envelope and lifted it to her lips. "Whoopee." She bounced back to her seat.

Gloria had a fleeting thought that she might one day regret the decision to build her friend a shooting range. She would have to worry about that another day.

The girls gazed at the small pile of gifts behind Margaret and Gloria.

A twinge of jealousy shot through Andrea, although she quietly dismissed it. This was a special day for the Garden Girls. Maybe someday...

Gloria reached down and grabbed the larger of the two boxes left on the floor. "We have something for you, Alice."

Alice pointed to her chest. "Me?"

Margaret nodded. She motioned her to come.

Alice looked at Andrea uncertainly and Andrea nodded. "Go," she urged.

Alice wandered to the front.

Gloria held out the box. "There are two things in this box." She turned to Margaret who held up a finger.

"First, there is a year's supply of ghost chili." Alice clapped her hands. "Oh, the dishes I can make."

"Second, is a simulated driving course so you can learn to drive while watching TV," Gloria added.

Alice beamed. "Oh, I will use it every day, Miss Gloria," Alice promised. She gave each of them a hug before she made her way to the back of the room.

Andrea picked up an empty dish and started for the door.

She took a step back when Gloria stopped her. "Wait, Andrea. We haven't given you your gift yet."

Andrea paused. "Me?"

Gloria smiled. "Why, of course."

All five of the friends turned to Andrea, still standing in the back. Gloria waved her up. "Come get your gift," she urged.

Andrea slowly made her way to the front as Margaret picked up the last box. It was the smallest of them all but it held the most significance to each of the five Garden Girls, for each of them knew what the box held. It was a special gift and they waited eagerly for Gloria to explain.

Gloria didn't explain. Instead, she simply handed the box to Andrea. "Open it."

The box was unlike the rest, meticulously and lovingly wrapped in a bright, shiny paper. Tied in the center was a bright green bow. Pictures of gardening gloves, packets of seeds and small green plants covered the outside.

The paper was beautiful. Andrea pried the tape off with her fingernail and carefully set the paper and bow to the side. She lifted the lid on the box and pulled out the only thing that was inside...a green hat. A Garden Girls hat, not unlike the one that Margaret, Lucy, Dot, Ruth and Gloria had purchased when they formed their Garden Girls Club.

"Welcome to the club," Gloria simply said.

Andrea stared at the hat, then up at her friend. "You mean..."

"Welcome to the club," the five women, who had unanimously voted to add Andrea to their small group, exclaimed.

Andrea popped the hat on her head and beamed with pride. The hat was the best gift ever.

The other three made their way to the front as each of them hugged their young friend. She had been a part of the group for a while now, at least in their hearts and minds, and now it was official.

Alice stood near the back and took a picture of the five – now six – women, with Andrea near the middle, grinning from ear-to-ear.

After Alice finished taking several pictures and the women cleared the clutter, Gloria stopped them one more time.

"We have one more gift," Margaret announced. "This one is for *all* of us."

Gloria nodded. "We commissioned an artist from Grand Rapids to paint The Garden Girls portrait and if Andrea doesn't mind, we would love to hang it here at Magnolia Mansion."

The girls were thrilled and Andrea, too, since she would be able to display it in the tearoom for all to enjoy. "After our painting, we commissioned him to paint one more – of Magnolia Mansion - and you can put that anywhere you like," Gloria said.

The chatter of excited voices filled the sunroom and spilled over into the rest of the house. This house promises years of wonderful memories for not only Andrea, but also the rest of the Garden Girls.

Margaret and Gloria were the last to leave. Gloria flung her arm around Margaret's shoulder. "Well done, my friend," she said.

Margaret paused. "You, too." She slid the tip of her high heel pump across the smooth tile floor. "You know, the best gift we have is each other."

"That is the truth." Gloria hugged Margaret and then watched as she made her way down the drive to her SUV before heading to the kitchen.

She wanted to thank Andrea one last time for making the day special.

Andrea, still wearing her green hat, was in the kitchen covering the leftovers.

Gloria tapped the tip of the hat. "I take it you are happy with our gift."

"I think she will sleep with it on her head," Alice predicted.

Gloria smiled.

Alice wiped her hands on her apron. "Oh. Miss, Gloria. In all the excitement, I forgot about the Acosta family. You know, the people with all the dogs."

Gloria frowned. She had forgotten as well. "You said you had a chance to talk to them."

"Si. Perhaps if you are free in a day or two, we can go out there to talk to the owners."

Gloria nodded. The sooner the better. She had vowed to help those poor animals and that was what she was going to do.

"How about tomorrow? If you can reach the owners, we can swing by there tomorrow."

"Yes. That is good," Alice agreed.

Finally, Gloria the last to leave headed to the car. The sun had set and with all the excitement of the last couple of days, she was ready to spend a quiet evening at home, kicking back in her recliner and watching her favorite detective show.

She pulled Annabelle into the drive and climbed out of the car. Brilliant streaks of cotton candy pink and tangerine orange filled the skies across the street... God's magnificent creation.

Gloria locked the car doors and headed inside. She smiled and looked back one last time at the sky. God had surely blessed Gloria and she couldn't wait for what tomorrow would bring.

***

The end...or is it? I tossed around the idea of leaving a taste of what was to come in Book #9...and decided to leave it up to you – my reader. If you are content with the tidy ending, read no further.

If you would like to take a peek at Gloria's upcoming adventure, feel free to scroll down for the second ending.

Happy Reading and Have a Blessed Day.

Hope

Alternate Ending

Gloria pulled Annabelle into the drive and climbed out of the car. Brilliant streaks of cotton candy pink and tangerine orange filled the skies...God's magnificent creation.

Gloria, distracted by the beauty that surrounded her, almost missed the police car and crime scene van parked in front of the farmhouse across the road. Almost.

The end, end!

Monster Cookies Recipe

<u>Ingredients</u>

½ cup brown sugar
¼ cup white sugar
½ cup margarine, softened
1 cup peanut butter
3 eggs
2 tsp. vanilla
4 ½ cup rolled oats
2 tsp. baking soda
4 oz. chocolate chips
4 oz. M&M candies
½ cup chopped walnuts or pecans

<u>Directions</u>

Preheat oven to 350 degrees.
Cream together sugars, softened margarine and peanut butter.
Add eggs and vanilla.
Beat well
Mix together oats and baking soda.
Add to creamed mixture.
Stir in chocolate chips, candy and walnuts.
Mix all ingredients thoroughly.
Drop by teaspoonful onto greased cookie sheet.
Bake at 350 degrees for 10 minutes.

Fall Girl – Book 9

Garden Girls
Cozy Mystery Series

Hope Callaghan

hopecallaghan.com

Thank you, Peggy Hyndman, for taking the time to preview *Fall Girl,* for the sharp eyes that catch my mistakes.

Visit my website for new releases and special offers: hopecallaghan.com

Chapter 1

Gloria Rutherford peered into the mirror that hung over the buffet table in her dining room. She turned her head from side to side, as she surveyed the camouflage face paint. "Lucy. I look like I'm ready to crawl through the trenches of the back 40."

Gloria had to wonder how in the world she had ever let her best friend, Lucy, talk her into deer hunting in the first place. She vaguely remembered agreeing to think about it. Next thing she knew, Lucy was on her doorstep with camo gear, face paint and a hunting rifle that weighed almost as much as she did.

"I'm hot." Gloria pulled on the collar of her jacket as a trickle of perspiration inched down her back.

"You don't want the deer to see you," Lucy patiently explained. She knew that once Gloria got used to the idea that she was going to try hunting, at least once, she would settle down.

Lucy patted her jacket pocket to make sure she still had the deer lure. If Gloria was putting up this kind of fuss over the face paint, she wondered how she would react when she got a whiff of the deer lure...

Lucy knew she had to take baby steps with the whole hunting thing. Once Gloria got accustomed to the rifle, the camo gear and the face paint, she would slip in the deer lure.

Maybe she should wait until they were out in the woods to spring that one on her friend.

The girls trudged through the kitchen as they made their way out onto the back porch.

Mally, Gloria's springer spaniel, met them at the door. "Sorry girl," Gloria reached down and patted her head. "You can't go this time."

Visions of someone accidentally shooting Mally filled Gloria's head. It wasn't that Gloria thought she would shoot her, or even Lucy, but there would be other hunters out in the fields and Mally liked to wander off.

They stepped out onto the porch and into the cool morning air. It was still early and the first rays of daylight peeked over the top of the barn across the street.

Lucy's eyes shifted to the old farmhouse across the road. Crime scene vans and police cars filled the drive. "What's going on over there?"

Gloria frowned. She had noticed the same vehicles across the street when she'd come home the night before. Her plan was to run over there this morning to try to find out what had happened but all that was forgotten when Lucy arrived on her doorstep with the hunting gear.

Gloria's late husband, James, and his family had owned the old farmhouse across the road for decades.

James' brother had lived in the house for years until one day he up and moved out. After he moved, the siblings decided to sell the house. A local farmer bought the property, lock, stock and barrel solely for the farmland. The house had stood vacant for many years.

A young couple had recently purchased the home and were in the midst of completing some much-needed major renovations before they moved in.

"I have no idea," Gloria replied. "The crime scene van was there last night."

Judging by the yellow police tape that wound around the trees and the front porch, Gloria could only guess that someone had died. She hoped it wasn't the Fowlers, the nice young couple who had purchased the place.

Gloria pulled the collar of her jacket around the nape of her neck as a brisk November gust of wind whipped strands of hair across her face. She stepped onto the sidewalk and started down the drive. There was only one way to find out what was going on.

Lucy picked up the pace and fell into step with Gloria. She knew her friend well enough to know that her curiosity had gotten the best of her.

Gloria looked both ways and darted across the road. She hoped that Officer Nelson, or better yet, her fiancé, Paul, was on the scene and that they would fill her in on what had happened.

Her heart sank when two investigators stepped out onto the narrow front porch. One looked vaguely familiar. She had never seen the other one before.

Gloria came to a halt at the bottom of the steps. "Hello. I'm Gloria Rutherford. I live across the street and was wondering what was going on."

The officer on the left, a burly man with a solemn expression, stepped forward. "Yes, ma'am. It appears there was a homicide. We are in the midst of a preliminary investigation."

He pulled a notepad from his front pocket, along with an ink pen. He flipped the lid of the pad. "You said you live across the street?"

Gloria nodded. "Yes. I'm Gloria Rutherford." She pointed toward the house. "The person who was found...dead. W-was it one of the new owners?"

The officer shifted his gaze and studied Gloria. "We are not releasing information about the victim at this time."

He went on. "We...err...aren't able to make a positive ID, yet. That may take some time. It doesn't appear to be the current owners."

Gloria wasn't sure if she should feel relieved.

"Can you at least tell us if you think it's a local resident?" Lucy piped up. The Town of Belhaven, where both Gloria and Lucy lived, was small. Everyone knew everyone else. If the victim was a local, there was a good chance the girls would know who it was.

"Sorry ma'am. I can't give out any other information." He turned back to Gloria and began to ask her if she'd seen anything unusual. Then he asked her where she'd been the night before.

"I can vouch for her," Lucy defended. "She was at a party. In fact, several others can vouch for her, too."

That was true. The girls had just celebrated Gloria's recent windfall, along with their other close friends: Ruth, Margaret, Dot and Andrea.

The cop shifted his stance and rubbed his jaw thoughtfully. "She was with you all night?"

Gloria swallowed hard. Did the officer think she was somehow involved? Surely, they wouldn't try to pin a murder on an innocent woman if they couldn't find the killer.

The officer asked a few more questions and Gloria had a hunch he was trying to incriminate her. He flipped the pad of paper shut and shoved it in his front pocket. "My name is Officer Fred Burnett. I have your information and will be in touch with you in the next day or so."

With the sweep of his hand, he dismissed the women, turned on his heel and walked back inside the house.

"What a jerk," Lucy hissed. She patted Gloria's arm. "Don't worry about it, Gloria. All of us girls can vouch for you."

The girls strode across the road as they made their way back to Gloria's farm. Gloria wasn't in the mood to hunt now. Not that she had been in the first place but now she wanted to go even less.

The corners of her lips turned down as she stalked to the backyard.

"Hunting will take your mind off this whole thing," Lucy promised her. "Maybe after we're out of the woods, we can run into town to see if Dot has heard anything." Dot was one of the girls' close friends. She owned Dot's Restaurant, the only restaurant in the small Town of Belhaven.

"Good idea," Gloria agreed.

The walk helped clear Gloria's head and by the time they reached the deer stand at the edge of the woods, she had almost forgotten about the entire incident.

Gloria owned more property than Lucy did and she had allowed her friend to build her tree stand on the edge of her favorite wooded area near the back.

It was not far from the spot where Gloria and Mally often came to spend quiet time. Gloria visited the special place when she needed to be alone.

Lucy stopped abruptly in front of a large oak tree. "We're here."

Gloria's eyes traveled up the tree, past the crude, wooden steps Lucy had constructed, to a small platform a good fifteen feet up in the air. "We...we're going to go up there?"

"Yep." Lucy grasped the first rung. "Trust me. It's not so bad once you get up there." Lucy scampered up the tree. When she got to the top, she turned around and looked down at Gloria. "C'mon."

Gloria sucked in a breath. "I don't know about this." She placed both hands on the first rung and began to climb. Her heavy farm boots scraped roughly against the tree bark as she ascended the rungs. The rungs were sturdy and even she was surprised at how easy it was to navigate.

Gloria took a quick glance at the ground below. Maybe now she could venture into the tree fort her grandsons had built in her front yard. When she reached the top, she crawled onto the platform and plopped down on her rear. "That wasn't so bad."

"See?" Lucy said. "I told you." She settled in next to Gloria, reached into her pocket and pulled out the small plastic container of deer lure. She flipped the top and squeezed a small amount into the palm of her hand.

The overpowering smell of urine filled the air and Gloria's nose. She gasped for fresh air as she frantically waved her hand across her face. "Good heavens. What in the world..."

Lucy calmly rubbed her hands together and then wiped the palms of her hands on the sleeves of her hunting jacket. "It's deer lure. It masks the human scent so the deer won't know that we're here," she explained.

Lucy poured another dose into her hand and began to wipe it on Gloria's pant legs.

Gloria jerked her leg back. "Stop. That smell makes me want to throw up." She pushed Lucy's hand away.

Lucy stopped wiping. "Okay." She lowered her head and slowly closed the lid of the lure. Her expression was so crestfallen that Gloria felt bad. She had hurt Lucy's feelings. "Okay. Wipe away," she groaned.

The smile returned and Lucy quickly began swiping the stinky substance on Gloria's jacket in an attempt to finish before Gloria had time to change her mind.

When she finished, she closed the lid on the bottle and slipped it back inside her jacket.

"Now what?" Gloria asked.

"We wait," Lucy said.

***

The girls sat as quiet as church mice. The woods were peaceful. The only sound was an occasional gunshot off in the distance. After the third time of hearing gunshots, Lucy set her rifle on the wooden deck and dropped her chin in her hands. "I wish that was me."

Gloria didn't. She had only come on this merry little hunting excursion for Lucy's sake. On top of that, she had no idea how the two of them would manage to drag a deer from the woods if Lucy did shoot one.

They stayed in the same spot for what seemed like eternity, although according to Gloria's watch, it had only been a couple hours.

Gloria shifted onto her knees and groaned. They hadn't seen hide nor hair of a deer.

Lucy could see that Gloria had reached her limit. "Wanna head back?"

Gloria opened her mouth to reply when Lucy whacked her in the arm. "Wait. There's a buck."

Lucy lifted her rifle. She stuck the butt of the gun on her shoulder and pointed the barrel at the buck, which lifted his head and looked around.

Gloria braced herself for the gunshot but dared not make a move lest she scare the deer.

"Pow!"

Lucy fired off a shot and then lowered the rifle as she tilted her head forward. "Darn. I missed. That was a five point buck." She sighed.

"We can stay a little longer," Gloria relaxed her body, her ears still ringing from the sound of the gun firing. She hadn't realized how much of a fanatic her friend was over deer hunting. Maybe if she stayed long enough, she would be off the hook for the next time.

"Nah." Lucy flipped the safety lever in place and slipped the gun into the carrying case. "It's a lost cause. Now that I fired a shot, all the deer in the area will be spooked. I won't get another shot in today."

Gloria followed her friend out of the tree. When she reached the bottom rung, she hopped onto the ground. "Well, that was interesting." She lifted the sleeve of her jacket and sniffed the surface. "Pee-yew." If anything, the smell had intensified.

"Don't worry. I'll take the jacket home and store it in the shed for next time." The jacket belonged to Lucy and Gloria was relieved she wouldn't have to worry about getting the stinky smell out.

The girls wandered out of the woods and made their way down the strip of grass that ran between the empty farm fields as they walked back to Gloria's place.

When they reached the driveway, Lucy loaded the stinky garments into the back of her jeep. "Do you still want to go to Dot's place?"

Gloria glanced across the street. All was quiet. The police vehicles were gone and the drive was empty. "Yeah. If you don't mind."

"Sure." Lucy climbed into the jeep and rolled down the window. "Stop by my place when you're ready and we can ride together."

Gloria waved at Lucy, who stopped at the end of the drive and then pulled out onto the road.

She could see Mally's head peeking through the glass pane of the door as she stepped onto the porch. She opened the porch door and Mally sprinted out.

Gloria stood on the porch and waited for her pooch to stretch her legs. She gazed across the street and shivered. The young couple who had bought the house had been there just the other day. That meant that someone had gone into that house and either killed someone or left a body in the last couple of days.

What were the chances that now that the house was in the midst of renovation, someone decided to use it to hide a body?

Gloria's blood chilled. Maybe the body had been inside for a long time, undiscovered until workers began renovation.

"C'mon girl." Mally and Gloria stepped inside the house. Gloria shut the door, clicked the deadbolt in place and then pulled on it, just to make sure it locked.

She walked to the bedroom, grabbed a pink sweater and pair of blue jeans and headed for the shower. While the water warmed, Gloria peeled off her sweaty flannel shirt and bib overalls, and climbed into the shower. Although she hadn't gotten "dirty" from hunting, she could still smell the lingering odor of deer urine.

After Gloria was squeaky clean, she headed out the door and climbed into Annabelle, her 1989 Mercury Grand Marquis.

When she got to Lucy's place, she pulled her car in behind Lucy's jeep, which was parked in the drive. She grabbed the handle of the door to open it when Lucy emerged from the house and darted down the steps.

Lucy slid into the passenger seat and reached for the seat belt. "I have a new strategy for next time we go hunting," she exclaimed excitedly.

Gloria grimaced. "What's that?"

Lucy smiled slyly. "It's a surprise."

Gloria rolled her eyes. She could hardly wait. "Does it involve baiting the deer with sweets?" Lucy was notorious for her sweet tooth and although Lucy ate excessive amounts of sugary goodies, she never seemed to gain an ounce.

Gloria pulled Annabelle into an empty spot in front of the restaurant. It was still early for the lunch crowd and they easily found a table near the back.

Dot darted over to the table. She set a Diet Coke in front of Gloria and a regular Coke in front of Lucy. "How did the hunting go? Did you get your deer?"

"Nope." Gloria pulled the wrapper off her straw and slid it into her drink. "But it wasn't because the deer knew we were there. Lucy smeared enough deer lure on us to last a month."

Lucy shot her friend a dark look. "I did not. I only put a little on you," she argued.

Dot stuck the empty tray under her arm. "I heard they found a body in that old house across the street from your place."

Gloria wiped at a speck on the tabletop. She took a deep breath and nodded. "That's why we're here. Well, one of the reasons. Have you heard anything?"

Dot shook her head. "Officer Nelson was in here earlier. When I tried to pump him for information, he clammed up. He said we'd find out soon enough."

"Let me guess. You're talking about the body found in the house across the street from Gloria's." Ruth, the girls' friend who was also head postmaster at Belhaven post office, had come up behind them.

Gloria turned her head. "Yeah. We wondered if maybe Dot had heard anything."

Now that Gloria thought about it, if anyone had insider information, it would be Ruth. Ruth was always one of the first to hear the scuttlebutt around town.

Ruth unzipped her jacket, slipped her arms out of the sleeves and hung it on the back of the chair before sliding into an empty seat. She eyed Lucy uneasily and then turned to Gloria. "Yeah. A few people were in this morning talking about it."

"And?" Lucy leaned forward.

Ruth dropped her eyes, a sure sign that what she was about to say was going to be unpleasant.

"Judith Arnett said she heard it was Bill Volk."

Chapter 2

Gloria's heart plummeted. Her eyes shifted to Lucy, who had turned as white as a ghost.

Dot gasped.

Bill Volk was Lucy's ex-boyfriend. They had dated for over a year and broken up just a few months earlier. The breakup hadn't been amicable but then it hadn't been nasty, either. Uncomfortable was the word Lucy used to describe the breakup.

Gloria reached out and squeezed Lucy's hand. "We don't know for sure."

She turned to Ruth. "Right? I mean, it's just a rumor."

Ruth nodded. "That's just the word on the street, Lucy. They found some identification on the body that may be Bill's. At least that's the gossip."

Lucy's face went blank. She started to stand and then sat back down. "Maybe I should try to call Bill."

She reached for her cellphone, switched it to on and peered at the screen. Her eyes widened in disbelief. "He...it looks like Bill tried to call me yesterday but he didn't leave a message."

Lucy pressed the call button and placed the phone against her ear.

The girls held their breath and waited, praying that Bill would pick up.

Tears welled in the back of her eyes as she disconnected the line. "There was no answer."

"Maybe you should leave a message," Dot suggested.

Lucy set the phone on the table. "And say what? 'Hey, I heard you were dead. Can you call me back?'"

She reached for the phone and dialed his number a second time. "Hello Bill. Lucy here. Can you please give me a call when you get a chance? Thanks."

Dot headed to the kitchen to grab a cup of coffee for Ruth. The trio sat in uncomfortable silence.

Gloria had a sudden thought. "Maybe you should try calling his store." Bill owned a small sporting goods store in the nearby Town of Green Springs.

"Good idea." For the third time, Lucy picked up her cell phone. "I'm not sure if I still have his work number programmed in my phone." She scrolled through the screen. "Yep. Here it is." She pressed the "call" button and put the phone to her ear.

The girls waited silently for someone to answer the other end of the line.

"Yes. This is Lucy. Lucy Carlson. Oh hey, Eric. I was wondering if Bill was around."

Gloria sucked in a breath.

Lucy listened silently for several moments. "No. No. I had no idea." She lowered her head into the palm of her hand. "I-I can't believe it. Okay. Thanks."

Lucy disconnected the line and looked up, her eyes brimming with unshed tears. "Bill's brother Randy just came into the store to tell the employees. Police think the body they found in the house across from Gloria's place was Bill."

A tear trickled down Lucy's cheek.

Gloria hopped out of her chair and rushed to her friend's side. She put an arm around her shoulder. "I'm so sorry Lucy." She didn't know what else to say. The other girls: Ruth and Dot gathered around her as they tried to comfort their friend.

"Let's go to the back," Dot urged. She led the way and the girls headed to the kitchen.

Ray, Dot's husband, stood in front of the fryer. "The food couldn't have been that bad," he joked when he saw the look on the girls' faces.

Dot stood next to her husband. "Bill Volk's body was found in the house across the street from Gloria."

Ray set the fryer basket in the holder. He wiped his hands on the front of his apron. "How do you know?"

Dot explained what Lucy had just found out. "We don't know any details. The only thing we know is police are saying it was his body they found."

"You don't think Lucy would be a suspect..." He turned to Lucy.

The thought hadn't occurred to Gloria - or Lucy for that matter. Would Lucy be a suspect? Their break up hadn't been that long ago.

Gloria had heard that Bill already had a new girlfriend. Lucy had moved on and was dating Max Field, a man Gloria and she had met when they were investigating the disappearance of Milton Tilton, a resident of nearby Dreamwood Retirement Community.

"We could both be suspects." Lucy frowned at Gloria.

It was true. Gloria suspected she was already on police radar due to her proximity to the location of where the body had been found. Lucy would be a suspect as a disgruntled ex...with a penchant for guns and blowing stuff up.

"We don't know how he died," Gloria pointed out. Paul might know. The investigators the girls met earlier had been from neighboring Kensington County but the two police departments often crossed paths and many of the officers and investigators knew one another.

"Let me ask Paul."

The girls headed out the back door and over to the picnic table. Dot brought out several bowls of chili and the girls ate their food in silence.

Ray popped his head out the screen door. "Margaret just walked in." Margaret was one of the Garden Girls and another close friend.

"Send her back," Dot told him.

Seconds later, Margaret emerged from the restaurant. She studied her friends' faces. "Looks like you heard." She settled onto the bench seat directly across from Gloria.

"Yeah. Can you believe it?" Ruth shook her head.

Margaret folded her arms on the table. "I was gonna tell you that Don had stopped by Bill's store to pick up some golf balls first thing this morning. One of the employees told him they had found the owner shot to death in an abandoned house."

***

"This is getting worse by the minute," Lucy whispered. "What if they think I killed him?" She remembered the phone call Bill had made to her the day before. Had he wanted to tell her something, that he suspected someone was after him?

"Especially since Bill tried to call you," Gloria grimaced. "But Bill owned a sporting goods store and they sold guns," she added.

She glanced at Margaret. "I wonder if Bill's new girlfriend likes guns."

Gloria had to believe the woman did. Bill was a gung-ho outdoor enthusiast and had gotten Lucy interested in all kinds of new activities. It had been one of the reasons for the break up.

Bill planned for Lucy to go hunting with him and when she told him she wanted to spend time with her friends, he told her she could spend all the time she wanted with them. That argument had been the beginning of the end of their relationship.

Dot stacked the empty chili bowls while Gloria picked up the dirty spoons.

Margaret patted Lucy on the back. "I'm sorry Lucy. I can just imagine how hard this must be."

"I-I'll be fine," Lucy reassured her friends.

Gloria opted to stick to the alley as they made their way back to the car.

When they were safely inside the car, Gloria turned to her friend. "Do you wanna come spend the night at my house?" She was concerned about Lucy staying alone.

Lucy shook her head. "No. Jasper is home waiting for me." Jasper was the dog Lucy had recently adopted during Gloria's investigation at a local puppy mill. "Plus, Max is going to stop by later."

Gloria backed the car out of the parking spot and onto Main Street. She shifted the car into drive. "I need to stop by Andrea's place to find out Alice's plan to help the puppies."

Gloria had recently sold some valuable coins. She had promised to use some of the money she had gotten from the sale of the coins to turn a puppy mill they had stumbled upon into a training center for dogs. The plan was to train the dogs and then sell or donate them to those with special medical needs.

Alice and Andrea had assured Gloria that with proper training, the Acosta family, who owned the dogs, could turn it around and into something special.

"We can go now," Lucy said.

Gloria glanced down at the clock on her dashboard. "If you don't mind."

Andrea's newly remodeled mini mansion was near Lake Terrace and just blocks from downtown.

Gloria turned into Andrea's drive and parked behind her young friend's pick-up truck. Brian, Andrea's boyfriend, was also there.

Brian was Brian Sellers, the owner of Nails and Knobs Hardware store. He also owned several other small businesses in Belhaven, including a grocery store and pharmacy.

Andrea and Brian had been dating for quite a while now and Gloria wondered if someday soon Brian might pop the question to Andrea. Gloria was dying to ask but didn't want to seem nosy. She also didn't want to put poor Brian on the spot.

If truth be told, it was none of her business.

The girls climbed out of the car and made their way to the front door.

Gloria grasped the lion's head doorknocker and rapped sharply.

Minutes later, the door swung open and Alice, Andrea's former housekeeper and current housemate, greeted them. "Oh Miss Gloria." She clapped her hands. "Andrea and I wondered if you forgot about us."

Gloria's eyes slid to Lucy, who stood next to her. "I got a little sidetracked earlier. I hope it's not too late to talk."

Alice reached for Gloria's hand and pulled her inside. "No. No. I spoke with Mr. Acosta today. He is still excited about our idea of turning his dog kennel into a training center."

The girls followed Alice down a small hall and into the library. "Miss Andrea and Brian are in here." She waved them into the warm, inviting room and then followed them in.

Andrea was sitting at a small desk in the corner. Brian was standing next to her. She quickly lowered the lid on the computer, which made Gloria instantly suspicious. Andrea reminded Gloria of one of her own children when they tried to hide something.

She took a step closer. "What are you doing dear?" she asked.

"Oh...just working on Thanksgiving and some minor details for your upcoming wedding," Andrea told her.

Gloria nodded. She certainly had her plate full. Thanksgiving would be the quietest affair. Gloria had invited her daughter, Jill, and Jill's family, along with Paul and his two children.

Christmas, on the other hand, was going to be the humdinger. Not only would all of Gloria's children be in town for the holiday, Gloria and her boyfriend, Paul Kennedy, planned to marry.

Andrea waved to the large, wingback leather chairs. "Have a seat."

Gloria slid into the seat closest to Andrea. She crossed her legs and leaned back in the chair. "Do you still want to visit the Acostas tomorrow?"

Andrea tucked a strand of blonde hair behind her ear. "Yes. Alice is driving me nuts."

"Good. Come by the house tomorrow morning and we'll ride together." Gloria turned to Lucy. "You can come, too."

Lucy wasn't paying any attention to the conversation. Her mind was a million miles away as she stared out through the library window at the backyard. "What? I'm sorry Gloria. I missed what you said."

"I said you can visit the puppy place with us, too."

Lucy frowned. "No. I think I'm going to hang around the house tomorrow."

She turned to Andrea. "I just found out that my ex-boyfriend, Bill's, body was found in the house across the street from Gloria."

Andrea's hand flew to her mouth. "Oh my gosh." Andrea had met Bill right after she moved to Belhaven. She knew that Bill wasn't one of Gloria's favorite people and that Lucy and Bill's relationship had ended not long ago. "That's the first I've heard."

Andrea had had to deal with her own share of deaths, including the death of her husband, Daniel.

"That place has been vacant as long as I've lived in Belhaven," Andrea remarked.

Gloria shifted in her chair. "A young couple just bought the place and started to fix it up."

In the back of Gloria's mind, she had to wonder if whoever had killed Bill Volk had intentionally set out to frame Gloria. If that was the case, they were succeeding. It would only be a matter of time before police tied Bill to Lucy and then in a roundabout way, to Gloria.

Lucy must have thought the same thing. She slowly turned to Gloria. "You don't think someone killed Bill and left his body in the house across the street to frame you..."

That was exactly what Gloria thought. Someone had it in for Gloria, or Lucy. "As soon as I get back home, I'm going to call Paul to see what he knows." She slid out of the chair and rose to her feet. "I should get back. Mally and Puddles will be wondering what happened to me."

Andrea and Brian walked the girls to the front door.

Gloria shifted her purse on her shoulder. She glanced at Lucy. Neither she nor Lucy had ever been the focus of an investigation. "We need to do a little snooping around, starting with Bill's business."

The girls rode in silence as they headed to Lucy's place.

Gloria pulled into Lucy's drive, shifted the car into park and turned to her friend. "You gonna be okay?"

Lucy reached for the door handle and nodded. "Yeah. I don't think it has sunk in yet," she admitted. "Max will be here soon."

Gloria suspected that Lucy was still in shock. She made a mental note to call her later, before she went to bed that night.

She backed out of the drive and eased Annabelle onto the road. Shadows from the trees crept across the two-lane road. It would be dark soon and she would be glad to be home.

Gloria no longer cared to drive on the roads after dark. It was hard for her to judge distance. Not only that, but a freezing drizzle coated the roads making them a little slippery.

She breathed a sigh of relief when she pulled into her drive and parked the car in the garage. Her eyes wandered to the house across the street. It was dark, empty and looked sinister. The only light was Gloria's mercury light on the other side of the barn.

Gloria picked up the pace as she headed up the steps to the back porch. Someone - a killer - had been only yards away from her own front door.

She let Mally out for a brief run and then quickly brought her back in. She would need to be on alert until police apprehended the murderer.

Gloria dropped her purse on the chair and pulled her cell phone out. She dialed Paul's cell phone number and he picked up on the first ring. "I've been wondering when you were going to call," he said.

Gloria stepped over to the kitchen window, lifted the blind and peeked out. "I guess you heard."

Gloria could envision Paul rubbing his temples as he talked to his fiancé, who had a penchant for getting caught smack dab in the middle of some doozy investigations. "Fred Burnett, Kensington County's lead investigator, called a short time ago. Somehow, he found out that my soon-to-be bride lives right across the street from a crime scene."

"And?" Gloria asked.

"He was snooping around, asking vague questions about you."

Gloria's heart sank. She knew that there was now a bullseye on her back, and that someone was trying to frame her. She thought about Lucy. "You know that the deceased was Bill Volk, Lucy's ex-boyfriend."

There was a long silence on the other end of the line. "No. I heard the name but didn't put the two together." Long sigh. "This doesn't look good," he said.

After they hung up, Gloria made her way into the dining room. Puddles, Gloria's cat, was napping on the chair. She gently picked him up, settled into the chair and lowered him onto her lap. Puddles opened one eye, purred contentedly and then promptly fell back asleep.

Gloria checked her emails, replied to messages from her two sons, who would be coming for a visit next month and then opened a new screen. Lucy had mentioned the name of Bill's sporting goods store. *All Weather, All Purpose...*

Gloria reached for her cell phone that was on the desk next to the computer. She dialed Lucy's home phone.

"Hello?"

"Hi Lucy. Gloria here. What was the name of Bill's sporting goods store? It was "All" something..."

"Seasons." Lucy lowered her voice. "I can't talk right now. The police are here."

Chapter 3

Gloria tightened her grip on the phone. "Call me when they're gone." She disconnected the line and set the phone down. She wondered if they would be on her doorstep next.

Her fingers flew over the keyboards as she typed in All Seasons Sporting Goods, Green Springs, Michigan." The image of a long gray building with large plate glass windows popped up on the screen. In the corner of the screen was a picture of Bill.

She clicked through the tabs at the top of the page. The store sold a variety of weapons, including rifles and handguns, along with duck calls and just about any other outdoors item under the sun.

The last tab she opened was the "about us." Gloria reached for her reading glasses and slipped them on. Front and center was a picture of Bill, surrounded by his employees.

None of the names meant anything to her, except for one – an employee by the name of Randy Volk. She wondered if perhaps Randy wasn't related to Bill.

Her eyes squinted as she studied his face. There were similar facial features and Gloria would bet money the two were somehow related.

Her eyes drifted to the woman standing on the other side of Bill. A little too close in Gloria's opinion.

Gloria squinted her eyes and leaned in. It almost looked as if Bill had his arm around the woman's waist.

She glanced down at the corner clock. It was getting late...too late to make a trip to All Seasons tonight.

Gloria jumped when her cell phone began to ring. She lifted the phone and stared at the screen. It was Lucy.

"Are they gone?

"Yes, but I think they'll be back...to arrest me."

Gloria ran her fingers lightly over the computer keys. "What makes you think that?"

"Because they searched my shed and found a gun that matches the one that was used in Bill's shooting."

The blood drained from Gloria's face and she began to feel lightheaded.

"They said something about a knife had been used, too." Lucy went on. "I think they're headed to your place next. They kept asking how close..."

Gloria jumped. Someone was banging on her porch door.

She pushed the chair away from the desk and set Puddles on the floor. "I think they're here. I'll call you back." She hung up the phone and headed to the back door.

Gloria peeked out the side window and caught a glimpse of a man in uniform. She closed her eyes. "Dear Lord, please help Lucy and me," was all she had time to say.

473

She calmly unlocked the deadbolt and pulled the door open.

The uniformed officer that stood in the doorway looked familiar. He was the same one she had met earlier.

He tipped his hat. "Good evening, Mrs. Rutherford. I'm sorry to bother you this late in the day, but wondered if you had a few minutes to spare. I would like to ask you some questions about the house across the street."

Gloria swung the door open and stepped to the side. "Please. Come in." She motioned him in. "Have a seat. Coffee?"

She knew she was jabbering at the jaws but she was nervous. She had never been on the receiving end of a police investigation. Well...maybe once, but that had been a huge misunderstanding.

Officer Burnett eased his tall frame into a chair near the door and removed his hat. "I just spoke with your friend, Lucy Carlson. It seems that Mr. Volk, the man whose body was found in the empty house across the street, was well-acquainted with Ms. Carlson."

Gloria nodded. "Yes. They knew each other." Gloria silently told herself to keep the answers as brief as possible so as not to incriminate Lucy or herself.

Burnett propped an elbow on the table. "Were you acquainted with Mr. Volk?"

"Yes. I met Mr. Volk some time ago."

"So you were aware that Ms. Carlson and Mr. Volk had dated?" he asked.

Gloria felt as if Fred Burnett were trying to trap her, to get her to say something to throw poor Lucy under the bus. She wondered if she should tell him that she wanted a lawyer present. Of course, that would make her appear guilty as all get out.

Gloria remembered hearing one time that if you didn't want to answer a question, to ask one of your own. "Is Lucy a suspect?"

Burnett shifted in his chair. "We are in the beginning stages of the investigation. No one has been ruled out as a suspect...including you."

Beads of perspiration formed on Gloria's brow. She met Burnett's gaze. She would not let this man intimidate her. She hadn't done anything wrong and neither had Lucy.

The tone of Burnett's voice and his obvious attempt at intimidation ruffled Gloria's feathers. She replied in a cool, even tone. "It seems to me that you're trying to insinuate that Lucy and I are somehow involved in Mr. Volk's demise and I can assure you that we had nothing to do with his death."

She calmly walked over to the door and yanked it open. "Now. If you don't mind, I have had a very long day."

Burnett pushed the chair back and slowly rose. He stepped onto the porch and turned back. "I had hoped to end this visit on a different note but you leave me no choice."

475

He shifted his gaze and stared across the street in the direction of the farm across the road, although it was pitch black. "I intend to solve this murder case, with or without your cooperation."

Gloria's eyes narrowed. That sounded like a threat to her. She waited until Burnett reached the sidewalk before she slammed the door shut. She clicked the deadbolt in place and reached for her cell phone to call Lucy.

Lucy picked up on the first ring. "He's gone."

"W-what did he say?"

Gloria repeated the questions Burnett had asked and then told her friend how she'd gotten angry and showed him the door.

Despite the gravity of the situation, Lucy giggled. "You didn't."

"I did," Gloria said. "But I'm not sure how much that will help our case. He'll be back. Mark my words."

Lucy said what Gloria already suspected. "He thinks that we're...or at least that I'm involved."

Gloria ran her hand through her hair. "Yes, Lucy. I'm afraid he does. That's why we have to get over to Bill's store first thing tomorrow morning." *Before they arrest one of us for Bill's murder*, she silently added.

***

Gloria tossed and turned all night. Visions of Lucy locked up behind bars filled her mind. Gloria had been behind bars once before, although it was only for one night and had been a huge misunderstanding. Lucy, on the other hand, had never been arrested.

Jail was not a pleasant experience and Gloria vowed to avoid a repeat, if possible.

She crawled out of bed early the next morning, wiggled her feet into her slippers and headed for the door.

Mally, who lay curled up in her doggie bed on the other side of the dresser, let out a low moan and rolled over to face the wall.

Gloria glanced in the dining room mirror on her way to the kitchen. Tufts of gray hair stood straight up and she patted them down as she walked.

When the coffee pot began to brew, Gloria reached for the well-worn Bible she kept on the corner curio cabinet. Bill's death lay heavy on her heart, not only for the predicament that the two women were now in, but also for Bill and his family.

She turned to 2 Corinthians 4:17-18 NIV:

"For our light and momentary troubles are achieving for us an eternal glory that far outweighs them all.

So we fix our eyes not on what is seen, but on what is unseen, since what is seen is temporary, but what is unseen is eternal."

Gloria closed her eyes and prayed for Bill's salvation, for her own salvation and her friends and family. She knew that she could be gone in the blink of an eye and vowed to take the time to tell her children and loved ones how much she loved them.

Gloria slid out of the chair and made her way over to the kitchen cupboard. She reached inside for a clean coffee cup and watched as Mally padded into the kitchen.

She filled her cup with piping hot coffee and then the two of them stepped outside and onto the porch.

A light frost covered the ground and wisps of mist escaped Gloria's mouth as she yawned. Her eyes drifted to the house across the street. Someone had intentionally left Bill's body in that house for the sole purpose of framing either Lucy or Gloria...or both of them. Someone who knew them well enough to know that the police would link the two together.

After Mally finished patrolling the perimeter of the farm and marking her favorite tree, the two of them headed back inside. Today was going to be a busy day and her first order of business was to visit All Seasons Sporting Goods.

Chapter 4

Gloria reached for the phone to call Lucy when she spied Andrea's truck as it pulled into the drive.

Gloria groaned. She had completely forgotten her promise to visit the puppy mill with Andrea and Alice that morning.

She quickly dialed Lucy's number. "I forgot I promised to visit the puppy mill this morning. Do you want to ride with me and then afterwards we can head over to Bill's store?"

Lucy paused. Gloria could hear her pup, Jasper, barking in the background. "I don't know...I'm not company material today."

"Neither am I," Gloria argued, "which is a perfect reason why the two of us need to get out of the house."

Lucy finally caved and agreed to hurry up and head over so that she could ride with Gloria.

Gloria met Andrea and Alice on the porch. The morning sun had popped up on the horizon and beamed brightly in her eyes. She shaded her eyes against the bright light. "Lucy is on her way."

While the trio waited for Lucy, Gloria explained how the police had questioned Lucy and her the night before.

Andrea frowned. "They think that you have something to do with Bill's murder?"

Gloria shrugged. She didn't have time to answer as she watched Lucy pulled into the drive and parked off to the side.

She could tell by the way that Lucy trudged across the drive that her friend was down in the dumps.

Lucy lowered her sunglasses as she headed to the steps. Gloria had a hunch that Lucy had been crying and her heart sank.

She stepped off the porch and met Lucy on the sidewalk. "I explained to Andrea and Alice that we would follow them to the Acosta's farm."

Lucy nodded.

Andrea stepped close. "I'm sorry Lucy. If there's anything I can do to help..." her voice trailed off.

"I-It's okay."

It was bad enough that someone Lucy had at one time cared deeply for had been murdered but it was even worse to be questioned by the police as a possible suspect.

Gloria vowed to get to the bottom of it. She glanced down at her watch. "It's time to get this show on the road."

With a purposeful stride, she made her way over to the garage and lifted the garage door. Lucy trailed behind and climbed into the passenger seat while Gloria started the car.

The ride to the Acosta farm was silent. Gloria wasn't even sure where to start to try to help her friend with the sudden turn of events.

Andrea and Alice were already on the porch talking to Mr. Acosta when Gloria pulled her car into the rutted drive.

"We talk inside." He motioned the women inside the house and over to the kitchen table.

Two young children hovered in the doorway. "These are my children, Robert and Emeline. I have a teenage daughter, too, but she is with her mother." The children smiled shyly and then darted into the other room.

"They are beautiful children," Gloria told him. "Is your wife here?" She looked around.

"No. My wife, Maria, she moved back to New York. She did not want to live in the country," Marco Acosta explained.

Open mouth. Insert foot. Gloria had a sudden urge to have the floor open up and swallow her. "I am so sorry."

She quickly changed the subject. "I'm sure that helping others will make this all worthwhile."

Gloria turned the meeting over to Alice, who had done a great deal of research on rescue dogs and their training.

Gloria listened with interest and almost, not quite, but almost forgot about the dark cloud looming over her head...namely Bill's recent demise.

Alice explained that start-up costs for the training center would be high unless they combined it with a dog sitting service. "We need a website," she told them.

Gloria raised both hands. "Not me. My internet skills are basic at best."

The group turned expectant eyes to Andrea, the youngest person sitting at the table. She shook her head. "I'm sorry folks, but I am no expert." She had a sudden thought. "But Brian is handy at creating websites."

Gloria lifted a brow. It was true. Brian owned several small businesses in the Town of Belhaven. Maybe they could recruit him.

Alice pulled several sheets of paper from a manila folder she had brought with her. "We visited a few of the local animal kennels and a larger training facility in Grand Rapids."

She outlined the general plan and Gloria was impressed with Alice's knowledge of kennels and the research she had done.

With a plan in place and Gloria's commitment to help with the first six months of expenses, the meeting ended.

Gloria got a good feel for Marco Acosta. She felt bad about his wife, Maria, leaving him.

Before they left, Gloria and the girls stopped out back to check on the pups. The conditions were as deplorable as

Gloria remembered and Alice vowed to come back first thing in the morning to start working on the living conditions.

Gloria scribbled out a check for the first month's expenses, handed the check to Alice and then climbed into the car.

Lucy climbed in next to her. She reached for her seatbelt. "You have the most generous heart out of anyone I know," Lucy told her.

"I-..." Gloria was about to disagree but quickly changed her mind. She did try.

Gloria was no saint and could be just as selfish and judgmental as the next person could. Still, it was nice to be on the receiving end of a compliment. "Thanks, Lucy," she simply said.

The girls stayed on the safe subject of the puppy project they had dubbed, "At Your Service Dogs," with Lucy volunteering a few hours each week to help the girls get the business up and running.

Lucy directed Gloria to All Seasons Sporting Goods in Green Springs. The first thing Gloria noticed when she pulled in the parking lot was that it was empty. "Is this place even open?" She shifted the car in park and turned the engine off.

Lucy grabbed the door handle. "Maybe they closed shop."

The women slid out of the car and wandered to the front door. The lights were on and when they pushed on the door, it swung open.

Gloria followed Lucy down the center aisle to the counter located in the back of the store. She glanced from side to side as she noted the wide variety of outdoor enthusiast items.

Behind the counter stood a man that Gloria recognized from the photo she had seen online. He was the man that resembled Bill.

Standing next to him was a younger man she guessed to be in his early twenties. The last person behind the counter was a woman. Gloria recognized her as the woman in the picture that appeared to cozy up to Bill.

When they got close, Gloria could read the man's nametag: *Randy.* She hung back and let Lucy take the lead.

Randy eyed the women with interest. His gaze turned to Lucy. "Hello Lucy."

Lucy tucked a stray strand of red hair behind her ear. "Hello Randy. I...we...stopped by to offer our condolences."

Randy's gaze turned to Gloria. "Thank you. We're still in shock."

Lucy nodded. "I'm sure. I still can't believe Bill is gone..." her voice trailed off.

"Police were by here earlier asking questions about Bill. They told us his body had been found in a vacant farmhouse not far from your place." Gloria could've sworn she noted a flicker of accusation cross his face.

Gloria didn't dare mention that the place he'd been found was directly across the street from her. "You're Bill's brother. Who do you think had it in for him?"

Randy shrugged. "I have no idea."

The dark-haired woman standing next to Randy suddenly spoke. "The only person I can think of would be Lucy," she blurted out.

Lucy began to shake her head. "No..."

Gloria lowered her gaze to read the woman's tag. *Barbara* stepped closer. The woman crossed her arms and shifted her stance. "Bill said that there was some bad blood between you and that you refused to return some of the guns he had loaned you."

Lucy rubbed the palm of her hand on the top of her jeans. "No. That's not true. I never borrowed anything from Bill. I own every single gun that I have and I can prove it." Lucy's face turned as red as her hair.

Barbara's eyes sparked. "I think that is a bald-faced lie and I told the police that they should take a close look at you."

"Why, I." Lucy pointed at the woman's nametag. "Hey. I know who you are. Bill told me months ago, before we broke up that you were chasing after him." She handed her purse to Gloria. "You're one of the reasons we broke up."

Gloria could tell by the wild look in Lucy's eyes that things were about to head south...to the Mexican border south. She slung both purses over her shoulder and reached for Lucy's arm. "Maybe we should go."

It was as if Lucy hadn't even heard Gloria. Her full attention focused on the woman on the other side of the counter.

"Why don't we step outside," Lucy challenged.

The woman – Barbara – rolled up her sleeves. "Why don't we?"

Visions of Lucy and this Barbara woman rolling around on the ground, punching each other and pulling each other's hair flashed across Gloria's mind.

Apparently, Randy had the same thought and he reached for Barbara's arm. "It's not worth it, Barb," he reasoned.

The young man behind the counter mysteriously disappeared in the midst of the conflict...*what if he was calling the cops?*

"Let's go, Lucy," Gloria urged. She tugged on Lucy's arm.

The women retraced their steps and exited the store. Gloria kept a firm grip on Lucy's arm as she led her to the car.

"Psst."

Gloria shifted her attention as she gazed over the roof of the car.

"Over here." The young man, who had been behind the counter, was motioning for Gloria to come over.

Gloria glanced inside the store and then casually made her way around the front of the car.

Lucy started to follow Gloria but Gloria waved her back to the car. She didn't want to draw attention...at least no more attention than they already had.

The young man, Zeke, according to the name embroidered on his shirt, motioned her forward. "Something funny was goin' on here right before Mr. Volk's death," he said. "Mr. Volk asked me to keep an eye on the cash register. He thought one of the other workers was stealing from him."

Gloria leaned in. "Did you tell the police that?"

Zeke plucked a pack of cigarettes from his front pocket. He tapped the pack on the side of his hand and pulled one out. "Nope. The police questioned us at the same time and I didn't want to say anything in front of the others."

Gloria nodded. Smart move. Otherwise, it might put a target on his back. "You need to talk to Officer Fred Burnett," she said.

Zeke clamped the cigarette between his lips and fumbled in his pants pocket for his lighter. "Yes, ma'am. I'm going to do that just as soon as I leave work today."

Gloria heard a car door slam in the distance. "Who do you think killed Mr. Volk?" she asked.

Zeke lit the cigarette and took a drag. "Could be one of the people that worked at the store. There was also a weirdo gun salesman that kept coming in. Every time he showed up, Mr. Volk would disappear in the back of the store and tell us to tell him that he wasn't here."

"Did you get a name?" This could be a huge clue.

"Maxim. Something Maxim." Zeke flicked a cigarette ash on the sidewalk. "All I know is he avoided this Maxim guy like the plague."

"Zeke." Someone from behind the store called Zeke's name.

"Look. I gotta go." Zeke dropped the cigarette on the cement and crushed it with the tip of his shoe. He jogged down the sidewalk that ran next to the building and disappeared from sight.

Gloria slowly walked back to the car. She opened the driver's side door and slid into the seat. "Did Bill ever mention someone by the name of Maxim?"

Lucy frowned. "Hmm. Maybe."

Gloria fastened her seatbelt and started the car.

"I think I remember..." Lucy rubbed her forehead. "Yeah. Bill hated the guy. He was some sort of salesman, always trying to pressure Bill into buying more guns and ammo."

Lucy gazed out the window as Gloria pulled onto the road. "He sold a special kind of gun. It was real expensive."

Lucy turned to face Gloria. "Oh my gosh, Gloria. The gun. The special gun. It was a Kahr® brand. It's the same gun that I have and the same one that the police told me killed Bill."

Chapter 5

Gloria's head was spinning. First, there were the employees at All Seasons Sporting Goods who may or may not have been stealing. The woman, Barbara, who all but accused Lucy of killing Bill, and now this "Maxim" guy who Bill did not care for and sold Bill the custom gun that had, in fact, killed him. She added all of them to her mental list of suspects and included the employee, Zeke.

He seemed eager to throw others under the bus, but he was an employee, too. Maybe he was under suspicion for stealing, as well. He said that Bill told him to keep an eye on the others, but why would Bill have ruled him out as a possible thief?

Lucy and Gloria discussed the list of suspects on their way home. The next step in the investigation was to get inside the house across the street to see if there were any clues investigators may have missed.

Lucy read Gloria's mind. "We need to sneak into that house. The sooner the better."

When they reached the Town of Belhaven, Gloria made a last minute decision to stop by Dot's Restaurant.

Dot spotted the girls when they stepped through the door. She met them at a back table with a cup of coffee for Gloria and a cup of hot water, along with a packet of hot chocolate for Lucy.

Gloria caught a whiff of chicken and dumplings. Dot's famous chicken and dumplings to be exact. Her stomach grumbled. "I'm starving." She had been in such a hurry to start the investigation she had skipped breakfast.

"Me too," Lucy said. "I'll take the chicken and dumplings."

"Ditto," Gloria agreed.

Dot pulled her order pad from her apron pocket and jotted their orders down. "How is the investigation going?"

Gloria lifted the coffee cup to her lips and sipped. "We're racking up more suspects than Carter has liver pills."

Dot snorted. "So I guess the case is in high gear."

Lucy dumped the packet of hot chocolate in her cup. She added hot water, three packets of sugar and picked up her spoon. "We're hoping to lock onto something before one of us ends up in jail, charged with Bill's murder."

Dot set the coffee pot on the edge of the table. "Are you serious? You two are suspects?"

At one time or another, each of the Garden Girls had been the subject of a criminal investigation. Everyone that is, except for Lucy and Gloria. And maybe Margaret.

Lucy lifted her mug of hot chocolate and sipped. "Needs a little more sugar." She reached for another sugar packet.

Gloria explained how the gun that had killed Bill was a custom gun, one that he carried in his shop and the same brand gun that Lucy owned.

Gloria told Dot about Officer Burnett's visit the evening before and how she had politely shown him the door. "I think I've managed to make it to the suspect list."

"Maybe the detective thinks that you're covering for Lucy," Dot pointed out.

"Or that I'm an accomplice," Gloria added. "That's why Lucy and I are going to sneak into the house across the street later tonight to search for clues."

She knew they were grasping at straws. The investigators had been across the street several times and she was certain they had probably turned up anything and everything that looked suspicious. Still, they had to try…

Dot picked up the coffee pot and turned to go. "I'm not sure that's a good idea. The last thing you need is to get caught inside that house."

In the back of Gloria's mind, the warning bells went off. Dot was right. It wouldn't look good.

Looking back, she wished she had heeded Dot's warning and her own feeling of foreboding.

***

The girls stepped out onto the back porch and Gloria stared up at the sky. It was pitch black. A thick layer of clouds hung in the air, obliterating the stars and moon.

Gloria took the lead as she and Lucy crept across the deserted street. She reached a hand inside her jacket pocket and touched the top of her 9mm handgun, safely tucked inside.

Gloria couldn't shake the feeling that the outcome of this covert operation was going to end badly.

At best, they ran the risk of getting caught and being charged with breaking and entering...but only if the new owners decided to press charges...she hoped not.

At worst, the killer could return to the scene of the crime and add two more notches to his belt: the two of them.

Gloria pushed aside the nagging thought of something going awry. After all, who in their right mind would show up this late at night?

The girls had decided not to share their plan with anyone and Dot swore she wouldn't breathe a word.

Gloria had even had to tell Paul that she would have to call him a little later than normal because something unexpected had come up.

He seemed curious but didn't press. He knew his betrothed well enough to know that she was more than likely up to something and that he more than likely did not want to know what that something was.

"You got it?" Gloria whispered to Lucy, who crept silently next to her.

Lucy nodded. "Yep." She lifted the mini flashlight and held it out.

A loud thumping echoed in the still night air. It sounded like it was coming from the old corncrib behind the barn.

Lucy tugged on Gloria's coat sleeve. "What was that?"

"I-I don't know," Gloria answered. The hair on the back of her neck stood straight out. Something felt wrong...terribly wrong. She prayed they weren't walking into a trap and the killer hadn't returned for some unfinished business, namely them.

Gloria swallowed the lump in her throat and pushed back the feeling of dread. "Let's get this over with."

The girls tiptoed across the gravel drive and around to the back door. Gloria reached for the handle. The door was locked.

"It's locked," Gloria hissed.

Lucy reached inside her back pocket. "That's okay. I think I can open it."

Gloria stepped to the side and Lucy stepped in front of the door. She shoved what appeared to be a credit card, in between the door and the jamb. She slowly slid the card down as she turned the knob.

"Pop." The door creaked open.

Gloria shook her head. "The Jill of all Trades," she joked.

Gloria reached inside her other pocket and pulled out a small flashlight. She turned it on and pointed the beam at the floor. "Where did you learn that trick? Never mind. Maybe I don't want to know."

She took a step inside the kitchen. The floorboards creaked under the weight.

"Shh," Lucy whispered.

"I can't shh," Gloria said.

"Then let's hurry up," Lucy urged. "What's the plan?"

Gloria didn't have a plan. It had been years since Gloria had been inside the old farmhouse. She vaguely remembered that the kitchen was located in the back.

"Time is of the essence." Lucy reached for her own flashlight and flipped the switch. "You start over there and I'll start here."

The girls methodically searched the small kitchen...or what was left of it. The house was in the midst of major renovations. A few of the lower cabinets were still there but all of the upper cabinets were missing.

Gloria made a mental note to try to find out the names of the construction workers on site. What if one of them had taken Bill out? It was a stretch but they certainly had access to the house...

"There's nothing here." Lucy turned to Gloria. "I wish we knew where Bill's...uh, where Bill had been found."

"Let's try the other room," Gloria suggested. She pointed her flashlight at the floor and crept forward.

Lucy was right on Gloria's heel as the women made their way into the living room.

Gloria beamed the light around the room. Furniture crowded the center. Large sheets of cloth covered each of the pieces. She guessed this was to keep them from getting dirty during construction.

Gloria lifted the corner of a sheet and peeked underneath. It was a chair and it looked vaguely familiar. She wondered if it was something James' brother had left behind.

Lucy stuck close to Gloria as she studied the small room. "This place is giving me the heebie-jeebies."

It was giving Gloria the willies, too. Just the fact that a murderer had been inside the house was enough to cause her stomach to twist in knots.

"Let's search the bedrooms," Gloria suggested. She led the way as the women quietly stepped into the first bedroom. Her eyes had adjusted to the lack of light and she pointed her flashlight at the floor.

The room was empty. Off to the far right was a closet, the door closed.

Gloria eyed the door cautiously. Did she really want to look inside?

Gloria pushed her fear aside. This was the whole reason they were there. She stiffened her back. "Let's finish this."

Before she could change her mind, she grabbed the handle of the door and yanked it open. Something large and black shot out at Gloria. She stumbled backwards. "Agh."

Lucy, certain that Gloria was under attack, bolted from the room.

The dark object whacked Gloria on the forehead. She clenched both fists and swung at it furiously. She wasn't going down without a fight.

When it didn't fight back, she opened her eyes. It was the handle of a broom.

Gloria shoved the broom back inside the closet. "It was just a broom," she hollered into the living room.

"Scaredy-cat," she mumbled under her breath.

Lucy scurried back inside the bedroom. "I was going for help."

"Sure you were," Gloria laughed. "I could've been dead by now."

The girls finished their search of both bedrooms and a small bath located between the two bedrooms.

Gloria flicked the flashlight off. "It's hard to tell if there's a clue or not. I'm gonna go with the place is clean."

"Yeah. Let's get out of here," Lucy agreed.

The girls turned back toward the kitchen when a noise on the front porch caused them to stop dead in their tracks.

"Did you hear that?" Gloria whispered.

"Uh-huh. W-what was it?" Lucy asked.

Gloria slowly turned her gaze to the front door. She could see the shadow of someone through the glass pane. "There's someone at the door."

Just then, the doorknob began to rattle. Whoever was at the door was trying to get in.

Chapter 6

"Hit the deck." Gloria grabbed Lucy's hand and dragged her down. The girls landed on the floor with a dull thud.

"Follow me." Gloria slithered along the scuffed wooden floor in a desperate attempt to reach the kitchen – and the back door.

She cast a furtive glance behind her. The shadowy figure was still there and the knob rattled again. It echoed loudly in the quiet of the house. It sounded to Gloria like the rattle of death.

Lucy, who was right behind Gloria and gaining quickly, grabbed the heel of Gloria's sneaker. "Get your gun out."

Gloria had almost forgotten she'd brought her handgun with her. She twisted to the side, fumbled inside the pocket of her jacket and reached for her gun. It wasn't there. "I-It must've fallen out of my pocket when I hit the floor," she gasped.

Lucy spun like a kid on a merry-go-round and headed back to where they'd made contact with the floor. The palms of her hands darted back and forth as she searched in vain for the cool metal of the weapon.

Gloria turned back, too, frantically sweeping her arm across the floor as she searched for the missing weapon.

499

Gloria glanced up at the door. The shadow was gone, along with whoever had been trying to get in.

She knew it was too good to be true. "You don't think..."

A beam of bright light shone in through the back door and illuminated a section of the living room floor. The girls froze. Gloria squeezed her eyes shut and offered up a silent prayer for protection.

***

"Hello?" The voice...male, was very familiar. "Gloria? Are you in here?"

Gloria's eyes shot open. "Paul?"

"Where are you?" The beam of light illuminated the living room and bounced off the wall. Finally, it came to rest on two sets of terrified eyes.

Gloria felt a wave of relief flood her body and sudden tears burned the back of her eyes.

The girls slowly rose to their feet.

"What are you doing here?" Gloria brushed at the sleeves of her shirt.

Lucy raised a hand in greeting. "Hi Paul."

"Hello Lucy," he answered and then turned to Gloria.

"What am I doing here?" Paul asked. "What are *you* two doing here?"

"We...uh..."

Paul shook his head. "I know what you're doing. Do you have any idea how much trouble you two could get into?"

Gloria had an inkling. But they were already in trouble so heaping a little more on top seemed insignificant, although she didn't tell Paul that.

"How did you find us?" Gloria brushed the dust bunnies from the front of her pants; her eyes casually scanned the floor in search of her gun, which was still MIA.

He nodded across the road. "I had a sneaky suspicion you were up to something so I thought I'd drop by. When I saw Mally wandering around the yard, Lucy's jeep in the drive and neither of you in sight, I put two and two together."

Lucy slid her foot across the smooth floor and made contact with the gun. She casually reached down and picked it up. "You sure got Gloria pegged," she joked.

Gloria shot her a death look as Lucy tried to slip the gun in the waistband of her pants.

Paul's sharp eye didn't miss a thing. "You brought your gun with you?"

"Well..."

"Not only did you bring your gun with you, you lost it? What if I had been the killer, found your gun and then shot you with your own weapon?"

This was as close Paul had ever come to scolding her errant behavior. Gloria looked properly contrite. "I'm sorry."

Paul, feeling bad for the tone he had just used and knowing that Gloria's heart was in the right place, wrapped an arm around her and pulled her close. "You're going to give me more gray hairs than I already have," he complained.

Gloria snuggled against Paul for a moment and then pulled back. "I think we're running out of time. My gut tells me that Officer Burnett is waiting to pounce," she predicted.

The trio wandered out the back door. Paul reached behind him, pulled the door shut and wiggled the knob to make sure it had locked. "How did you get in?"

Lucy pulled her local grocery store rewards card from her pocket. "I used this."

Paul led the way across the drive and to the edge of the road. "Lucy Carlson, I do believe you have missed your calling."

Lucy grinned. "Me too." Her smile vanished and she turned to her best friend. "I'm sorry to drag you into all of this," she apologized.

Gloria patted her arm. "You know that's not true. I was more than willing to jump into this investigation with both feet. On top of that, I'm sure I'm on the suspect list too," she pointed out.

Back inside the house, Gloria started a fresh pot of coffee while she explained to Paul what the All Seasons Sporting Goods employee, Zeke, had told her.

Paul poured a small amount of milk into his coffee cup and stirred. "Sounds to me like this Zeke character is throwing everyone under the bus but himself."

Gloria thought the same thing. There was no way to corroborate his story, especially the part about Bill telling him to keep an eye on the other employees.

Gloria dropped into the chair next to Paul and turned to Lucy. "That woman...Barbara. What's her story?"

Lucy explained that she had started working at Bill's store a few months before the two of them broke up. She said that Bill had told her the woman flirted with him all the time and that he had started to avoid her.

He had been trying to figure out how to let her go without bringing an unlawful termination of employment suit against him...or worse yet, sexual harassment.

Lucy turned the coffee cup in small circles. "Next thing I know, we break up and the two of them are dating."

"What about Bill's brother, Randy? Any bad blood there?" Gloria probed.

Lucy shrugged her shoulders. "He never said anything negative about Randy but I sometimes got the feeling that the two of them didn't get along."

Gloria tapped the tabletop with her fingernails. "So far we've got Zeke, Randy, the brother, Barbara, the on-again-off-again girlfriend and this Maxim guy that Bill didn't like."

Paul slid his chair back and stood. "I need to get back to the station." He pulled Gloria close and kissed her soundly on the lips.

Lucy covered her eyes and lowered her head. "Get a room," she teased.

Gloria giggled. "Won't be long now 'til wedding bells ring." She frowned. "Unless I'm too much to handle."

"No way," Paul said as he reached for the doorknob. "I kinda like you keeping me on my toes." He sighed as he pulled the door open. "Although it would be nice if maybe you took up something safe, like crocheting or pottery..."

Lucy snorted. "Pottery? I'd like to see that."

Gloria walked Paul out to his patrol car. He slid into the driver's seat, pulled the door shut and rolled down the window. He cast an uneasy glance in the mirror at the dark house across the street. "Call it a cop's intuition or just worrying about the love of my life, I have an uneasy feeling about this."

Gloria did, too, and Paul just confirmed her own thoughts. She leaned her head inside the window, closed her eyes and savored the sweet, tender kiss. When she pulled away, she lifted her hands above her head and stretched her back.

"Dinner tomorrow?" She had promised to make him a home-cooked meal. It would be nice to have quiet evening at home.

Paul nodded. "Can't wait. I've been looking forward to it all week." He blew Gloria a kiss, backed the patrol car out of the drive and waved as he drove off.

Lucy met her on the sidewalk, purse in hand. "I should get going. Jasper doesn't like to be left home alone after dark."

Lucy climbed into the jeep and slid the key into the ignition. She cast a wary glance back. "Better lock the doors as soon as you get inside," she warned.

Gloria nodded. "I will. Talk to you in the morning." She watched until Lucy's taillights disappeared from sight before she slowly shuffled back into the house.

***

Gloria dreamt that her grandsons, Tyler and Ryan, were visiting. They had decided to remodel the tree fort out front.

She was in the backyard hanging clothes on the line. She clipped the last clothespin to the edge of her blouse and picked up the laundry basket. Mally ran ahead and Gloria brought up the rear.

Gloria followed the sound of the hammering but when she got to the front yard, it was empty. The boys weren't in the treehouse but the pounding continued.

Through the haze of the dream, Gloria realized that the noise was real and it wasn't her grandsons at all. Someone was tapping on her bedroom window.

Gloria bolted upright in bed. She swung her feet over the edge of the bed and scooted to the window. She lifted the edge of the blind and peeked out.

Margaret was on the other side. She motioned frantically for Gloria to let her in.

Gloria cupped her hands to her mouth. "Go around."

Margaret disappeared and Gloria headed for the door. She grabbed her robe as she passed by the bed and glanced at the clock. It was 7:15 in the morning.

Gloria's heart began to race as she picked up the pace. Something was terribly wrong for Margaret to be pounding on her bedroom window at the crack of dawn.

Mally was already waiting at the door.

Gloria opened the door to let Margaret in and Mally out.

Margaret reached out and patted Mally's fur as the dog made a beeline for her favorite tree.

"Is everything okay?" Gloria asked as she swung the door open.

"No," Margaret said. "The police picked Lucy up first thing this morning. Ruth just told me they took her to jail."

Chapter 7

Gloria's mouth dropped open and she stared at Margaret, speechless. She had feared this moment was coming and had prayed before she went to bed the night before that it wasn't but that nagging feeling that something bad was about to happen hung in the back of her mind.

"What..."

"Ruth was on her way to work and saw the cops putting Lucy in the back of the cop car," Margaret blurted out. "When I stopped by the post office to drop some stuff in the box out front, Ruth met me at the door. She said Officer Nelson had just been by and he told her they picked Lucy up. He said they were going to charge her with Bill's murder."

The blood drained from Gloria's face. Poor Lucy. She had never been booked before, unlike Gloria, Margaret and Gloria's sister, Liz. It was an unpleasant experience and one that Gloria hoped she would never have to go through again.

Gloria motioned her into the kitchen and slowly walked over to the coffee pot. She poured the leftover coffee from the night before into clean cups and put both cups in the microwave. Normally, Gloria would have brewed a fresh pot but her mind was numb.

Margaret pulled out a kitchen chair and plopped down. "What are we going to do?"

"Call Paul." Gloria reached for her phone. The call went right to voice mail and Gloria had a hunch he was sleeping since he had worked the night before. "I'll have to wait. Maybe we should run down to the station. I can post bond."

"We need a lawyer," Margaret said.

"Right." Gloria nodded. "Brian should be able to point us in the right direction."

Just then, Dot's van pulled in behind Margaret's SUV. News sure did travel fast in the small Town of Belhaven. "You talk to Dot while I go get ready."

Gloria disappeared into the dining room and raced to the bedroom to grab some clean clothes. Her mind spun recklessly. What kind of evidence could the police possibly have to arrest Lucy?

Gloria emerged from the bathroom a short time later. Not only was Dot and Margaret there, Andrea and Ruth had arrived and the group of Garden Girls, minus Lucy, gathered around the kitchen table.

The girls looked at Gloria expectantly.

Dot spoke first. "This is a 911 Garden Girls emergency. What do we do?"

"Coffee. We need coffee to clear the cobwebs." Gloria made a beeline for the coffee pot. She filled the pot with water, popped a new filter into the basket, poured fresh coffee grounds inside the basket and then filled the reservoir before turning it to on.

The girls slid their chairs to the side to make room for Gloria. "The first thing we need to do is pray."

The girls promptly reached for each other's hand and bowed their heads. "Dear Lord. You know that our friend, Lucy, is in jail this morning, charged with a crime she didn't commit. Lord, we ask You to help us solve the murder and track down the true killer." Gloria didn't know what else to add so she ended it with, "Amen."

Dot uncovered a box of tasty looking pastries and donuts as Gloria set a cup in front of each of her friends. She poured freshly brewed coffee into each cup.

All of them eyed the tempting treats with the same thought in mind. Lucy was the sweet tooth of the bunch and just the sight of the goodies made Gloria's stomach churn.

"I don't think I can eat these," she admitted.

Andrea shook her head. "Me either."

They unanimously agreed that the sight of Lucy's favorite food caused them to lose their appetites.

Dot replaced the lid on the treats and pushed them off to the side. "What do we do?"

"The first thing we need to do is see if we can get Lucy out of jail," Gloria said.

She went on. "Then, we have to get serious about solving this case." She left the words unspoken that it was either that, or chance one of their closest friends being convicted of a crime she didn't commit.

Ruth lifted her cup to her lips and eyed Gloria over the rim. "What about Paul?"

"I left him a message." Gloria glanced at the clock above the sink. "Don't you have to work?" It was just after eight in the morning.

Ruth shook her head. "Kenny is holding down the fort." Kenny was Ruth's right hand man at the post office. When he found out one of the girls was in trouble, he offered to cover for Ruth until she could make it in.

Andrea nodded. "Maybe I should call Brian to see if he can recommend an attorney."

"Great minds think alike," Gloria said. "Margaret said the same thing."

Andrea reached for her cell phone while Gloria poured the last of the coffee and headed to the kitchen counter to brew another pot. While the coffee was brewing, she told the girls what had happened so far and ticked off the list of suspects.

Margaret wiped an imaginary crumb off the table. "Someone needs to do a little snooping around All Seasons Sporting Goods."

Ruth raised a brow. "Maybe look into ordering one of those guns. Like the one that killed Bill," she suggested.

Gloria wandered over to the counter and reached for the pot of coffee. "I'd love to but Lucy and I were in there yesterday. They would recognize me."

"True." Andrea dropped her chin on top of her fist. "I know enough about guns. Not as much as Lucy, for sure. But I'll go if one of you will go with me."

Ruth shook her head. "I'd go but I have to work."

"I can go in a pinch," Dot offered.

Margaret held up a hand. "The most obvious choice would be me. I can go. Besides, Don and I have been talking about buying a gun for protection, what with the way the world is today."

All heads turned to Margaret.

"You don't have a gun?" Gloria was surprised. Margaret and her husband, Don, were two of the wealthier residents in their small town. Don had retired a couple years earlier as vice president of a local bank. "Why that's your second amendment right."

Margaret frowned. "There was never a need."

She had a point. The Town of Belhaven was relatively crime free...except for the murder of Andrea's late husband, whose body had been discovered in the woods out back of the old elementary school. Or the time there was a large drug trafficking ring operating out of the post office. Then there was the time...

"I take that back," Margaret thought about her answer. "Yeah. It's probably time to buy a weapon."

The girls decided to divide and conquer. Andrea and Margaret would head over to All Seasons Sporting Goods to do a little investigative work.

Dot would stop by Nails and Knobs, Brian's hardware store, to see if he could recommend a good attorney.

Ruth had to head back to work so Kenny could start his route but promised she would keep her ear to the ground.

Gloria would be the one to drive to the police station to see if she could spring Lucy.

The girls agreed to meet at Dot's Restaurant around five and each of them headed out.

Dot was the last to leave. She reached for her purse and then paused. "I know you love Lucy with all your heart. You love all of us, and that you're worried sick. Just be careful, Gloria. Sometimes I think you carry the weight of the world on your shoulders."

Dot impulsively reached over and hugged her friend's neck. A lone tear trickled down Gloria's cheek as she watched Dot make her way back to her van. The stress of the last couple of days was wearing on her and at that moment, she felt every single one of her sixty some years.

Gloria slowly closed the door, leaned her head against the glass pane and let the tears flow. When she lifted her head, she wiped the wetness from her cheeks and stiffened her back. Lucy needed her and Gloria was not going to let her down.

Gloria grabbed her purse from the chair, her car keys from the hook near the door and stepped out onto the porch. It was time to bring Lucy home.

***

The Kensington County Sheriff's station was abuzz with activity. Gloria had to circle the parking lot twice before she was able to squeeze Annabelle into a spot near the back.

She shut the engine off and reached for the door handle before she paused to bow her head and pray a quick prayer that they would allow her to post Lucy's bail and take her home.

It was 11:45 in the morning, which meant that, according to Ruth, the police had picked Lucy up over four hours ago.

Gloria hoped that the interrogations had ended and Lucy had been booked. She frowned as she wondered if bail had even been set. If not, this trip would be a waste of time.

Gloria stepped inside the cold, drab lobby and approached the counter. A dark-haired woman in a police uniform looked up from her computer. "Yes, can I help you?"

Gloria nodded. "I'm looking for my friend, Lucy Carlson." She didn't know what else to say so she closed her mouth and waited.

She lowered her gaze and read the woman's tag. Her name was Lisa. "Let me check to see if we have anyone here by that name." The woman turned her attention to the computer screen in front of her and began to tap on the keyboard.

She frowned and then looked back up. "You said Ms. Carlson was a friend of yours?"

Gloria nodded. "I-I'm not certain if she's been arrested or was picked up for questioning..." her voice trailed off. She wasn't sure on the police lingo.

Although Gloria's favorite TV show was *Detective on the Side* and she hardly missed an episode, she wasn't sure if she had explained it right.

The woman, Lisa, nodded. "Yes. She's here."

Gloria set her purse on the counter. "Can I see her?"

The woman held up an index finger. "I'll check."

Lisa stepped over to a door on the far side of the lobby area and disappeared behind it.

Gloria wandered over to the "Wanted Posters." Her mind must have been playing tricks on her because several of the people in the mugshots looked familiar, although she wasn't sure why.

514

She shrugged her shoulders, certain that she was under extreme duress and the people in the pictures could not possibly be anyone she knew.

"Yes, ma'am."

Gloria spun around. Lisa had returned.

"Ms. Carlson is free to leave. She's in the waiting room across the hall."

Lisa pointed to a door on the right.

Gloria smiled. "Thank you...Lisa."

The woman returned the smile and switched her attention back to the computer screen.

Gloria crossed the room, grabbed the door handle and pulled it open. On the other side of the door was a small hall and across the hall was another door.

She stepped inside the room and gazed around. Her heart sank when she caught a glimpse of Lucy's bright red head bent down, her hands covering her face.

Gloria tiptoed over to the corner chair. She eased down in the chair next to Lucy. "Hey, Lucy."

Lucy's head popped up. Her eyes, red and bloodshot, met Gloria's eyes.

Gloria reached out and grabbed her friend's hand. "I'm here to take you home," she simply said.

The two women rose to their feet and silently walked out of the Kensington County Sheriff's station.

Chapter 8

Lucy stared out the window the entire ride home. Gloria, determined to give her friend the space she needed, focused on the road ahead.

When they reached the outer edges of Belhaven, Lucy spoke. "Can we stop by the cemetery?"

"Sure." Gloria nodded. Gary, Lucy's first husband, was buried in the cemetery.

Gloria's husband, James, was buried in the same cemetery, but his grave was in a different section.

Gloria pulled Annabelle into the cemetery grounds and eased down the narrow dirt path. She stopped the car adjacent to Gary's headstone.

She shifted the car into park and watched as Lucy climbed out of the passenger seat.

The wind had picked up. Lucy pulled her jacket tightly around her thin frame and lowered her head.

Gloria's heart broke as she watched the frail, broken figure shuffle to the gravesite.

Lucy dropped to her knees. She rubbed a light hand across the letters, *Gary Carlson*. Lucy took a deep breath and spoke to the man who had been the love of her life for decades. She poured out her heart and explained her situation.

When she finished, Lucy wiped the tears on her face with the back of her jacket. She placed both hands on the cold, hard ground and pushed herself to a standing position. She stood, looking down at the grave one final time before she turned on her heel and made her way back to the car.

She opened the door of the car, eased into the passenger seat and reached for her seatbelt. "Thank you for waiting for me, Gloria. I feel much better now."

Lucy clicked the lock in place and turned to Gloria. "It's time to stop messing around and track down whoever it is that's trying to frame me."

The old Lucy was back and Gloria shifted the car into drive as they headed out of the cemetery. "You betcha Lucy. That's exactly what we're going to do," Gloria vowed.

The girls swung by Lucy's place so she could let Jasper out for a run before they drove to the farm.

Gloria parked in front of the garage and the girls headed inside the house where they hung their jackets on hooks just inside the door.

Lucy dropped her purse on an empty chair and eyed the box of baked goods that Dot had left behind.

Gloria slid the box toward her friend. "Help yourself." She headed to the fridge to scrounge up something for lunch.

By the time Gloria had fixed two roasted turkey and Swiss cheese sandwiches, along with bowls of piping hot chicken noodle soup, Lucy had wolfed down one Bavarian cream donut, two pumpkin spice donuts and topped it all off with a tangy lemon bar.

She reached for a napkin and dabbed at her lips. "Those were delicious."

Gloria set the sandwich and bowl of soup in front of Lucy. "You sure you don't want to finish it off with a cup of hot chocolate?" she teased.

Lucy shrugged as she reached for her sandwich plate. "Maybe for dessert."

Gloria eased into the seat across from her and unfolded a napkin in her lap. The girls bowed their heads in prayer and Gloria thanked the Lord that Lucy was home safe and sound.

When she finished praying, she explained to Lucy all that had happened that morning and how the girls had come up with a plan.

Lucy gazed out the window. Tears began to well in her eyes. "I don't know what I would do without my friends," she whispered in a soft voice.

Gloria lifted her soupspoon. "You would do exactly what we are doing for you."

She silently hoped that Andrea and Margaret were able to glean some information from their trip to All Seasons Sporting Goods.

***

Andrea turned into All Seasons Sporting Goods parking lot and pulled into a spot on the end.

Margaret unbuckled her seatbelt. "What was the name of that gun again?"

"It's a 9MM Kahr®," Andrea said. "I think I have enough questions the employees won't be able to answer and they'll have to call in that gun rep...what was his name?"

Margaret reached for her purse. "Maxim something."

The girls had decided to let Andrea do the talking. Margaret knew next to nothing about guns. Andrea had a small handgun for protection. Lucy was the weapons expert of the bunch.

The store was busy and the two women wandered around while they waited for one of the employees, a woman, to approach.

If this was Barbara, Margaret has to wonder what Bill had seen in the woman. She was short...shorter than Margaret, who stood a mere 4' 8" tall. She wore wire-rimmed glasses and her long, dark hair hung limp around her shoulders.

Lucy was a thousand times prettier.

"Can I help you?" Her green eyes peered at them through the thick frames.

Andrea shifted the purse on her shoulder. "Yes, my..."

"Mother," Margaret blurted out.

Andrea slid a sideways glance at Margaret. "My mother is looking for a handgun. Something small and easy to handle. Price isn't a concern," she added.

The woman, Barbara, lifted a brow. Andrea could almost see the commission cha-ching in her head. "Follow me."

She motioned them over to a display case off to one side. Several handguns sat on the top shelf while several larger pistols were displayed on the lower level.

Barbara fished inside her pocket and pulled out a keyring. She inserted one of the keys into the lock on the back panel, turned the key and slid the door to the side.

"This would be a good choice." She pulled out a small, silver gun and handed it to Margaret who motioned for Andrea to take it.

Andrea picked up the weapon and slowly turned it over in her hand. It was a Ruger®. "I don't like the way this one handles. Anything else?" she asked as she handed the weapon back.

Barbara nodded and reached for another gun. "This one has a different grip. You may like it better but it's more expensive." She handed it to Andrea. It was the Kahr®.

Andrea ran the tip of her finger over the cool metal of the gun. The gun was lighter than the other one and the grip was comfortable. Actually, Andrea liked the gun. "Do you have any others in this model?" Andrea knew they didn't. She had done her research on line before she left the house. There were several stair step models but the one in her hand was only one of two that All Seasons stocked.

Barbara smiled. The store carried the cheapest version of the Kahr®. The others were much more expensive...and special order. "We have two but the other one...isn't here."

Barbara took the gun from Andrea and placed it back inside the case. "Artie Maxim, our Kahr® rep, comes by every Thursday."

Tomorrow was Thursday. "Perfect." Andrea turned to Margaret. "Mom, do you have time to come back tomorrow?"

Margaret shifted her purse. "I think I can squeeze it in." She turned to the clerk. "What time?"

Barbara lifted a finger. "Let me check. I'll be right back." She disappeared in the back of the store.

Andrea turned to Margaret. "Can you come back tomorrow?"

Margaret didn't have time to answer. Barbara had returned. "He'll be here in the morning; around 9-ish is when he usually shows up."

The girls told the woman they would come back the next day and then turned to go when Andrea paused. "Say. I heard that the man who owned this place was murdered." Her eyes widened innocently.

Barbara locked the gun case and shoved the keys in her pocket. "Yeah." Barbara's expression grew solemn. "It looks like his ex-girlfriend may have been involved," she stated.

"Interesting." Margaret set her purse on the counter and leaned forward.

Andrea was certain that Margaret was ready to pop the woman in the jaw. She reached over and touched her arm.

"Why do you say that?" Andrea asked.

"I know for a fact that the ex-girlfriend had recently purchased a gun identical to the one that killed Bill," she answered. "On top of that, his body was discovered in a dilapidated old farmhouse just down the road from where the ex lives."

"Maybe someone set her up," Margaret theorized.

Barbara tapped her fingers on the top of the glass. "True. Never thought about that. Course, one of those exact same guns came up missing a couple days before Bill was murdered."

She went on. "Randy, Bill's brother, told the police about the missing gun, but I guess police uncovered more evidence that pointed to the ex. What was her name...Trudy."

Barbara rubbed the palm of her hand across the glass top. "No. That wasn't it. I can see her face." She stared up at the ceiling as if Lucy's name would magically materialize. "Kinda homely woman with bright red hair."

Andrea felt the tips of her ears burn. She slid Margaret a sideways glance.

Margaret appeared to be on the verge of lunging across the counter to attack the woman. "What about his brother, Randy?"

Barbara shrugged. "Randy. He's a nice enough guy, although now that I think about it, the two of them had a knockdown, drag out argument a couple weeks back." She shook her head. "It was a pretty tense work environment."

"What were they fighting about?" Margaret asked through thinned lips as she tried to blot out the image of Barbara's eyes bulging as she squeezed the life out of her.

Barbara shrugged. "Money. Not that I know for certain, but I do believe they were arguing about money." Barbara must have decided she had said too much. She quickly changed the subject. "So you'll be back tomorrow morning? I won't be here," she added.

Andrea fumbled with the clasp of her designer bag and reached for her truck keys. "Yes and we'll be sure to let the gun rep know that you helped us today," she assured the woman.

"Thanks. I appreciate that."

The girls stepped out of the store and made their way to the edge of the parking lot where Andrea had parked the truck.

Margaret jerked her head toward the store. "What do you think?"

Andrea clicked the key fob and unlocked the doors. "That we have too many suspects with too many motives. Maybe talking to this Maxim guy tomorrow will help."

The women climbed into the truck and headed back to Belhaven. When they turned onto Main Street, Andrea spotted Gloria's car parked in front of Dot's Restaurant. "Want to stop by?"

Margaret nodded. The girls had agreed to meet up later in the day. They were early but Margaret was starving.

Andrea pulled into an open spot and shut the engine off. She reached for the driver's side door. "Don't mention..."

"That the nasty store clerk described our Lucy in a most unflattering way? It took everything I had not to punch her in the face," Margaret admitted.

Andrea giggled. "I could tell. Just remember, the woman was after Bill while he and Lucy were dating," she reminded her.

"True." Margaret climbed out of the truck and shut the passenger door. "Still. I would've loved to inflict a little pain on that woman's pig face."

Andrea, if she were honest, would have liked to, too. Nothing was worse than having to remain silent and unable to defend their friend in the face of a blatant attack.

The girls picked up the pace as they stepped inside. It was a mini reunion as the girls celebrated Lucy's release. They hugged Lucy and thanked God that she hadn't been booked but just detained for questioning.

Dot and her husband, Ray, made their way over with glasses of ice water. "The only one missing is Ruth," she said.

Gloria reached for an ice water to lighten Dot's load. "We'll be sure to fill her in."

Lucy reached for a water and turned her attention to Andrea and Margaret. "What did you find out?"

Margaret bent down and shoved her purse under her chair. "That one of the guns, the same gun that killed Bill, came up missing from the display case a couple days before his death."

Lucy's eyes widened. "Really? The Kahr® is missing?"

Andrea nodded. "Yep. And Mom and I are going back tomorrow to talk to Maxim, the dealer."

Gloria frowned. "Mom?"

Margaret chuckled. "Yeah. We told Barbara that I was Andrea's mother and that we were in the store to shop for a handgun for me."

Margaret could easily pass for Andrea's mother. They both had light colored hair and Margaret was a good 25 years Andrea's senior. "Good cover," Gloria said. "Smart thinking."

She turned to Dot, who had stopped by Brian's hardware store earlier to ask him about attorneys, just in case Lucy would need one, although she hoped not. "What did Brian say?"

"Oh. I almost forgot." Dot reached inside the front pocket of her apron and pulled out a slip of paper. "According to Brian, this guy is the best around. He said if you need to hire him, mention Brian's name and he'll give you a discount."

Lucy took the slip of paper, briefly glanced at the information and then shoved it in her front pants pocket. "I hope not."

Dot jotted down Margaret and Andrea's lunch orders and the group waited for her to return before they turned the conversation back to the investigation.

Dot slid into an empty seat and looked at Gloria expectantly. "Now what do we do?"

Gloria frowned as she swiped at a stray strand of hair. She didn't have a plan. They had already searched the house across the street and came up empty handed.

It looked like Margaret and Andrea had a good handle on the list of suspects.

The only thing she could think of was to get inside Bill's house to search for clues. "Too bad we can't search Bill's place," she said aloud.

Lucy grasped the end of her straw and jabbed the ice cubes inside her glass of water with the tip. "We could...I still have a key to his house."

Chapter 9

Gloria gasped. "Lucy. Why didn't you mention that before?"

Lucy fidgeted in her seat. "Well, if the police knew I had a key to his house, wouldn't that make me even more of a suspect?" she pointed out.

Gloria frowned. It was true. If the police knew that Lucy had access to Bill's house, it would certainly be a piece of incriminating evidence.

Ruth wandered in and to the back of the restaurant. "Well? What happened?" She slid into the last available chair and dropped her purse on the floor next to her.

Gloria brought her up to speed and finished with the last tidbit of information – that Lucy still had a key to Bill's house.

Ray and restaurant employee, Holly, carried two trays laden with food to the table. The girls waited until the food was on the table before picking up where they left off.

Andrea reached for an onion ring and dipped it in her ketchup. "Are there a lot of neighbors close to Bill's place?"

Lucy shook her head. "Nope. He owns some 20 acres of land and his ranch sits smack dab in the middle of the property."

That made sense. Someone like Bill who had been an avid outdoorsman his entire life probably craved the solitude and quiet of living in the middle of nowhere.

"So it would be fairly easy to...say...stop by his place and have a look around?" Ruth inquired.

Lucy nodded. "Yep. He had a couple hunting dogs that guarded the property but I'm sure that by now, someone has picked them up."

Gloria glanced around the table. "I'm a sucker for an adventure. Who wants to go with me to have a look around?"

"I'll go with you," Lucy offered.

"But..." Gloria started to argue.

Lucy lifted a hand to stop her. "It makes sense for me to go. I know the layout of the property and house. You'd be going in blindly without me," she pointed out.

Lucy was the most logical choice to go. Still, if they were caught trespassing and Lucy was with them, it would be one more nail in Lucy's coffin, so to speak. She thought back to the close call they'd had at the farm across the street the night before.

"I'll go with you," Ruth piped up. "I can bring my drone along to do a little reconnaissance beforehand. You know, make sure the coast is clear before we try to get inside the house."

Gloria narrowed her eyes. She remembered the last time Ruth had used her drone to try to help solve a mystery and it had turned into a disaster when the drone had run out of power and gone down behind enemy lines.

But that was before Gloria and Margaret had gifted Ruth a new Phantom II drone. It had longer range and a heavy-duty battery.

Ruth noted the look of concern on Gloria's face. "Don't worry. I've been practicing with the drone you guys bought me." She rubbed her hands together. "This will be my first chance to test 'er out."

There was no way Gloria could tell her friend "no." And, it *was* one of the reasons they had bought Ruth the drone in the first place. So that she could, at some point in time, help them out if need be. She hadn't realized it would be only days later that they would put Ruth's new toy to the test.

Gloria gazed out the large picture window thoughtfully. "So when should we go?"

Ruth popped the last piece of the BLT sandwich in her mouth and dropped the napkin on her empty plate. "The drone is hard to use when it's dark so it will have to be during the day."

She went on. "Kenny can cover for me if you want to go first thing tomorrow morning."

The trio agreed to meet at Ruth's place first thing in the morning.

While Gloria, Lucy and Ruth were breaking in...err, searching Bill's place, Andrea and Margaret would head back to All Seasons Sporting Goods to try to glean information from Artie Maxim, the sales rep.

"I guess I'll hold down the fort," Dot said. "Come back tomorrow when you're done and you can be my taste testers. I've been working on a new strawberry donut."

"Cool." Lucy rubbed her hands together. "I'll be the official taste-tester."

Gloria glanced at her watch. "I should get going."

Gloria and Lucy climbed back in the car. She stopped at Lucy's place to drop her off before heading home.

As soon as Gloria opened the porch door, Mally darted out into the yard.

Gloria dropped her purse on the chair, just inside the door and stepped back onto the porch. "Want to go for a walk?"

Mally, who had been sniffing around the edge of the garage, bounded across the lawn and skidded to a halt in front of Gloria. "Woof."

Gloria took the "woof" for a yes and the two of them crossed the yard as they made their way between the empty farm fields and toward the woods out back. There were still a few hours of daylight left and it had been quite some time since their last visit to their favorite quiet spot.

Forecasters had predicted a light dusting of snow for later that evening and Gloria knew her days of long, leisurely walks in the woods would end soon. Not only would the walks end, Gloria's days of living alone were almost over.

Next month, just before Christmas, Gloria and Paul planned to marry at Andrea's place. They had originally planned an intimate affair with only family and close friends, but the guest list had ballooned and they now had over 75 confirmed guests. They were still waiting on another 40 responses but Gloria had a hunch most of them would be coming as well.

She needed to get Lucy's crisis behind her so she could focus on the wedding and the much-anticipated visit from her children and their families.

With everything that had been going on, she hadn't even had time to worry about Thanksgiving. Paul and she had decided a small turkey day would be best, but the more Gloria thought about it, she wondered if maybe instead of that, all of the girls could get together, share the cooking duties and make it a more friends and family affair. She made a mental note to discuss it with Paul before mentioning it to the girls.

Ruth had one sibling, a sister who lived in Florida. She would most likely spend Thanksgiving Day alone and that was the last thing Gloria wanted.

Dot and Ray were childless and although they had each other, it would still be a quiet day.

Lucy had told Gloria that her children planned to spend Thanksgiving with their spouses' families this year. It would be just her and her boyfriend, Max.

That left Andrea. Gloria knew her young friend had no intention of flying to New York to be with her parents. Instead, she would remain in Michigan with her former housekeeper, Alice, and Andrea's boyfriend, Brian.

The more she thought about it, the more she liked the idea of a potluck-kind-of Thanksgiving. After all, her friends *were* her family.

Mally and she had reached the edge of the woods and Mally darted off to check out the creek. The water was still low but soon, the snow would pile up and the creek would fill.

Gloria settled onto "her" log nearby and watched Mally frolic in the frigid water. She shook her head and grinned as Mally chased a bunny rabbit that had been scampering back and forth, teasing Mally, if Gloria had to guess.

Her mind drifted to Lucy's dilemma. Right now, there were several suspects. Bill's brother, Randy, who had been arguing with Bill just days before his death. Barbara, the employee who had chased after Bill and eventually dated him, even though Lucy claimed Bill never cared for the woman.

Next on the list was Zeke, the young man who seemed all too eager to throw Randy, Barbara and even this unknown Artie Maxim under the bus.

Then there was the missing gun. One of the store employees, possibly even the gun dealer, had access to the gun.

The police lacked a murder weapon, not counting Lucy's gun, which was probably why Lucy was the main suspect. She actually owned a gun exactly like the one that had killed Bill.

Gloria knew that if she could figure out what happened to the missing gun, she could figure out who had murdered Bill.

She jumped to her feet. "C'mon girl. We have some more digging to do."

Gloria zigzagged through the trees as she made her way out of the forest.

The wind had picked up and cold air blew right through her jacket. She picked up the pace as she headed back to the farm. There was a piece of the puzzle missing. If only she could figure out what it was...

Back at the house, she settled in at the desk and turned her computer on. After it warmed up, she checked her email and then started a search of the list of suspects.

She opened a second screen and pulled up the picture of Bill and his employees. She jotted Barbara Coleman's name down and last, but not least, Zeke Waren, the young employee Gloria had talked to.

She researched both of their names but came up empty-handed.

Frustrated, she clicked out of the screens and glanced down at her watch. It was time to start dinner.

Margaret had recently shared her secret meatloaf recipe and Gloria was anxious to try it out on Paul.

Gloria assembled the ingredients for the meatloaf and mixed them all together. When she finished, she placed the loaf inside a metal baking dish and set it on top of the stove.

She had been craving her homemade cheesy hash brown casserole. The dish would be a perfect side for the meatloaf.

Gloria pulled a large glass dish from the cabinet. Next, she mixed the thawed hash browns with a can of cream of chicken soup, sour cream, shredded cheddar cheese and melted butter. After she mixed the ingredients together, she dumped the mixture into the square casserole dish and popped both the meatloaf and casserole in the oven.

Gloria untied her apron and hung it on the hook as she glanced at the clock on the way out of the kitchen. Paul would be here in an hour and a half. It would give her plenty of time to take a long, leisurely bath.

After her recent windfall, Gloria had splurged on a bathroom remodel. The remodel included double sink granite counters, a new water saver toilet and her favorite thing of all, a large, luxurious jetted tub.

She filled the tub with hot water; added jasmine scented bath oil, peeled off her clothes and then slipped into the tub.

Gloria closed her eyes and leaned her head against the pillow rest. Should she tell Paul about the girls' plan to snoop around Bill's place in the morning?

He had been upset when he caught Lucy and her inside the house across the street. She knew he would not be happy with her if she told him their plans.

Technically, they wouldn't be breaking and entering. Lucy had a key. Bill had given it to her. If he had wanted it back, he would have asked for it. On top of that, she was certain that Bill would want someone to track down his killer. Gloria knew that if it was she, she sure would.

Gloria savored her quiet bath time until Mally began to paw at the bathroom door. She lifted her head and pulled herself to an upright position. "I'm done," she grumbled.

She let the water out of the tub and reached for a clean bath towel.

Gloria slipped into her robe and tied it tight before she let Mally outside for a brief run before she headed back to the bathroom to finish primping.

Their wedding was only a few weeks away now and Gloria was starting to have minor anxiety attacks. What if he got cold feet and left her at the altar? What if she got cold feet?

She pushed the dark thoughts aside as she popped the top off the tube of lipstick and spread the pale pink cream across her lower lip. She rubbed her lips together and nodded at her reflection in the mirror. Finally, she was ready.

"Honey, I'm home."

Gloria set the tube of lipstick on the counter and grinned. It was Paul. She had given him a key to the house a while back and told him he might as well get used to letting himself in and making himself at home.

She wandered into the kitchen and watched as he hung his jacket on the hook by the door. He held a card in his hand and when she got close, he handed it to her.

Gloria took the card. "What's this?"

"For you. Just a small treat to spoil my girl." Paul pulled Gloria close and circled his arms around her waist. He lowered his head and gently kissed her lips. "So that's what a proper kiss feels like," he teased. "It's been so long, I forgot what it felt like."

"Ha," she snorted. "If you weren't so darn busy at work all the time." She quickly changed the subject. "So what's in the card?"

"Open it," he urged.

Gloria slid her fingernail under the edge of the envelope and lifted the lid. She slipped the card out of the envelope. On the front was a portrait of a beautiful rose garden. The inside of the card spoke words of love.

Gloria blinked back the tears. Tucked inside the envelope was a gift card for a day at the spa. "Paul. What…"

"You need a break, Gloria. You deserve a day to be pampered and spoiled and I thought this would be perfect."

Gloria pulled Paul's head toward her and kissed his lips. "You are going to spoil me rotten, if it's not already too late," she warned.

"Nah. No chance."

The timer went off and Gloria headed to the stove. She pulled the oven door open and peered inside. The cheesy hash brown casserole bubbled merrily. She pulled the dish from the oven and then lifted the pan of meatloaf.

Gloria spread a thick layer of ketchup across the top of the meatloaf and placed it back inside the oven. "Fifteen more minutes and it'll be ready."

"It smells delicious. I can't wait 'til there's no more TV dinners," he said.

"Don't be so sure about that," Gloria warned.

She poured two glasses of tea and settled in at the table. As she sat there, she thought how comfortable it felt. How good and perfect this moment was. If this was how their marriage would be, Gloria could hardly wait.

They chatted about Paul's job and he asked how Gloria's day had gone. She was careful to avoid bringing up the incident from the night before when he had caught Gloria and Lucy inside the house across the street.

He, however, wasn't. Paul sipped his tea and set the glass on the table. "How's it going with Lucy?"

Gloria averted her eyes and studied her sparkling engagement ring. "Oh...okay," she answered. "The police questioned Lucy at length this morning but let her go. Brian gave us the name of a good attorney," she added.

Paul rubbed the faint five o'clock shadow on his chin thoughtfully. "Do you think that will be necessary?"

Gloria explained all that she knew. The suspects, the missing gun and she even told him about the gun dealer.

"Are you going to confront this Maxim fellow?" Paul could see his spunky bride-to-be doing exactly that.

Gloria shook her head. "Nope. Andrea and Margaret are going to meet him in the morning."

Paul slid out of his chair and stepped over to the fridge to refill his glass. "What will *you* be doing?" He knew there was no way Gloria would stand on the sidelines. She would most definitely be right in the thick of things.

Gloria decided to answer his question with a question. "What should I do?"

Paul brought the pitcher to the table and filled her glass. "You're up to something." After he filled her glass, he placed the pitcher back inside the fridge and closed the door. "I probably don't want to know."

"Probably not," she agreed.

The oven timer sounded a second time and Gloria was thankful for the interruption.

Paul set the table while Gloria carried the food and set it in the center.

They bowed their heads to pray and Gloria said a special prayer for Lucy, who was at home...alone.

She sliced a large piece of meatloaf from the center and set it on Paul's plate. "I hope you like it. This is Margaret's super-secret recipe. It took me years to wear her down and she finally shared it with me."

Paul scooped a large spoonful of cheesy hash browns on the side and then set a piece of crusty bread on his napkin.

Last, but not least, he added a pile of green beans. Gloria had canned the beans a couple months ago. She had had a bountiful crop this year and her stockpile of canned goods would last both of them through the winter, until it was time to start a garden again in the spring.

The evening flew by and before Gloria knew it, dinner was over and the kitchen cleaned. They even had time to kick back and relax in the living room with a bowl of chocolate ice cream.

When the ten o'clock news started, Paul reluctantly got to his feet. "I better head out. The kids will be waiting up for me."

Gloria frowned. Paul's son, Jeff, and his daughter-in-law, Tina, had recently moved back in with him after being evicted from the apartment they had been renting. If ever there was a problem looming on the horizon for Paul and Gloria's relationship, she guessed it would be these two.

It seemed that whenever they got into a pickle, they turned to Paul to bail them out. It wasn't that Gloria didn't want to help family, but these two seemed to cause their own difficulties. Both had steady jobs and made good money. They just did not know how to manage their finances.

Gloria had suggested several times that Paul get involved and to his credit, he had tried, but nothing seemed to change.

She had a hunch that they knew good ole dad would be there no matter what and that there were no consequences for their actions. Someday Paul...and Gloria...would be gone. She wondered who would take care of them then.

Gloria bit her tongue and let it go. She walked him to his truck and waited for him to climb in and fasten his seatbelt. He rolled down the window and leaned out. "I love you. Please try to stay out of trouble tomorrow, whatever it is you have planned."

Gloria nodded. "I'll try," she answered honestly. "Sometimes it's hard." She leaned in for a long, tender kiss and blinked back the tears that burned the back of her eyes.

Paul waited for her to wander back up the sidewalk and into the house before he backed out of the drive and pulled onto the road.

Chapter 10

Gloria woke early the next morning. It was still dark out. She could hear a hoot owl off in the distance...the same owl that returned every November. She had come to expect the owl, to wait for his call.

The first time she had noticed his haunting hoot was the same year that James died. Maybe she hadn't noticed before because she never paid close attention to the noises. After James was gone, she would lie awake in bed for hours listening to every creak, every groan and every sound, both big and small.

The owl could have been around for years but just the past few she had noticed him. Other things seemed to have magnified in her mind after James' death. There were the smells. Several times, she had been convinced she smelled something burning but every time she checked, there was nothing. Just her overactive imagination, she supposed.

Gloria slid out of bed, grabbed her robe and padded to the kitchen. She started a pot of coffee, slipped her jacket over her bathrobe and then stepped out onto the porch with Mally.

The dusting of snow forecasters had predicted covered the ground. It was pretty to look at and it put her in the holiday spirit. She had remembered to ask Paul the evening before if a potluck Thanksgiving was okay with him and he told her he would leave it up to her.

His main priority was to enjoy some turkey and dressing, followed by a long nap on the couch and maybe watch a little football.

Mally, who wasn't used to the cold yet, was happy to head back into the warmth of the kitchen. She settled into her doggie bed by the door while Gloria fried a few slices of bacon, scrambled a couple eggs and then toasted some bread.

Puddles had been sleeping on the sofa but now he slunk into the kitchen and sniffed the air. Gloria cooked some extra slices of bacon and she shared it with her beloved pets before she settled in at the kitchen table with the morning paper.

Her mind zipped back and forth between the upcoming visit to Bill's place and the grocery-shopping list for turkey day. She wasn't keen on the crowded stores and planned to stock up on all the necessary supplies in advance.

She had just finished her breakfast and set her dirty dishes in the dishwasher when her phone rang. Gloria picked it up expecting Lucy or Ruth to be on the other end.

It was Gloria's daughter Jill. "Hello dear."

"Hi Mom. I just dropped the boys off at school and thought I'd give you a quick call."

Jill, her husband, Greg and grandsons, Ryan and Tyler had recently moved into a new home, with a little help from Gloria and her recent windfall. There had been a minor issue with the house before they closed and with the determination of a mother on a mission and some of Gloria's friends, it had been resolved.

Jill and her family were happy as clams in the new, spacious home. Gloria couldn't wait to stop by to see it finished and decorated for the holidays.

"Have you decided on a time for Thanksgiving Dinner?" her daughter asked.

"I'm glad you mentioned it," Gloria replied. "I was thinking about inviting Ruth, Dot and Lucy since none of them have family nearby." Or none at all she silently added.

"That's a great idea, Mom," Jill said. "That's very thoughtful of you."

The mother and daughter talked for several long moments and Gloria promised to stop by soon to check out the house.

Today, though, she had her hands full and the first thing on her list was to meet up with Ruth and Lucy.

***

Lucy was pacing back and forth in front of Ruth's van when Gloria pulled in the drive.

Gloria pulled off to the side and slid out of the driver's seat.

"I don't get a good feeling about this," Lucy warned when Gloria got close.

"Is the feeling as strong as it was the other night?" Maybe Lucy had developed a sixth sense now and Gloria should pay closer attention.

Lucy stopped abruptly. "It's different. Kind of like...I dunno a feeling that we're being watched." She shivered as she looked around.

Gloria's heart skipped a beat. In all the years the two women had been friends, this was the first time Gloria could recall Lucy saying something like that. She took it very seriously.

"Do you want to call it off?"

"But," Ruth piped up.

Gloria motioned her to be quiet. "This is your call, Lucy. After all, you're the one the police suspect." Now that she thought about it, who was to say that the police weren't keeping tabs on Lucy, even now?

Gloria narrowed her eyes and surveyed the house and surrounding yard. Maybe they *would* be walking into some sort of trap.

She tried to remember everything she'd ever watched on *Detective on the Side,* and how police set up a sting. If they thought Lucy was hiding something, wouldn't they want to keep her under surveillance...watch her every move?

Ruth snapped her fingers. "I've got a plan." She darted up the side steps and disappeared inside. A few moments later, she motioned them in.

When they got inside the kitchen, she shut the door behind them and pulled the shade. "Stay here and out of sight," Ruth instructed.

Gloria had no idea what Ruth was up to but had to trust she had a plan, which was more than Gloria had. It seemed like they sat there forever and Gloria was getting anxious. "What..."

Tap, Tap. There was a light tap coming from the back of the house.

"Be right back." Ruth zigzagged around the table and out of sight.

"I wonder what she's up to," Lucy said.

When Ruth returned, she wasn't alone. Judith Arnett, a Belhaven local and motor mouth to boot, stepped into the kitchen.

Gloria's eyes widened at the sight of Judith. She was wearing a bright red wig on her head as she followed behind Ruth.

"Oh my goodness." Gloria's hand flew to her mouth. "Where did that wig come from?" she gasped.

"Just some extra costume stuff I had boxed up in the basement." Ruth pointed to Lucy. "You two need to swap clothes," she said.

Lucy pointed at herself. "Me?"

"Let's go." Ruth waved them into the other room.

On the dining room table was a row of mannequin heads. On each of the heads was a different colored wig with different hair shapes and lengths. Some were short while others were long. One of the mannequins was bald. Gloria correctly guessed that the missing wig was now on Judith's head.

Gloria was dying to know where the wigs had come from. She didn't buy the "boxed up in the basement" story.

"Here." Ruth grabbed a medium length, light colored wig and handed it to Lucy. "Put this on."

Lucy stared at the wig in her hand, her mouth open. "Why, I..."

"Okay. I'll do it for you." Ruth snatched the wig from Lucy's hand and stuck it on her head. She tugged on the sides and stood back to inspect her handiwork.

"That red hair. We have to hide it." Ruth shoved her hand along Lucy's hairline as she pushed strands of red hair under the rubbery shell of the wig. "You've got some wiry hair there, Lucy," she commented.

Gloria hid a grin as Ruth circled around to work on the other side of Lucy's face.

Ruth stood back and studied Lucy. "Yep. I think this will work."

Lucy traipsed off to the bathroom. She flipped the light on and examined her new "do." She turned her head from side to side. "Not bad. I think I could pass for a blonde."

Ruth waited for Lucy to emerge from the bathroom. "Judith is the decoy. She's going to walk out of this place pretending to be you. If the cops are trailing you, they'll go after Judith instead."

"I didn't sign up for this," Judith argued.

Ruth gave her a hard stare. "You want me to tell everyone about..."

"No. I do not." Judith cut her off. She wrinkled her nose.

Ruth narrowed her eyes as she studied Judith and Lucy critically. The women looked to be about the same size. "Time to swap clothes." She motioned at Lucy to follow her to the bedroom.

Judith headed into the bathroom and Lucy to a bedroom next door.

Lucy shut the door. Moments later, the door opened. Lucy snaked her hand around the partially closed bedroom door and handed her pants and shirt to Ruth.

Ruth took the clothes to Judith, who was waiting for her behind the bathroom door.

Next, Judith handed Ruth her blouse and slacks through the crack in the door.

Ruth took the clothes to the bedroom door. "Knock-knock. Your pretty princess attire has arrived," she teased.

The door opened a fraction. Lucy snatched the clothes from Ruth's hand and shut the door.

Gloria could hardly wait to see how they looked.

When Lucy emerged, Gloria giggled at the sight of her friend, who was now wearing a pink frock with a thick layer of ruffles along the front. Her slacks, a shiny, polyester brown, hung loosely on Lucy's thin hips and scrawny legs.

Lucy thrust her hand on her hip and pouted. "You have no sense of style, Judith."

Judith, who had emerged from the bathroom, looked none too happy with the sudden turn of events. She tugged at Lucy's plaid, flannel shirt. "You call this style? Why even Carl wouldn't wear this outfit," she declared. Carl was Judith's husband.

There were several unflattering bulges in the too tight pants but at least Judith had managed to get them on.

Ruth stood between the two warring women and extended her arms. "Now ladies." She stressed the word "*ladies.*"

"So now what?" Judith snapped.

"Lucy, give Judith your car keys," Ruth commanded. "Judith will have to drive your Jeep home. We can call her later to bring it back."

"How did Judith get here?" Gloria asked.

"Carl dropped me off out back," Judith mumbled. "How do I get myself into these messes?"

Lucy plucked her keys from her purse and dropped them into Judith's outstretched hand. "Please be careful with my baby. I hope you know how to drive a stick shift," she added.

Judith's eyes widened. "A stick shift?" She narrowed her eyes and turned to Ruth. "Ruth..."

Ruth crossed her arms in front of her. "Surely you know how to drive a stick."

Judith clutched the keys in her hand. "Thirty years ago. No one drives a stick anymore."

"I do," Lucy argued.

Judith, fed up with the entire situation, adjusted her wig, marched across the kitchen floor and stomped out the door and down the steps. The girls peeked out the window and watched as Judith hopped into Lucy's jeep.

The jeep jerked out of the drive and stalled in the middle of the road. Gloria could see Judith's lips moving and would bet the farm that she was cussing them out.

Ruth leaned over Gloria's shoulder and watched Judith. "She'll get over it," she predicted.

Finally, Judith was able to get the jeep moving forward and it lurched to the corner. Judith squealed around the corner and disappeared from sight. "I hope she's careful with Beep," Lucy whispered.

Gloria stood upright. "Beep?"

"That's my jeep's name. Beep."

Gloria thought she was the only one that named her vehicles. She turned to Ruth, the master planner. "Now what?"

"You and I head out smooth and easy, then we circle around and pick Lucy up in the alley," she said.

Lucy frowned as she glanced at the pink pumps...Judith's pink, sensible pumps that were now on her feet. "I-I've never walked in heels before."

Gloria patted her on the back. "You can do it Lucy. Think of them as barn boots with a small heel," she suggested.

Lucy took a few tentative steps, her ankles turned as she attempted to balance. "I don't know about this."

"You'll be fine," Ruth waved an arm, grabbed a cardboard box from the table and headed to the door.

Gloria followed Ruth out the front door while Lucy stumbled to the back. Lucy wasn't kidding when she said she wasn't used to heels.

Gloria hopped in the passenger seat of Ruth's van while Ruth opened the rear door and slid the box in the back. She closed the door and made her way to the driver's side. "Looks like the coast is clear," she said.

Ruth backed out of the drive, circled around the block and pulled into the alley where Lucy was hovering behind a large evergreen bush.

She slid into the back of the van, or maybe it was more like tripped into the back of the van. She yanked the door shut and crawled across the floor.

Lucy wrenched the pastel pink shoes from both feet and dropped them on the floor. "I'd rather walk on shards of glass than spend one more second in those toe pinching, heel grinding weapons of agony," she moaned dramatically.

They had just made it past the village limit sign when Ruth's cell phone beeped. Gloria glanced down at the screen. "It's Judith."

"Answer it," Ruth said.

"Hello?"

"Ruth?" Judith gasped.

"No. This is Gloria. I have you on speaker. Ruth is driving," she explained.

"Yeah. Well, I just wanted to let you know that a four-door sedan with tinted windows followed me home. They're parked across the street from my house. What should I do?"

"Stay there until I tell you to come back to my house," Ruth instructed.

"But I planned to meet some friends at Dot's for breakfast," Judith whined.

"Judith..." Ruth warned.

Silence.

"Okay, but you owe me one."

Judith hung up before Ruth could reply.

She shrugged as she turned the corner at the stop sign. "She can be such a baby."

Lucy directed Ruth out of town, past the Montbay County line and onto a dirt road, that Gloria was certain she'd never noticed before. "Bill lives...err, lived out here?" The place was desolate.

"Yep. I think we have another quarter mile to go," Lucy guessed.

The road quickly turned into a narrow, rutted path that jostled the van and caused Gloria's stomach to feel queasy. She clutched her middle section. "I hope we're almost there."

"Turn in here." Lucy pointed to an even narrower road, which was more like a two track or dirt path.

Ruth peered through the front windshield "Are you sure?"

"Yep. This runs along the back of Bill's property. Not many people know you can get to his place from here."

This would work out perfect to stay incognito.

Ruth drove until the van couldn't move forward without taking off chunks of paint. She shifted the van in park and shut the engine off. "End of the road. Literally."

Lucy shoved her feet in Judith's shoes. "I can't believe I have to put these back on," she grumbled.

Gloria grabbed the passenger door handle. "Time to roll."

Chapter 11

The cold November morning air nipped at the tip of Gloria's nose. The dusting of snow that had covered the ground earlier had disappeared. In its place was a blanket of wet, sticky leaves along with some downed tree limbs and branches thrown in for good measure.

"This way." Lucy pointed to a row of tall pine trees. She led the way with Gloria close behind. Ruth brought up the rear with her box of goodies.

Gloria hadn't asked what all Ruth had determined was necessary for their mission. She figured she would find out soon enough.

The girls wound their way around the trees. A light breeze rustled through the trees and it made a low, moaning sound that Gloria decided sounded like, "Whoa..."

Gloria shivered involuntarily. "You sure we're headed in the right direction?" It seemed as if they were going in circles.

Lucy nodded but didn't slow her pace. "We're almost there," she promised.

Moments later, they reached a large clearing and a brick ranch house. On the front porch were a couple of old wooden ladder-back chairs. In one corner was a planter, the plant inside shriveled and limp.

Gloria stepped into the clearing and stood next to Lucy.

"Wait," Ruth said. "We need to make sure the coast is clear."

Her eyes studied the house and then traveled upwards as she scanned the tree line. Her shoulders slumped. "It's not safe for the drone. Not sayin' it's gonna happen but I'm afraid it'll get caught in the trees."

She set the cardboard box on the ground, lifted the flaps and folded them back. Ruth peered inside the box and pulled out what looked like a small satellite dish. The base was solid black. The front part, shaped like a cone, was a frosted white color.

Ruth carefully set the device on the ground and then reached inside the box again. She pulled out a headset, slid it over the top of her head and adjusted the earpieces snugly against her ears.

With her index finger, she spun the dial on the side. Next, she flipped a small switch on the side of the dish and held a finger to her lips. "Shhh."

Gloria and Lucy watched quietly as Ruth fiddled with the headpiece. Moments later, she slid the headphones down so they rested against the nape of her neck. "The coast is clear. I heard a few birds and maybe a couple squirrels but that's all."

Gloria pointed to the cone. "Is that what I think it is?"

Ruth ran her finger along the rim of the cone. "It's a supersonic listening device. This baby can pick up noises up to

100 yards away, even inside a house." She tapped the top. "Just got this in the mail yesterday."

"I think you missed your calling." Gloria grinned. Ruth was accumulating quite an arsenal of spy equipment. "What will they think of next?"

Ruth's eyes lit. "I'm waiting on this handheld fogger device. It masks the human scent, say for example, if you were being chased by a K9 unit." She rubbed her hands together. "It should be here next week."

She went on. "My goal is to cover the five senses. I haven't been able to nail down taste." Ruth wrinkled her nose. "So far what's out there on the market hasn't worked for me. I'm waiting for something good to come along."

Gloria wondered how it "hadn't worked" for Ruth and who exactly Ruth had tested it on. She frowned. Why in the world would Ruth need to try to hide her scent and avoid the police?

Gloria handed her the portable monitor. That was a question to save for another day. First things first.

Ruth set the monitor and headphones inside the box and closed the lid. "I'll pick this up on our way out."

Lucy waved them forward. When they reached the front porch steps, she came to an abrupt halt and lowered her head. Her hand shook as she reached for the knob.

Gloria put a hand on Lucy's shoulder. "Are you sure you're ready for this?"

Lucy nodded. "Yeah. Bill wouldn't want me to have to go through this, no matter how badly our relationship ended."

Lucy pulled a key from her front pocket. She inserted the key in the lock and turned. It wouldn't budge. "Uh-oh. It doesn't work." She pulled the key back out.

"Here, let me try." Gloria took the key from Lucy and slipped it inside the deadbolt. She jiggled it back and forth and finally, it turned. "It was just a little sticky."

The door creaked loudly as Gloria gingerly pushed it open and stepped inside. Lucy was right behind her. Ruth brought up the rear.

The house smelled musty.

Gloria wrinkled her nose. "Do you smell that?"

Ruth nodded. "Yeah. Smells damp."

Gloria took a tentative step forward. The floorboard creaked and Lucy jumped. She pressed a hand to her chest. "Oh my gosh."

Gloria took another step. The hair on the back of her neck bristled.

A sudden, muffled thump echoed through the house.

"Wh-what was that?" Lucy whispered.

"It sounded like it was coming from the kitchen," Gloria murmured. She rubbed her sweaty palms on the top of her jeans. Should they high tail it out of there or press on to the kitchen?

They had come too far to turn back now. She took a firm step forward, determined to see this mission through, no matter what the outcome.

They finished crossing the living room floor.

Gloria stopped in the doorway that led to the kitchen. The kitchen was modern and spacious. She wasn't sure what she expected since Bill was pure outdoorsman. Maybe a faucet shaped like a grizzly bear.

The kitchen was far from rustic. In fact, it was a little too modern for Gloria's own taste with its sleek lines and flat cabinets. The walls were a light gray. The backsplash a pale green subway tile. "This wasn't at all what I expected."

Lucy had to agree. "Yeah. He was kind of a stickler for cleanliness."

A small movement over the kitchen sink caught Ruth's eye. "The kitchen window – it's open."

Sure enough, the window above the kitchen sink was wide open.

Lucy slipped past Gloria and approached the sink. She leaned across the sink, put both hands on the sill, pulled down and snapped the lock in place. "Bill would never have left the window open."

Gloria stepped over to the sliding glass door and peered out. "You think someone else was in here?" It was possible that someone in Bill's family had opened the window and forgot to close it before they left.

She glanced down at the expensive oak floors. Humidity and moisture had warped several of the boards. Gloria rubbed her shoe over the bumpy surface. "What a shame. These will have to be fixed."

Lucy led them from the kitchen, across the dining area and into the hall. "Bill used the first bedroom for storage and the second one was his office."

Lucy grasped the handle on the first door they came to. She turned the knob and pushed the door open.

Gloria peeked over Lucy's shoulder and gasped when she looked inside. The room was in shambles. In one corner were floor-to-ceiling boxes. Strewn across the floor were piles of wrinkled clothes. The closet doors were wide open and shoved off to one side was a row of wire hangers.

Pushed up against the far wall was a black futon. On top of the futon was a navy blue sleeping bag, unzipped. It looked as if someone had been sleeping on it.

A camo-patterned strip of material caught Gloria's eye. She stepped over to the bed, reached underneath and tugged on it. It was a backpack. Something a hunter or possibly a college student might use to carry supplies.

Gloria held the backpack in her hand. "You said this room was for storage? It looks like someone was sleeping in here."

Lucy frowned. "Yeah. Last time I was here, Bill used the room for storage. I've never seen that futon before."

Did that mean that someone had been living with Bill? Gloria vaguely recalled that Bill had divorced his first wife years ago and that they had had two daughters. She couldn't remember their names. "What about Bill's daughters?"

Lucy scrunched up her nose. "One of them lives in Wisconsin and the other one lives overseas where her husband is stationed in the military."

It was possible they had just arrived in town and were staying at Bill's place. If that were the case, there would be suitcases and other travel bags.

Gloria shoved the backpack back under the bed and followed Lucy into the hall.

Lucy closed the door behind them and made her way to the room across the hall. The door was open and Gloria peeked inside. The room was empty. There was nothing inside...not a stick of furniture, not a picture on the wall. Nothing.

"That's odd. This used to be Bill's office. It was full of office furniture."

If Bill had removed everything from the room, what had he done with it?

The trio passed by a hall bath on their way to the master bedroom at the end. Double doors opened to the spacious master suite. The room was clean, the bed made. A door on the far end led to a small screened-in porch.

Gloria glanced out the window. Centered against one wall was a white wicker loveseat with navy blue cushions. A matching wicker table sat next to it. On top of the wicker table was an ashtray.

Lucy opened the door and stepped out onto the porch. She pointed at the ashtray. "Huh. That's odd. Bill quit smoking years ago. In fact, he hated the smell."

The girls finished their inspection of the master bedroom and adjoining bath.

They retraced their steps as they made their way to the end of the hall. At the end of the hall was an open staircase leading down to the basement. Although the steps were carpeted, they still creaked – loudly - when the girls stepped on them.

Gloria wondered how a house that was only a few years old could have so many creaks and groans.

At the bottom of the steps, Lucy fumbled with the light switch on the wall. A bare bulb in the center of the ceiling cast a dim glow and illuminated the open space. The room was empty except for a desk, chair, bookcase and file cabinet squeezed against the far wall.

Gloria glanced around. The basement was small, much smaller than she thought it would be for a house that large. "This is it?" she asked.

Lucy nodded. "Yep. For some reason, Bill didn't see the need for a large basement. He said the only thing basements were good for was storing junk. He always said if he did anything, he'd build a bomb shelter."

She pointed to the wall. "There is his office equipment."

Gloria frowned. Why would Bill move his office downstairs and into a dark, dreary basement instead of leaving it upstairs in a bright, airy bedroom? It didn't make sense.

Lucy slipped into the chair and settled in behind the desk. She turned the computer on and waited until the login screen appeared. "I'm not sure if Bill's password is the same." Lucy clicked a few of the keys and hit enter. An error message appeared.

She tried again, and again she got an error message. "Nope. He must have changed it." She tried to guess the password but nothing worked. Finally, it locked her out. "I have no idea what his password is."

While Lucy worked on the computer, Ruth searched the bookcase and Gloria rifled through the cabinets. Nothing popped up as suspicious. There were folders for receipts, bills and other important papers.

Not once did Gloria's internal radar go up. She shut the cabinet door and took a step back. Ruth joined her. "The place is clean."

"Looks like we just wasted our time." Lucy pushed the chair back. Her fingers pressed against a desk calendar and it shifted forward. The corner of a small slip of paper appeared.

Lucy reached down and pulled on the paper. "What's this?" She flipped the piece over and squinted at the words scribbled on the back.

"12 Grand Marais Drive, Detroit, MI 49962"

A smudge of what appeared to be blood stained the corner.

"I wonder if that's Bill's blood." Gloria's stomach churned at the thought.

"Let me get a plastic baggie so we can take it with us." Lucy darted up the stairs without waiting for a reply.

She returned moments later. Using the corner of the clear, plastic bag, she slid the slip of paper inside and pulled the tab across the top to seal it shut.

They finished their search of the basement and utility room, which turned up nothing. At least they had something...the small slip of paper.

Disappointed, the trio trudged up the stairs. Ruth was the last one out and she flipped the light switch on her way up.

The women retraced their steps through the living room and exited through the front door. Lucy glanced toward the kitchen. "Do you think whoever has been inside the house will notice that we closed the window?"

Gloria's brows formed a "V." True...if someone was staying in the house, there was a good chance they would notice. Then again, if they didn't close the window and the house was vacant, wild animals and the elements would damage much more than a section of the kitchen floor.

When they reached the edge of the yard, Ruth stopped to pick up her surveillance equipment. Gloria and Ruth followed behind Lucy as they zigzagged through the pine trees.

The tops of the trees began to bend and sway as the wind picked up. The wind whistled through the treetops and it began to rain.

The freezing rain pelted their faces and clothes. The girls picked up the pace in an attempt to outrun the sudden storm.

By the time they reached the van, they were soaking wet.

When they were safely inside the van, Ruth switched the motor on, turned the center dial to heat and cranked it all the way up. "That was fun."

Warm air blasted from the ducts and Gloria stuck her hands in front of the warm air. "I'm not sure I'm ready for winter," she admitted. She loved fall and loved having a white Christmas to put her in the holiday spirit but after New Year's, the winter weather was for the birds…or the outdoor enthusiasts.

Lucy wiped her forehead with one of the ruffles from the front of Judith's fancy pink blouse. "Since Paul is retiring, maybe you guys can become snowbirds…maybe spend the winter months somewhere warm like Florida."

Lucy leaned forward in her seat. "I'll be the first one to come visit," she promised.

Gloria's sister, Liz and her best friend, Frances, had recently moved to Florida. It was a thought. The idea of warm, sunny weather was appealing. "We might just do that," Gloria answered.

"First, we have to get out of the woods, literally," Ruth grimaced. She shifted the van into reverse and slowly backed out of the woods.

Sharp branches scraped the windows and the sides of the van. Gloria cringed each time a branch scraped the side. This had been her idea and she would never forgive herself if Ruth's van were damaged during one of her investigations.

Finally, they reached the main road and turned toward home.

Gloria hoped that Andrea and Margaret had better luck with the mysterious gun rep, Maxim, than they had searching Bill's house.

Chapter 12

Ruth handed Gloria her cell phone. "Call Judith and let her know we're on the way."

Gloria dialed the number and switched it to speaker-mode.

Judith picked up on first ring. "Please tell me you're on your way back."

Gloria smiled wickedly. "We're on our way back."

"Good," Judith gasped through the line. "These clothes are downright itchy. Lucy must wash her clothes in poison ivy."

"I do not." Lucy leaned forward in her seat. "I use only all natural ingredients."

"I'll be waiting in the drive." Judith hung up before Ruth could reply.

Ruth dropped Lucy off one street over, circled around the block and pulled into her drive.

Judith, true to her word, was waiting for them. She swung the jeep door open and hopped out of the driver's seat. She didn't look at all happy as she trudged up the drive, scratching at her arms, her stomach and her neck as she walked.

Gloria could see large red welts covering her skin. "Wow. That looks bad," she commented.

The women traipsed up the steps and into the house. Ruth made her way to the back door to let Lucy in.

The two women swapped clothes. Lucy handed Judith her shoes. "Those are the most uncomfortable shoes I have ever worn."

Judith grabbed the shoes. "Can't be any worse than your clothes," she snapped.

Judith shoved her foot into the shoe and pointed at Ruth. "I've paid my dues and upheld my end of the bargain."

Ruth nodded solemnly. "Yes, you have Judith and I thank you for your cooperation."

Judith snatched her purse off the table, turned on her heels and stomped out the door, slamming the door shut behind her.

Lucy grinned. "I would give anything to know what Ruth had on her to make her agree to the swap."

They watched Judith hustle down the sidewalk and disappear around the corner.

Ruth shook her head. "No can do. Judith held up her end of the bargain and I need to uphold mine."

Lucy reached into her purse and pulled out the plastic bag with the small piece of paper inside. "Do you have time to check this out?"

Ruth glanced at the clock on the wall. It was almost lunchtime. "Yeah. Kenny isn't expecting me to come in until after lunch."

She waved the girls past the small eat-in area and down the narrow hall off to one side. She stopped in front of the first door and they followed her inside.

The room was dark and the curtain drawn tight with nary a sliver of light coming in.

Ruth shuffled over to the other side of the room and switched on a small desk lamp that sat on top of the desk.

Gloria had never been in the back of Ruth's house. She'd only seen the kitchen, dining and living room.

If Gloria had an inkling that Ruth was obsessed with surveillance equipment, she was now 100% convinced of the fact.

The room was floor-to-ceiling monitors. Every square inch of wall space was filled with electronic gadgets and boxes.

A giant map of Michigan covered one entire wall. Circled in bright red pen was the Town of Belhaven.

Round, color-coated tacks dotted the map. Gloria reached into her purse, slipped on her reading glasses and peered at the map. "What do all those colored dots represent?"

"Uh, just a little map for tracking different post offices," Ruth explained.

Gloria wasn't convinced. Down in the lower right hand cover was a legend. She bent down and leaned in.

"That is of no interest to you," Ruth blurted out. "We have more important things to worry about."

Gloria was itching to find out what the colored dots and legend meant, but she didn't want to put Ruth on the spot.

"You're right." Gloria looked longingly at the map and then turned her attention to Ruth. "We need to get down to business."

Ruth slid into the seat at the desk. She wiggled the mouse until the computer came to life.

Lucy read the address on the small sheet of paper.

Ruth typed in the address and clicked the "search" button. Several results popped up...all of them listing the same place: East Michigan Swap and Shop, a Detroit area gun shop that took guns in trade and bought used guns.

What did that mean? Obviously, it meant something to Bill...or whoever was using Bill's computer. But why Detroit? It was almost 200 miles away.

***

Gloria climbed in Annabelle and started for home. She made a last minute decision to stop at Nails and Knobs, Brian Sellers' hardware store.

The parking lot was full. Gloria turned down a side street and parked behind the building.

Brian had recently painted the hardware store, along with the small pharmacy and grocery store...stores that he also owned. All three buildings now matched and it somehow helped make the cozy Town of Belhaven appear uniform and even quainter.

She made her way inside and walked to the back of the store. Brian was waiting on a customer. He smiled when he caught a glimpse of Gloria.

Gloria waited off to one side while Brian rang up the customer's purchases. After the customer left, she wound her way around the light fixtures and garden hoses and over to the counter.

She set her purse on the edge of the counter and hopped up on one of the barstools. Brian reached behind him for the pot of coffee and a cup. "I was beginning to think you were avoiding me," he teased.

"Me? Avoid you?" Gloria snorted. "More like the other way around." It was true. She hadn't seen much of Brian lately.

He had taken a brief vacation to visit his father, who had suffered a minor stroke. Other than seeing him at Andrea's the other day, it had been quite some time since they'd had a chance to chat.

He slid the piping hot cup of coffee across the counter and then leaned both elbows on top. "Doing a little sleuthing this morning?" he guessed.

Gloria lifted the coffee cup to her lips and took a sip. "How did you know?"

"I stopped by the post office to mail some packages and Ruth was MIA. When I asked Kenny what happened to her, he mumbled something about an unexpected emergency so I put two and two together and figured you two were trying to crack Lucy's case."

Gloria fiddled with the handle of the mug. "What do you think?"

Brian shrugged his shoulders. "Judging by the gossip around town and what I've been told, it looks like someone is trying to frame Lucy."

"That's what I think," Gloria agreed. "We have some suspects but nothing solid. No smoking gun so-to-speak."

She listed the suspects and gave Brian a brief rundown of each of their motives.

"I think Bill rejected that Barbara woman. Maybe she went crazy with jealousy and murdered him," she theorized.

She went on. "Next is the brother, Randy. One of the employees told me that Bill and his brother had a huge blowout a couple days before his death."

Gloria shifted in her chair. "Last, but not least, is the gun dealer that Bill seemed to be somewhat intimidated by." That reminded her she needed to do a little snooping around on him once she got a report back on Andrea and Margaret's findings.

"What does Lucy think?" Brian asked. She knew Bill better than the rest of them combined.

"Lucy is in a haze." Not that Gloria could blame her. This whole thing reeked of a set up. Someone who was close to Bill knew that Lucy would be a prime suspect. She remembered the employee, Zeke, who seemed all too willing to throw everyone else on the tracks.

"I should go." Gloria glanced at her watch and slid off the barstool. "Thanks for the coffee."

Brian reached for the empty coffee cup. "How are the wedding plans going?"

The wedding plans weren't "going" anywhere. They were almost at a standstill. Not that there was much to do at this point...the invitations had been sent, the wedding party and location ready to go, along with the food. The only thing left to do was pick out a dress and flowers.

"It's right on track. Speaking of that, are you and Andrea ever going to settle down?" Gloria blurted out.

"Now that you mention it." Brian opened the cabinet drawer behind him, reached inside and pulled out a small box. "What do you think?"

Gloria smiled. "Well, I know that this box isn't for me."

Brian and Paul had tricked Gloria into thinking the engagement ring Paul had bought for her was one that Brian intended to give to Andrea. Paul had been so nervous about her liking the ring, that he had her give her "seal of approval," in a roundabout way.

Brian lifted the cover off the box and pulled out a second box, covered in white velvet. He lifted the lid and held it out. A large, marquise cut diamond ring was nestled inside.

Gloria picked up the box and set it in the palm of her hand. "Oh Brian. This ring is beautiful." She shifted her gaze and stared at Brian. "When..."

Brian grinned. "I was thinking of taking her on a romantic carriage ride in downtown Grand Rapids and popping the question."

"How romantic," Gloria gushed. She handed the ring back and clapped her hands. "Oooh. I hope I can keep my mouth shut. This is so exciting," she babbled.

"You better keep quiet or we won't make you the godmother of our children," he threatened.

"Godmother? Oh my gosh." Her hand flew to her chest.

The front bell chimed and an elderly couple that Gloria vaguely recognized made their way to the back.

Brian closed the lid on the box, popped it back inside the outer box and then slipped it into the drawer. He made a zipping motion across his lips.

"I promise." Gloria zipped her own lips. "I better go." With a spring in her step, Gloria headed down the center aisle and out onto the sidewalk.

The day had started out rough around the edges, but Brian's exciting news made Gloria want to explode into a million tiny pieces. She could hardly wait to tell someone, anyone, but she knew she couldn't.

Chapter 13

Andrea pulled her truck into the parking lot, eased into an empty spot and shut the engine off. The place was deader than a doornail. The only other vehicle in the parking lot was a four-door late model sedan. She wondered if it belonged to the gun dealer...

A shiver of fear raced down her back. Was this gun dealer also a killer? Andrea cast a wary glance toward the store. It was possible that any of the employees inside the store could be Bill's murderer.

Andrea grabbed the edges of her jacket and pulled them tight. "I'm a little nervous."

Margaret shifted her purse on her shoulder. "Yeah. I get a bad feeling about this place." Her eyes wandered around the empty parking lot. She had a nagging feeling that they were being set up. She made a vow to stop watching so many creepy movies.

The store bell chimed as Andrea pushed on the door and the women stepped into the shop. Margaret followed Andrea to the counter in the back.

A young man that Andrea vaguely remembered from the day before approached them. "Can I help you?"

Andrea set her handbag on the edge of the counter. "Yes. We were in here yesterday talking to..."

"Barbara," Margaret prompted.

"Barbara," Andrea continued, "and she said the Kahr® handgun rep would be here this morning."

The young man with the jet-black hair nodded. "Yep. He's talking to one of the owners now."

Margaret glanced at his nametag: *Zeke*. She frowned. "I thought the owner recently died."

Zeke shook his head. "Yeah. He did." Zeke left it at that and quickly changed the subject.

"I'll go get Mr. Maxim."

He opened a door that led to the back and disappeared from sight. "That's interesting," Andrea muttered under her breath.

Zeke returned. With him was a bald-headed man. "This is Artie Maxim, our Kahr® representative."

The man sported a gray goatee and wore a brown trench coat that brushed against the floor. It reminded Andrea of a coat killers wore while walking down a dark alley in the dead of night, stalking their prey.

Andrea mentally shook her head to clear the thought. There was nothing odd about a man wearing a trench coat on a drizzly November morning. "Yes. We were here yesterday and one of the guns my mother and I wanted to take a look at was not in stock."

He nodded. "Barbara left a note. It was a Kahr®." He tapped his finger on the glass case where there was an empty spot. "There's only one model left. Have you seen it?"

He motioned for Zeke to unlock the cabinet.

Zeke shoved his hands in his front pockets. "Uh. I don't have a key to this case. Barbara is the only one who has the key and she's not here," he said.

"What about Randy? Maxim frowned.

"Nope. Not even Randy. We're gonna get another key made but haven't gotten around to it yet."

Andrea remembered Barbara telling them yesterday that the Kahr® gun, identical to the one that had killed Bill and the same one that Lucy had at home, had come up missing from the case.

Maxim folded his hands in front of him. "How do customers look at guns if there's no key to unlock the case?"

"They don't," Zeke replied. "I mean, it's only been a month or so. It wasn't a problem before. Bill had a key and Barbara had a key. One of them was always working."

"What about Bill's key?" Andrea couldn't help asking the question.

Zeke nodded. "Yeah. We checked his key ring and for some reason, it's missing. Just like the model gun that killed him."

***

"That is no way to run a business." Maxim whacked his open palm on the counter. "I could be losing thousands of dollars in commission with this shoddily run operation," he fumed.

Andrea shrank back. Maxim was turning out to be as sinister as she had suspected. She could even imagine him taking Bill out back and shooting him. But where was the motive? She wondered if Gloria had had a chance to do a little preliminary research on him yet.

He narrowed his eyes and scowled. "Never mind."

Maxim shifted the duffel bag he was holding. He reached inside the bag and lifted out a lumpy roll of canvas. He set the canvas on the glass top and unfolded it.

Inside the canvas was a whole arsenal of guns. The girls spent the next hour learning about each weapon and their pros and cons. To Andrea it was fascinating. It was boring Margaret to tears.

Lucy would have loved it.

After Maxim explained each weapon in detail, Andrea took his card and promised to discuss which one would work best with her mother.

The women thanked Maxim and Zeke for their time and wandered out of the store.

The skies had opened up and hard rain, almost a hail, pelted the truck. "I hope the roads haven't started icing over yet," Andrea fretted. The truck was a dream to drive except when it came to ice. Andrea hated driving on ice.

Andrea fumbled around inside her bag, pulled out her keys and unlocked the truck doors. The girls hurriedly climbed inside and yanked the doors shut.

Andrea backed the truck around, pulled out of the drive and onto the main road.

The wind picked up and the rain turned into freezing rain. She slowed the truck, gripped the wheel and focused on the road. It was going to be a white-knuckle drive home.

Finally, she turned the truck onto a side road and let out the breath she had been holding. She could feel the truck slide as they rounded the corner.

Margaret sat quietly in the passenger seat. She didn't want to distract Andrea, who focused all her attention on the road in front of her.

Instead, Margaret prayed a silent prayer they would make it home safely.

Suddenly, a car that had been following Andrea's truck, a little too close in Margaret's opinion, zipped around them and attempted to pass on a double yellow line.

"Jerk," Andrea muttered. She took her foot off the gas so that the car could get by. The red car, a beat up two door, rusting around the bottom, started to lose control and fishtail in front of them.

Andrea instinctively hit the brakes, which caused the truck to lose control on the ice. The vehicle spun in a wide circle and hit the edge of the gravel road where it gained a little traction.

It was too late. The front tire bounced off a large rock causing the vehicle to shift sideways. When the truck stopped spinning, the girls were smack dab in the middle of an open field, facing the opposite direction.

The car that had caused them to spin out was long gone.

Andrea sucked in a breath and put her forehead on the steering wheel.

Margaret reached over and patted her arm. "Good job, Andrea," she said.

Andrea opened her eyes and lifted her head. "Thanks. What a jerk," she fumed.

She looked around the open field. "Let's see if I can get the truck back on the road." Andrea pressed a button on the dashboard and switched the truck to four-wheel drive. She shifted the truck into reverse and pressed lightly on the gas pedal.

The truck made a sudden jerking motion as it began to move backward. They made it about halfway out of the field when the truck began to sink in the soft dirt.

"Oh no." Andrea pressed the gas pedal harder, which caused the vehicle to sink further into the field.

"Try rocking it," Margaret suggested. She knew that trick sometimes worked with a manual transmission. She wasn't sure if it would work with an automatic.

Andrea shifted the gears from drive to reverse several times. They went nowhere, except maybe a little deeper in the mud.

She rolled down the window and stuck her head out as she inspected the tires. "This isn't going to work. We'll have to call a tow truck."

"Give Gus a call," Margaret suggested. "He can pull us out." "Gus" was Gus Smith, a Belhaven resident who owned a small towing and automotive shop.

"Good idea." Andrea pulled her cell phone from her purse. She pressed the "on" button, switched to search mode and typed in "G.S. Towing and Automotive, Belhaven, Michigan." When she found the number, she pressed the call button.

Thankfully, Gus picked up on the second ring. Andrea explained her – their - situation and Gus told her was on his way.

Andrea disconnected the line and slumped down in the driver's seat. "This sucks. I wish I could get my hands on that driver."

Gus showed up half an hour later. He waded across the mucky field and approached the driver's side door.

Andrea rolled down the window.

"You dug yourself a hole," he observed.

"Yeah," Andrea groaned. "Some moron decided to not only pass on a double yellow line but on an icy road. When he started to spin out in front of me, I hit the brakes and here we are."

Gus nodded. "Yeah. It takes some of these blockheads a while to figure out the roads are slippery."

He went on. "Let me get you hooked up."

Gus lumbered back to his wrecker. He unwound a long cable from the back of his wrecker. On the end of the cable were two long hooks. He hooked the large metal hooks to the underneath of her truck and then climbed behind the wheel of his tow truck.

The cable slowly retracted as the winch wound the cable around the metal cylinder.

Andrea let out a sigh of relief as the truck began to inch its way out of the field and back onto the road.

When the truck was safely off to the side and parked in the gravel, she climbed out of the truck and waited while Gus removed the hooks. "Thank you, Gus. How much do I owe you?"

Gus fastened the hooks on the back of the wrecker. "You get the family discount," he teased. "Twenty-five bucks. You can just meet me back at the shop. I forgot to bring my portable card scanner."

Andrea frowned. "That seems too cheap, Gus. I think you should charge me more."

Gus snorted. "Most people think I charge too much." He shrugged. "Okay. Forty bucks."

"Deal. I'll meet you back at your place." She climbed in the driver's seat and fastened her seatbelt.

They followed Gus to his shop and both women met him at the door and followed him inside.

Andrea glanced back at her truck and frowned. A thick layer of mud covered the lower half of her driver's side door, the trim and the running boards. "Great. I guess our next stop will be the car wash."

They stepped inside the repair shop and over to the small counter where Gus was writing up a ticket. "Nice truck," he commented as he handed her a receipt and took her card to swipe it through his credit card machine.

When he had finished processing the transaction, Andrea shoved her card back inside her wallet and glanced at Margaret. There was a red bump on the side of her forehead. "Margaret, did you bump your head?"

Margaret touched her forehead. "Yeah. I think I might have."

Andrea leaned in for a closer inspection. "I think that is going to bruise. I am so sorry."

Margaret shook her head. "It's not your fault, Andrea. You didn't cause the accident. I'll be fine," she reassured her young friend.

Andrea felt terrible. "Let's stop at Dot's and get a bag of ice."

Andrea hopped in the driver's seat and Margaret slid into the passenger seat. She backed out of the parking out and turned the truck toward Main Street.

Thankfully, there was an empty parking spot right out front. Andrea pulled the truck into the empty spot and shut the engine off.

Andrea waited for Margaret near the front of the truck. "Do you feel dizzy? Light headed?"

Margaret waved her hand and opened the door to the restaurant. "I'm fine. It's just a little bump."

"What if it's a concussion?" Andrea fretted.

"Who has a concussion?" Dot rushed over. "Oh gosh." A large lump had begun to swell on Margaret's forehead. "You should sit down."

Dot led Margaret to a chair in the back. "Ray. Grab a bag of ice!" she hollered into the kitchen. She turned to the girls. "What happened?"

Andrea shifted her purse. "We ditched the truck after some moron tried to go around us on the slippery roads."

She slid into the seat next to Margaret and studied the swelling. "I am so sorry Margaret," she whispered. "I wish it had been me, not you."

"Nonsense," Margaret waved her hand. "You two are making too much of a fuss over me. I'll be fine."

Ray made his way over to the trio. He handed the bag of ice and a clean, dry rag to Margaret. "How'd you get that goose egg?"

Andrea frowned. "We had a run in with the ditch and Margaret bumped her noggin."

Margaret covered the bag of ice with the clean rag and placed it against her forehead. "It feels better already."

Dot changed the subject. "Well? How did it go at the store? Did you find anything out?"

Andrea explained what had happened. "I don't know what to think. I'm not ruling out Barbara, who is the only employee with the key, or Bill's brother, Randy." She crossed her arms in front of her and leaned back in the chair. "Who knows? Maybe even the gun rep was involved."

Dot glanced at her watch. "Gloria and the rest of the girls should be here anytime. I wonder if they found anything over at Bill's house."

Andrea and Margaret ordered hot tea and a plate of decadent desserts. They munched on the sweet treats and discussed the case. This was the first time that Gloria had sent them out on their own covert operation and it was exciting to be right in the middle of the investigation.

Margaret reached for a strawberry donut and nibbled on the outer ring. "This is delicious. I've never tasted a strawberry donut. Here. Try this." She broke off a piece and handed it to Andrea.

Andrea bit into the donut. "Wow. This is so good. Are these new?"

Dot nodded. "Yep. I've been experimenting with strawberries for a while and think I finally got the recipe right."

"It's a winner." Andrea popped the last of the shared donut in her mouth.

She stared at the door anxiously. "I wish Gloria would hurry up. I'm dying to know what happened."

Margaret nodded and lifted her teacup to take a sip. The cup slipped out of her hand and clattered against the saucer. She put a hand to her head. "I'm not feeling good." She slumped over in the chair and laid her head on the table in front of her.

Chapter 14

Andrea shot out of her seat. "Margaret." She shook her arm gently. Margaret didn't respond.

"Call 911!" Andrea shrieked to no one in particular. "Margaret. Margaret! Can you hear me?" Her eyes frantically searched the restaurant. "Does anyone here have medical training?"

A young woman rushed to Margaret's side. "I'm a nurse." The woman dropped to her knees and gently turned Margaret's head. Next, she placed her cheek close to Margaret's mouth and then glanced at Margaret's chest. "She appears to be breathing."

Margaret jerked her head. "I'm just a little dizzy," she mumbled. Her words were slurred and it was difficult to understand what she had said.

"We're going to move you into a more comfortable position." The woman placed a hand under each of Margaret's arms and gently pulled.

Andrea wrapped her arms around Margaret's middle. The women lowered Margaret to the floor of the restaurant and then placed her on her side.

The nurse tipped Margaret's head to ensure her neck and windpipe were in an unobstructed position. The young brunette glanced at Andrea. "What happened?"

"She bumped her head a short time ago when we slid into the ditch," Andrea explained.

Margaret placed a hand on the side of her head. "I'll be fine. I just need to go home and rest," she protested.

The fire department arrived moments later, followed by an ambulance. Despite her protests, paramedics gently lifted Margaret onto a gurney and wheeled her toward the front door.

The gurney was on its way out the door as Gloria, Ruth and Lucy were on their way in. Gloria did an about face when she saw Margaret on the gurney. "What in the world..."

"We had a small accident." Tears began to burn the back of Andrea's eyes. "Margaret hit her head on the passenger side window of my truck. She insists that she's fine but she's not."

Dot, Ruth, Gloria, Lucy and Andrea all climbed into Ruth's van.

Gloria promptly called Don, Margaret's husband, to let him know that Margaret was on the way to the hospital. She left a message on his cell phone and another on the home phone.

They followed the ambulance to Green Springs Memorial Hospital, the small community hospital in nearby Green Springs.

On the way, Andrea explained what had happened at Bill's shop and then told them about the reckless driver who had caused them to spin off into the ditch.

"Stupid jerk. I wish I could get my hands on the driver," Andrea clenched her fists in her lap. "I'd wring their sorry neck."

When they reached the ER entrance, the girls all climbed out of the van while Ruth drove off to find a parking spot.

They found a small cluster of chairs off in the corner of the lobby and settled in to wait for a doctor to come out.

Don arrived shortly after. The girls briefly explained what had happened and Don, accompanied by a nurse, strode down the hall in search of his wife.

Gloria watched until he disappeared from sight. "Let's pray."

The girls gathered in a small circle and held hands while Gloria prayed. "Lord, we lift up our friend, Margaret. We know that You are the God of healing and we ask that You heal Margaret's body and if there is something wrong, the doctors are able to find it right away. Thank you. In Jesus' name, we pray. Amen."

Gloria felt a sense of peace as she lifted her head. Margaret was in safe hands...God's hands.

Time passed slowly. Finally, Don emerged from the back. The girls rushed forward and crowded around.

"What did the doctors say?" Andrea asked.

Don rubbed his forehead. "She has a mild concussion and seems highly disoriented so they want to keep her overnight, just to be safe."

He went on. "I have to run home and pick up a few things for Margaret."

"I'll stay," Gloria offered.

Dot needed to get back to the restaurant. Ruth needed to get back to the post office. That left Andrea, Gloria and Lucy.

"Why don't I have Ruth drop me off at my truck and then I can come back to cover the shift," Andrea suggested.

They agreed that Andrea and Gloria would take the first shift and then a little later, Don would return to spend the night by his wife's side. "Call me immediately if anything changes," Don said before he headed out the double sliding doors.

Gloria promised she would. The rest of the girls promised to check in later and Gloria made her way to Margaret's hospital room.

She tiptoed to the edge of the door and peeked around the corner. Her heart sank when she saw her friend's still body covered in sterile hospital sheets.

Margaret propped herself up on one elbow when Gloria stepped inside the room. "Lucky you. You get babysitting duty," Margaret joked.

Gloria slid onto the hard, plastic chair that was next to the bed. "I wouldn't want to be anywhere else."

Margaret eased back down and shifted on the mattress. "I don't know why I have to stay here. Other than a little dizziness, I feel great."

"Better safe than sorry," Gloria said. She changed the subject. "I heard that you and Andrea had a successful trip to All Seasons Sporting Goods."

Margaret ran a hand through her hair. "Yeah, it was great except for the accident," Margaret quipped. "What did you find out?"

Gloria told her about Ruth's handy dandy listening device, how they suspected someone had been living inside the house and might still be there.

She told her about the small slip of paper with a Detroit address handwritten on it and that there appeared to be a spot of blood on the edge. "It's a gun shop in Detroit."

Gloria pulled her notepad and pen from her purse. She flipped the pad of paper open and clicked the button on the pen. "We can work on the list of suspects and motives." She glanced up from the pad. "Unless you would rather rest."

"What I'd rather do is leave," Margaret grumbled. "Working the case will take my mind off this place."

"Good." Gloria nodded. "So first on the list is Randy, Bill's brother. The two had been fighting days before Bill's death and now Randy is acting like he owns the place."

"Check," Margaret agreed.

Gloria scribbled his name at the top of the notepad. "Next is Barbara, the worker that Bill didn't seem to care for but ended up dating after Lucy and he broke up. She's the only one who has a key to the gun cabinet. The case where the gun went missing and the same model that killed Bill."

"Yep," Margaret nodded.

"Then we have this Maxim, the sales guy who had access to that type of gun. Bill didn't care for him and on top of that, he hits the suspicion radar."

Margaret shivered and pulled the blanket closer. "Yeah. He was an interesting fellow, for sure. Very cagey."

Gloria tapped the end of the pen on top of the pad of paper. "Maybe Bill caught him doing something he shouldn't have been...like selling guns on the black market," she theorized.

"It's possible," Margaret agreed. "What about that young man that works at the store?"

"Zeke," Gloria said. "Yeah. He told me Bill was suspicious of all his employees and had asked Zeke to keep an eye on things when he wasn't at the store." Of course, that was Zeke's version. Bill was no longer around to corroborate the story.

"What about the funeral? I always heard that killers love to attend the funerals of their victims. They get some kind of buzz from being there." Margaret pointed out.

"True," Gloria hadn't thought about that. She wondered if Lucy would go. She hadn't been charged with Bill's murder, only questioned. "I'll check with Lucy later. I wonder when visitation or funeral services will be held."

Gloria popped out of her chair. "I bet it's listed in the local paper. I'll be right back." Gloria darted out of the hospital room and sped down the gleaming hospital corridor.

She remembered seeing a small gift shop on the first floor.

When she got to the gift shop, she was relieved to find the shop was open.

Gloria stepped inside and made a beeline for the stack of newspapers near the entrance.

She was surprised at the variety of items the store stocked. Gloria headed for the checkout counter and then circled back to pick up a bouquet of fresh flowers to take to Margaret.

After she paid for her items, she stopped by the hospital cafeteria where she grabbed a couple chicken salad sandwiches and two bags of potato chips.

Gloria juggled her purchases as she made her way back upstairs to Margaret's room. On the way to the room, she stopped at the nurse's station to make sure it was okay for Margaret to eat the food she had just purchased.

Margaret had dozed off and was startled by the sound of Gloria setting the vase of flowers on the bedside tray. "You took so long, I got sleepy."

Margaret rubbed her eyes and stared at the flowers. "Gloria. Now why did you do that?" she scolded.

"Because this place needs a splash of color." She glanced around. "Why do hospital rooms have to be so stark? A little color goes a long way."

Gloria placed a bag of food on the tray in front of Margaret. "This is for you in case you're hungry."

Margaret reached for the bag. "I'm starving. All I had were some donuts at Dot's."

The girls unwrapped their sandwiches, bowed their heads to pray and then bit into the food. It wasn't gourmet but it was more than edible and Gloria quickly devoured her sandwich. She opened the bag of chips and then unfolded the newspaper.

Bill's murder was no longer on the front page. It was three pages in. Gloria slid her reading glasses on and brought the paper close to her face. "Bingo. I found something." She leaned in to read the article. "They're having a candlelight vigil tonight. It starts at 7:00 p.m."

She lowered the paper and gazed at Margaret. She was on the fence about mentioning it to Lucy. "Should I tell Lucy?"

Margaret shrugged and then popped a chip in her mouth. "Let Lucy decide. I'm sure she already knows about it."

True. Margaret had a point.

Gloria finished her bag of chips, crumpled the empty wrapper and tossed it in the nearby trashcan. She wiped her hands on the napkin and reached for her cell phone.

Lucy didn't answer and Gloria left a message for her to call.

"I'm back." Gloria whirled around to find Andrea standing in the doorway.

Andrea was holding three bags of food in her hand. "I thought you all might be hungry."

Gloria groaned.

Margaret patted her stomach. "I'm starving." She winked at Gloria and reached for one of the bags.

Gloria thought Margaret was just being nice until she noticed that Margaret finished eating the entire second sandwich. "Now, I'm full," she declared.

Andrea plopped into the empty seat on the other side of Margaret's bed. She turned to the woman in the bed. "What did the doctors say?"

"That I'm too crotchety to be going anywhere anytime soon," she joked. "Seriously, I have a mild concussion but they decided to torture me by making me stay overnight."

Andrea turned to Gloria for confirmation.

Gloria nodded. "It's true. All of it except for the crotchety part."

Gloria unwrapped the turkey wrap Andrea had given her. "Thanks for the sandwich, Andrea. That was very thoughtful." She lifted the wrap to her mouth and took a big bite. "Do you have any plans later?"

Andrea shook her head. "Nope. I dropped Alice off at the Acosta's farm earlier this morning so I'm on my own until later this evening when I have to run by there to pick her up. Why?"

"I was thinking about attending a candlelight vigil they're having this evening for Bill."

Andrea arched a brow. "The killer always returns to the scene of the crime...or goes to the victim's memorial or funeral."

"It's worth a shot," Gloria said. "Don is coming back around six so we can go right from here to the park." She glanced down at her outfit. She was wearing her standard spy gear from when the girls had gone to Bill's house earlier, which consisted of a black turtleneck, black slacks and dark brown flats.

Andrea always looked nice. She was wearing a pink cashmere sweater and black slacks. They would definitely pass muster for grieving attire.

Lucy returned Gloria's call a couple hours later and when Gloria explained that Andrea and she wanted to attend Bill's vigil, Lucy paused.

"You don't have to go," Gloria told her.

"I'm torn," Lucy admitted. "On the one hand I want to pay my respects." There was silence on the other end. "Do you think it will look odd if I don't at least make an appearance?"

Gloria picked at a piece of lint on her pants. "Like an admission of guilt? Maybe." She wasn't sure if it would look suspicious if Lucy went or if Lucy didn't go.

"I can meet you there," Lucy said in a small voice. "What time?"

Gloria glanced at her watch. "How does 6:30 sound? The candlelight vigil starts at 7:00. They're holding it in Besterman Park." Besterman Park was one of the larger parks in Green Springs. In the summertime, the city held concerts, Saturday night movies under the stars and other fun family events in the park.

The girls agreed to meet in the parking lot at 6:30 on the dot.

Andrea and Gloria stepped out of Margaret's room when the doctor stopped by to check on her.

He shut the door for privacy and the girls headed to a small visitors area at the end of the hall.

"Do you think Margaret will be all right?" Andrea fretted.

Gloria patted her hand. "She'll be fine, dear. Like she said, she's too cranky to go anywhere."

She glanced at Andrea's hand. Andrea was wearing a silver band with a row of sapphires on her third finger.

Gloria touched the top of the ring. "That's a beautiful ring, Andrea. Where did you get it?"

Andrea twisted the band between her thumb and forefinger. "Brian surprised me with it a few months back. At first, when he handed me the box, I thought it was an engagement ring," she admitted.

Gloria could not help herself. "Were you disappointed that it wasn't?"

Andrea lifted her hand and gazed at the band. "Yes and no. I mean, Brian and I have talked about settling down." She wrinkled her nose. "It's just that we both have homes that we love and both of us are too stubborn to move in with the other."

"Kind of silly, huh," Andrea added.

"No. That's not silly at all." Gloria and Paul had run into the same complication. Both of them had farms that had been in their respective families for decades. Farms that they hoped to pass on to the next generation.

In Gloria's case, her two sons weren't at all interested in farming or the farmhouse.

Gloria's oldest son, Eddie, lived in Chicago with his wife, Karen. Her middle child, Ben, lived in Houston, Texas with his wife Kelly and their twins. That left Jill, Gloria's youngest child. Jill wasn't interested in living on the farm.

Jill's two young sons, Gloria's grandsons, Tyler and Ryan were a different story. She would bet money the two of them would fight over the farm. Just the thought of her two beloved grandsons made her smile.

"Do what Paul and I are going to do," she suggested. "Share time between both. Eventually, the living arrangements will work themselves out." At least Gloria hoped they would.

It reminded her that Paul's son, Jeff, and Jeff's wife, Tina, had recently moved back in with him. Maybe it wouldn't be an issue for them, after all.

Andrea sighed. "Yeah, you're right. Maybe we're putting too much emphasis on material things."

Gloria quoted a favorite Bible verse:

"Do not lay up for yourselves treasures on earth, where moth and rust destroy and where thieves break in and steal, but lay up for yourselves treasures in heaven, where neither moth nor rust destroys and where thieves do not break in and steal. For where your treasure is, there your heart will be also." Matthew 6:19-21 ESV

Andrea closed her eyes and nodded. "Yeah. I need to remember that. Life is so temporal."

Gloria thought about Andrea's first husband, Daniel Malone, who had been murdered.

Andrea tugged on a strand of blonde hair. "Every time I think about Daniel and how important material possessions were to him, I try to remind myself that I don't want to end up like that."

Andrea impulsively reached over and hugged Gloria. "That's what I love about you. You have a way of putting everything into perspective without even trying."

Gloria hugged her back. "I believe that it is God speaking through me, that's all."

Andrea looked over Gloria's shoulder. "The doctor just came out of Margaret's room. Time to find out what he has to say."

Chapter 15

They quietly made their way over to the doctor, who was standing outside Margaret's door scribbling notes inside a chart.

"Hello..." Gloria paused. She nodded toward Margaret's room. "How is she?"

The doctor looked up. "She appears to be doing much better now but we'll still keep her overnight for observation. I'll check on her one final time before my shift ends."

He went on. "Doctor Gillivray will be here later to check on her."

Andrea and Gloria would be long gone by then. At least Don would be here to keep Margaret company.

Gloria thanked the doctor for the update and the girls stepped back into the room. Margaret, who held the TV remote in her hand, glanced up. "The TV shows here leave much to be desired."

Margaret loved to say that idle hands were the devil's tools and she rarely watched TV. She was a movie, buff, though, and loved to watch movies in the theater room Don and she had built in their basement.

Every once in a blue moon, when a hot new release came out, they hosted a movie night and would invite a bunch of friends over to watch it. The guests would play board games and munch on finger foods. Afterwards they would settle in with huge bowls of popcorn and soft drinks to watch the movie.

She jabbed the "off" button and tossed the remote on the end of the bed. "Nothing but a bunch of junk."

"Have Don bring your e-reader," Gloria suggested.

Margaret snapped her fingers. "Great idea. Why didn't I think of that?"

The girls settled in again to wait for Don and the rest of the afternoon flew by.

"There's my girl," Don's loud voice boomed from the doorway.

He was carrying a large bouquet of zinnias, marigolds and sunflowers. There were even a few crimson-colored roses tucked into the arrangement.

Margaret's eyes lit up when she saw her husband and noticed the bouquet. "For me?" she gushed.

Don set the arrangement on the table and bent down to kiss his wife.

Gloria and Andrea silently slipped out of the room.

Gloria gave Don a quick wave as they made a hasty exit.

Margaret was in safe hands now and Gloria was thrilled that Don had been thoughtful enough to bring his bride flowers.

Gloria nodded to the nurses as they passed the nurses station and stepped over to the bank of elevators on the other side.

When they reached the main level, Andrea led the way to her truck, parked in the visitor parking lot.

Andrea had not taken the time to wash the mud off her truck. It was still covered with a thick coat of caked mud. She hopped into the driver's seat. "Do you mind if I stop by the car wash and rinse some of this mud off?"

Gloria reached for her seatbelt. "Not at all dear. Be my guest."

Andrea drove to the nearest car wash and ran her truck through twice.

When they finished washing the truck, they turned onto the main road and headed toward the park, which was on the edge of the downtown area.

The parking lot was packed. Andrea drove around several times before she was able to find an open spot.

Lucy wandered over as Andrea and Gloria climbed out of the truck. She tugged on the edge of her jacket sleeve and cast a wary eye toward the clusters of people who started to gather near the fountain, located in the center of the park. "I'm nervous," she admitted.

Gloria wrapped an arm around her shoulder. "We're right here with you. Don't worry. We don't have to stay long." Just long enough to study the mourners.

The trio walked across the parking lot and through the wrought iron gate entrance.

"Can you believe how many people are here?" Lucy whispered. "I didn't know that Bill even knew this many people."

They had just entered the park when Andrea came to an abrupt halt. "That's it."

"What's it?" Lucy asked.

Andrea pointed to a beat up, rusted out, red car outside the gate. "That is the car that ran me off the road."

***

The girls hurried out of the park and made their way over to the jalopy.

Gloria peered inside the driver's side window. "Are you sure?"

"Positive." Andrea walked around the back and studied the bumper. "I remember this sticker." She lifted her foot and kicked the back of the car with the heel of her shoe. "Piece of crap."

Her eyes blazed as she gazed through the gates of the park. "Whoever tried to run me off the road is inside."

Andrea marched through the gates as she made her way over to the fountain. She had no idea who she was looking for but she vaguely remembered the vehicle had one lone occupant and that person was wearing a dark hat or had dark hair. That left the field wide open.

Gloria cupped her hands together and pressed them against Andrea's ear. "You'd be better off watching the vehicle to see who gets into it," she whispered.

"Right." Andrea nodded. "I'll be out on the sidewalk if you need me."

She turned on her heel and stomped out of the park. Gloria shook her head. "I don't believe I have ever seen Andrea so fired up," she said.

Lucy had to agree. "Me either." She turned her attention to the crowd of people. "We don't have candles."

Lucy had a point. They didn't have candles. She glanced around. Others were "candle-less," as well.

Lucy's eyes darted back and forth, as she studied the growing crowd. "I have cold feet."

"You can do this." Gloria propelled her forward and they joined the outer fringe of mourners.

"I think I'm going to throw up," Lucy groaned.

"Do you want to take a walk?" Gloria wasn't sure if that would help. It certainly couldn't hurt.

"No."

Gloria glanced at Lucy's face, which was pale and pinched. Maybe this hadn't been such a great idea, after all. "We can leave if you want."

"No. It's too late. We're already here."

"Focus your attention on possible suspects," Gloria suggested. "That will take your mind off the other."

Lucy nodded. "Good idea." She studied the faces. Lucy recognized several people. Some of them were Bill's hunting and fishing pals. Bill's daughters and their spouses stood close to the fountain.

The employees from All Seasons Sporting Goods gathered in a small cluster near Bill's family.

"Over there...near the angel statue," Lucy pointed.

Gloria's eyes drifted to the angel.

"The lady with the hoochie mama outfit. That's Bill's ex-wife, Victoria."

Lucy had given an accurate description of Bill's ex. She was wearing a tight fitting, hip hugging, super short black dress that showed too much cleavage, at least in Gloria's opinion. "Where does she live?"

"Detroit, I think."

Detroit. The same place where the gun shop was located. Gloria wondered if there was a possible connection. Was Bill's ex-wife somehow involved in his death? Had she hired a hitman?

Surely, Bill had a will and that would be the first place investigators would look.

The girls wove their way through the throng of people and studied the faces as they worked their way around the cement fountain. Hundreds of lit candles lined the ledge.

The glow from the candles bounced off the tranquil water that surrounded the fountain. It was peaceful and serene.

Someone began to sing, "Amazing Grace." Gloria and Lucy joined in. A tear rolled down Lucy's cheek and she hastily brushed it away.

"You." A woman's shrill voice cut through the solemn reverence of the song.

All eyes turned as Victoria Volk marched across the grass and stopped in front of Lucy. She lifted a blood red fingernail and pointed it at Lucy. "What are *you* doing here?" she shrieked.

"I'm paying my respects," Lucy answered in a calm even voice.

"Out!" Victoria shouted, her fists clenched at her sides. "Get out!"

The crowd parted and Lucy and Gloria shuffled to the park's entrance. Every eye was on the two of them as they made their way down the sidewalk and through the gates.

Gloria opened her mouth to speak but was interrupted by the sound of tires squealing. She looked up just in time to see a car swerve off to one side. It almost sideswiped another car before it careened out of the parking lot and onto the road.

She could hear the roar of the car's engine as it raced off into the dark night.

"I know who you are!" A voice screamed. The voice, a woman's voice, sounded very familiar. It was Andrea. She was standing near the center of the parking lot, shaking her fist in the direction of the car.

"Looks like Andrea found the car's owner," Gloria commented.

Andrea stomped over to the spot that the car in question had just vacated. She nearly collided with Lucy and Gloria. "Oh. There you are."

She waved her arms wildly in the air. "I know who ran me off the road."

"Who was it?" Gloria asked.

"That kid. The one that works at All Seasons Sporting Goods...Zeke something."

Chapter 16

Gloria was stunned. "Zeke?" Why would Zeke try to run Andrea and Margaret off the road?

Andrea's chest heaved as she tried to catch her breath. "Yeah. When I confronted him, he shoved me to the ground, hopped in his piece of crap car and drove off. He knew he ran me into the ditch."

Gloria shifted her feet and stared at the exit. At the very least, Zeke was a terrible driver and inconsiderate to boot. Maybe there was more to the story. Gloria remembered how he had said that Bill told him to keep an eye on the other employees. That someone was stealing money.

Bill's key to the gun case was missing...or was it? What if Zeke was staying in Bill's house? Maybe he was in cahoots with Maxim, the gun dealer?

There were still Randy and Barbara. Gloria wasn't ruling anyone out.

She turned to Andrea. "Do you have time to swing by All Seasons?"

Andrea reached for her keys. "Absolutely. I want to punch that little punk's lights out."

Gloria smiled. The visual of tiny little Andrea punching anyone was hilarious. The girl had spunk. Gloria had to give her that.

"I'll ride with you," Lucy offered. "We can stop back by here and pick up my jeep on the way home."

The girls piled into Andrea's truck and maneuvered out of the packed parking lot. When they reached the road, Gloria turned to Andrea. "If we track him down, under no circumstances are you to approach him. He may have a weapon."

Andrea tightened her jaw. "I know. I'm just so dang mad." She pounded the steering wheel in frustration. "That moron hurt Margaret."

Gloria shook her head. Zeke had seemed like a nice kid. Maybe she had him all wrong.

Andrea pulled the truck into the dark, deserted parking lot of the store and drove around back. The lot was empty. There was no sign of a rusted out two-door car. Gloria was relieved. A confrontation this late at night behind a deserted building was a bad idea.

She knew Andrea carried a concealed weapon. Not that she believed Andrea would use it unless she absolutely had to. Of course, if this young man was a killer, then maybe they would need it.

"We should head back," Gloria suggested. It had been a very long day and she was exhausted. So much had happened in such a short amount of time, she wasn't sure if she was coming or going.

"Do you think this Zeke guy is living at Bill's place?" Lucy asked.

Gloria had had the same thought. It was quite possible. "Maybe."

Lucy turned to Gloria, her expression anxious. "It wouldn't take long to take a quick run by there to check it out."

"I'm game," Andrea blurted out. More than anything, she wanted to confront this character, to demand an explanation for purposely driving her into the ditch.

Gloria stared out the front windshield. If Zeke thought they were onto him, he might bolt. They may never catch Bill's killer.

If he was the killer, and he knew they were onto him, would he lie in wait, expecting them to show up? She wasn't keen on walking blindly into a dangerous situation.

Maybe he was just a dumb kid who did a dumb thing and then got caught. Maybe not.

Andrea patted her purse. "I'm packing heat."

Gloria groaned. "That's what I was afraid of."

Lucy directed Andrea to Bill's street and then pointed to the long, winding drive that led to his house.

Andrea slowed the truck. "Should we or shouldn't we?" She didn't wait for an answer as she cranked the wheel and started down the narrow drive.

"Kill the lights," Lucy suggested.

Andrea promptly shut off the headlamps but left the fog lights on.

The closer they got, the louder Gloria's heart pounded in her chest. Were they driving right into a trap?

Technically, they were trespassing. If there were someone living in Bill's house with his permission, that person would have every right to call the cops.

Gloria decided to keep that thought to herself.

When they reached the end of the drive, the ranch house came into view.

Curtains covered the large front picture window. Small rays of light beamed out from the edges. "Someone is in there," Lucy said.

Andrea let off the gas and the truck coasted the rest of the way. Parked next to the house was a vehicle, but it wasn't Zeke's rust bucket. It was a newer sedan and one that Gloria didn't recognize.

"I wonder who that belongs to," Gloria said. She reached inside her purse and pulled out her cell phone. She switched the phone to on and handed it to Lucy, who was in the passenger seat. "Take a picture of the license plate."

Lucy reached for the phone. "We're not close enough."

"That can be arranged." Andrea tapped the gas pedal and the truck lurched forward. When they got close, Lucy lifted the phone and snapped a photo. "I hope it turns out. It's awfully dark."

"Four TX E71," Gloria repeated the numbers in her head. "Text that to me."

Lucy handed the phone back. "I have no idea how to operate your phone."

She reached in her pocket, pulled out her own phone and began tapping the screen. "Done."

"Uh-oh," Andrea moaned. "Someone is coming."

"Burn rubber lady!" Gloria shouted.

Andrea obeyed Gloria's instructions, literally, as she jammed the truck into reverse, skidded to a halt, shoved it into drive and stomped on the gas pedal.

The truck sailed along the drive at a good clip and even went airborne a couple times, as the truck zoomed over several ruts in the drive.

"Someone should fix that drive," Gloria said. She glanced behind her. There were two lights. Headlights. "I think they're following us."

Andrea squealed out of the drive and careened onto the street. She pressed her foot down on the gas and the truck roared off down the road. Gloria was glad she wasn't driving. She didn't do too well driving after dark.

Andrea had no problem at all.

Gloria tugged on the edge of her seatbelt to make sure it was securely fastened. She glanced behind her.

Off in the distance was a set of dim lights. She wasn't certain if it was the same vehicle from Bill's place or perhaps someone else.

When they reached Green Springs' city limits, Andrea slowed. "Now what?"

"I need to pick up my jeep," Lucy reminded her.

"Right." Andrea turned onto the main road and pulled into the park. The lot was still half-full and Lucy's jeep was parked in the back.

Andrea stopped in front of Lucy's jeep. Lucy opened the door and started to climb out.

"We'll follow you home," Andrea offered.

"She's not going anywhere," Gloria stated.

"Huh?" Lucy frowned.

Gloria pointed at the jeep. "Your tires. They're flat."

Sure enough, all four of Lucy's tires were flatter than pancakes. "Victoria Volk," Lucy fumed. "I'll bet money that woman flattened my tires."

"Hopefully she just let the air out of them." Gloria saw dollar signs at the thought of Lucy having to buy four brand new tires.

"I have a flashlight." Lucy stepped over to her passenger side door and pulled it open. She reached into her glove box and pulled out a flashlight.

Andrea and Gloria climbed out of the truck. The girls inspected all four tires and were relieved that they hadn't been slashed.

Andrea shuffled over to her truck, leaned against the front quarter panel and crossed her arms. "Now what?"

Lucy frowned. "No repair shop for miles around is open this late."

"What about Gus?" Andrea asked. He had been a lifesaver earlier when Andrea had been in the ditch.

"Smart thinking." Gloria pulled her phone from her purse, switched it to "on," scrolled through the screen and tapped Gus' cell phone number.

Lucy prayed he would be able to help.

"Hi Gus. It's me Gloria. We have a little emergency," she said.

She went on. "We're down here at Besterman Park. Someone let the air out of Lucy's tires." She paused. "Uh-huh. Yep. Okay we'll be here."

Lucy grabbed the phone from Gloria's hand. "Gus. You're a lifesaver. I love you. If Mary Beth ever leaves you, I want to marry you. Okay. Bye."

She handed the phone back. "He said he'll be here in less than half an hour."

Gus, the sweetheart, arrived right on time. He was driving a tow truck but it wasn't the same one that he had used earlier to pull Andrea's truck out of the ditch. This wrecker had a flat bed.

He slid out of the driver's seat and made his way over to where the girls were waiting. He nodded at Gloria and glanced at Andrea. "You again."

Andrea blushed. "Yeah. I'm having quite a day," she admitted.

He turned his attention to the jeep. "What'cha got?"

"Someone let the air out of my tires," Lucy explained.

Gus walked over to the jeep. He inspected the tires.

Lucy hovered nearby.

Gus shook his head and rose to his feet. "There's no way to air them here. I'll have to load 'er on the back and take her back to the station to air them up."

He lowered the flatbed of the truck and then hooked a hook, connected to a towrope to the front of the jeep. Next, he pulled the jeep onto the bed and secured all four tires with tire chains.

He tugged on each of the tire chains to make sure the car was secure and then leveled the platform. They were ready to roll.

Lucy rode with Gus while Gloria and Andrea followed behind.

When they got to Gus's shop, he wasted no time airing her tires. Gus told her he was only going charge her $50 but Lucy insisted it was more.

Gus held up both hands. "Nah. You know I can't charge you more, Lucy. After all, you proposed to me," he joked.

He wouldn't take another dime so Lucy paid the $50.

On the way out, Gloria slipped another $50 in his jacket pocket.

Gus shook his head and reached for the money. "Gloria…"

Gloria put a hand on his arm. "Gus, you're a sweetheart…salt of the earth. You deserve it."

Gus clamped his mouth shut and then grinned. "Thanks Gloria."

The long day and chain of events had taken their toll and the girls were exhausted.

Andrea yawned and lifted her hands over her head. "I better get going. I still have to pick up Alice."

Gloria hugged Andrea and patted her back. "Be careful." She crawled into Lucy's passenger seat and placed her head on the headrest. "I'm exhausted."

"Me, too," Lucy agreed.

Thankfully, they weren't far from home.

Lucy pulled the jeep into Gloria's drive and circled around until the passenger door faced the side porch. "Talk to you in the morning."

"You got it." Gloria unfastened her seatbelt and opened the door.

She slipped out of the passenger seat. "Be careful going home."

Lucy rubbed her eyes. "I will."

Gloria closed the passenger door and slowly walked up the porch steps.

She could see Mally's face peeking out through the lower glass pane. Poor Mally had been home alone for most of the day. A wave of guilt washed over Gloria.

Lucy waited until Gloria was safely inside before she pulled out of the drive.

Inside the kitchen, Gloria peeked out the kitchen window and watched as Lucy turned onto the road.

As soon as Lucy's jeep turned onto the road, a vehicle appeared out of nowhere and began to tailgate Lucy. From the mercury light on the far side of the barn, Gloria caught a glimpse of the vehicle as it zoomed by.

Her blood froze. Gloria recognized the vehicle.

Chapter 17

Gloria, keys still in her hand, yanked the porch door open and raced down the steps. Lucy was in trouble. She could feel it in her bones.

All this time Gloria had been foolish to think that someone's main objective was to frame Lucy. Not only did they want to frame Lucy, they wanted her gone. As in six-foot-under gone.

Her mind raced. She did the only thing she could think to do as she slammed Annabelle in reverse and barreled out of the driveway.

With one eye on the road and the other on her phone, Gloria dialed Paul's cell phone and prayed he would pick up.

"Hello?"

"Lucy is in trouble," she blurted out. "She just dropped me off at home and when she pulled out of the drive, a vehicle raced up behind and began tailgating her."

"Did you recognize the vehicle?"

"I did," Gloria said. She told Paul who owned the vehicle and gave him the make and color.

"Where are you going now?" Paul, who had stopped by the Montbay County Sheriff station to drop off some paperwork, headed for the door.

"To Lucy's house." Gloria glanced in the rearview mirror. "Whoever it is - is out to harm her. I feel it in my bones."

"Don't do anything, rash, Gloria."

"I-I'll do whatever I can to save Lucy," Gloria replied. She wouldn't make a promise that she couldn't keep.

Gloria disconnected the line and dropped the phone in her lap. When Lucy's place was in sight, she eased her foot off the gas and slowed the car. It was too dark to see.

Gloria drove to the corner, turned around and did another drive by. Lucy's jeep was parked close to the house.

Directly behind Lucy's jeep was Bill's truck. Someone, most likely the killer, had the nerve to move into Bill's house. Not only that, they had somehow managed to steal his truck.

She remembered the backpack sitting next to the bed. Then she remembered Zeke, who had run Andrea off the road. Maybe Zeke was trying to kill them all.

Gloria began to feel lightheaded and her pulse raced. Now was not the time to feel faint.

She gripped the steering wheel tightly. "Think, Gloria, think," she whispered aloud.

She pressed on the gas pedal and drove past. At the next corner, she turned onto the side road and glanced down at the clock on the dashboard.

Paul was at least 20 minutes out...Lucy might not have 20 minutes.

Gloria studied both sides of the dirt road in search of a place to pull off. When she found an even spot where the tall grass had been trampled, she pulled off the road.

Gloria fumbled with her cell phone as she dialed Lucy's number. She prayed her friend would answer, and that everything would be all right but it went right to voice mail. She didn't dare try the house phone.

She put the car in park, killed the lights and switched the engine off. She shoved her purse on the floor and eased out of the driver's seat.

The weeds pressed against the side of the car and she batted them away as she eased the driver's side door shut.

The quarter moon, along with what seemed like a million stars, gave off a little light. Other than that, the country road was pitch black.

Gloria shoved her cell phone in her back pocket and waited for a moment to give her eyes a chance to adjust to the lack of light.

She was too far away to see Lucy's house, hidden by a row of tall trees that lined the edge of the farm field.

Gloria studied the edge of the field. She had two choices: either she could take to the field and chance stumbling on a rock and injuring herself, which wouldn't help Lucy at all, or she could walk along the edge of the road.

She opted for the path of least resistance…the road.

"Please God. Protect Lucy," she whispered. "And me," she added.

Gloria jogged down the road as fast as she dared. When she reached the corner, she made a sharp right and headed to the house.

She could see the corner of Lucy's house now and she slowed her pace, just a little. Gloria knew the layout of Lucy's place almost as well as her own.

She tiptoed to the edge of the yard and prayed that Jasper, Lucy's dog, wouldn't spot her and start barking.

She let out a sigh of relief that the front of the house was dark.

Gloria snaked around the back of the house and darted to the shed…Lucy's weapons shed. Gloria knew that the shed was loaded with guns. Gloria just needed one.

When she got to the edge of the shed, she dropped to her knees and turned to face the kitchen window.

Lucy passed in front of the window. Gloria narrowed her eyes and studied the pinched expression on her face.

Lucy turned to face whoever was in the kitchen with her and her lips moved. She shook her head violently.

Gloria's blood grew cold. If she had to guess, Lucy was pleading for her life.

With renewed determination, Gloria hustled around the side of the shed and over to the entrance door. She grabbed the handle and turned the knob. The door was locked.

She rattled the handle in desperation and prayed that somehow God would unlock the door for her.

Frustration spilled over and Gloria whacked her open palm on the door.

"Dummy," she scolded herself...nothing like drawing attention to herself.

She crept to the back corner of the shed and began to pace. "I need to find a way into that shed."

Gloria remembered not long ago that Max, Lucy's boyfriend, had accidentally shot out one of the shed windows. Lucy had boarded it up and was now waiting for repair people to install a special order piece of glass.

Gloria retraced her steps and made her way over to the boarded up window. With both hands, she pressed against the thin piece of paneling that covered the opening. It bowed under the pressure. She pushed harder and it gave a little more.

Gloria closed her eyes, offered up a prayer and pushed with all of her strength.

Pop!

The flimsy piece of material popped out and clattered on the cement floor inside the shed. Gloria frowned at the square window frame and then looked down at her body. It would be a tight fit but she had to try.

Gloria placed both hands on the windowsill and pulled herself up onto the frame. Her feet dangled in the air while her head tottered back and forth inside. *I really need to hit the gym.*

Finally, gravity took over and Gloria landed on the cement floor of the shed with a loud thud. Her knee cracked. She gingerly rubbed her kneecap and hoped the noise was a joint and not a bone.

She scrambled to her feet and limped to the other side of the room. The only light was the light from the window she had just come through.

"Handguns, Gloria. Where does Lucy keep her handguns?" She forced herself to focus on the task at hand, as she reached for the large upper cabinet. Although there was a lock, it wasn't latched.

She quickly slipped the lock from the door latch bracket and set it on the workbench. She opened the cabinet door and peered inside. It was too dark to see anything.

Gloria stuck her hand inside the cabinet and felt around. The shelf was full of guns. How was Gloria to know which one would work best? The only gun she'd ever handled was the one small handgun she had at home. Lucy's guns seemed a whole lot bigger.

She didn't have time to decide which gun would work best. Any gun that would fire would have to be good enough. She reached for the nearest gun, ejected the clip and checked for bullets. The gun was loaded.

She snapped the base back in place, shoved the gun in the waistband of her pants and glanced around. There was no way was she going to crawl back out the window. Instead, she unlocked the shed door and slipped outside.

Gloria inched along the side of the shed and around to the back. She lowered down and tiptoed across the open yard until she reached the edge of the house. She dropped to her knees and crawled along the white lattice that covered the bottom of the porch.

When she reached the other side, she slithered to a standing position and peeked in the corner of the window.

Lucy was still standing near the window, her face pale and her lips drawn in a tight line.

Gloria's eyes widened when the barrel of a gun came into view. The gun was pointed right at Lucy. A tall shadow flitted back and forth but Gloria couldn't see who it was.

There was no way Gloria could sneak in, not with the killer guarding the door.

Gloria bit her lower lip. In the back of the house was a set of steps that led to the basement. It was Gloria's only hope.

She crept along the side and then the front of the house until she reached the steps. Gloria leaned against the side of the house and plucked her cell phone from her back pocket.

She turned her cell phone on and it gave off just enough light for Gloria to creep down the steps to the basement door.

Gloria had been nagging Lucy for months to get the basement door fixed. The door lock was broken and if you wiggled the knob just right, the lock would pop. She prayed that Lucy hadn't gotten around to fixing it yet.

Gloria grasped the handle and jiggled it back and forth. She prayed that Lucy and whoever was upstairs wouldn't hear.

Woof! Woof! Off in the distance, Gloria heard a dog bark. It was Jasper. Lucy's dog, Jasper, had heard her.

Desperate to get inside, Gloria frantically twisted the handle and finally, it popped. She turned the knob and slowly pushed the door open.

The mixture of garlic and mothballs assaulted Gloria's nose. Lucy had had a problem with mice a short time ago and read online that if she combined the two smells, it would drive out any rodent. Or vampires.

She waved her hand across her face. Gloria took a step across the threshold when something dark and moving at the speed of light crashed into the side of her leg almost knocking her over. It was Jasper. Lucy had let him outside. He wagged his tail and nudged Gloria.

Gloria knelt down and patted his head. "Good doggie, Jasper. Don't bark at Auntie Gloria," she warned.

Jasper licked the side of her face and then darted back out into the dark yard.

Gloria let out a sigh of relief, stepped inside the basement and quietly closed the door behind her.

Lucy's basement was crammed from floor to ceiling with boxes and discarded furniture. Storage shelves lined an entire wall. On those shelves were tidy rows of canned goods.

Centered between two shelves was the door leading to the upstairs. The door was ajar.

Gloria stepped over to the door and gently pushed. She slipped through the crack in the door and pressed her body against the wall.

She pulled the gun from her waistband and put one foot on the bottom stair tread. "Dear God, protect us."

Chapter 18

Gloria dropped down on all fours and crept up the steps. The safety was still on the gun and she was careful to keep the trigger away from her trembling fingers.

The old shag carpet, threadbare in spots caused Gloria's knees to ache. Or maybe it was the tumble she had taken while breaking into the shed.

A sharp nail jutted up from one of the steps and stabbed her thumb.

Gloria lifted the wounded digit for a quick inspection. A small trace of blood appeared and she wondered how long it had been since her last tetanus shot. She briefly decided that if she couldn't remember, it was probably time for a booster.

This would only matter if Lucy - and she - made it out alive.

She had a fleeting thought that Paul should only be minutes away. Would Paul come in, guns blazing? Would he decide to surround the place and the girls would end up in a hostage situation? She hoped not.

Gloria was halfway to the top when she heard the sound of voices as they drifted down the basement steps.

It was Lucy's voice and a male voice. The two of them were arguing.

As Gloria neared the top, she realized she recognized the deep voice. It was a voice from beyond the grave.

At the top of the stairs, Gloria eased along the far wall as she made her way through the pantry and peeked around the edge of the door and into the kitchen.

Bill's back was to Gloria as he faced Lucy, his gun pointed at her chest. "There's no point in discussing this any further, Lucy. I already have blood on my hands. The FTA was hot on my trail. The only loose end right now is you."

Bill's hollow laughter filled the room and sent a shiver down Gloria's spine. "Now that you've written your suicide note, explaining that you killed yourself because you were so distraught over my death, the only thing left is for you to finish the job."

Bill pulled a handkerchief from his front pocket and wrapped it around the metal grip. He lifted the gun and pointed it at Lucy's head.

At that precise moment, Gloria launched her body at Bill.

Bill lost his balance and stumbled forward.

Lucy lunged at him as she reached for the gun, which fired into the air.

Bill staggered to the side, the gun still tightly gripped in his hand.

Lucy dove for his knees.

Gloria lifted her own gun and flipped the safety lever. She pressed the barrel against his temple.

"Freeze!"

"Drop the gun!" she shouted. "Drop the gun or I'll shoot you dead! I swear I'll do it!"

Bill dropped the gun and it clattered to the floor.

Lucy dove for the gun.

Bill kicked it away and at the same time, kicked Lucy in the head.

For a brief second, Gloria shifted her attention to Lucy.

Bill, seeing that Gloria was distracted, seized his opportunity to overpower Gloria and swiped at the gun in her hand.

The two of them struggled for the weapon. Bill was bigger and stronger than Gloria and although she fought with all that she had, she was no match.

Gloria's grip loosened, and Bill started to get the upper hand when the kitchen door burst open and Paul plowed in. "Freeze!"

Bill let go of the gun.

Gloria quickly stumbled backward and fell to the floor.

Lucy lay on the floor, curled up in a ball, her head in her hands. When she pulled her hands away, Gloria could see a large smear of blood near her temple.

Two uniformed officers stormed into the kitchen and quickly handcuffed a very-much-alive Bill Volk.

Gloria crawled over to her friend. "Lucy! Lucy, are you okay?"

The crimson blood was a stark contrast to Lucy's ghostly white complexion. "I-I think so."

The two crawled over to the cabinets and leaned against them as the shock of what had just happened began to sink in.

The two officers led Bill Volk out of the house. Paul followed behind.

It was several long moments before Paul appeared back inside the kitchen. "You could've been killed," Paul said.

"Lucy was almost a goner," Gloria argued. "A few more seconds and she would have been dead. Bill was cleaning his prints off the gun when I surprised him."

Paul bent down to examine Lucy's injury. "Do you want me to call an ambulance?"

Lucy slowly shook her head. "Nah. My noggin is thicker than that."

"I'm just glad it's finally over," she added.

"Me too." Gloria couldn't agree more.

The girls slowly rose to their feet and made their way over to the kitchen table. It was still hard to believe that Bill was alive...and a killer. A killer who had staged his own death.

The police questioned Lucy at length and then asked Gloria several questions. After they left, Paul stayed behind. "You'll need to come by the station tomorrow to fill out some paperwork."

Lucy nodded. "I'll be there."

"I'll be with you," Gloria reassured her friend.

Paul stayed long enough to check the entire house and grounds to make sure there wasn't another person hiding out, waiting in the wings to finish the job.

When he finished his search, Gloria walked Paul out to his patrol car. "Thank you for saving my...saving our lives."

Paul pulled Gloria close and set his chin on top of her head. "Why can't you take up something safe like origami or stamp collecting," he groaned.

"Or pottery," she reminded him.

Despite the gravity of the situation, Gloria giggled. "Maybe I'll take up martial arts instead."

Paul snorted. "Well, that would at least be useful."

He kissed her tenderly and then made her promise to give him a call when she was safe and sound at home.

Jasper had wandered back in the kitchen and looked up at Gloria when she stepped inside. She reached down and hugged his neck. "Good dog. You didn't even bark at me."

"He didn't?" Lucy turned to Jasper. "What kind of watch dog are you?"

"The best," Gloria said.

Lucy fixed a pot of tea while Gloria hovered over her. After what had happened to Margaret earlier, she wanted to make sure her friend was all right before she left.

"Bill told me that he was in trouble with the law so he staged his own death. I asked him whose body was discovered in the house across from yours and he mumbled something about a traitor." Lucy shuddered.

"He went into great detail on how he had used a gun, just like mine, to kill the guy and then disfigured his face so that he couldn't easily be identified." Lucy went on. "In his demented mind, he figured by the time police found out it wasn't his body, he'd be long gone."

Gloria finished her cup of tea. "That is just unbelievable. You think you know someone and then something like this happens."

Gloria's eyes drooped and she began to nod off at the table.

"You should go home," Lucy urged. "It's late."

Gloria nodded. She didn't have an ounce of energy left to fight her. "Can you take me down to get my car? It's in the field next door."

Lucy frowned. "That's right. I forgot all about it." She shook her head as if to rid herself of the cobwebs.

The girls climbed into Lucy's jeep and headed to the next street. Gloria's car was where she had left it and Lucy waited until her friend was safely inside the car before she pulled back onto the road.

Lucy turned off into her drive and Gloria finished the short drive home.

When she got back to the farm, Gloria let Mally out for a short run.

She let her beloved pooch back in the kitchen, shut the door and clicked the lock in place.

Gloria barely had enough strength to brush her teeth. She turned off the bathroom light, stumbled to her bedroom and fell into bed, clothes and all.

Chapter 19

Gloria was out like a light. It was 9:45 a.m. before she heard Mally, who stood in the bedroom doorway and began to whine.

Gloria flung back the covers and reached for her robe. "Okay. I hear you loud and clear."

She let Mally out onto the porch and then made her way to the kitchen counter to start a pot of coffee. She added an extra half scoop of grounds. Today would be another long one and Gloria knew she would need that extra shot of caffeine to make it through.

She had almost finished her first cup of coffee when a movement out of the corner of her eye caught her attention. Five eager faces stared at her through the glass pane of the kitchen door: Dot, Margaret, Lucy, Ruth and last but not least, Andrea.

She clutched her robe around her and shuffled to the door.

"Good morning, sleepy head," Margaret teased.

Gloria reached out and hugged her. "You're out of the hospital."

"I'm fit as a fiddle," Margaret proclaimed. "We've been trying to call you for over an hour now. We decided to call an emergency meeting what with everything that has happened in the last 24 hours."

Gloria swung the door open and motioned them in. "Make yourselves at home. I'll be right back."

She darted into the bedroom, grabbed a pair of blue jeans and purple sweater from the closet and then headed to the bath. She quickly showered, dressed and finger fluffed her hair in place.

Next, she dabbed a little makeup on. Gloria turned to the left, then to the right as she studied her reflection. Despite the lack of sleep and the stress of the last few days, she didn't look too shabby, if she had to say so herself.

The girls had settled in at the table. They were feasting on bagels, muffins and a variety of other baked goodies that Dot had brought with her.

Dot reached for a pecan swirl. "I made another pot of coffee. I hope you don't mind."

"Not at all." Gloria settled into the last empty chair and reached for an "everything" bagel.

Lucy shifted in her seat. "The girls have been dying to know what happened but I told them they would have to wait until you were here to hear the whole story."

Between the two of them, Lucy and Gloria shared the chain of events that had occurred the night before, starting with the moment Gloria caught a glimpse of Bill's truck as it followed Lucy after she pulled out of the drive.

Ruth poured a splash of cream in her coffee. "Did you think it was Bill?"

Gloria drummed her fingers on the tabletop. "No. I thought that whoever had been living in Bill's place had taken his truck."

Lucy shook her head. "All that time, I felt terrible about Bill's death and here he was, faking his own death and then trying to pin it on me."

"When the police didn't arrest you, he got desperate and decided to take you out," Andrea guessed.

"Making it look like a suicide," Dot finished.

Gloria popped the last bite of cream cheese coated bagel in her mouth and wiped her hands on her jeans. "Yep. I can hardly wait to hear what Paul has to say."

Ruth glanced at her watch. "I gotta get back to the post office. If I keep making Kenny hold down the fort, he's gonna want a raise."

Andrea stood, too. "Yeah. I need to go. Alice is chomping at the bit to get over to the puppies."

The rest of the girls headed for the door.

Gloria held it open and followed them out. "How is that going?"

Andrea pulled her keys from her purse. "Great. Thanks to your generous donation, the place is shaping up. You wouldn't even recognize it."

She went on. "A trainer is scheduled to come Monday morning to start his first training session."

Andrea squeezed Gloria's hand. "Thanks to you, they can afford the trainer."

"Are they still going to turn it into a boarding kennel?" Gloria thought that made the most sense. Maximize the use of space and keeping the cash coming in.

Andrea nodded. "Yep. Marco and Alice are working on the website and online ads, too. Alice is turning into quite the website guru."

She pressed a hand to her cheek. "And I think there may be a budding romance between Alice and Marco."

Margaret shook her head. "Well, I'll be darned. Wouldn't that be something?"

Dot glanced at her watch. "I should go. Ray is holding down the fort at the restaurant." She reached for the railing.

The word restaurant reminded Gloria of food, which reminded her of Thanksgiving. "Wait. I almost forgot. Thanksgiving. Would any of you be interested in a potluck Thanksgiving here at the farm? I'll make the turkeys and you all bring sides."

The idea was a hit and all agreed they would love to spend the special day with their best friends. Each promised to tell her what they planned to bring by weeks end.

After the last Garden Girl pulled out of the drive, Gloria wandered back inside the house. She had a lot to be thankful for this year, not the least of which was her close-knit group of friends.

Chapter 20

Gloria darted from the oven to the roaster then back to the oven. She hadn't realized that cooking two very large turkeys, along with three pans of stuffing and four large dishes of her made-from-scratch macaroni and cheese would be so much work.

She glanced frantically at the clock on the wall. It was almost time. Almost time for her 20+ guests to start arriving.

The tables had been arranged and her dining room ready for guests. The buffet gleamed from a small spritz of furniture polish and a heavy dose of elbow grease.

The festive fall plates were stacked, the silver polished.

She froze in her tracks when she heard a tap on the backdoor. She thought someone had come early, but it was only her backup troops. Or "troop." It was Paul.

She yanked the door open and dragged him into the kitchen. "Good. You're early." She thrust an apron in his hand. "Put this on."

Paul lifted the apron and stared at the pink pansies that dotted the front. "You have got to be kidding me."

"Fine. Let's switch." Gloria quickly untied her apron, lifted it over her head and handed it to him.

She snatched the one with pretty flowers and dropped it around her neck, quickly tying the back.

Paul wound an arm around her waist. "You need to take a deep breath. Everything will be fine."

Gloria nodded but the wave of panic continued to wash over her. She wasn't sure what had stressed her out so much. After all, it was only friends and family.

Gloria sucked in a breath and forced herself to calm down. "Okay. I'm better now." She gave him a list of chores and then headed to the deep freeze on the front porch in search of corn she had frozen during harvest season.

She had just finished putting her last stick of butter in the butter dish when the guests started to arrive. Soon, the house was brimming with people.

Jill and her family were the last to arrive. Tyler and Ryan raced over to their beloved Grams and wrapped their arms around her waist. "We're starving," they told her.

"I'm hungry enough to eat a whole turkey by myself," Ryan declared.

Gloria swiped a hand across Ryan's blonde locks and planted a kiss on his cheek. "Good. At least I won't have to worry about leftovers," she teased.

Each of the Garden Girls arrived laden with goodies for the Thanksgiving feast. There were pots of mashed potatoes, green bean casseroles, sweet, buttery yeast rolls and homemade cranberry sauce.

Dot arrived with every type of dessert conceivable. There was a traditional apple pie, pecan pie, chocolate pie and chocolate cake. Last, but not least, she brought her now famous cream cheese pumpkin pie.

There was so much food, Gloria almost ran out of counter space.

After everyone had arrived, they all assembled in the dining room for a prayer of thanks.

Gloria decided that since Paul would soon be head of the household, it was time to turn over the reins and she asked him to pray.

The room grew silent as the guests bowed their heads in prayer.

"Dear Lord. We are thankful for this day You have given us. Lord, we thank You for each and every one of our family and friends that are here in body and those that are here in spirit. We pray for blessing in each of their lives and ask You to guide us and direct us in the paths You will lead us."

Paul went on. "On this day, we thank You most of all for our Lord and Savior Jesus Christ. In His name we pray amen."

The prayer ended and total chaos ensued.

Gloria stood off to the side and watched as the people who mattered most to her celebrated the day of Thanksgiving.

Gloria loved Christmas. It was her favorite holiday of the year, but Thanksgiving was a close second. It was a time that she could stop and reflect on all of her many blessings.

Paul and Gloria were the last two to fill their plates, and fill them they did. This was the one day of the few days of the year where Gloria gave herself permission to eat anything and everything she wanted.

They settled in to the two empty places near the head of the table. Gloria had managed to fit the children at a card table off to the side while all the adults gathered around two tables she had placed in the shape of a large "L." It was a perfect fit.

Talk of the wedding was the main topic of conversation. When the conversation drifted to Lucy's recent dilemma, everyone quieted down and listened to Paul's explanation of why Bill Volk had faked his own death and tried to frame poor Lucy.

He explained that Bill had recently gotten involved with Artie Maxim, a known criminal who was also a gun salesman. Not only did he sell guns legally, he sold them on the black market, making a tidy profit.

Maxim had somehow convinced Bill that he could make millions by taking in used guns and then reselling them on the streets.

It had worked for several months. Bill had gotten greedy, upping his illegal sales and looking into different avenues to secure more guns. The ATF was onto him and when Bill began to feel the heat, he masterminded his own "murder."

Bill had harbored bitterness towards Lucy for weeks after their break up and he saw the perfect opportunity to frame Lucy, all the while staging his own death.

He had built a secret hideaway underneath his house where he hid out when someone showed up.

Bill had moved into his spare bedroom, where the secret room was located in case the ATF raided the house. He was in the process of buying a home in Mexico and was only days away from leaving the country. Permanently.

Lucy's eyes widened. "So that time we went to his house to snoop around...he was there? Hiding?"

Paul sipped his Coke. "It would seem so."

Gloria reached for a warm roll. "What about the car that ran Andrea off the road? The kid, Zeke, who worked at the store?"

Paul shrugged. "He was just a little thug. He had nothing to do with Bill's scheme. Bill used him to throw suspicion onto Barbara and his brother, Randy."

Gloria turned to Lucy. "We need to do a better job of screening your boyfriends." She winked at Max, Lucy's new boyfriend, who was sitting next to Lucy.

Gloria liked Max. He seemed more "normal" if that made any sense. He wasn't the least perturbed when Lucy shopped or had lunch with friends, unlike Bill who had always insisted that Lucy do what he wanted...mostly hunting, fishing and camping.

Lucy was a tomboy through and through but she still liked to do the girlie stuff.

Jill, Gloria's daughter, reached for the butter. "Did you ever get that deer, Lucy?"

Gloria frowned and gave her daughter a warning look.

It was too late.

Lucy dropped her fork. "Yeah. Hey, Gloria, we only have a few days left for gun season. You want to go tomorrow?"

"Uh..."

Paul reached over and patted Gloria's hand. "Of course she does, Lucy. That's all she can talk about is how much fun she had last time."

Gloria slapped the front of her forehead with the palm of her hand. She vowed that later, after everyone was gone, Paul was going to pay for that comment.

After the last morsel of food that anyone could bear to eat, including the scrumptious desserts Dot had brought, was consumed, the girls made quick work of kitchen clean up while the guys headed to the living room to watch the football game. At least they pretended to watch the game. Every single one of them promptly fell asleep.

Gloria's grandsons darted outside to inspect the tree fort.

Gloria packed the last baggie full of turkey she was sending home and dropped it into Andrea's grocery bag.

"Thanks for the leftovers," Andrea said. "Next is the wedding," she reminded her.

"How's the dress shopping going?" Ruth asked.

Jill snorted. "It's not. I don't believe Mom has even looked for one yet."

"Gloria," Margaret chided.

Gloria shrugged. "I've been busy," she said. "Besides. I don't want to go alone."

Lucy tapped her on the shoulder. "We'll go with you. How 'bout day after tomorrow?"

Gloria sucked in a deep breath and nodded. Time was running out. The wedding was less than a month away. "Okay."

Alice clapped her hands. "Oooh. This will be so much fun, Miss Gloria."

Margaret dried the last dinner fork and dropped it in the silverware tray. "Great. I have the perfect boutique store in mind. It's in Grand Rapids. We can look for a dress and then have lunch."

Ruth nodded. "Perfect. Even I can go since it's on a Saturday."

Jill headed to the living room. "It's time to round up my troops. We still have to stop by Greg's parents." Jill and her family were the first to leave.

Next was Andrea, Brian and Alice.

Andrea hugged Gloria on her way out the door. "Thanks for the leftovers."

Alice hugged her next. "Everything was delicious, Miss Gloria." She paused. "But if I may suggest, the stuffing...it could use a little more zip." She pinched her fingers together. "Maybe you could add a little jalapeno."

Andrea tugged on her sleeve. "Alice."

Alice grinned. "It was just a suggestion."

Lucy and Max were the last to leave. The four of them stood on the porch and chatted. "What do you think will happen to Bill?" Lucy asked.

Paul shifted his tall frame and leaned against the porch post. "He will be gone for a very long time. I doubt he'll live long enough to see the light of day again."

Lucy nodded. She wondered how she could have been such a poor judge of character. "I had no idea."

Paul shoved his hand in his pants pocket. "Don't be so hard on yourself, Lucy. Greed changes people. Greed got the better of him."

"Thanks for saving Gloria and me that night," she said.

Paul grinned at Gloria and winked at Lucy. "She sure does keep me on my toes."

He glanced at Max. "You sure you know what you're getting yourself into?" he joked.

Max shuffled his feet and lifted his head to meet Lucy's eyes. "She's a firecracker, I'll give you that."

Lucy rolled her eyes. "We better get out of here before they decide to take away our car keys," Lucy joked.

Paul and Gloria stood on the steps and watched Lucy and Max drive off in Max's sports car. "He sure does have his hands full," Paul commented.

"Just like you," Gloria teased.

Paul nodded. "Yep. Just like me."

The end.

If you enjoyed reading "Garden Girls Cozy Mysteries Anthology III (Books 7-9)", please take a moment to leave a review. It would be greatly appreciated. Thank you.

List of Hope Callaghan Books

Audiobooks
(On Sale Now or FREE with Audible Trial)

Key to Savannah: Book 1 (Made in Savannah Series)
Road to Savannah: Book 2 (Made in Savannah Series)
Justice in Savannah: Book 3 (Made in Savannah Series)

Cozy Mystery Collections

Hope Callaghan Cozy Mysteries: Collection (1st in Series Edition)

Made in Savannah Cozy Mystery Series

Key to Savannah: Book 1
Road to Savannah: Book 2
Justice in Savannah: Book 3
Swag in Savannah: Book 4
Trouble in Savannah: Book 5
Missing in Savannah: Book 6
Book 7: Coming Soon!

Garden Girls Cozy Mystery Series

Who Murdered Mr. Malone? Book 1
Grandkids Gone Wild: Book 2
Smoky Mountain Mystery: Book 3
Death by Dumplings: Book 4
Eye Spy: Book 5
Magnolia Mansion Mysteries: Book 6
Missing Milt: Book 7
Bully in the 'Burbs: Book 8

Fall Girl: Book 9
Home for the Holidays: Book 10
Sun, Sand, and Suspects: Book 11
Look Into My Ice: Book 12
Forget Me Knot: Book 13
Nightmare in Nantucket: Book 14
Greed with Envy: Book 15
Dying for Dollars: Book 16
Book 17: Coming Soon!
Garden Girls Box Set I – (Books 1-3)
Garden Girls Box Set II – (Books 4-6)
Garden Girls Box Set III – (Books 7-9)

Cruise Ship Cozy Mystery Series

Starboard Secrets: Book 1
Portside Peril: Book 2
Lethal Lobster: Book 3
Deadly Deception: Book 4
Vanishing Vacationers: Book 5
Cruise Control: Book 6
Killer Karaoke: Book 7
Suite Revenge: Book 8
Cruisin' for a Bruisin': Book 9
High Seas Heist: Book 10
Book 11: Coming Soon!
Cruise Ship Cozy Mysteries Box Set I (Books 1-3)
Cruise Ship Cozy Mysteries Box Set II (Books 4-6)

Sweet Southern Sleuths Cozy Mysteries Short Stories Series

Teepees and Trailer Parks: Book 1
Bag of Bones: Book 2
Southern Stalker: Book 3

Two Settle the Score: Book 4
Killer Road Trip: Book 5
Pups in Peril: Book 6
Dying To Get Married-In: Book 7
Deadly Drive-In: Book 8
Secrets of a Stranger: Book 9
Library Lockdown: Book 10
Vandals & Vigilantes: Book 11
Fatal Frolic: Book 12
Sweet Southern Sleuths Box Set I: (Books 1-4)
Sweet Southern Sleuths Box Set: II: (Books 5-8)
Sweet Southern Sleuths Box Set III: (Books 9-12)
Sweet Southern Sleuths 12 Book Box Set (Entire Series)

Samantha Rite Deception Mystery Series

Waves of Deception: Book 1
Winds of Deception: Book 2
Tides of Deception: Book 3
Samantha Rite Series Box Set – (Books 1-3-The Complete
Series)

Get Free Books and More!

Sign up for my Free Cozy Mysteries Newsletter to get free and discounted books, giveaways & soon-to-be-released books!

hopecallghan.com/newsletter

Meet the Author

Hope Callaghan is an author who loves to write Christian books, especially Christian Mystery and Cozy Mystery books. She has written more than 50 mystery books (and counting) in five series.

In March 2017, Hope won a Mom's Choice Award for her book, "Key to Savannah," Book 1 in the Made in Savannah Cozy Mystery Series.

Born and raised in a small town in West Michigan, she now lives in Florida with her husband.

She is the proud mother of one daughter and a stepdaughter and stepson. When she's not doing the thing she loves best - writing books - she enjoys cooking, traveling and reading books.

Hope loves to connect with her readers! Connect with her today!

Visit hopecallaghan.com for special offers, free books, and soon-to-be-released books!

Email: hope@hopecallaghan.com

Facebook:
https://www.facebook.com/hopecallaghanauthor
/

Margaret's Magnificent Meatloaf Recipe

<u>Ingredients</u>:

1-1/2 lbs. ground beef (I substituted with ground turkey)
1 cup milk
1 egg, slightly beaten
¾ cup soft bread crumbs (I used Club crackers instead)
1/2 medium yellow onion, chopped
1 tbsp. chopped green pepper
4 tbsp. ketchup
1-1/2 tsp salt
1 tsp. sugar (Optional. I think it could be omitted. The sweetness from the Club crackers was enough)

<u>Directions</u>:

-Preheat oven to 350 degrees.
-Combine all ingredients: (Set aside 2 tbsp of ketchup.) Ground beef, milk, egg, bread crumbs, onion, green pepper, ketchup, salt and sugar. Mix well.
-Press into 4" x 8" ungreased load pan.
-Bake at 350 degrees for one hour.
-Remove from oven. Drizzle remaining 2 tbsp. of ketchup over top of loaf. Return to oven and bake an additional 15 minutes.

Easy Cheesy Hash Brown Casserole Recipe

<u>Ingredients</u>:
1 – 8 oz. container of sour cream (regular or light)
1 - 10.75 oz. can cream of chicken soup
3 – Cups shredded sharp cheddar cheese
1 – 2 lb. bag of shredded frozen hash browns (THAWED)
¾ stick melted butter
1 tsp. salt
¼ tsp. pepper

Preheat oven to 350 degrees.

Mix all ingredients. Pack ingredients into 8-1/2 x 11 glass baking dish. Bake uncovered for one hour.

*You can also add ½ cup chopped yellow onion. For less bitter taste, sauté onion and then add to mixture before baking.

**I haven't tried it but, I think bacon bits would taste great!

84900655R00392

Made in the USA
Middletown, DE
22 August 2018